ÇALIKUŞU

(THE WREN)

REŞAT NURI GÜNTEKİN

THE COMPLETE ENGLISH TRANSLATION

PARTS 1-4 TRANSLATED FROM THE TURKISH BY SIR WYNDHAM
DEEDES
PART 5 TRANSLATED FROM THE TURKISH BY TUGRUL ZURE AND
EDITED BY ANGEL GARCIA

Cover design: Angel Garcia

Second Edition, 2020, Alma Angela Garcia

ISBN: 978-1-9994809-2-9
First Edition published in 2018
Copyright © Reşat Nuri Güntekin 1922
English Translation Copyright for Parts 1-4 © Sir Wyndham Deedes 1949
English Translation Copyright for Part 5 © Angel Garcia 2018

To my mother Sabrina Lucia Risma Garcia, whose fondness for Feridé and Kâmran provided the spark that turned into this book.

TABLE OF CONTENTS

PREFACE

This book is the result of an unexpected journey down a rabbit hole.

My mother loves foreign dramas. She fell in love with Feridé and Kâmran, the main characters of a Turkish drama that is available on Netflix. The drama is based on a Turkish book and she pleaded with me to find an English translation (if you know Filipino mothers, you will know the power of their soulful dark eyes and singsong voices). I figured the task would be an easy one, and the perfect Christmas present.

On Netflix, the drama is called *Lovebird* in English and *Çalıkuşu* in Turkish. A bit of digging online revealed that "çalıkuşu" actually means "wren" and that the book is a Turkish classic written by Reşat Nuri Güntekin in 1922. An English translation by Sir Wyndham Deedes was written in 1949 but I could not find any available hardcopies. More digging, however, led me to an online file of the English translation, on which I spent many post-workday evenings manually typing it up and formatting it into a manuscript. Mission accomplished! I printed an actual physical book for my overjoyed mother that Christmas.

But I wasn't fully content. My investigation also revealed that the English translation was incomplete. Fortunately, my engineering colleague and good Turkish friend, Tugrul Zure, was willing to check. I purchased the original Turkish version for him to compare with my manuscript and it was confirmed: the English version of Part 5 had left out many, many pages. Having now watched all the episodes on Netflix and also having read Deedes' translation, I was intrigued and emotionally invested in Feridé's 1920's Turkish life. The Netflix version of the story has deviations from the Turkish classic novel and ends much earlier than the classic novel, omitting Feridé's teaching adventures. How did *Çalıkuşu* really end? If I could somehow procure a complete Part 5, would I even be allowed to put it together with Deedes' Parts 1 to 4?

Luck was on my side. I began a search for the rights holder to Deedes' work. Sir Wyndham Deedes passed away in 1956 without a wife or children. I instead found his grandnephew, Jeremy Wyndham Deedes, who was kind enough to allow me to use his great uncle's work in assembling a complete English translation of *Çalıkuşu*. To top it all off, my friend Tugrul was willing to help me translate the complete Part 5. Despite having moved away and preparing to have a baby with his wife on the other side of Canada, he continued to help me remotely.

So, a gigantic thank you to Tugrul Zure and also to Jeremy Wyndham Deedes, who has graciously given his permission on behalf of the Deedes' family. I can only hope that Reşat Nuri Güntekin and Sir Wyndham Deedes would approve.

Mom, enjoy! That goes for you too, Netflix *Lovebird* fans.

Angel Garcia
Edmonton, Alberta
September 2018

EDITOR'S NOTE

I went through Deedes' work and touched as little as possible. Aside from fixing a few typos, some words have been stripped of their hyphens or put together in order to provide better "flow" for the modern reader. For instance, "to-day" has been simplified to "today." Also, capitalization was enforced for the beginning of most sentences.

Updated words (In Order of Appearance)
To-day = Today
Sea-shore = Seashore
Head-dress = Headdress
Hand-work = Handwork
Class-room = Classroom
Candle-light = Candlelight
Chatter-box = Chatterbox
Tip-toe = Tiptoe
To-night = Tonight
Hand-bag = Handbag
Fairy-tale = Fairy tale
To-morrow = Tomorrow
Jewel-case = Jewel case
For ever = Forever
Tap-water = Tap water
Week-end = Weekend
Shoe-lace = Shoelace
Any one = Anyone
School-book = Schoolbook
Ear-ring = Earring
Arm-chair = Armchair
School-teacher = Schoolteacher
Paint-brushes = Paintbrushes
Sea-weed = Seaweed

Dove-cot = Dovecot
Cheek-bone = Cheekbone
Knee-cap = Kneecap
Home-made = Homemade
Water-colour = Watercolour
Eye-glass = Eyeglass
Maid-servant = Maidservant
Tear-drop = Teardrop
Fire-place = Fireplace
Guest-room = Guest room
Living-room = Living room
Bird-cage = Birdcage
Eye-brows = Eyebrows
Drawing-room = Drawing room
Match-boxes = Matchboxes
Carob-trees = Carob trees
Half-way = Halfway
Worth-while = Worthwhile
Heart-Breaking = Heartbreaking
Easy-going = Easygoing
Light-heartedness = Lightheartedness

❧ PART ONE ❧

I was in the fourth form. I must have been about twelve years old. One day our French teacher, Sister Alexei, had given us a composition. "Try," she said, "to write down your earliest recollections. Let's see what discoveries you make. It will be a fine exercise in imagination for you."

I shall never forget it; the nuns, who were tired of my naughtiness and chatter, had separated me from my companions in the class, and had sat me down in a corner on a little seat made for one. I was condemned to be exiled there until (in the words of the head mistress) "you have learnt not to talk to your companions during lessons, and to listen quietly to your teacher."

On one side of me was a great wooden beam, a soundless, voiceless, serious and very tall companion, who made it impossible for me to raise my head, and who bore with stoic pride the wounds I inflicted on him from time to time with my pocketknife. On the other side of me was a long window, the venetian blinds of which were never open and seemed to have been made to maintain the cool and gloomy darkness demanded by the discipline of the convent.

I had made an important discovery. By leaning on the desk, if I raised my chin a little, I could see through the blinds a piece of sky, and between the leaves of a big acacia tree, the window of a single room and the railing of a balcony. To tell the truth, it was not a very splendid view; the window was always shut, and there was always a child's mattress and blanket hanging over the balcony railing. But I was grateful even for that.

During lessons, if I turned up my eyes to the sky—the real sky which I could see through the blinds—my attitude, with my hands locked together under my chin, must have seemed a very spiritual one to the Sisters; and they readily ascribed it to the beginnings of good behaviour. While I, feeling that I had got the better of them, kept my eyes, as it were, on the life they were somehow concealing from us, and experienced a sense of revenge, as if I had tricked them successfully.

1

Çalıkuşu

When Sister Alexei had finished her explanations, she left us to get on with our work. The serious-minded ones at the top of the class who adorned the forms in front set to at once. Although I was not sitting near them, I knew what they were writing as well as if I had looked over their shoulders: "My first memory is the golden head of my dear little mother tenderly bending over my small bed and smiling at me with her sky-blue eyes," or some poetic little untruth of that kind. . . . In point of fact, little mothers must be some other colour than golden and sky blue. But for the girls at the convent school, those were the colours in which mothers could be painted; they were quite essential to them, so for us it was a matter of routine. As for me, I was quite another kind of child. I could not remember very much about my mother, whom I had lost at a very early age; but in any case it was quite certain that she was not golden-haired and blue-eyed. That being so, no power on earth could force me to love her or to think of her with any other countenance than her real one.

I wondered what to write. The cuckoo clock which hung under the coloured picture of the Virgin on the wall went on ticking, but I procrastinated. I loosened the ribbon around my head, and began to let my hair fall slowly over my eyes. Holding my pen in my mouth with one hand, I kept biting it and turning it round and round between my teeth. When philosophers and poets write, they have strange habits like scratching their noses and pulling the skin of their chins; the fact that I was biting my pen and letting my hair fall between my eyes was a sign that I was plunged deep in thought. Mercifully my periods of thinking were rare: because otherwise I should have preserved a continual appearance of disheveled locks, like the well-known witch of the fairy tales.

Years have passed since those days, and now, as I begin—in a strange town, in the bedroom of a strange hotel, simply as a defence against the loneliness of a night that seems unending—to record my memories, one hand is pulling at my hair again in the manner of a small child, and trying to make it come down over my eyes. As to the reason for this, it seems to me that I am still a child—a light-minded and inattentive child, all too easily carried away by the life going on around her. Certainly, in times of stress, in order to be left alone with myself and my own thoughts, I used to try to draw a curtain with my hair between myself and the world. As for turning my pen holder round and round in my mouth like a meat-

2

skewer, I really haven't solved that mystery. All I do know is, that at a period when I was beginning to look like a young lady, and yet had lips never free of ink-stains, I presented myself one day before someone who had come to visit me at school, looking as though I had on a painted moustache, and was thoroughly ashamed of myself in consequence.

What was it I was recounting? Oh yes: the first memory test that Sister Alexei gave us. In spite of racking my brain, I remember that this is all I was able to write that day: "Perhaps I was born in a lake, as fishes are. It's not that I don't remember my mother . . . my father, my nurse, our orderly Hüseyin . . . a little black dog that made me run one day in the street . . . the bee that stung my finger the day I secretly stole some grapes from a full basket . . . the red lotion they dropped into my eyes when they ached . . . my arrival at Istanbul with dear Hüseyin . . . and a great many other things of that kind. But not one of these is a first memory. They are not as old as my recollection of splashing about stark naked among the big water-lilies in the lake that I loved . . . a lake which was as boundless as the sea. . . . But if it had leaves on it and big trees on its banks, how could this lake be as big as the sea, you will ask? I swear I am not telling lies, and I'm as much surprised as you are, but it's a fact; how can I help it?"

When my composition was read in class, all the others looked at me and burst out laughing, and poor Sister Alexei found it very hard to quieten them and restore silence. Sister Alexei!—in her black dress, her snow-white collar, her pimpled bloodless face framed in a headdress like a palace *yashmak* pulled up to her forehead, with her lips as red as a pomegranate flower—the strange part of it is, that if she were to appear before me now and ask me that question again, I doubt if I could find a very different answer. I should begin again by saying I'd been born like a fish in a lake.

I heard later from someone or other that the lake is quite close to a little village in the direction of Mosul, the name of which I can't remember; my boundless sea is nothing more than a strip of water set in a clump of trees, the remains of a river run dry.

My father must have been in Mosul at the time. I was no more than two and half years old. It was so hot in summer that it was impossible to stay in the town, and my father was obliged to take my mother and me to this village. He used to go down to Mosul every morning, and return in the evening after sundown.

3

My mother was ill; so ill that she was unable even to see me. For a time I was in a very miserable state. For months together I dragged my life out in the servants' rooms; and then they found in one of the villages, an Arab woman named Fatma, who had no belongings. Fatma gave me her heart and her breast, both left unwanted by her child who had died.

During my early years I grew up like a child of the desert. Fatma used to tie me to her back like a bundle; she used to take me around in the heat of the sun, and carry me up to the very tops of the palm trees. Well, it was just at this time that we came to the village I mentioned just now. Fatma would take me every morning to this oasis, with food for both of us, and put me naked into the water. . . . And until the evening we would eat our food, sing songs and romp together. Then, when we felt sleepy, we would pile the sand up and make a pillow of it; and with our bodies in the water and our heads out of it, we would go to sleep in each other's arms, cheek to cheek! . . .

I got so used to this kind of life that when we returned to Mosul I was like a fish out of water! I would feel very sorry for myself, and in a burst of temper and a high state of nerves, I would throw off my clothes without hesitation at the first opportunity, and run out into the street stark naked.

Fatma had decorations tattooed on her nose, on her cheeks, and on her wrists. I got so used to these, that faces not tattooed really seemed to me to be ugly. The first time I ever seriously went into mourning was on the occasion of Fatma's departure. Wandering here and there, we had reached Kerbela. I was then four years old, an age when one more or less remembers everything. Fatma had met her fate and the day my nurse became a bride and a lady in her own right is as clear in my mind as if it were today. In a house full of women (who seemed to me the most beautiful in the world, as their faces were tattooed like Fatma's) I was passed from one lap to another, and then set down beside Fatma. And I remember how we ate our food, tearing it to pieces with our fingers, on large copper trays placed in the middle. Stupefied at last by the tinkling tambourines and the hollow kettle-drums, and the fatigue of the day, I went off to sleep early, on my nurse's knee. I don't know if our Mother Fatma was alive when they killed her son Hussein in Kerbela, but if the poor woman did live to that unhappy day, her cries of anguish would have been nothing compared with my cries, when on the morning following the wedding night I found myself in that house, in the arms of a strange woman. Indeed, since Kerbela became Kerbela, I don't fancy it had

4

witnessed such a lamentation. And when I stopped howling, I did a hunger strike for whole days, just like a grown-up person.

Months afterwards, a cavalry soldier called Hüseyin helped me to forget my grief over my nurse. Hüseyin was a soldier who had been lamed by a fall from his horse during exercises. My father had brought him to the house as his orderly. Hüseyin was a real sport. He quickly learnt to love me, and I responded to this love with an unbelievable and quite unforgivable lack of loyalty! It's true I didn't sleep with him, as I had done with Fatma. But in the morning, at cockcrow, the very moment I opened my eyes, I would dash into his room at once, and sit on his chest as if riding a horse, and open his eyes with my fingers. Just as Fatma had accustomed me to the garden and the countryside, so Hüseyin accustomed me to the barracks and life of a soldier. I have never seen in anyone else so much skill in inventing games as this great long-moustached fellow had. What was really lovely about these games was that most of them were dangerous and exciting. For instance, he would take me and throw me up in the air like a rubber ball, or sit me on his astrakhan fez, and take me by the legs and jump me up and turn me round and round. Nothing gave me so much pleasure as to yell at the top of my voice, with my hair tousled and my eyes starting out of my head.

It was not that there were no accidents. But there was a firm compact between Hüseyin and me. If I were hurt while playing, I was not to cry; and he was not to complain about me to anyone. I got used to keeping a secret like a grown-up person, because I was afraid that he wouldn't play with me again, rather than from any sense of duty. When I was a child, they called me a tomboy. Maybe they were right. I would hurt anyone I was playing with, and make him scream. That certainly was a habit that arose from the games I played with Hüseyin. In the same way, if I hurt myself and met the misfortune with a smile without grieving much, that too was a legacy from him.

Sometimes Hüseyin would get the Anatolian soldiers to play the tambourine, and setting me on his head like a pitcher he would start his weird games. At one time too, I acquired the habit of horse-stealing with him. When my father was away from home, Hüseyin would steal the horse from the stable, and then he would sit me on his lap and take me out into the country for hours on end. But this amusement of ours didn't last long. I don't wish to malign her, but it seems likely that we were given away to my father by our woman cook. After a couple of beatings, Hüseyin never dared approach the horse again.

5

There is no pure love, they say, without quarrels and rows; and in the course of the day I would have at least four or five bouts with him. I had a strange way of showing my anger. I used to squat down in a corner of the room and turn my face to the wall. Hüseyin would leave me in this position for three or four minutes, and then he would have pity on me; he would seize me by the waist and toss me up in the air, till he made me shout again and again. After sitting on his lap and acting peevishly for a little, I would finally consent to kiss the fellow on the chin, and we would make friends.

My friendship with Hüseyin lasted two years. But those years are not like these. They were long—so long!

Shouldn't I be a little ashamed of talking so much about Fatma and Hüseyin, in recounting my childhood memories?

My father, whose name was Nizamettin, was a cavalry major. The year he married my mother they sent him to Diyarbakir, and he never came home again. He never returned to Istanbul. From Diyarbakir he went to Mosul, from Mosul to Hanikin, thence to Baghdad and to Kerbela. He never stayed more than a year in any one place. They said I was very like my mother. Well, there's a picture of her dating from the year when she married my father, which is exactly like me. But from the point of view of health we were very unlike. She was very thin. She hadn't the kind of constitution to withstand the ceaseless journeys, the hard weather in the mountains and the heat of the desert. Then, too, she must have had some complaint or other. But the whole married life of the poor soul was spent in trying to conceal her illness. What else could she do? She dearly loved my father. She seems to have been afraid that they would take her away from him by force. . . .

And my father, as he travelled further and further away from Istanbul, used to say to her every time they set out afresh, "Let me send you to your mother, at any rate for a season—or for two months? Poor old dear, she is getting on. . . . Think how she must be longing to see you!" But my mother used to pretend to scold him, and answer, "Wasn't this part of the bargain?—weren't we going to return to Istanbul together?"

As for her illness: "There's nothing wrong with me. . . . I am a little tired. . . . The weather changed a couple of days ago; that's the trouble; but it will pass . . ." she would say, or something of that kind. She seems to have concealed from my father the fact that she was longing to see

Istanbul . . . but was it possible? Only two minutes after falling asleep, she would wake him up and relate a long dream in which she had been in our country house in Kalender, in the little wood nearby, or on the shores of the Bosphorus. . . . To cram such long dreams into a few minutes' sleep surely showed a very strong desire to see the places in question?

My grandmother, I believe, used to protest in tears to the Chamberlains, and at the War Office, but these entreaties had no kind of effect. In the end, when my mother's illness got worse, my father asked for a month's leave, to take her, at any rate, to Istanbul; he set out without waiting for an answer. To this day, I can remember our crossing the desert by camel. On reaching the sea at Beyrut my mother seemed to revive a little. She put me in her own bed in the house where we put up, combed my hair, and because my hands were dirty and my buttons half off, she hid her face in my shoulder and wept.

One day, she roused herself completely: she took some new clothes out of her trunk and dressed herself up. Towards evening we went below, to meet my father. My memory of him suggests a stern soldier, somewhat wild in character; but when he saw my mother up and dressed, I shall never forget the joy with which he ran to her. Taking her by the wrists like a child that has just learnt to walk, he began to weep.

That was the last day we spent together. The next day they found my mother dead beside an open trunk, with her head fallen upon a bundle of clean linen, and with the stain of blood on her lips.

A child of six should be able to understand a good deal. But for some reason or other I didn't grasp the situation at all. The house we were in was crowded. I know that on many days I played with other children in the garden, and wandered around with Hüseyin in the streets, along the seashore, and under the domes and in the courtyards of mosques. After leaving my mother on foreign soil, my father could not face returning to Istanbul. It's probable that he rather recoiled from meeting my grandmother and my aunts. On the other hand, he felt it a duty to send me to them; furthermore, it was natural, no doubt, that he should reflect upon the impossibility of educating in barracks and at the hands of soldiers a little girl who was getting bigger and bigger every day.

Our orderly Hüseyin took me to Istanbul, a tiny little girl on a first-class steamer, sitting on the lap of an Arab soldier dressed anyhow. . . . Just think what a queer pathetic sight we must have presented to a great

7

many people! But if I had done the journey with anyone but Hüseyin I shouldn't have been so happy.

In a copse at the back of our country house there was a stone fountain, and on the edge the statue of a naked child, broken off at the shoulders. During the first days of my arrival, this broken statue, blackened by sun and moisture, looked to me like a crippled desert child. The greenish water of the fountain was covered with red leaves, so the season was probably autumn. As I looked at these leaves, I saw that there were a few goldfish swimming about below them; I started walking into the pool in my new shoes and the silk dress that my grandmother (making much ado about it) had got ready for me. Suddenly there was a shout; and my aunts, without waiting to see what I was up to, grasped me in their arms and carried me up to change my clothes, kissing me one moment and scolding me the next. And because I was frightened of the wailing and the fuss, I didn't dare enter the pool again, but would stretch myself face downward on the pebbles, and lean my head over the water.

One day I was busy watching the fish again, in the same position. I can picture the scene to myself even today, so clear it is. A short distance behind, my grandmother was sitting in a garden-chair, in the black shawl she always wore round her shoulders. Hüseyin was kneeling beside her as though saying his prayers. They were slowly discussing something between them. In any case they must have been talking Turkish, because I could not understand what they were saying. But their voices and their occasional glances at me aroused my suspicions. I pricked up my ears like a hare. I lost sight of the goldfish that swarmed round the breadcrumbs I had broken up with my teeth and thrown into the pool, and I stared at the reflection of my grandmother and Hüseyin in the water. As he looked at me, Hüseyin was wiping his eyes with a great big handkerchief. It sometimes happens that children have a keenness of perception beyond their years. From that *tête-à-tête* conversation I scented an attempt on myself. They were going to take Hüseyin from me. Why? I was not of an age to understand delicate matters of that kind; only I very well understood that when the time came to part, it would be a disaster which could no more be prevented than the setting of the sun or the falling of the rain.

That night as I lay in my small cot alongside my grandmother's bed, I suddenly opened my eyes. The red night-light that stood at our heads had gone out. But the room was quite bright in the moonlight which came through the windows. I couldn't sleep any more. I felt an intolerable grief. Propping myself up on my wrists for a minute, I looked at my grandmother, and made sure she was asleep; then I slowly got out of bed and went out of the room on tiptoe. Unlike other children, I was not afraid of the dark or of being alone. When the stairs creaked, I stood still with all the caution of a grown-up person, and slowly went down to the ground floor. The doors were bolted. But as the window beside the garden door had been left open, it only took me a moment to climb out. Hüseyin used to sleep in the gardener's hut, right at the other end of the garden; and there I ran, with the long skirts of my white nightgown twisting round and round my legs. I jumped on to Hüseyin's bed, which was spread out on a bench. He was a heavy sleeper. In fact, while we were in Arabia, it used to be quite a business to wake him. In order to get him to open his eyes, I had to sit on his chest and jump about as if I were riding a horse, and then take hold of his moustaches and pull them as though they were reins, shouting a good deal the whole time. But on this particular night I was afraid of waking him. If he woke, I was quite sure he would not let me sleep on his lap as he used to do, but would take me in his arms and hand me over to my grandmother. In fact, all I wanted was to spend one more night with him.

My unseemly behaviour on that night was still, up to a short time ago, being talked about in the family. When my grandmother woke early in the morning and saw that I was not in my bed, she nearly went mad. . . . Within a few minutes the whole house was astir. Off they went into the gardens and down on to the beach, with lamps and candles in their hands. . . . From the roof down to the street, from the boat-house down to the two feet of water in the pool, they searched and dragged every corner. They hung lamps down the well in the next door garden. After some considerable time, my grandmother remembered Hüseyin, and ran off to his room, and there she saw me fast asleep with my arms clasped round his neck.

I still remember the tragedy of the day of his departure, and I smile. I don't know that I ever remember grovelling to anyone as I did that day. Hüseyin with his great moustaches was squatting down by the door and weeping unashamedly, while I was kissing the skirts of my grandmother and my aunts, beseeching them with the prayers I had learnt from the Arab beggars in Baghdad and Syria.

A novel will describe a grief-stricken person as dumb and inert, with bent shoulders and unseeing eyes; someone, in fact, who's in a really bad way. I was always exactly the opposite. When I am really worried my

9

eyes sparkle, my whole attitude is lively, and I feel as pleased as possible with myself; I am convulsed with laughter, as though the world meant nothing to me, and I talk inconsequently and do every kind of mad thing. All the same, I think this is better, if you have no one near you in whom you can confide. After parting with Hüseyin I remember I did the craziest things, and used to bully my cousins, whom they brought in the hopes of amusing me.

With a lack of constancy that would have shocked a stranger, I quickly forgot all about Hüseyin. I don't feel very sure, but it's probable that I really was angry with him. If his name were mentioned in my presence, I would make a face, and say (in the Turkish words I had just begun to learn) "Dirty Hüseyin! Ugly Hüseyin! Bad-mannered Hüseyin!" and spit on the ground. At the same time, a box of dates which the poor, unfortunate, dirty and ugly Hüseyin sent me the moment he got to Beyrut seems to have assuaged my wrath. Although I looked on their coming to an end as a disaster, I cleared the whole lot off at a sitting. Fortunately the stones remained, and with them I played for weeks. I mixed them with some of my lucky beads, strung them on a thread, and hung them round my neck like a splendid cannibal necklace. The others I planted here and there in the garden, and for months I used to water them every morning with a small bucket, awaiting the growth of a clump of date palms.

My poor grandmother was sorely troubled. It was impossible to do anything with me. I would wake before it was light in the morning, and until I gave in exhausted at night I spent all my time in making disturbances and getting into mischief. If my voice were stilled for a time everyone in the house became anxious, because this meant either I had cut myself somewhere, and was trying to stop the bleeding without saying a word, or that I had fallen down from somewhere and was doing my best not to howl, or else that I was doing some kind of damage, such as sawing off the legs of the chairs, or painting the coverings of the divans.

One day I climbed to the top of some trees to make nests for the birds with pieces of linen and little bits of wood. Another day I climbed to the top of the roof in order to throw stones down the chimney of the kitchen fireplace, and frighten the cook. Now and again a doctor used to come to the house: one day I jumped into the empty carriage which was waiting for him at the door, and whipped up the horses; and another day I rolled a big wooden washing tub down to the sea and let myself go with the current. I don't know whether it's the same with others, but in our family it was considered a sin to lay hands on an orphan. When I reached the limit, the punishment they chose was to take me by the arm and lock me up in a room.

We had a strange relative whom all the children called "Uncle Whiskers." This uncle used to call my hands "the railings round a saint's tomb;" for my fingers were never free of wounds and scratches; they looked as if they had been dipped in henna and tied up afterwards.

I couldn't get on at all with my companions. I even used to frighten the cousins who were older than I was. If by an out-of-the-way chance a wave of affection swelled within me, that proved another misfortune. I couldn't learn how to love like a human being, or to treat those I did love with kindness. I would throw myself like a little wild animal upon the ones I felt most for; I would bite their ears, scratch their faces, and thoroughly torment them. It was only with one of my cousins that I had an inexplicable feeling of hesitation and want of courage—Kâmran, the son of my aunt Besimé. But it would not be right to call him a child. In the first place, he was older than I was, and he was very well-behaved and serious. He didn't care to bother with other children. He used to walk about alone with his hands in his pockets along the seashore, or read a book under the trees.

Kâmran had curly fair hair, and a pale, delicate, bright complexion. So bright was his skin, that I felt that if I had had the courage to seize him by the ears and put my face close to his cheeks, I should see myself reflected there, as if in a mirror.

All the same, in spite of my backwardness, I had a row with Kâmran too, one day. I had a piece of rock which I had put in a basket and was carrying up from the sea, and I dropped it on his foot. Was it that the stone was very heavy or that he was particularly sensitive? I don't know. But suddenly there was a yell and a howl of lamentation. I was alarmed. With the agility of a monkey, I climbed a big plane tree which stood in the garden; and neither scoldings nor threats nor even supplications would make me come down again. In the end they sent the gardener up after me. But the higher he climbed, the further up I went. So much so, that the poor man perceived that if he went on, I shouldn't hesitate to climb into the thinnest branches, which would not bear me, and that there would then be an accident. So he came down again. In the end, I roosted on the branch of the tree that night until it got dark.

I gave my poor grandmother no chance to sleep. The good woman had lavished all her love upon me. Some mornings, before she had recovered from her tiredness of the day before, she would be wakened by the noise I was making; thereupon she would sit up in bed and hold me by my arms, and shake me, scolding my mother as she did so, saying: "Why did she go and die, and leave me in my old age at the mercy of this wild animal?" But this much was certain, that if at such moments my mother had appeared before her and had said: "Will you have this wild animal or me?" my grandmother would have had no hesitation in choosing me, and sending my mother back to the place she had come from.

Yes; it's hard on a delicate old lady in poor health to be roused from her sleep before she has recovered from her previous day's fatigue. But we must remember too what it is to wake with a rested body, a brief memory, and a soul thirsting for further trouble. In a word, in spite of all the trouble I gave, I am sure that my grandmother found me a consolation for her, and was, in her heart, contented.

I was in my ninth year when we lost her. My father happened to be in Istanbul as well. They had transferred the poor man from Tripoli to Albania, and he could only stay one week in Istanbul. My grandmother's death left him in a difficult situation. An officer who was also a widower could not have dragged around with him a nine-year-old little girl. But for some reason or other he did not fancy leaving me with my aunts. He probably feared that I should fall into a position of dependence on them. However that may be, he took me by the hand one morning, on to the steamer, and across to Istanbul. At the bridge we got into another carriage, and climbed endless hills passing through the bazaars until we came to a halt at last before the door of a big stone building.

This was a convent school, in which I was to be shut up for ten years. They took us into a gloomy room near the door, the windows and the shutters of which were all closed.

Everything must have been discussed and arranged beforehand, because a woman dressed in black, who came in soon after, bent over me and looked me closely in the face, stroking my cheek, while the flaps of her white headdress touched my hair like the wings of some strange bird. I remember that my very first appearance at school began with an accident and a bit of naughtiness on my part. While my father was talking with the Mother Superior I began to wander round the room and to finger one thing after another. A vase, with coloured pictures above it that I wanted to touch with my fingers, fell to the ground and was smashed. My father leapt from his seat, his sword rattling, and seized me by the arm, in a great state of concern. The Mother Superior, on the other hand, who proved to be the owner of the broken vase, simply laughed, and tried to calm my father, waving him aside.

How many more things like this vase was I not to break at school? The untamable nature I had shown at home persisted here too. Either those Sisters were really angels, or else there must have been a pleasanter side to my nature. Or was it that there was no other way of putting up with me? I was always talkative in class and given to wandering all over the place. It was not for me to go up and down stairs as other people did. I would be sure to hide in a corner and wait for the others to come down, and then, jumping on to the banisters as if mounting a horse, I would let myself go from top to bottom. Or I would hop downstairs with my legs together. There was a withered tree in the garden: one of the teachers saw that whenever I got the opportunity I climbed up it, and heedless of warnings would jump from branch to branch till I had no breath left. She called out one day, "That child isn't a human being: she's a wren (Çalıkuşu)!" And from that day on my real name was forgotten, and everyone began to call me Çalıkuşu.

I don't know how it was, but thereafter this name caught on in the family, and my real name Feridé remained an official one, used on special occasions, like clothes that one wears on feast-days.

I liked Çalıkuşu, and it served my purpose. When they complained about some impropriety, I would shrug my shoulders helplessly and say: "What can I do? What can you expect from a 'Çalıkuşu'?"

Now and again a spectacled priest with a small, goat-like beard round his chin used to come to and fro to the school. One day I cut a piece of my hair with the handwork scissors, and fixed it to my chin with glue. When the priest looked in my direction I hid my chin in my palms, and when he turned his head in the other direction, I withdrew my hands and wagged my beard, mimicking the priest and making all the others laugh. The teacher couldn't make out what was amusing us, and began shouting at us all at the top of her voice, in a rage. I happened to turn my head for a moment towards the window of the classroom which opened on to the corridor. And what should I see but the Mother Superior looking at me through the glass? What do you think of that?—and what was I to do? I was horror-stricken. I bowed my head, put my finger to my lips to signify "silence," and then I blew her a little kiss with my hand. The Mother Superior was the senior Sister of the school. From the oldest teacher

13

down, everyone treated her like a god. All the same, my inviting her to be my accomplice against the priest tickled the good woman, and as though afraid she would not be able to maintain her composure if she came into the class, she laughed, shook a warning finger at me, and disappeared in the darkness of the corridor.

The Mother Superior caught me one day in the dining-room. I was busy putting the scraps from the table into a paper basket I had stolen and brought along from the classroom.

She called to me to her rather severely: "Come here, Feridé," she said; "what's that you're up to?"

I couldn't understand what harm there was in it, and raising my eyes to her face, I asked: "Is it wrong to feed the dogs, Mother?"

"Which dogs? And with what food?"

"The dogs in the ruins. Oh Mother! If you only knew how pleased they are when they see me! Last night they came to meet me right from the street corner, and began to go round and round my feet. . . . 'Steady, now. Hi! What are you doing? I shan't give you a thing till you get back there!' The creatures don't understand a word you say to them. They pulled me down. . . . But I was obstinate, and hid the basket in my skirts. They very nearly tore me to pieces, but thank Heaven a street bread-seller was passing by, and he saved me."

The Mother Superior fixed her eyes on mine, and listened.

"All right then; but how did you get out of the school?"

Without any hesitation, I explained that I had jumped over the wall at the back of the laundry.

The Mother Superior put her hand to her head, as though she had had some very bad news.

"However did you dare?" she asked me.

With the same innocence, I said to her: "Don't worry, Mother. . . . The wall is very low . . . and how do you expect me to go out by the door? . . . Do you think the porter would ever let me? The first time I went, I took him in, by saying: 'Sister Thérèse is calling you,' and got through that way. Please don't give me away . . . because there's such a danger the dogs might starve. . . ."

What strange creatures those Sisters were! I imagine that if I'd done the same in any other school, I should either have been shut up, or I should have got some other punishment. But in order to avoid coming face to face with me, Mother Superior knelt down on the ground.

"My child, to care for animals is a good thing; but to be disobedient is not. . . . Leave the basket with me . . . I will have the scraps taken to the dogs by the porter."

In all my life perhaps no one loved me as that woman did. Actions of this kind on the part of the Sisters seemed to make about as much impression on my behaviour and bad manners as the tide makes on the rocks. But with time they worked secretly within me, and I fear they have left indelible traces: an incurable weakness, and a sediment of pity.

Yes, I was indeed a strange child, difficult to understand. I had probed the weaknesses of my teachers, I had thoroughly explored what it was that would worry each one of them, and I prepared my tortures accordingly.

For instance, we had an old and extremely fanatical music teacher called Sister Mathilde. While she was praying, with tears in her eyes, before the figure of the Holy Virgin Mary, I would call attention to the flies buzzing around her; I would attack where it would most hurt, by coming out with something of this kind: "Sister, the angels have come to visit our dear Mother!" Then again I had noticed that another of the teachers was very spick and span: so I would pretend that my pen would not write properly, and shake it hard as I passed her, and her snow-white collar would be sprinkled with ink.

There was yet another of them, who was very much afraid of insects. I found a coloured picture of a scorpion in one of the books, and cut it out with scissors. Then I glued this piece of paper to the back of a great big horse-fly which I caught in the dining-room; and during preparation I went up to her on some pretext, and left it on her desk.

As I engaged the Sister in conversation, the fly began to walk. When the poor girl saw, by the light of the gas, a dreadful scorpion crawling across her desk with its pincers and tail in the air, she started to scream; seizing a ruler that lay beside her, she squashed the fly with a single blow, and then, leaning her back against the wall and covering her face with her hands, she fainted away.

That night, I too, for a brief half-hour, twisted and turned in my bed from one side to the other. This would be when I was about twelve years old. By now, feelings of compunction and modesty had developed within me a good deal. I was ashamed of what I had done, and I understood afterwards that this fault was not one of those that would easily be passed over. I should certainly be cross-questioned the next day, and who knows what might not happen then? Several times in my sleep, I saw the Mother

15

Superior before me. She seemed to be descending on me and shouting, with a frown on her face, and her eyes wide open.

Next day, however, the first lesson passed off uneventfully. Towards the evening of the following one, the door was opened; a Sister who came in said something to the teacher, and then beckoned to me to come with her. There was going to be trouble. I stamped out, hunching my shoulders and putting out my tongue, while the children laughed and the teacher tapped her desk with her ruler, to bring them to order.

A few minutes later I was in the Mother Superior's room. But wonder of wonders, the expression on her face was not in the least like the head mistress I had seen in my dreams; so much so, that I felt it was not I, but she, who was guilty of inventing the scorpion horse-fly game and making the teacher faint.

Her face was sad, and her lips trembled. She took me by the hand and drew me towards her.

"Feridé, my child . . . I have news for you . . . sad news. Your father has been rather ill. . . . I say 'rather,' but he has been very ill indeed. . . ."

The Mother Superior was crumpling a piece of paper in her hand; she found it impossible to finish her sentence. I saw the teacher who had fetched me from the classroom suddenly cover her face with her handkerchief, and go out of the room.

I understood. I tried to say something. But like the Mother Superior, I too was tongue-tied. I turned my head; I looked at the trees opposite through the open window. Swallows were flying above the sun-kissed tops of the trees. Suddenly I felt as full of life as they.

"I understand, Mother," I said, "don't grieve. What can we do? We must all die."

This time the Mother Superior pressed my head to her breast, and did not let me go for a long time.

Soon after, although it was not a visitor's day, my aunts came to see me. They wanted to get leave for me and take me home. But I would not agree. I told them the examinations were very near. Nevertheless, the approach of the examinations did not prevent me from being more mischievous than ever that day. So much so, that during the evening session I had a violent fever, and put my arms on my desk, just as lazy children do, and went to sleep; and ate nothing all that night.

When I woke the next morning I was the old Çalıkuşu again.

I spent the summer holidays at my aunt Besimé's house, in Kozyatak.

I had no use for the children there. My cousin Nejmiye was a child who would never leave her mother's side; she seldom uttered a word, and was always ailing. Kâmran was almost her double. Thank heaven there were some refugee children about the place. I used to collect them in my garden, and lead them into the maddest adventures all day, till evening. At one time my poor little friends got into trouble, and were turned out, thanks to the gardener. But they were docile children; they ignored this indignity, and came back to help me escape. We used to wander all over the countryside and climb over garden hedges to steal the fruit. By night time, with my face all blistered from the sun, I would be trying to hide the rents in my frock with my torn hands. When I got home my aunt would tear her hair and hold up Nejmiye as an example to me—Nejmiye, opening her pink mouth and yawning, like a lazy yellow cat, under a pile of feather down. And Kâmran, too, was always one to throw at my head, every other moment, his studiousness, his delicacy and good manners, and all the rest of it.

It didn't so much matter in the case of Nejmiye. After all, she had grown up at her mother's knee; a soft, warm, docile little cat. I was not above admitting, inwardly, that girls ought to be like that.

But what about the great Kâmran, now nearly twenty, and beginning to grow a bit of a moustache on his long, thin lips? I would get really angry with him, for looking more like a girl than a man, with his small feminine feet in their white suede shoes, and silk socks, his slender body swaying like a branch as he walked, and his white throat rising from the collar of his silk shirt. I was enraged at his virtues, which were continually being extolled by his neighbours and masculine relatives. I can remember how I would run and fall on top of him, pretending I had slipped; how I would tear his books, and try to pick a quarrel with him on some imaginary pretext.

"But for heaven's sake, do show a bit of emotion some day! Get angry; say something contrary; and I'll roll you over on the ground and attack you as I would a cat—I'll pull your hair, and I'll threaten those yellow snakes' eyes of yours with my fingers. . . ." Trembling with rancour and delight, I would call to mind those early days when I used to throw stones at his feet and hurt him.

But he considered himself a grown-up person; he would look me up and down, and say with a sly smile in his eyes, "How long is this childishness to go on, Feridé?"

17

"All right: but how long are you going to keep up this shyness, and these old-fashioned poses and affectations?" . . . But how could I say that to him?—I, a girl of thirteen or fourteen. . . . A girl of that age can't say all she likes to a young man, if he treats her uncouth behaviour with so much politeness. I would put my fingers on my lips, as though I feared some forward remark would escape me involuntarily; and in order to be able to malign him at my ease, I would run off to some nice corner of the garden.

It was a rainy day. Kâmran was discussing clothes, with a few of the women-folk downstairs. The ladies were asking his opinion about the colour of the winter clothes they were going to have made. I was busy in a corner, patching with great care the sleeve of a torn blouse, my tongue out and my eyes screwed up. I couldn't restrain myself: and I began to giggle.

"What are you laughing at?" demanded my cousin.

"Nothing," I said, "something came into my mind. . . ."

"What came?"

"I won't say."

"Come on, now, don't smirk. . . . In any case, you can't keep a secret. Whatever happens, you'll give it away in the end."

"If that's the case, don't get angry . . . while you were talking clothes with the ladies, I was thinking: God made a mistake when He created you. You were meant to be girl—not at the age you are now—but when you were about thirteen or fourteen. . . ."

"Well—what then?"

"By the time I've finished sewing a bit of stuff, my fingers are in such a state, that I might be a man of twenty."

"And then?"

"What do you mean, 'and then'? Then by the will of Allah and the word of the prophet, I'd have married you, and that would have been the end of that."

There was a peal of laughter in the room. I raised my head and saw that everyone was looking at me.

One of the guests went and put her foot in it.

"All right! But you can do that as things are, Feridé."

I was at a loss; and opening my eyes wide, I asked: "How?"

"How?—Why, you can marry Kâmran; he'll busy himself with your clothes. He will do your mending, and you will look after things out of doors."

I got up, infuriated. But it was with myself that I was really angry. I had asked for this kind of talk. I didn't as a rule talk such nonsense as this, but it looked as though the thankless mending business had made me forget my surroundings. However, I took the offensive, with the desperation of someone well aware of his guilt.

"That's possible, but it would be a pity for Kâmran, I think," I said, "if there were a row in the house, which God forbid, what do you think would happen to my cousin? I don't expect he's forgotten the stones I threw at his delicate legs not long ago." I started to go up to my room, unusually serious in the middle of all the laughter. But at the door I turned around again.

"I've behaved badly," I said, "really badly, for a girl of fourteen; but please forgive me." Kicking the stairs with my heels and slamming the door, I went up to my room. I threw myself on my bed like a ball. The laughter downstairs continued. Who knows, they were probably still laughing at me? They'd see! Perhaps it would have been a good thing to marry Kâmran; because we were gradually growing up, and the opportunities of having rows with him were getting more remote. Even if it were only for a moment, let there be a real battle; and then, to have my revenge, there'd be nothing for it but marriage.

At the end of the summer holidays the school was in a great state of ferment, which would only end when the terminal examinations began. The reason was this. My Catholic school friends who had reached their thirteenth or fourteenth year made their first communion at Easter; in white silk dresses down to the ground, with their heads wreathed in sheaves of muslin like brides' veils, they were betrothed to their prophet Jesus. The whole wedding ceremony was very impressive; it was performed in church, by candlelight, with prayers sung to an organ, amid clouds of incense which mingled with the scent of spring flowers and pervaded the air of the whole place.

The pity of it was, that during the holiday months which followed the ceremony, my faithless schoolmates were at once false to their betrothed, and betrayed the waxen-faced blue-eyed Jesus with the first man they met; and indeed with more than one. When school re-opened, what a number of letters, photographs, flowery keepsakes and the rest of it did they not bring with them, concealed in the corner of a trunk. When they took a stroll in the garden, in twos and threes, I used to know quite well what they were talking about. I had no difficulty in understanding that underneath those pictures of angels, and the coloured prints of their

19

prophet (which had been presented to the most innocent and religious girls) were hidden the photographs of young men. The story one girl whispered in the ear of another in a corner of the garden, in a voice inaudible even to the insects buzzing around her in the air, did not escape me.

About this time, the girls would divide themselves off into groups of twos and threes, and stick to each other tenaciously. I, poor dear, was left all alone in the garden and in the classroom. The others seemed like so many mystery boxes to me. They avoided me even more than the nuns; you will ask why? Because I was a chatterbox, and (as my be-whiskered old uncle would say) I could not keep a secret. For instance, if I got to know that one of them had effected a little innocent exchange of flowers with one of the local young men through the garden railings, I would broadcast it all over the garden; and more than that, I was fanatical about things of that kind.

I shall never forget how one winter's evening, we were doing lessons in the classroom. A hard-working girl called Michelle had got permission from the Sister to study Roman history, and had gone to the seat at the back of the room. Suddenly, in the silence of the classroom, a sob was heard. The nun raised her head, and exclaimed: "What is the matter, Michelle? Are you crying?"

Michelle's face was wet with tears, and she covered it with her hand. I answered for her:

"Michelle has been moved by the defeat of the Carthaginians; that's why she's crying," I announced. The class burst out laughing.

The truth was, they were well advised not to admit me to their confidence. All the same, to be set apart from everyone, and for a girl of my age to be treated as a little chatterbox, was not a very pleasant experience.

I was approaching the age of fifteen, about the age when our mothers became brides and when our grandmothers would go off in a great state to the wishing wells at Eyup, exclaiming "Preserve us from having to stay home unmarried!" I had not grown much in height. But in spite of my crudity, my body had begun to develop, and strange colours and lights had begun to come and go in my face. Now and again my bearded uncle would seize my hands and pull me to the window; and then, drawing my face close to his, as though he were going to drink it in with his short-sighted eyes, "Girl," he would say, "what sort of complexion is this? What does this colour mean? It's just like a piece of cambric; it will neither fade nor grow old."

Now is this what a girl ought to look like?—a dumpy little body and a face that looks as though it had been painted with a brush?... On looking in the glass I felt as though I was looking at a doll in one of the shop windows in the Bonmarché; and I would amuse myself by putting out my tongue and squinting at my reflection.

I loved Easter above all the holidays. When I went to Kozyatak to spend those two weeks there, the cherries were ripe, and the cherry trees, which covered the whole of that side of the big garden looking on to the main road, were resplendent with fruit. I was very fond of cherries. During that fortnight I lived almost entirely on cherries, like the sparrows, and did not intend to go back to school until I had finished the ones that still remained at the top of the highest branches.

One day towards evening, I was again on the top of a tree eating cherries and amusing myself by flipping the stones as far as I could. And would you believe it, one of these happened to encounter the tip of the nose of a middle-aged neighbour who was passing that way.

The good fellow couldn't make out what had happened to him. He looked all round in a great state of mind, but it didn't occur to him to look up at the tree. If I had said nothing and hadn't moved from where I was, perhaps he would never have seen me, and would have gone on his way, thinking, maybe, that some ill-mannered bird had dropped a stone while passing over his head. But although I was in an awful state of fear and very much ashamed, I couldn't restrain myself and began to laugh. To see a girl seated astride a large branch and laughing shamelessly was too much for the good man. With a face convulsed with anger, he said: "Bravo, young lady! I never would have believed such a thing of a fine grown-up young woman like you...."

Would that the earth had opened and swallowed me at that moment. Goodness knows what colour the cambric had become. In spite of the risk of falling out of the tree, I clasped my hands across the front of my school blouse, and slightly bowed my head:

"Forgive me, Sir," I said. "I swear it was an accident: or rather it was carelessness." The innocent gesture of supplication was the one assumed by the nuns and the more religiously minded pupils, when praying before Mary and Jesus. At all events it had long proved successful. For centuries both Mother and Son had been deluded by this form of approach; surely it would appease this old fellow?

I had not been wrong in my calculation. My neighbour was taken in by my hypocritical repentance, and the tremor in my voice, and he softened. Anyway, for whatever reason, he felt constrained to say something nice to me. "Does it not occur to you that this kind of carelessness may be dangerous for a grown-up young woman?" he asked.

Although I knew very well what he meant, I opened my eyes wide and said: "Why should it, Sir?"

Shading his eyes from the sun with his hand, he looked me attentively, and laughed.

'Well—for one thing, I might hesitate to ask for you—for my son?"

I laughed too. "I'm insured against that, Sir. Even if I were a well-mannered girl, you wouldn't have me."

"How do you know?"

"Because I have far worse faults than that of climbing trees and throwing cherry stones. . . . In the first place, I am not rich. . . . From what I hear, a girl who is not rich is not much sought after. . . . Then I am not pretty; and if you ask me, that is a greater fault than poverty."

My words greatly amused the old gentleman. "Are you ugly, my dear?" he inquired.

I made a face. "Whatever you may say to the contrary, do you think I don't know myself? Do you think *this* is what girls look like? Tall, fair-haired with blue or green eyes . . . that's what's wanted."

I believe the old boy had been a bit of a dog in his day; with a significant look and a change in his voice, he said: "Ah! My poor child, are you old enough to know what beauty is, and be aware, as well, of what you are yourself? But never mind. . . . Let's see now, what's your name?"

"Çalıkuşu. . . ."

"But what sort of name is that?"

"I beg your pardon. That's what they call me at school. My real name is Feridé. But this one expresses roundness and lack of grace—as I do."

"Feridé Hanim, your name is as pretty as you are. You can be sure of that. I trust I shall find someone like you for my son. . . ."

I don't know why, but I was enjoying my talk with this gentlemanly, pleasant-spoken man. "That means, then, that I can throw cherries at him?" I asked.

"Of course—of course; there can be no doubt about that."

"But for the moment, please allow me to give you a few cherries. Whatever happens, you must accept them, to prove that you have forgiven me. Wait a couple of minutes." I began to climb the branches with the agility of a squirrel. My old neighbour clasped his hands across his chest, and shouted out: "Oh Lord! The branches are cracking—I'll be to blame—you'll fall, Feridé Hanim!"

I took no notice of his excitement, and called out: "Don't worry. . . . I'm so accustomed to falling . . . if you were near enough, you could see the scar on my temple; it puts the finishing touch to the rest of my charms."

"Look out girl! You'll fall. . . ."

"It's all over, Sir. It's done . . . the only thing is, how am I going to give them to you? . . . I know what I'll do, Sir; I've got it." I took my handkerchief out of the pocket of my tunic, filled it with cherries, and tied it up like a parcel.

"Don't worry about the handkerchief . . . I haven't wiped my nose on it yet . . . it's perfectly clean. Now I beg you to catch it without dropping it: one—two—three!"

My old neighbour caught the handkerchief full of cherries with the most unexpected agility. "Thank you very much, my dear," he said, "only how am I to return your handkerchief?"

"It doesn't matter . . . I'll make you a present of it."

"But that won't do!"

"Why not? And there's something else . . . I shall be going back to school in a few days. . . . There's a custom at the school . . . The girls flirt with young men all through the holidays, and then when school re-opens they tell one another about it. I've had no success of that kind yet, so I'm rather looked down on. They don't dare to say anything to my face, but it's quite certain they laugh at my simplicity. This time I have had a success. When I get back to school, I shall bow my head deep in thought, as though I had a great secret, and I shall smile sadly. They'll say, 'Çalıkuşu, is there anything the matter?' I shall say, 'No, what could be the matter?' They won't believe me; they'll persist . . . and then I shall say, 'Well, all right. But swear not to tell anyone'—and I shall invent a story."

"What story?"

"My making your acquaintance will facilitate that. I shall say, 'I flirted over the wall with a tall fair man . . .' of course I shan't say he had white hair; and when you were a young man you must have had fair hair

. . . I know their characters. They will ask: 'What did you talk about?' I shall swear he said he thought me pretty. But it would never do to say I gave him cherries in a handkerchief . . . I gave him roses, I shall say. But no: that won't do either . . . It's not the custom to give roses in a handkerchief. . . . I'll say I made him a present of my handkerchief, and that will be that."

Although we had been within an ace of fighting, now I was laughing with the old fellow and waving my hand to him as we parted.

In the summer of that year, something else happened to me as a result of this tree-climbing infirmity of mine. It was a moonlit night in August. A number of guests had come to the house, among them a widow of about twenty-five called Neriman, who occasionally honoured us with a visit. From my aunts, who liked no one else, to the simple servant girls, everyone admired her. Her husband, whom it was said Neriman had loved very much, had died a year ago; that was why she always wore black. But I had a feeling that if black had not been particularly becoming to this blonde lady, the mourning would not have lasted so long, and the clothes would have been thrown away a good deal earlier.

Neriman tried to pursue me, behaving rather as though she were caressing a dog or a cat. But for some reason I didn't care for her. There was a certain frigidity between us; I always used to meet her advances rather coldly. In spite of the fact that the coolness persisted, I must still admit that Neriman was dangerously pretty. And what I couldn't stand about her was that she was a dreadful flirt. When she was alone with women, she was as demure as could be. But if by chance a man appeared, her face would change, and her voice, her looks, and her laughter altered completely. In a word, she went one better than my contemporaries at school, though they were up to all kinds of deceptions.

The moment there was any talk about her husband, she would adopt a rather studied sentimental role, saying: "Ah well! Life for me is over . . . ;" which used to be too much for me. When she acted like this, I would boil with rage, and reflect: "You wait: if someone better than you should come along, you'd be taught a lesson."

There was no one in our house who could be regarded as a rival to Neriman. It would not have been correct to reckon the passive Nejmiye a human being. My aunts were really elderly now; they had no conversation except an occasional malicious remark, about this person or the other. Consequently . . . ! I somehow grasped what it was that

24

attracted Neriman to the house. It looked as though she had taken a fancy to my imbecile cousin. Did she want to marry him? I don't think so. That a widow nearing her thirties would want to marry a lad of twenty would be very unseemly; and even if she didn't refrain from that kind of behaviour, it was not likely that my spiteful old aunts would willingly surrender their boy to this bird of prey.

In that case . . . in that case—

Was there a case?

Until the merry widow had succeeded in running to earth another man who would minister to her whims and indulgences, she would amuse herself by wasting time on my cousin. . . .

I called Kâmran an imbecile just now, out of irritation. I really feel like calling him a sly, insidious . . . *insect*! He did his best not to give himself away as he talked to Neriman, but do you think he could escape me? Whether I was romping about with the children, or skipping by myself, or lying on the ground telling fortunes with cards, my eyes were always on him. Wherever my cousin might be, it would be somewhere near the woman. . . . Now and then, pretending not to be aware of it, I would go past them; at once they would lower their voices . . . or change the conversation. "Let them do as they like," you will say, "what's it got to do with you?" What's it got to do with me? Even if Kâmran is my enemy, he is my cousin too. Is it likely that I should want a woman (and who knows what sort of a woman?) to ruin his character?

Let me see—what was I saying?—Oh, yes; it was a moonlit night in August. They were talking and laughing in a crowd on the verandah in front of the house, by the light of a quite unnecessary Japanese lantern. Neriman's laughs, which were as measured and harmonious as notes of music, so tried my nerves that I moved off and plunged into the darkness of trees in a corner of the garden. Right at the other end there was an old plane tree, some of the branches of which hung over our neighbour's grounds. Although the poor thing had no fruit of any value to me, I loved its ancient appearance, and would climb its great flat branches and explore them. That is what I did that night; I climbed to a fairly high branch and sat there.

Soon afterwards I heard a light footstep, followed by a muffled laugh. I opened my eyes at once, and pricked up my ears . . . And what do you suppose I saw? My cousin, with the merry widow, coming straight towards me.

Çalıkuşu

Like a fisherman who sees a fish approaching his bait, I was alive with expectation. I was terribly afraid I should make a noise where I was sitting. I needn't have worried. They were so taken up with one another, that even if I had beaten a drum where I sat, I believe they would never have heard it.

Neriman was walking in front, my cousin four or five paces behind her, like an Arab slave. As they couldn't continue their walk beyond the wall, they stopped below my tree.

(Come along, little ones: come along, my lambs. . . . Allah has sent you to me. We'll have a word or two, in a minute. . . . We'll do our best to leave you with an unforgettable memory of this lovely moonlit night.)

At that moment, a cricket had to start chirping. I was going out of my mind. I wouldn't be able to hear the speech my cousin was making to the merry widow.

If it had suited my purpose, I should have called out: "Wretch! What is there to be frightened of? Who is there to hear you? Raise your voice, Sir!"

The only few words that reached my ear from the speech were "Neriman—my pretty! My angel!" I began to tremble all over. I was afraid that even if I didn't fall, I should make a noise and rustle the leaves. Meanwhile I caught a few of Neriman's words. . . . "Please, Kâmran Bey; please—" she was saying.

Finally the voices died away. Neriman was walking towards the wall and raising herself on tiptoe as though there were something she wanted to see in the darkness of the neighbour's garden. Standing like this of course, she had her back towards Kâmran, who seemed not to know what to do. . . .

Suddenly I could see my cousin walk up to her and lift his hands. . . . My heart was beating: "At last he's come to his senses; he's going to give the creature a thorough shaking," I said to myself; "if only he would, I should throw myself down from the tree in tears, and make my peace with him till the day I die."

But that beast did nothing of the kind. With those thin arms of his, and his white, feminine hands, he seized her first by the shoulders, and then by the wrists, with the most unexpected strength. There they were in each other's arms: I could see them through the leaves of the tree, in the glimpses of the moonlight, with the hair of their heads touching.

Oh, dreadful, dreadful scene! My body was trembling from head to toe. Although it was only a moment since I'd wanted to trap them, I was terribly afraid now that they would detect me. How I longed to change into a real bird!—to fly up skyward over those branches, and be lost in the arms of the moon, far above; and never again to contemplate the faces of the men of this world.

In spite of pressing my lips with my fingers one sound escaped me. It might have been a cry of alarm; but as those two listened it turned into a laugh. You should have seen the surprise and dismay of the shameless creatures at that moment. The merry widow (who but a moment ago had seemed to move softly, like a moonbeam, without touching the ground with her feet), now made off as hard as she could, running into trees, and twisting her ankles. My cousin wanted to do the same thing. He started after her a little way, and then, for some reason, sheepishly turned back.

As I could find nothing else to do, I was still laughing; and he, like the fox in the well-known tale of the fox and the crow, began to walk warily up and down under the tree. In the end, abandoning his confusion and embarrassment, he said to me:

"Feridé, my child, will you climb down a little?"

I stopped laughing, and asked in a serious voice: "What for?"

"Oh, nothing. . . . But there's something I want to say to you."

"I've nothing to say to you . . . don't disturb me."

"Feridé, stop joking."

"Joking, you say? What next?"

"Look here: you're going too far . . . if you won't come down, I can climb up."

"Do you want to kill yourself? How surprising! My delicate simpering cousin, who gets into a state if he's out for a walk and comes to a puddle, so that he has to look at his shoes and the water three or four times before deciding to jump it; and who can't sit down without pulling up his trouser-legs with the tips of his fingers—*he* wants to climb a tree!"

But he was wild that night. He seized one of the nearest branches and sprang on to the trunk of the tree, ready, indeed to go higher still. . . .

For some reason or other, it made me desperate to think of coming face to face with him on that night, and in a tree. It would be disastrous for that to happen. If I were to see his green, venomous eyes looking closely at me, we should turn into two birds of prey, struggling with one another among the branches. After putting out his eyes, I should be sure to throw him down; either him or myself.

27

But for some reason I didn't think it right to give any sign of this desperate feeling. I drew myself up, where I was, and commanded sternly: "Stop a minute, where you are!"

He took no notice, and didn't even answer. He straightened himself on the branch to which he had climbed, and began to look up still further.

"Stop!" I ordered. "This will end badly. You know I'm a wren. The trees are my property.... I can't allow anyone else to set foot in them."

"What are you talking about, Feridé?"

What a strange conversation it was! Preparing to climb still higher if he came on, I said: "You know I respect you. I should be very sorry to have to send you hurtling down from the tree. It will be dreadful if that voice, which was reciting poetry just now, should suddenly change into cries of 'Help! Help!'" I mimicked him, and laughed.

"Now we'll talk," I told him.

Fear had made him brave and agile. Ignoring my threat, he started to climb the branches below me. We began a game of hide-and-seek on the tree. The nearer he got to me, the higher I went; but the branches got thinner and thinner. At one moment I thought of jumping over the wall and running away. But if I did, there was a chance of failing to escape by injuring myself, so that I should end by crying out myself, instead of my cousin.

None the less, whatever happened, we must not approach one another tonight. Changing my policy, I asked him:

"May I be told why you are so anxious to talk to me?"

At these words he changed his tactics too, and adopting a serious attitude, he paused.

"I am joking with you; but the question is important, Feridé ... I am afraid of you...."

"Is that so? What is there about me that you are afraid of, I wonder?"

"Of your chattering."

"Isn't that something I do every day?"

"But tonight's not the same as other nights."

"What's extraordinary about tonight?"

Kâmran was very tired and troubled. With no further thought of his trousers, he seated himself on one of the branches. Although he still seemed to be joking, he was in fact bordering on tears. It was not that I was sorry for him, but because, come what may, I couldn't stand talking to him any longer, and wanted to escape at once, that made me say:

28

"Don't bother; you may be sure that there's nothing to be afraid of. . . . Go back at once to your guests. It's disgraceful to leave them like this."

"Is that a promise Feridé? Will you swear?"

"It's a promise. I swear . . . whatever you like. . . ."

"Am I to believe you?"

"I think you must believe me. After all, I'm not as much of a child as I was. . . ."

"Feridé!—"

"And how do I know what you're afraid of my saying? I'm just sitting alone on my tree. . . ."

"I don't know; but somehow, something tells me not to believe you."

"Of course, I must point out that I'm much older now; nearly a grown-up person. Listen, my dear cousin . . . don't be so worried. There are some things a child can see, but a young girl who's just begun to grow up can't distinguish them. . . . Come on, set your mind at rest."

It seemed as though Kâmran's feeling of fear was slowly turning into one of surprise. Raising his head, as if determined at all costs to see me, he said: "How very differently you are talking, Feridé."

If this conversation went on, we should never put a stop to it. With simulated anger, I let out: "Oh, stop! That's enough. If you go on, I shall take back my promise. You think a minute!"

This threat alarmed him. Heavily he climbed down the tree, and as though ashamed of going off in the same direction as Neriman, he began to walk towards the other end of the garden.

After that night the merry widow wasn't seen at the house again. As for Kâmran, I felt, for a long time, that he was afraid of me. Every time he went down to Istanbul, he used to bring me presents—a coloured Japanese sunshade; silk handkerchiefs; silk stockings; a heart-shaped mirror; a chic handbag. What was the point of his giving me these things which were more suitable for a grown-up girl than an uncouth child like me? What reason could there have been, except to throw dust in the eyes of Çalıkuşu, to keep her little beak shut, and prevent her from chattering?

I had come to the age when I could appreciate the pleasure of being considered by others; and moreover, I liked the lovely things. But for some reason or other I didn't wish to show either Kâmran or anyone else that I attached any importance to the offerings. When my sunshade, adorned with pictures of bamboo houses and slant-eyed Japanese girls, fell on the ground or into the dust, I didn't pick it up; and I used to hear my aunts scolding me: "Feridé, is this the value you attach to presents people give you? And I roused them to protest one day, when I started to put some fresh fruit into the handbag, for which, as I rubbed its bright soft leather case, I really felt a kind of awe. If I had been astute enough, I might have profited still more from Kâmran's fears, and I might have got a whole lot of other things from him by exploiting the situation. But even these treasures, which from one point of view I liked having so much, I somehow wanted to tear up or destroy; and longed to stamp them underfoot, and then burst into tears. The anger and disgust that I felt for my cousin persisted. In other summers, as I saw the days approaching when the school would re-open, my head would ache, and my eyes would lose their brightness. But that year, I longed for the day when I should be quit of the house and all the people in it.

It was a Sunday, during the first weeks of school. The nuns had taken us for a walk in the direction of Kağithane. The Sisters themselves were not very fond of walks in the street, but somehow or other we had stayed out late that evening.

I was walking at the rear of the column. I don't know how it happened: at one moment, without having noticed it, I found that the distance between myself and the rest had increased to an alarming degree. They must have thought I was far ahead of them, as usual, because no one called out. Just at that moment I saw a shadow beside me. I looked; it was Michelle.

"Is it you, Çalıkuşu?" she said, "How is it you're walking all alone and so slowly?"

I pointed to the handkerchief wound round my right ankle, and answered: "Perhaps you didn't notice that I fell and hurt my foot just now when we were playing."

Michelle isn't a bad girl. She was sorry for me. "If you like, I'll help you," she said.

"You're not going to offer to carry me?"

"No, of course not. I can't do that . . . but I can take your arm, can't I? Not like that; put your arm on my shoulder. Lean heavier . . . I'll put my arm round your waist. It'll take some of the weight off you. . . . How's that?—don't you feel less pain now, when you walk?"

I did as she asked. It really was better. "Thank you, Michelle," I said, "you're an awfully good sort."

After walking a little, Michelle said: "Do you know, Feridé, what the others will think when they see us walking together?"

"What will they think?"

"That Feridé has fallen in love too. . . . She's telling her trouble to Michelle, they'll say. . . ."

I stopped at once. "Do you really mean it?" I asked.

"Of course!"

"If that's the case, let go my arm at once." I said this with all the sternness of an officer giving a word of command.

Michelle kept hold of me, and said: "You idiot, how can you really believe that?"

"Why idiot?"

"Doesn't everyone know what you really are?"

"What do you mean?"

"Oh, nothing. Only that *you'll* never have that sort of adventure . . . that there's no chance of *your* ever attracting anyone. . . ."

"Why? Do you think I'm ugly?"

"No . . . not ugly . . . pretty, even, perhaps. But you're so hopelessly simple and stupid."

"Is that how you think of me?"

"It's not only me. Everyone thinks like that. In the matter of love, Çalıkuşu is a regular 'gourde.'"

I'm not quite sure of the Turkish word, but in French, "gourde" has some sort of meaning like "hanging pumpkin," "water pumpkin," or "sweet pumpkin." Whichever it may be, it's something unpleasant. In fact, with my short stature, and my rather thick-set body, I'm not altogether unlike one of those pumpkins. . . . How awful, if instead of calling me Çalıkuşu, they started calling me "Gourde." . . . Whatever happened, I must avert that danger, so damaging to my *amour-propre*. I put my head on Michelle's shoulder, with a gesture I had learnt from her, and smiled sadly, with a sidelong glance that was full of meaning.

"You go on thinking that."

"What do you mean, Feridé?" Michelle stopped and looked at me with amazement. I confirmed my statement, and nodded slightly.

"Unfortunately, that's how it is," I said, and to make my lie a little easier to swallow, I sighed. . . .

This time Michelle was so surprised she made the sign of the cross. "Good . . . very good, Feridé. What a pity I can't bring myself to believe it." Poor Michelle! She was a girl obsessed with love; so that it was a pleasure for her even to detect it in another. But as she herself said, what a pity it was that she did not dare to believe in the reality when she met it! I had done something awful; but it was a matter of honour to go through with it.

"Yes, Michelle," I said, "I'm in love as well."

"It's just—that *you* love—someone?"

"Oh, the someone else is involved as well, of course—'grande gourde!'" (I gave her back the word "gourde" which she'd used just now, with the adjective "great" attached to it; but it never occurred to her to say: "That's you. That's *your* name." Which meant that I'd no sooner started to lie, than I had succeeded in making her resemble me. What luck!)

Michelle took my arm with a great show of affection. "Explain, Feridé. Explain how it happened! You mean that you, too—? Isn't it a lovely thing, to love?"

"Of course it's lovely."

"Who is it? Is he very handsome, the young man you love?"

"*Very.*"

"Where did you see him? How did you get to know him?"

"—"

"Come on; don't be so secretive."

I longed to be less so. But I didn't know what story to invent. It's very difficult to find an honest man one can really love. It's so difficult, so difficult to even imagine one—

"Feridé! . . . Don't hesitate . . . I'll say you're making it all up."

Suddenly I got into a state. Making it up? God forbid. Was I a mere pumpkin or what? I'd invent such a love story that it would astound even Michelle . . . And who do you think came into my mind to present to her as a lover?—Kâmran.

"My cousin and I are in love with each other," I said.

"That fair-haired cousin I saw last year in the school parlour?"

"Yes. That one."

"Oh—how *lovely!*" It was just as I said; Michelle was born to love. Kâmran had been over to the school twice, up to now, perhaps three times. Wasn't it odd that Michelle, who would nose out a young man as a cat noses out liver, should have come running into the parlour and caught sight of us there?

The stars were out. In spite of its being autumn, it felt so like summer that one could almost catch a breath of harvest. All the weight of my body hung on Michelle's shoulders; our hair and our faces were close together, as I started to tell her the fairy tale.

"It was an even brighter night than this," I was saying. "We were some way from all the others, outside the door. I was in front, my cousin a step or two behind me. . . . He was saying lovely things to me; I shan't be able to repeat what he said . . . because I'd rather not. The crickets were making so much noise . . . we walked and walked. From the open spaces that the moonlight turned into pools, we went into the darkness of the trees. . . . Then we came out again into the light . . . and then again into darkness. . . ."

"But how long is your garden, Feridé?"

I was afraid I had struck a false note. "Oh, it's not so long as all that: but we were walking slowly," I said, and continued, "Well, here we reached the end of our journey. Where the garden ends there's a big plane tree, overlooking our neighbour's grounds. When we got underneath it we paused . . . I was standing on tiptoe, as if I were looking over the wall into the next door garden. . . . He put his hands together . . . he was going to move . . . but he didn't dare. . . ."

"But you had your back turned to him. How did you see all that?"

"My cousin's shadow fell across the wall: that's how I knew." I must have played my part very well, because all the time I was telling the story, I was trembling; my voice choked; tears crept into my eyes. . . .

"And then, Feridé?—then?"

"Then . . . my cousin suddenly seized my wrists—"

"Oh, how lovely!—and then?"

"Then. . . . How do I know what happened?"

"But you're stopping just at the best place!"

"Then a bird began to sing in the tree . . . an ugly, coarse kind of bird . . . we were afraid—we ran away. . . ." I couldn't restrain my tears now. I put my head on Michelle's breast and sobbed bitterly. . . . I don't know how long this crying went on. Thank goodness, at last someone discovered that Michelle and I were lost; and they came shouting and looking for us, till my companion called out to them:

"We're coming; but we can't hurry . . . Çalıkuşu's foot is hurting her. . . ."

"That's right, Michelle. That's really why I'm crying. . . . But we can go a bit faster now."

When everyone had gone to sleep that night I wept in bed. But this time I wasn't crying on purpose, but because I was so angry with myself.

33

If I'd decided to invent a lie to convince the others I wasn't a "gourde," why on earth had I picked on Kâmran, as if there was no one else in the world? Kâmran, whom I disliked above all the rest? I swore to myself that no sooner was I awake tomorrow than I would take Michelle by the hand and drag her into a corner, and tell her that what I'd related the evening before had been a lie.

But alas, next morning, when I awoke, I found that both my indignation and shame had gone completely. I didn't dare tell the truth to Michelle, who now regarded me with quite different eyes, and treated me like an ailing child. The tale gradually spread among the others. Michelle must have strictly warned them against it, because no one said a word to me. But from their looks and their giggles, I knew what they meant. It gave me a strange sense of pride. For a time I had to give up my chatter and mischief. After all, I was now in everyone's eyes the girl who was in love with her cousin. That she should skip and jump about like a child, and play the fool, would never have done. However, they say a man's character doesn't change till he dies. In the evenings, during the final break from lessons, I would hang on to Michelle's arm, and the devil would tempt me, now and then, to go on in a slow voice inventing stories.

Once more, we were on our way back from a country walk. Michelle, who for some reason hadn't come with us that day, met me at the door, and taking me by the hand, ran off with me to a corner of the garden.

"I've got news for you," she said, "you will be both glad and sorry."

"Why?"

"Your fair cousin came to school today. I'm sure he came for you. . . . If only you had stayed with me!"

I didn't believe it. It wasn't likely that Kâmran would come to see me without some serious reason. Michelle must certainly have been mistaken. All the same, I didn't express my doubts to her.

"Could anything be more natural than that a young man should come and see the girl he's in love with?"

"You're sorry you weren't here, though, aren't you?"

"*That* I am!" Michelle stroked my cheek: "All the same, he'll come again," she said, "if he really loves you."

"There's no doubt about that."

That evening after supper, Sister Mathilde called me. She handed me two coloured boxes of sweets tied up with gold cord, and explained: "Your cousin brought these for you." Sister Mathilde is a type I don't care for; but as she handed me the boxes, it was as much as I could do not to put

34

my arms round her neck and kiss her on the cheeks. So Michelle was not wrong, it seemed. It was my cousin who had come to the school. If any of my friends doubted the truth of my story, they would have to change their minds when they saw those two boxes. How satisfactory! One of the boxes was filled with *fondants* of all colours, and the other with chocolates wrapped in gold tinfoil. Had it been three or four months ago, I should have carefully hidden them even from my closest friends. But that night, my boxes passed from hand to hand in the classroom, and each one helped herself to one, two, or even three pieces, according to the dictates of her conscience.

Some of them made significant signs to me from where they were sitting; but I pretended to be rather confused, and turned my head away with a laugh. How lovely again! When Michelle returned me the boxes, the gold bottoms of which were, alas, now beginning to be visible, she whispered: "These boxes are sort of engagement boxes of sweets, Feridé." My story had cost me a good deal, but what was I to do?

It was three days later; I was preparing a coloured geography map for the exams. Painting was not at all my strong point. Being rather clumsy, I used to smudge the colours now and again, and get paint on to my fingers and mouth. On that day, when I was engaged on this too, the porter's girl came into the class, and announced that my cousin had come, and was waiting to see me in the parlour. I remember I looked confusedly about me, and at the teacher who was taking the class, as though I didn't know what to do.

"Come now, Feridé," she said, "leave your map as it is, and go and see your visitor."

Yes, I could go and leave my map—that was all right—but what sort of a face was I going to present to the visitor? The girl next to me had taken a little mirror out of her overall, and put it in front of me, as though to make fun. My face and my mouth were in an awful state. Just as I used to stick my pen in my mouth when I wrote, now I'd put the paint brush in it; my lips were lined with yellow and red and violet paint. I knew there was no chance of washing it off either with my handkerchief or even with soap and water; in fact, I should only make it worse. Kâmran of course was of no importance; I didn't mind what sort of face I presented to him. But *vis-à-vis* the others, who wanted to know who the bridegroom was to be, and who were laughing hard, I represented a girl in love, who was, indeed, about to be betrothed. Devil take them all!

35

Çalıkuşu

As I left the corridor, a looking-glass that happened to catch my eye greatly added to my discomfort; so much so, that if there had been no one outside the parlour, I should perhaps not have gone in at all. But as luck would have it, there were people about, and they prevented any action of this kind. Well! There was no going back. I opened the door quickly, and burst in.

Kâmran was standing near the window. Was I to go straight up to him? I didn't know. I supposed I would have to shake hands with him; with the paint on my wet fingers, I should make a dreadful mess of the clean, elegant, feminine hands of my cousin. I caught sight of some parcels on the table, tied like the others with a gold cord. I knew they were meant for me. If there wasn't to be trouble, there was nothing for it but to hide the paint on my hands and mouth, under the pretext of some childishness. I took hold of the corners of my black overall, and made a reverent and slow obeisance to both boxes. At the same time I took the opportunity of wiping my fingers a bit on the corners of my coverall. Then, blowing the boxes a couple of kisses with my fingers, I took a little of the paint off my lips.

Kâmran came up to me, laughing. I somehow had to show a little goodwill.

"How good of you to do this, Kâmran Bey," I said. "It's true I have some right to chocolates and *fondants*; all the same, you make me feel quite embarrassed. In the box you brought the other day there was a certain kind of *fondant*. . . . If only I can find one like it in these new boxes! But it's really impossible to describe what it was like. As it melted in your mouth, your heart melted at the same time."

"This time," Kâmran said, "I think you'll find something even more worth having, Feridé."

With excitement and impatience I opened the box he was pointing at, and two brightly-coloured books emerged. They were the kind of childish fairy stories you give small children at Christmas. It was obvious that my cousin, for some reason or other, must have wanted to make me look foolish. If that was all he had come for, it was cruel indeed. Had the time come, I wondered, to teach him a little lesson? I don't know; but at any rate I couldn't help myself. With a seriousness that scarcely accorded with my paint-covered lips, I said:

"One must be grateful for any kind of present. But if you'll allow me, I should like to make a brief observation. A few years ago you were a child as well. It's true that you were quite grown-up in your manner and

36

your serious behaviour, even then, but in spite of that, you were a child; isn't that so? And while you are growing up, year by year, into a superb fellow like the hero of an illustrated novel, why am I always supposed to remain stationary?"

Kâmran opened his eyes in surprise: "Excuse me, Feridé; I don't understand," he said.

"There's nothing difficult to understand; you grow up, but why do I remain a baby who reads fairy tales from Bibliothèque Rose, and why am I not considered good enough to be treated with the respect due to a girl of fifteen?"

Kâmran continued to look at me, more and more surprised: "I still don't understand you, Feridé."

I compressed my lips and made a gesture as though amazed at this inability to understand. But to tell the truth, I didn't really know what I meant. By now I'd repented of what I had said, and was trying to find a way out. I was nervously cutting the string of the second box. There were *fondants* in this one, too.

Kâmran bowed slightly, in a way that was almost official. "It's given me great pleasure to hear from your own mouth that you ought to be treated as a grown-up girl, Feridé," he said, "I see it's no good apologising about the books, because the *fondants* are enough to show that the books were only meant as a joke. If I had really meant to bring you books, I might perhaps have chosen one of those novels you mentioned just now."

I was convinced that Kâmran was simply mocking me by his attitude and his words. None the less, I was pleased that he should express himself to me in those tones and in that sort of language. To avoid having to answer him, I clasped my hands as though in prayer, and assumed an attitude of deep admiration. When he stopped talking, I looked into his face, and with a shake of the head, I threw back the hair that was falling into my eyes.

"I haven't heard a word you've been saying," I said, "the *fondants* are so lovely. . . . Anyway, when I see *them*, we are friends again. Everything's all right. Thank you, Kâmran."

He was probably annoyed to think I hadn't been listening. Anyhow, he wasn't going to let me know it. He sighed, and said with a sanctimonious expression: "What am I to do? If presents for children are no longer welcome, from now on I shall have to pay you my compliments with some serious tributes, only suitable for grown-up people."

It now seemed I was absorbed in the *fondants*. I was looking at the box with as much pleasure as one would look at a jewel case, and was setting the chocolates I took out in a row on an illustrated paper. At the same time I was talking a lot of nonsense:

"Eating these is an art, Kâmran, and your humble servant has discovered this art. Look! For instance, you'd see no harm, would you, in eating this yellow one before the red?—But what a pity it would be! Because the red is sweeter and it's got a slight taste of *menthe*. If you eat that one first, it's so hard on the delicate flavour and the poetic scent of the yellow. Ah! What sweets. . . ."

I picked up one and put it in my mouth. I stroked it as though I were fondling a young bird, and murmured to it. My cousin stretched out his hand:

"Supposing you give it to me, Feridé," he said.

I looked into his face with curiosity. "What do you mean?"

"I want to eat it."

"I think it was a mistake on my part, to open the box when you were here. If you begin to eat the things you've brought, I've got something else to do."

"Just give me that one!"

Good gracious! What did this mean? Not to mind tasting something from another person's lips? . . . What ideas came into my mind . . . ! Anyhow, I must have shown a momentary surprise and hesitation, because my cousin suddenly put out his hand, and tried to snatch the *fondant* out of my fingers. But I was too quick for him. I saved the sweet, and stuck out my tongue at him.

"You're no good at sleight of hand; how did that happen?" I asked mockingly. "Look, let me show you how lovely *fondants* like these are eaten—*then* snatch. . . ." Throwing my head back a little and putting out my tongue again, I placed the *fondant* on it. As the sweet slowly melted, I shook my head, and as I couldn't use my tongue I indicated with my hands how delicious it tasted. My cousin was looking at my mouth with such surprised curiosity, that I couldn't help beginning to laugh. Then becoming serious again, I held out the box.

"Now that you may be considered to have learnt your lesson, I can offer you one."

Kâmran pushed the box away half jokingly and half in anger, saying: "I don't want it. You can have it all."

"Thank you very much for that."

After this we really had nothing more to say to one another, and having asked after those at home, as politeness demanded, and sending them my compliments, I put the boxes tightly under my arm, and was preparing to go. Suddenly there was a slight noise in the room next door to the parlour. I stopped, like a cat with its ears pricked up. The door of the room in question, which was kept for school notice boards and maps, had opened a minute before, and then I heard a sound like one of the notice boards falling down. Finally I detected a sound, and movements not unlike a mouse scratching behind the dividing glass door. What should I see, without my cousin noticing it, on looking at the door, but a great shadow of a head, behind the frosted glass. At once I tumbled to it. It was Michelle. She must have got round the simple-minded nun, by saying that she wanted to look for a map, and then come to spy on us from the room next door to the parlour.

The shadow disappeared. But I had no doubt that the girl was watching us through a keyhole under the glass partition. What was I to do? She would certainly be expecting something out of the ordinary from two people alleged to be in love. If she were to see me go out of the door like a fool, with a mere "Goodbye, salaams to those at home," she would understand everything; she would seize my head in her arms in the corridor and rumple my hair, and say with a laugh, "You've been telling me tales!" It was the fear of that which put a piece of wickedness into my mind at that very instant. It wasn't right; but I had begun to play a part, and I must play to its conclusion.

Michelle, like many of the other girls, didn't know Turkish. I decided it didn't matter what we said to one another. All that mattered was that by our voices and gestures we should *look* like two people in love. So I said to Kâmran:

"I'd nearly forgotten. Is our nurse's grandchild at home?" This grandchild was an orphan, who had grown up in the house for years. Kâmran looked surprised at my question.

"Of course, she's at home. Where would you have her go to?"

"Yes, of course . . . I know. . . . Only—how was I to tell? I'm so fond of that child. . . ."

My cousin smiled. "What's all this about? You've never once even looked at the poor little thing."

With a rather unexpected gesture, I said: "Oh, not looking at her proves nothing. Does it prove that I don't love her? That's absurd! On the contrary, I'm so devoted to the child that—" I kept repeating the world "love," bending my head and clasping my arms across my breast, rather like an actress in the title-role of "La Dame aux Caméllias," and at the same time glancing at the door out of the corner of my eye. Michelle only knew six words of Turkish; at least three of them were sure to be "To love—love—passion." But even if I were wrong, at any rate she could look in a dictionary or learn from someone who knew Turkish, what tremendous meaning the world "love" possesses.

But I had to control the situation not only as it affected Michelle, but also Kâmran. It looked as though I had not succeeded with the latter, because Kâmran began to laugh, both at my words and at my manner of expressing them.

"Where's this suddenly blown up from, Feridé?" he asked.

"Never mind where it's blown from." Was this moment to weaken? With the same warmth I insisted:

"Anyway, there it is; I love her. You must promise me something . . . the moment you get home, as a souvenir from me to that poor child . . . as a souvenir . . . do you understand? . . . a souvenir *d'amour*. . . ." How I longed to give Kâmran something for the nurse's grandchild, under Michelle's eyes. Most annoyingly, I had nothing in my pockets except some pieces of paper I'd screwed up ready to throw at the old nun, as she dozed during the evening session. But this lack of suitable means inspired me to something even better. I suddenly seized Kâmran's hands, and made a gesture as if I were going to hug him:

"You'll give the child a hug from me; you'll kiss her cheeks and eyes again and again, do you understand? Will you promise?"

Kâmran and I were almost in one another's arms. We could feel each other's breath. My poor cousin, who was completely in the dark, couldn't make out what all this exuberance meant.

My part had been successfully played, and it was over. The curtain could be rung down. I dropped Kâmran's hands, and flung myself out of the room without waiting any longer. I expected Michelle to come and throw her arms round me in the passage. But there wasn't a sound to be heard anywhere; I paused, turned round and went slowly towards the door of the room where the school notices were kept. And what should I see but old Brother Kasavier, who used to come and give us music lessons, from time to time. With his legs shaking, he had got on to a chair, and was looking for some music scores in the top drawer of the cupboard!

Oh, the devil take Michelle!—She had been a complete illusion, and I'd gone and disgraced myself before Kâmran forever.

I felt my eyes burning, like someone who's just had an attack of fever. Instead of returning to the classroom, I went into the garden and across to the fountain. I turned on the tap, and put my head beneath it. Not only did I feel hot all over, but I was trembling too. As the tap water ran through my hair and over my face into my shirt, I kept thinking: "If this is what comes of just acting the thing they call love, whatever can love itself be like in reality?"

Kâmran often came to school that year. So often, in fact, that every time the door opened I thought they were coming to call me to the parlour, and my heart would beat.

I can really say that the whole class lived on the chocolates, cakes and pastries that he brought me. Marie Pirlantaciyan, who was renowned as much for her greed as for her hard work, could not conceal her envy and admiration, as she nibbled my sweets with her great white teeth. "Your young man shows how much he must love you, bringing you all these lovely things," she used to say.

All the same, all this myth-making began to disgust me. Sometimes I used to think to myself: "Wasn't it dishonourable to show all these things to the others in one light, when really they were only brought to a chatterbox of a child, as the price of her silence?" And why did Kâmran come so frequently to the school? Each time he used to find some reason like the following: "I've come to ask after a friend who lives in the neighbourhood. . . ." "I wanted to hear a little music in the Taxim Gardens." One day, without my saying anything at all, he said again: "I'm on my way back from seeing an old friend of my father's in Nişantaş. My father was very fond of him."

I couldn't control myself, and suddenly took the offensive. "What's his name? What does he do? What's the address of the house?" I demanded.

My cousin became so confused he couldn't even invent a name and address. He changed colour, and laughed, trying to put me off by asking: "What are you after? Why all this interest?"

There seemed to be something significant in all this. When I said: "I shall ask my aunt, at the weekend," he grew still more shamefaced, and began to urge: "Be careful. Don't say anything to my mother about it. She doesn't want me to see him."

"Insidious creature! He thinks he can take me in. I can see right through you." I got up angrily, hiding my hands, which he tried to seize, in my pockets. "If you think your father's friends or your friends are any concern of mine, you're quite wrong." That was all I would say.

From that day on, whenever Kâmran came to the school, I invented an excuse and didn't go to him; I used to tear open the boxes he continued to bring in the classroom or in the garden, and dole them out to the other girls without touching a single one. The truth was as clear as day. Not a doubt of it, the merry widow lived somewhere in the neighbourhood. They must certainly have come to an understanding that night. My cousin was going to her house, from time to time, and looking in on me when he did so.

They could carry on as they liked with each other . . . what did it matter to me? But to have them treat me like a plaything was the final indignity! Whenever I thought of it, I got into a regular fever, and had to bite my lips till they bled, to prevent myself crying. It should have been a small matter to ask at home where Neriman lived. But to mention the woman's name seemed to be more than I could stand.

The day came when I set off for home, on holiday. A visitor happened to say to Nejmiye, "I had a letter from Neriman two days ago; she sounds very happy." I was just going out to give the little poodle a bath in the pond, when I heard the words. I stood by the door and crouched down on the ground to let the dog drop slowly from my lap. I couldn't ask any further questions about the merry widow, but no one could prevent my listening, you know. . . .

The visitor went on: "Neriman seems to be very happy with her husband; let's hope she will be, this time, poor dear. . . ." Nejmiye, echoing another's sentiments as usual, said: "Yes, of course, poor dear! I hope she'll be happy this time, anyway." Why must she repeat what the visitor had said, and so put an end to the conversation? Well, there was nothing else for it. So I asked with a touch of mockery in my voice, "So the lady's married again, has she?"

"What lady?"

"The one you had the letter from—Neriman Hanim."

Nejmiye answered instead of the visitor. "What, hadn't you heard? *Long* ago. . . . Neriman married an engineer. . . . She's been in Smyrna with her husband for the last five or six months."

Now it was my turn to repeat: "May she be happy this time, at any rate" (for the third time); and pressing the little dog to me, I fled. But I didn't go to the pond after all. I leapt over the hedge borders and the trunks of the vine trees, and ran right round the garden.

I went on a journey that summer. Not far—as far as Tekirdăgi. As you know, in my life, God had treated me very liberally in the matter of aunts. One of them lived in Tekirdăgi. Her husband, my uncle Aziz, had been provincial Governor there for years. They had a daughter named Müjgan who was older than I was; among my younger relatives I think perhaps I liked her best of all.

Müjgan was ugly, really. But that didn't make any difference to me. Although there was only three years between us in age, even as a child I always looked on her, somehow, as a grown-up person. And although the difference between us is even less now, I still look upon her in the same way, and call her "abla" (elder sister).

Müjgan abla is the very opposite of me. She is just as serious-minded as I am harebrained and mischievous. More than that, she's autocratic. It was always she who got what she wanted, although I sometimes took her advice with bad grace; and if I went against her wishes, I had to give in, eventually. Why? How can I tell? If you've the misfortune to love someone, you soon find you're a slave.

Once every few years Müjgan would come to Istanbul with my aunt Ayşe and spend a few weeks at our house, or go and stay with one of my other aunts. That summer, a semi-official invitation came to me from Tekirdăgi. In a letter which my aunt Ayşe wrote to aunt Besimé, she said: "I know it's no good asking *you*, but we insist on having Feridé these holidays for at least two months. Don't forget I am her aunt too. If she doesn't come, her uncle and I and Müjgan will be really annoyed."

Aunt Besimé and Nejmiye looked on Tekirdăgi as the other end of the world, so they screwed up their eyes as though peering at some distant stars, and asked: "But can it be arranged? Is the thing practicable?"

With mock humility, I made them a bow, and announced: "I should like, with your permission, to have the honour of proving it's not impossible."

Among my school friends there were a number who travelled during the summer holidays with their families, and who boasted to the rest of us about their adventures when they returned. This meant that when school opened again, I should have some opportunity of doing the same thing. It was going to be an agreeable indulgence, this year, to add a travel story to the tale of my flirtation of last year. Only I claimed the right to carry my own bag and go on board alone, just as American girls did in the novels I had read. But my aunts met this wish with cries of alarm, and wouldn't agree to my starting at all unless I took one of the men-servants with me. Indeed, even so, they hurt my feelings by giving me advice of this kind: "Don't hang your head over the deck-rail in the dark. . . . Don't talk to anyone. . . . Don't go rushing madly down the ship's stairs. . . ." Just as though that worn out old steamer, about the size of a shoe, which does the journey to Tekirdăgi, had a staircase sixty yards wide, like some transatlantic liner. . . .

Müjgan, whom I hadn't seen for two years, I found had grown, and was now so very dignified that I hardly dared talk to her. But we soon got to know one another.

Aunt Ayşe and Müjgan had a host of friends. Every day we were invited to some party or some house or someone's vineyard. They told me I was now a grown-up girl, and that if I played the fool I should disgrace myself; so it was necessary to walk circumspectly. As I paid my respects to strange ladies and tried to give them serious and polite replies, I couldn't help thinking of the way small children play at "visitors." All the same, I won't pretend that going into society didn't flatter my vanity.

Although these parties amused me, the times when I was happiest were the hours I spent alone with Müjgan. My uncle's house was on the top of a high hill by the sea shore. At first Müjgan abla thought it was dangerous for me to go down some of the cliff paths to the beach, which were sheer as a wall; and she tried to prevent me. But in time she got used to my doing it. We would spend hours lying on the sand, playing ducks and drakes, or walking long distances along the shore. At that time of year the sea was very lovely and calm, but we found it rather lifeless. Sometimes hours would pass without our seeing a sail or even a thin cloud of smoke on it. And towards evening the waters seemed so vast and lonely that they really brought a pang to the heart. Fortunately, I was already alive to this danger, and I would make the beach echo with my cheerful laughter.

One day Müjgan and I decided to make for a little headland a good distance away. We really wanted to go through a village on the far side of the rocks which formed the headland. But most tiresomely, the road was closed. There was nothing for it but to take off our shoes and stockings, and wade. For my own part, I was glad enough to do so. But what could you do with a grown-up young lady like Müjgan? I knew that whatever I said, I shouldn't get her to take off her shoes and stockings, so I made her an offer:

"Come on Müjgan abla," I said, "I'll carry you on my back. Let me get you across that way."

She wouldn't agree: "You mad child," she said, "how are you going to carry a great grown-up person like me?" Poor Müjgan! As she was both older and taller than I was, she thought I shouldn't be strong enough to carry her. I went up to her warily.

"We'll see; let's try, anyway," I said, "if we succeed, well and good." And I seized her by the waist and lifted her up. Müjgan thought at first this was really only a trial trip of a few yards, and doing her best to escape, she said with a laugh: "Don't be a fool. Drop me! How can you carry me?" But when she saw that I was going into the water with my bare feet, she nearly went out of her senses. "You're as light as a feather abla," I said, "if you struggle, we shall fall full length, and that would be a pity for both of us. But if you stay quiet there's nothing to be afraid of."

The poor girl went as white as a sheet. She seemed to be afraid of saying a word in case she lost her balance; she shut her mouth and her eyes, and clung to my hair with her hands. Wretched Müjgan! For the sake of a foot or two of water, she kept her eyes shut and didn't dare move in my arms, just as though we were crossing a precipice.

And what should I see as we rounded the cliff? Three sailors watching us, as they ate their food alongside a boat they had drawn up on the beach. Müjgan got alarmed at once, and gripped my hands as though she wanted to dislocate them.

"Well! You've done what you wanted, Feridé," she whispered, "and now what are we going to do?"

I laughed. "Fishermen aren't cannibals," I said to her. All the same, our situation was truly ridiculous; my own legs were bare to the knee; with my stockings in my hand I wasn't dressed for company. Müjgan was getting ready to run with those thin legs of hers, like a spider scurrying before a broom. I felt this cowardice was a disgrace, and taking my courage in both hands, I began to talk to the fishermen. I asked them why the sea had covered the tracks on the beach that day, and at what time and in what part of the sea they caught their fish. Not very intelligent questions; but one must say something, I told myself. Two of the fishermen were young men in their twenties or a little more, perhaps, and one was an old man with a beard. The young men looked rather sheepish. It was the old man who answered my questions. But like myself, he was hard put to it to find anything to say, and he asked me who I was.

45

After a moment's hesitation, I answered: "I'm a girl called Marika. I've come from Istanbul to stay with my uncle," and walked off.

Müjgan took me by the arm and pulled me along as she ran, "Confound you!" she said, "Whatever did you go and do that for?"

"How was I to know?" I asked. . . . "My aunts in Istanbul said 'Keep your mouth shut. Don't talk nonsense. In the place you're going to, there's a lot of talk;' and they warned me repeatedly. I didn't want the fishermen to say: 'What sort of Moslem girl is this? She exposes not only her face, but her legs as well.'"

The fact is, Müjgan, in her cowardice, made a good deal of fuss over a very trifling matter.

Towards evening, as I was strolling arm in arm with Müjgan, I noticed that a young cavalry officer was going up and down beside us. Ostensibly this officer was putting his horse through its paces; but just as though there were no other spot in the countryside, he kept coming back and fore on the road in which we were walking, looking at us whenever he passed; and with so much interest that he seemed to want to stop and talk. Another day, still schooling his horse, he lost us among the trees along the wall; when he had gone by, I laughed a bit, gave a little cough, and said: "Tell me about it, Müjgan."

Müjgan stared at me. "What do you mean, Feridé?" she asked.

"I mean this: that . . . well, I'm not the child I was, abla. You're getting on very well with that officer."

Müjgan began to laugh. "What—I? You crazy child!"

"If you'd deign to treat me as a colleague, madame, what harm would it do?"

"Do you think that officer is pursuing *me*?"

"One would have to be rather obtuse not to think so."

Müjgan laughed again. But this time there was a little pain in her laugh. Then she sighed. "My child, I'm not the sort of girl who's run after . . . it's round you he keeps coming and going. . . ."

"What are you talking about, abla?" My eyes were popping out of my head.

"Yes, it's you. . . . Before you arrived I often saw him. But he used to go by without distinguishing me from these trees by the roadside, and he never used to turn back again."

That evening after supper, Müjgan and I had gone out in front of the house, and we were walking down to the sea, without talking to one another.

Presently Müjgan said: "There's something wrong with you, Feridé. You haven't said a word."

After a moment's hesitation, I admitted: "I can't get out of my head the thing you said earlier in the day. I'm grieved about it."

Müjgan was concerned: "What was it I said?"

"I'm not the sort of girl men run after, you said."

Müjgan gave a little laugh: "All right; but what's that got to do with you?"

I took her hands; my eyes were full and my voice unsteady, as I asked: "Are you ugly, abla?"

She laughed again, and tapped my cheek. "Neither ugly nor pretty. . . . Let's put an end to the discussion by saying I'm neither one nor t'other. As for you, do you know that as you grow up you're becoming quite unusual?"

I put my hands on Müjgan's shoulders and pressed my nose against hers as if I were going to kiss her. I said, "Let's say I'm about the same, and leave it at that."

We had come to the edge of the cliff. I began to pick up stones and throw them into the sea. Müjgan copied me; but the poor dear didn't know how to throw, and she had no strength in her arms. The stones I threw were lost for a moment in the air, and then lit up the water with a flash of phosphorus; but hers either fell on the side of the cliff or on to the beach below. We both laughed a good deal. That was not the kind of inspiration a moonlit sea should have given two young girls: but what of it?

However, Müjgan soon got tired and sat down on a large rock, and I settled myself at her feet. She began to ask me about my school friends. I told her about one or two incidents with Michelle, and then unconsciously I began to talk about the stories I had invented. Why did I do it? Did I confess to Müjgan just for the sake of chattering about something? I don't know. But now and again as she listened to my absurdities, I was quite unable to restrain myself. What I related to Müjgan was in fact the story of how I had taken in the others with a fairy tale. But just as I had been upset, at the time, to find myself acting a part, now, when there was no need to play it, I had the very same feeling. My voice faltered; my looks became confused, and I avoided meeting

47

Müjgan's eyes. First I played with her skirt, or her buttons, and then I put my head on her knees, and looked out to sea the whole time. I tried to conceal from Müjgan who the hero of my story was; but at last I let it out.

Müjgan said nothing; she just stroked my hair, and listened to me. When I'd finished my story and had admitted how disgraceful it was to take the others in with inventions of that kind, what do you think she said?

"Poor little Feridé! You really are in love with Kâmran."

I gave a cry, and threw myself on her; rolling her in the dry grass, I began to pummel her hard. "What's that you said, abla? What's that you said? That creepy crawly *insect*! . . ."

Müjgan struggled to free herself, and said: "Stop it, you lunatic. You'll make me in such a mess, they'll see us from the road, and then there'll be a scandal. . . . *Do* stop it!" she implored me.

"You've got to take back what you said."

"I promise I will," she said. "I'll do whatever you like, if you'll only leave me alone."

"Yes, but not just to please me . . . not just to take me in!"

"All right, not just to please you and not just to take you in. It's the truth." Müjgan rose and brushed herself. "Feridé, you really must be mad," she said with a laugh. I hadn't got up, and I said to her in a trembling voice:

"How can you calumniate me, abla, without fear of God? I'm still a child." I couldn't help it; I burst into tears.

That night in bed I was seized with a violent fever. I couldn't get to sleep; I was delirious. I threw myself first one way and then another, like a fish caught in a net. Thank God my nights were short. Müjgan didn't leave me until it got light. I had a feeling of insuperable terror and disgust; it was as though my body had undergone some kind of change. Every now and again I hugged Müjgan with the natural clumsiness of a small child, sobbing: "Why did you say that, abla?" She evidently feared I might attack her again, and said neither "Yes" nor "No." She only stroked my hair, and pressed my head to her bosom, trying to pacify me. It was only towards morning that she grew irritable, and rebelled, and scolded me roughly.

"You mad creature, it is any disgrace to love, then? Nothing dreadful has happened . . . and if nothing worse happens, you will marry, and the thing will be all over. Come now, go to sleep at once . . . I don't want any more of this disobedience."

Faced with this unexpected attack from Müjgan, this time I kept quiet. After struggling the whole night long, I had turned myself into Monsieur Ségen's cat by morning. As I dropped off to sleep, I heard Müjgan whisper in a voice that had softened again: "Maybe he's not indifferent to you;" but I had no more strength to resist, and went to sleep.

Next day we were invited to a farm belonging to one of our wealthy neighbours. I don't believe I've ever been as irritated or amused as I was that day. I left my aunt Ayşe and Müjgan on the edge of the pond, talking scandal with the grown-ups; and got the children to follow me, gathering them round for a romp. And indeed, at one point I dared to get on a horse bareback, and nearly got into trouble. When my aunt and Müjgan saw me, they started making a lot of signs with their heads and hands. I didn't quite know what they wanted; but as it didn't suit me to understand, I pretended not to see, and hid myself behind the trees again.

Yes, it really was a disgrace, as they said, for a grown-up girl to behave in this vulgar way, barelegged and dishevelled before all the servants and workmen. I was well aware of this, but I couldn't make myself talk sense. At one moment I found Müjgan alone, and seized her by the arm, saying: "Do you understand all these women dressed up like Armenian brides? Come along with me!"

She seemed annoyed. "You wore me out, last night, till daybreak," she said, and added:

"You really are a surprising creature; you're like a wild animal, Feridé. What sort of state were you in yesterday evening? You didn't even sleep for a couple of hours this morning, but insisted on getting up. There's not a trace of fatigue about you. Your complexion is as fresh as can be, and your eyes are shining. But just see what a condition you've reduced me to!"

It was true; Müjgan was in a pitiable state. After a sleepless night, she had a face like wax. "I don't even remember the night," I said, and ran off again.

We were walking home in the evening, as our carriage was late. That was better, of course. In any case, the farm was not far away. . . . My aunt was following us, with two neighbours of her own age. I was a good

way ahead, and arm-in-arm with Müjgan, who had decided at last to
rouse herself a little. On one side of the road were broken-down walls,
and gardens surrounded with fences, and on the other the listless sea,
without a sign of sail or smoke on it. Traces of an unusually early autumn
were visible in the gardens; the green creeper that covered the fences was
dried up, and here and there a wild flower showed itself, crushed and
wilted in the dust. The dry leaves were falling on the dusty road, together
with the light dancing shadows of the alder trees, which we passed at rare
intervals. But far away in the distance, in the heart of those uncultivated
gardens, there were a few touches of red. Those were the raspberry
bushes, which God surely created especially for wrens to peck at. That
was why I gave up looking at the forlorn sea; and I took Müjgan by the
arm, and began to drag her off to the raspberry bushes.

By the time those behind us had passed us and reached the corner of
the road at their snail's pace, we should have done the job sixty times
over; but Müjgan abla drove one mad with impatience, she walked so
carefully. As she went down the middle of the field she was afraid of
spraining her ankle or getting a bit of dry straw into her foot, and she
hesitated when it came to jumping the fence. At one moment we were
attacked by a dog; a dog which would have gone comfortably into
Müjgan's handbag! When Müjgan saw it, she started to run away and
shout for help. Finally she was afraid of the raspberry bushes: "You'll be
ill; they'll upset you!" she told me, and tried to snatch the fruit out of my
hand. More than once we had a bit of a scuffle; the raspberries were
crushed, and got on to my face and made great stains on my white sailor
blouse with its wide gold-braided collar. We ought to have finished the
business by the time those behind had reached us, but while I was trying
to settle accounts with Müjgan and the raspberry bushes, they had
reached the bottom of the road. In fact, they wondered what we were
doing, and didn't turn the corner, but stood there looking back at us; and
with them was a man.

"Who's that?" asked Müjgan.

"Who would it be?" I asked, "—a traveler, perhaps, or a villager."

"I don't think so."

To tell the truth, I didn't think so either; although it was hard to
distinguish anyone in the twilight and the shadow of the big trees along
the side of the road, it didn't seem to be anyone of that kind. Soon after,
he waved his hand, and leaving the others, came straight towards us. We
couldn't make it out.

"Anyway, it must be someone we know," said Müjgan, and then added excitedly: "Feridé, it looks very like Kâmran. Be careful!"

"Impossible," I said. "What would Kâmran be doing here?"

"I swear it's he." Müjgan began to run. I, on the other hand, slowed down a little. I felt a catch in my breath and a weakness in my knees. At the edge of the road I waited, and put my foot on a large stone; I bent down and loosened my shoelace, and then slowly began tying it again.

When we came face to face, I was calmer and in a rather provocative mood. "I'm surprised to see you here," I said. "How is it you embarked on a long journey like this?"

He didn't say anything, but looked at me with a shy sort of smile, as if he were confronted by a stranger. Then he put out his hand. I drew mine back at once, and hid them behind my back. "Müjgan and I have been giving ourselves a feast of raspberries. My hands are sticky . . . and there's a lot of dust on them too. How are the aunts, and how's Nejmiye?"

"They send you kisses, Feridé."

"Merci!"

"How sunburnt you are, Feridé; you're all over freckles."

"That's the sun." Müjgan broke in at this point. "So are you, Kâmran," she said.

I couldn't resist it. "Who knows?" I said, "He may have gone for a walk in the moonlight, and not taken a parasol to protect him." We all laughed, and walked on. A little later, my aunt Ayşe and Müjgan got my cousin to walk between them. Their neighbours, bearing in mind that they were women of forty and that Kâmran was a man, walked a little distance apart. I was in front with the children; but my ears were behind me. I was listening to my cousin explaining to my aunt and Müjgan what wind it was that had blown him here.

"I got tired of Istanbul this summer; you don't know how tired. . . ."

I stuck my heels into the ground with annoyance, and said to myself: "Of course. What could be more natural, after letting the merry widow fall into the hands of a stranger?" He went on:

"The other night—it was the fifteenth of the month—I went to Alemdaği with some friends. It was a wonderfully beautiful night; but I can't stand tiring amusements. Towards morning, without telling anyone, I came back to town on my own. The truth is, I was absolutely fed up. I thought I'd leave Istanbul for a few days; but where was one to go? It's not the season for Yalova; Bursa is hot as hell just now. Suddenly you came into my mind. I was longing to see you, anyway."

That evening my uncle and aunt detained Kâmran for a long time in the garden; and although Müjgan was so tired that she could hardly stand, she stayed with them all the time. I, on the other hand, kept away, and disappeared every now and then, either into the house or to the far end of the garden. At one moment, I forget why, I had to pass quite near them; and Kâmran, with a gesture that showed he was conscious of my behaviour, said:

"Someone's showing a lack of respect to the guest."

I laughed and shrugged my shoulders. "They say 'Guests are jealous of each other.'" Müjgan took me firmly by the wrist and skirt, as if she didn't want me to run away again. I shook her off, and went up to my room, saying I wanted to go to bed.

When Müjgan came up a good deal later, I was already in bed and half asleep. She sat on the edge of the bed, and looked at me. Feeling sure I should laugh, I turned over to the other side and began to snore. She lifted my head, with some difficulty, and said, "There's no need to try and take me in; open your eyes."

"I swear I was asleep," I said, and opened my eyes wide. But we couldn't keep it up, and we both began to laugh. Müjgan stroked my cheek and said: "I was right in my calculations."

I stretched myself out in bed, while the springs creaked.

"What do you mean?"

She drew back suddenly. "Oh, nothing—nothing," and then added with a laugh, "For goodness sake don't say I'm going to make a row. I'm dead tired," and putting out the lamp, she got into bed. A few minutes later, I went over to her bed, and lifted her head from the pillow, and took her in my arms. But the poor thing really had gone to sleep. Without opening her eyes, she said beseechingly, "Don't do it, Feridé."

"All right," I said, "but there's something on the tip of my tongue, and if I don't say it now I can't go to sleep."

In spite of the darkness of the room, and the fact that Müjgan's eyes were shut, I hid my face in her hair, and whispered in her ear: "Senseless things are passing through your mind. I know. . . . If you say a word to him, I shall take you by force, and I'll hurl the two of us into the sea."

"All right—all right," Müjgan said. "Whatever you like!" And although I kept on giving her head little shakes, she went to sleep again.

Kâmran's arrival really spoilt my pleasure. The mingled sense of anger, fear and loathing that I felt towards him grew from day to day. When we met face to face I used to be rude, without any obvious reason, and run away. Thank heaven, my uncle Aziz hung on to his guest like grim death. He used to invite all kinds of people to the house to meet him, and would take him for a long drive in the carriage almost every day; or they would be invited to a neighbour's garden or vineyard.

One morning, as my cousin was getting ready to go out in answer to one of these invitations, I met him at the top of the stairs. He stopped me; and after looking about him as though anxious not to be overheard, he said: "Feridé, this excess of hospitality will kill me."

I wondered whether I could pass between him and the banisters without touching him. "What's wrong?" I asked, "They're taking you out every day."

Kâmran smiled in a comically despairing way, raised his eyes to the ceiling, and said: "They say 'One guest is jealous of another' but it's a tradition that one guest can criticise his host to another, too, and you must let me do it."

He had been annoyed, for some reason, on the first night, when I'd used the expression, "Guests are jealous of one another," and now and again he'd remind me of it. "That's all right," I said, "but there's nothing to complain of. You get to know fresh people and places every day."

Again he compressed his lips: "The people I get to know aren't very exciting."

I couldn't help it: "Poor wretches! Where can they find anyone to entertain *you*?"

Kâmran understood very well who it was I thought could amuse him; he stretched out his hands impulsively: "Feridé!" he said. But his outstretched hands remained empty. I jumped through the opening between him and the banisters, and escaped. I went down the stairs two at a time, and ran off into the garden, singing.

At last, one day, Müjgan had her way with me. I was walking with her on the cliff by the sea shore. It had rained the night before, and there was a lovely autumn coolness in the air. A vague cloud suggestive of fog or smoke hid the sun from us, and a pale light from somewhere unknown quivered on the dull surface of the sea. In the distance a few fishing boats with their sails furled rode motionless, like shadows.

I saw Kâmran go down the road; somehow or other he had been left free that day. Müjgan was sitting on the root of a tree, and she had her

53

face turned towards the sea; she didn't notice him. I too pretended not to see him, and half turned away in the same direction. But although I could see and hear nothing, I knew he was coming towards us, and I felt a prickle of fear at the nape of my neck. Müjgan asked: "Why have you suddenly stopped talking?" She turned her head, and saw Kâmran ten or fifteen paces away. Now there was nothing for it but a few moments' morning conversation.

Kâmran began by teasing Müjgan. "You haven't forgotten your umbrella today," he said.

She answered with a laugh: "No. But really there's a danger of rain. . . ." He began explaining that he liked that kind of weather, which was so like his own dull and indecisive character. Müjgan objected, and amused herself by opening and closing the umbrella.

"That's all very well," she said, "but it makes one depressed. When the season is over, almost all the days are like this. Then comes winter. You don't know how hard the winter is here. . . . All the same, my father has got so used to it, that he's afraid they'll go and appoint him somewhere else."

Kâmran said lightly, "Don't be too much against that, either. Who knows? Perhaps you'll go and marry someone who lives here."

Müjgan took his words seriously, and shook her head. "God forbid." At that moment a bare-legged fisherman came past us. It was the old fisherman to whom I'd introduced myself that day as Marika. He had the same handkerchief round his head. He greeted me, and said:

"I haven't seen anything of you for a long time, Marika."

"I'm waiting to go out fishing with you one day," I said; and we began to walk towards the edge of the cliff, talking hard.

Presently I went back to the others again, and found Müjgan telling my cousin the story of Marika. When she had finished, she took me by the wrist, and said, "It's not me, but Feridé, perhaps, whom we shall leave behind in Tekirdaği. She's met her fate. They want her for the son of a fisherman called Captain Isa. Never mind about his being a fisherman. He's a very wealthy man."

Kâmran was laughing. "Even if he were a millionaire, we can't be quite as democratic as all that," he said decidedly. "In my capacity as her cousin I should never agree to it."

What the devil was it that was prompting the sensible and staid Müjgan today? What do you suppose she went and said in answer to that? "There's more to it than that. Feridé has better chances. For instance, there's a cavalry officer, bright as the sun. He comes past the house every evening, and does a number of dangerous tricks, just to amuse her."

Kâmran was really laughing now; but there was something strange, something broken, in his laugh, too, which belied the smile of a few minutes before. "I've nothing to say to that. It's for her to answer," he said.

With a secret sign to Müjgan that meant "I'll show you," I said: "You're going a bit too far. You know I don't like this kind of talk."

She got behind Kâmran's back, as a precaution, and said with a wink at me, "That's not what we say when we're alone."

"Liar! Calumniator!"

This time Kâmran took the matter into his own hands. "You can tell me, Müjgan," he said, "I'm not a stranger. . . ."

Angrily, I stamped on the ground. "It's quite obvious. One can't talk without quarrelling with you. Goodbye!" I cried, and started walking towards the sea, in a fury.

I began to walk, but I had a feeling that going away wouldn't enable me to drop the conversation we had begun. After going to the edge of the cliff, I started to throw stones violently into the sea. Now and again, as though I were bending down, I looked behind me. What I saw was not very reassuring. Müjgan was going to be the undoing of me, and I had no means to hand whereby I could prevent it.

At first they laughed and talked, and then grew serious. Müjgan seemed to be finding her words with difficulty, and was making lines on the ground with her umbrella; and my cousin was standing there like a statue. Finally, I saw that both of them had turned round and were looking at me, and worse still, had begun to walk in my direction.

The situation was quite clear. I hurled myself as fast as I could from the steepest spot on the cliff-top, down to the beach below. I still marvel how it was that I didn't roll over the edge that day, and how I got to the bottom without even giving myself one injury. However, this act of madness didn't save me from them. On turning my head, what should I see but that they were coming slowly down the cliff by another path. If I were to begin running, it was quite certain those delicate creatures wouldn't be able to catch me not even on horseback. But there was just this to it: my running away would be significant, and would show that I understood everything, or at all events had my doubts about *something*.

So, as if I had no worries or cares, I walked quickly on, throwing a stone into the sea from time to time. If I could get round the promontory ahead, I should have gained safety. But as bad luck would have it, the tide was low that morning, and at the edge of the rocks, it was possible to cross dry shod.

I had my plans ready. After walking a bit further along the shore, I would begin to climb the cliff again by a goat track leading from it. As even goats climb that path with difficulty, they would have to give up chasing me; and they'd lose my tracks. But suddenly, on the other side of the promontory, a comedy (or rather a tragedy) faced me, which made me forget everything else for several minutes. The old fisherman who had passed us a short while ago could be seen armed with an oar, chasing a black street dog. The dog was howling and dodging first this way and then that, while the old man hit the poor beast with the oar whenever he could catch him. At first it occurred to me that the dog might be mad, and I stopped. But then it seemed to me that the fisherman was madder than the dog; he was struggling and yelling as though out of his mind. Not daring to approach him too suddenly, I called out: "What's up? What's wrong with the poor beast?"

The old boy had no breath left. Stopping his beating for a moment, he leant on the oar, and began, almost in tears: "What am I to do? The wretch has upset thirty piastres' worth of pitch. But I'll see he doesn't come near you."

The cause of his anger was plain. The dog had overturned a tin of pitch which the fisherman was boiling over a thorn fire on the beach. Awful crime!—but hardly such as to justify killing the animal with a boat oar. The dog had taken refuge in a cave in the rocks, a place where he thought he would be safe. Shortly after, when his enemy, armed with the oar, made his second attack, he began howling like anything, without trying to escape from the trap he'd walked into himself. But if he'd made off along the shore, or climbed the cliff by the path I meant to use, he would undoubtedly have got away.

If I'd had time, I should have done something to try and save the poor animal. Unhappily I had troubles enough of my own. I too was being pursued. Still fearful that Müjgan and my cousin might come round the promontory, I walked my fastest for a while, and then began to climb the cliff. All the same, I wasn't altogether content to run away, as I had at first intended. I stopped and looked furtively behind me, or rather below;

the little tragedy seemed to have diverted Müjgan and Kâmran. They were talking excitedly beside the overturned tin of pitch.

At last I saw my cousin take his purse out of his pocket and give the fisherman some money; and stranger still, the fisherman cheerfully threw down his oar, turned towards me and began to make signs. The dog was saved, and so was I. Taking no notice of the fact that they were calling out to me, I made my way home.

When I remembered what Müjgan had done, I lost my temper, and grew hot all over. Every now and then I would clasp my hands and exclaim, "You've disgraced me, Müjgan, and I'll pay you out." I was in such a state that I believe I might even have gone back to Istanbul; but my uncle Aziz met me outside the door.

"Hullo, girl! What's wrong with your face? You're the colour of beetroot. Has someone been chasing you?" he asked, standing in my way.

"Nonsense, uncle," I said with a rather uncertain laugh, and ran off to the back garden, where I heard children's voices.

In the back garden there was a swing, hung on a large elder tree. Some days I would collect the children of the neighbourhood, and turn the place into a kind of fun fair. Today my little friends had crowded in, without being invited, large and small, and they were all round the swing. What a lucky chance! I'd thought I would come home and go up to my room and lock myself in. But the other two would be sure to follow me, and when they tried to force the door open, there would be a scene on the landing. As it was, I should get in among the children and turn the place into a bear garden, so that I could prevent them approaching me.

There had been quarrelling among the children as to who should get on the swing first. I threw myself among them at once and divided them into two with my arms. "Line up, all of you!" I said. "I'll swing you in turn." I jumped on to the swing, and putting one of the children in front of me, I slowly started swinging.

Before long, the other two turned up, and stood behind the children. Müjgan was out of breath and pressing her hand to her breast every now and then; my cousin must have run her off her legs. I said to myself, "I hope you'll get worse," and worked the swing to a greater speed. The children waiting their turn in a row began to get impatient, and shouted: "You've swung enough. Us too! Us too!" But I took no notice. With the leaves of the tree rustling about my head, I swung faster and faster through the air.

This action absolutely infuriated the children. In their impatience, they threw themselves in front of the swing, crossing the line I had set them as a boundary. Müjgan and Kâmran seized them by the arms, and covered their faces and eyes to prevent their scattering. Worse still, the child swinging with me had given in. I'd begun to fear that this little wretch, who sat between my knees yelling for all she was worth, would let go the ropes, and fall to the ground and be killed.

Inevitably, I had to stop the swing; and then I began to scold her. What was she doing on a swing at all, if she was afraid of going fast? Children of that kind had better stay at home, to be swung in their small brother's or sister's cradle.... That was the kind of thing I told her. Quite frankly, I spoke spitefully and made an uproar, to give Kâmran no chance of speaking to me. Thank goodness the other children were making a row of their own, too, and playing the fool to their own tune, turning the garden into a bedlam.

"Me too, Feridé abla! Me too ... me too ... me too ... !"

"No, I won't take any of you! You're all afraid."

"We're not afraid, Feridé abla! We're not afraid! We're not! We're not!"

At that moment my aunt's voice was heard from the window. "Feridé! Do for goodness sake give in to them a little!"

At once I turned in that direction and started a long argument. "Auntie, it's all very well for you to say that, but if they fall and hurt themselves, you'll scold me."

"But my dear, you're not obliged to let them fall! Swing them slowly."

"But auntie, please don't talk as if you didn't know what you were talking about. Don't you know your old Çalıkuşu yet? Do you think you can depend on me? I begin quietly, and then, as the swing begins to go up and down, the devil gradually rouses me, with the words 'Come on, now, come on!—a bit more, a bit more!' ... 'Don't, don't! I've got children with me,' I answer.... But he goes on saying 'Come on now, come on! A bit more, a bit more. Nothing will happen.' And while he's saying it, the branches and the leaves of the tree say his words over like a chorus: 'Come on, Feridé. Come on, Feridé!' How can a wretched Çalıkuşu stand up to so much provocation? Be fair, now!"

My chatter was running out; but although my back was turned to him, I could feel my cousin at my shoulder. I'd no doubt that as soon as I stopped talking, he would begin. What was I to do? I must get away without facing him. I saw that a child had caught hold of my skirt; taking him under the arms, I picked him up. He was a baby of seven of eight, the youngest of my visitors. Putting our faces together, I said, "It doesn't much matter, but how would it be if we were to put some colour into those fat little cheeks?"

A shadow fell on the child's shoulders. It was Kâmran. When I took my head away from the child's, I had no doubt that he and I would come face to face. Well, there was no way of escape. To run away and be afraid of him was not a thing my pride would ever let me do.

So I let the child slip out of my arms, and looked straight into Kâmran's eyes: "Now then, child; go up to your big brother Kâmran. He's as kind and polite as a lady. He'll swing you quietly, without shaking you or tiring you, as if he were your nurse, and you wouldn't need a lullaby. Only don't move about too much. Because his delicate arms won't be able to hold you, and you'll both fall."

My intention, with my eyes fixed on his, was to make him lower his head; and to persist in my insolent, domineering mockery to the very end. But he would not take his eyes off me. He looked at me as though he were saying, "It's no good; do what you may, I know everything."

Then it was that I understood that I had lost the game. I looked down, and began to wipe my hands with my handkerchief; they were covered with dust.

Kâmran said: "You are amusing yourself, aren't you? You good-for-nothing little thing. All right! Now we'll see; we'll swing together."

He promptly took off his jacket, and threw it into Müjgan's arms to hold. My aunt was calling out of the window: "Kâmran, don't play the fool. You'll never be able to compete with that wild creature. You'll only hurt yourself." The children, who perceived they were going to witness something amusing, seemed to understand a little. We two remained alone by the swing.

My cousin said with a laugh, "What are you waiting for, Feridé? Are you afraid?"

Not daring, this time, to look him in the face, I said, "What nonsense!" and jumped on to the swing. The ropes creaked, and it was slowly set in motion. I acted cautiously; and to conserve my strength on a swing that I felt was going to be difficult, I contented myself with slightly bending my knees. The pace began to quicken; the elder tree began to sway, and there was a great rustling of leaves. We both set our teeth and said nothing, as though afraid to utter even a word, in case we were to weaken. The swaying motion was gradually getting the better of me, and making me lose control. Kâmran's head was suddenly plunged into a mass of leaves; his long hair was all over his forehead. In a mocking voice I asked him: "Do you regret having started, I wonder?"

He laughed as well, and replied, "We shall see who's going to do the regretting, soon enough." His piercing green eyes shining through his dishevelled hair, aroused in me a strange feeling of hatred and a desire to hurt.

Bending my knees with all my strength, I set the swing off at a wild pace. At its every turn, our heads were plunged in and out of the leaves, and our hair entangled. For a moment, as if in a dream, I could hear my aunt's voice, shouting "Enough, enough!"

Kâmran repeated it too. "Have you had enough, Feridé?"

"That's a question for you," I retorted.

"Not as far as I am concerned," he said, "after the lovely thing I heard from Müjgan, there's no chance of *my* getting tired. . . ."

My knees suddenly gave way. I was afraid I should let go the ropes. Kâmran went on: "I never expected that. I came here for your sake, Feridé." Although I had been afraid to move, the speed of the swing had not slackened. I put my arms round the ropes and locked my hands together. "Let's get down; I shall fall!" I begged him.

He didn't understand that I was beat, and said, "No, Feridé, unless I hear from your own lips that you're willing to marry me, I shan't let you go, not till both of us fall and are killed." His lips were touching my forehead and my eyes, through my hair. My knees were bent; my hands were locked together, but my arms were slipping on the ropes. If Kâmran hadn't taken hold of me at that moment, I should certainly have fallen. Even so, his strength wasn't enough to save me. The swing lost its balance, the ropes became twisted, and the next moment we were rolling on the ground.

I lost consciousness for a moment, and then opened my eyes to find myself in the arms of my aunt. She was wiping my temples with a damp handkerchief.

"Have you hurt yourself anywhere, dear?" she asked me.

I raised my head. "No, Aunt."

"Then why are you crying?"

"Crying, aunt—me?"

"What are those tears in your eyes?"

I buried my head in my aunt's lap. "I must have been crying before I fell," I told her.

Three days later we were on the way back to Istanbul, with my aunt Ayşe and Müjgan and the whole family. Aunt Besimé had heard the news from her son, and hurried to meet us at the pier, accompanied by Nejmiye.

The first weeks of my engagement were spent in trying to get away from everyone; and most of all from Kâmran. He wanted to be alone with me, to go out with me, and to talk to me; and I suppose he had as much right to this as any other engaged man. But alas, I was the world's strangest and wildest fiancée. Whenever I saw Kâmran approaching, I went off like a horse that's shied, and there was no catching me. I had sent him an ultimatum by Müjgan; when we met he was not to talk to me as if we were engaged. If he didn't promise, I swore I would break the whole thing off.

Here, as at Tekirdăgi, Müjgan would tackle me, now and again, when I was in bed. "Why behave in this mad way, Feridé?" she used to ask. "I know you love him desperately. These are your best days! Who knows what lovely things he has to say to you. . . ." Sometimes she went further. She would stroke my hair with her delicate hands, and talk to me with his lips.

Curling up in bed, I would protest: "I don't want it. I'm afraid. I'm ashamed. There's something strange about it; I can't explain. . . ." And if she went too far, I would complain, and cry. Then, when she left me and went to bed, I used to repeat to myself things Kâmran had said, and fall asleep to the sound of them.

My aunt insisted on having an engagement ring made for me, so valuable and attractive a stone that it in no way became my fingers, which were always covered with scratches. She showed it to me as a surprise, on her return from Istanbul, drawing me to one of the windows just when the trees opposite were lit up by the sun sinking behind them. I shut my eyes and drew back, putting my hands behind me and shielding my face in the shadow of the curtain, to hide the blush that came to it. My aunt couldn't understand me, and seemed surprised that I didn't hug her with pleasure.

"Don't you like it, Feridé?" she asked.

"It's very nice, aunt. Merci," I replied in a cold voice. It was evident that my action upset her. But not for long. Beginning to smile again, she said, "Stretch out your hand; let's try it on. I gave your old ring as a pattern. Let's hope it won't be too small, or anything." My aunt looked as if she were going to take hold of my arm, and I clenched my fingers, hidden behind my back.

"It's impossible just now, aunt," I said, "a bit later on. . . ."

"Don't be childish, Feridé!" Obstinately, I bent my head, and began tapping the floor with my foot.

"In a few days, we'll invite some of your friends in; and that will be the moment to wear the ornament."

My heart was beating fast. "I don't want that," I said, "or if you think it's absolutely necessary, do it when I've gone back to school." I really deserved a good scolding; but my aunt wanted to maintain her dignity. She smiled again, pursing her lips, and said with a touch of sarcasm, "What! Are we to have a substitute in your place at the engagement party? That's all right at the time of your betrothal, my dear, but no such custom has yet been observed when there's an 'engagement.'"

There was no answer to this; I continued to look straight in front of me. As if to help me to accept the severity of the lesson I had to learn, my aunt put one arm round my waist, and stroked my cheek and my hair with the other hand, saying: "Feridé, I think it's about time you gave up these childish ways; I'm not only your aunt now, but your mother as well . . . I needn't say, need I, how glad I am of that. You're very much better for Kâmran than any other strange girl would be, about whose character we'd know nothing. Only . . . only you're just a bit too harum-scarum. In a child it would be harmless. But you are gradually growing up; and as you get older, you should, of course, become more serious and sensible. There are still about four years before you will leave school and get married. It's a very long time. All the same, you are engaged now. I don't quite know what it is I am trying to say, but you do understand? You must be more serious in mind and in behaviour; you must stop this childishness, this mischievousness, this obstinacy. You know how sensitive and refined in feeling Kâmran is. . . ."

Was there really anything to hurt in those words, every one of which still remains in my memory? Even today I can't tell. But the fact remains that I got the impression my aunt thought I was not quite good enough for her son. And then, as if she wanted to see what effect her advice had had, she went on: "Well now, we understand one another, don't we? We'll have an engagement party—just a few relations and close friends."

I saw myself sitting beside her, at a brightly-lit table decorated with flowers, dressed up as I'd never been before, with my hair done in a different way, looking quite changed, with everyone staring at me. . . . I shuddered suddenly. "That's absolutely impossible, aunt!" I said, and made off downstairs as hard as I could go.

Müjgan was something more than an elder sister to me, these days; she was more like a mother. When we were alone in my room, I would put out the light and hug that body of hers, which had endured so much ill-treatment from me: and closing her mouth to prevent her from answering, I would make this demand: "The people I'm most sorry for, and laugh at most, in the whole world, are girls who get engaged. I've become one of them. Do beg the others, every one of them, not to call me 'fiancée.' I should sink into the ground. I'm afraid! I'm still a child! I've still got four long years ahead of me. Don't let anyone treat me as if I were engaged now!"

At last, when I let her speak, she answered, "All right, but on one condition, or rather two. First, that you won't squabble with me; and secondly, that you'll repeat to me just once more, that you love him very much. . . ."

My face was hidden in Müjgan's lap at the time; but I made a sign with my head, assenting.

Müjgan kept her promise. Neither those within nor those outside the house spoke of my engagement to my face. If, now and again, someone tried to make a joke of it, they caught it from me, and were reduced to silence. In fact, one day I gave someone a good box on the ears; fortunately, though, it wasn't a stranger, but my cousin himself; and a well-deserved box on the ears it was, too. But heaven forbid that my aunt Besimé should hear of it. If she had, who knows what she would have done to me?

All the same, I can't say I was very happy at home. For instance, I was now a person of more importance, so they transferred me to a better bedroom; they changed my curtains, my bed, and my wardrobe, but of course I didn't dare ask why.

One day we were to go to a village wedding at Merdivenköyü. The carriage was pretty full; I stood there alone, and announced, "I'll get up beside the driver." There was a laugh. I was annoyed, and climbed up, smiling to myself. It used to be the same in the old days, when I went to steal dried apricots or something of the kind from the kitchen; that wretch of a cook would tease me, and say: "Ask openly for what you want, young lady. It's unbecoming for you to steal." As no one had said anything, I didn't dare call in children from the street; once in a blue moon, I felt constrained to hide in a corner and wait for darkness, until I could climb a tree. But among them all, the most difficult to escape from was Kâmran. I may say that the last days of the holidays were spent in my playing a game of catch-as-catch-can with him. He was looking for an opportunity to catch me alone, and I had recourse to every kind of devilry to prevent it. I declined the outings in the carriage that he suggested now and again, and if he became insistent, I would take someone else—besides Müjgan—with us, and talk to them all the time we were out. I say "besides Müjgan," because there was no guarantee that Müjgan would not leave me alone with him while we were out, or start talking a lot of nonsense.

One day Kâmran said to me: "Do you know Feridé, you're making me very unhappy."

Unable to resist it, I asked, "Hasn't that ever happened before?" I asked the question with such strange surprise, that we both began to laugh.

"I want, just once, to hear from your own lips what you once told Müjgan. I think I have a right to ask that."

I pretended not to remember what I had said to Müjgan, and gazed at the sky as though deep in thought. Then I answered:

"Oh yes, but then Müjgan's a girl; and so, I believe, is your dutiful servant. We can't repeat everything we say to one another to everyone."

"Am I, then, 'everyone?'"

"Don't misunderstand me. Although you're very woman-like in some ways, you are, in fact, a man. And one can't repeat to a man everything one says to a girl friend."

"But aren't I engaged to you?"

"Now we shall probably quarrel; you know I can't stand that word." (You see, now, I had a perfect right to call myself unhappy. I daren't use the word lest you cast it in my teeth. But I have a special feeling for you, which I have for no one else.)

For a long time I realized I was about to be caught in the trap I had escaped so far. If I were to speak, either my voice would tremble, or I should do something foolish. I left Kâmran with the words on his lips, and ran out into the street. I thought he would follow me; but I heard nothing, and slowed down, and after a little while I looked round cautiously.

He had seated himself, quite simply, in a cane chair under a tree.

64

I couldn't help feeling, "Perhaps I've rather disgraced myself." I believe if Kâmran had looked at me then, he would have understood my remorse, and come up to me again. And I don't think I should have run away. As my cousin sat there, he looked really unhappy. To encourage myself, I began to say to myself, "Crafty yellow creature! I haven't forgotten how he hung on to the skirts of the merry widow in this very garden. I know I'm doing the right thing."

I can't go on without relating the misfortune that befell me during the last days of the holidays. One day the members of the family saw that there was a great bandage round one of the fingers of my right hand. When I was asked about it, I said: "It's nothing. Only a slight cut. It's of no consequence—it will heal itself." My aunt noticed that I was obstinately trying to hide the wound, and said: "I'm quite sure you've been up to some mischief. You're concealing something important. Let's show it to a doctor. We don't want any trouble."

The truth of the matter was, my aunt had sent me one day to fetch something—a handkerchief, I think it was,—from the chest of drawers in her room. In the open drawer, I saw a blue velvet-covered jewel-box. It was my engagement ring. I couldn't resist the satisfaction of seeing it on my finger, for a moment. But the caprice cost me dear. The ring, as my aunt had feared, had been made a little small, and I was quite unable to get it off. In an absurd state of excitement, I pulled as hard as I could; and then I tried to pull it off with my teeth. All in vain! The more I forced it, the more my finger swelled and the more the ring seemed to contract. If I were to tell the others, they would be sure to find some way of getting it off. But somehow it seriously hurt my pride to be caught with it on. Then it was that I put the bandage round my finger. For two whole days, whenever I found time, I shut myself up in my room and took off the bandage, to wrestle with the thing for hours on end. On the third day, just when I was about to confess the truth shamefacedly to my aunt, what should the ring do, but come off on its own! I imagine I must have got thinner from the last two days' worry and struggle!

On the last day of the holidays I began to get ready to go. Kâmran objected:

"Why all this hurry, Feridé," he asked. "You can stay another day or two?"

But as though I were a model student, I resolutely declined, making childish excuses, such as: "The nuns warned me to return the day school reopened. And the work this year is very stiff. . . ."

In the face of my insistence, Kâmran fell into a sad and angry mood.

Next day, as he took me back to school, he didn't talk at all, and just as we were about to leave each other, he said reproachfully, "I never would have believed you'd want to run away from me so soon."

In reality, I was not so very serious and industrious a pupil. Besides, this new trouble had completely upset me. During the first three months I got very bad marks; unless I made an effort and pulled myself together, I should "stay put" in the same form. The day the reports were given out, Sister Alexei drew me into a corner and asked me, "Are you pleased with your marks, Feridé?"

I shook my head gloomily. "They're rather awful, Sister," I admitted.

"Not *rather*; *very*! I don't remember your ever having fallen as low as this, and this year I was hoping there would be a big change in your work."

"You're right; I'm a year older than I was last year."

"Is that all there is to it?" Strange! Sister Alexei was stroking my cheek and laughing. What was she going to do next? I avoided looking at her. Oh, these nuns! Although they seem to be quite unconscious of what's going on in the world, they know very well; they get to hear the very slightest rumour or gossip. How do they get it, and from whom? Although I lived with them for ten years, and am not altogether unintelligent, I was never able to understand it.

As I tried to shield myself with some excuse, Sister Alexei began again. "I fancy you will not care to show everyone the marks in your report," she said. And this was followed by an even more significant warning. "If you can't get out of the class this year, there's a risk of having to spend another long year in this one."

I saw that unless I took the offensive, I should not be able to defend myself against Sister Alexei. So, as there was no other way, I resorted to impudence, and innocently inquired, "Risk? Why risk?"

Sister Alexei had reached the limit of her conversation as a woman. To go further would mean, more or less, to become too familiar with me. She cheerfully patted my cheek, as if admitting that she was defeated; "You know that best, yourself," she said, and walked away.

Michelle was not at school this year. If she had been, she would certainly have forced me to talk; and that would have intensified my misery of mind. In marked contrast to the freedom and frivolity of last year, when I was inventing all those stories, was the fear that I felt this year, now that I was really and truly engaged. The girls who congratulated me I dismissed with a short dry "thank you" and I didn't give a chance to those who showed an inclination to pester me. Only one of them, the daughter of an Armenian doctor who lived near us, succeeded in overcoming my obstinacy. I used to spend the weekend holiday at school. I had only been home for a night two or three times in three months. This obstinacy, whose origin I didn't very well understand myself, annoyed aunt Besimé and Nejmiye. And Kâmran didn't know what to think or what to do. During the first few months he used to come to the school every week. Although the nuns didn't dare say anything, they were shocked to find one of their pupils being visited by a fiancé; and when they announced that my cousin was waiting in the parlour to see me, their looks very clearly expressed their displeasure.

I would lean against one wing of the parlour door, which I purposely left open, and, with my hand stuck in the leather belt of my school overall, I would stand and talk for perhaps five minutes at most. My cousin had suggested writing to me occasionally. But I put him off doing that by telling him that the nuns had a habit of getting letters written in Turkish read by someone else, and then throwing them away.

I remember on one of these visits, a not very pleasant conversation took place between us. Kâmran, irritated by my standing at a distance, wanted to shut the door by force: but as he approached me, I showed I was quite ready to throw myself out of the room, and said in a low voice, "I beg you, Kâmran; you know that we're no sooner in this room than the eye is fixed on us from every aperture in the place."

He stopped at once, and said, "But how's that, Feridé? Aren't we engaged?"

I shrugged my shoulders slowly. "Well, there you are; that's the trouble," I told him. "You don't want, do you, to have them saying 'Your visits are becoming rather too frequent. Forgive us, but you must remember that this place is a school'?"

Kâmran went as white as a sheet, and after that he never came again.

What I had done wasn't really right; but what else could I do? This business of going back to the classroom after leaving Kâmran, and having everyone turn round to look at me, was more than I could stand.

Let me see, what was I saying? Oh, yes: one day, the doctor's girl came back after the weekend holiday, and said to me:

"So Kâmran's going to Europe, is he?"

I was taken by surprise, and said, "Who told you that?"

"My father. It seems his uncle in Madrid has invited him." My pride would not let me say, "I didn't know."

"—Yes. He has some such idea. Just a short journey," I said.

"Not so very short. It seems he's going as secretary to the Embassy."

"He won't stay long." I said no more, and we parted. My friend's father came pretty often to our house. I think he was our family doctor, or something of the kind. The news might conceivably be true. But how was it they had said nothing to me? I counted up the days; it was twenty since I had heard from home. That night I thought the whole thing over. I forgot my distant attitude to Kâmran, and was annoyed at his not telling me about an important thing like this. After all, we were two creatures bound to one another.

The next day was Thursday. The weather was fine, and we were to go for a walk in the afternoon. I was so glad. The idea of spending another night with thoughts like these alarmed me. So I went to the Mother Superior, and asked for leave of absence, explaining that my aunt was ill.

When I got home with my small valise in my hand, it was just getting dark. The house dog met me at the door. This old dog was very wide-awake, and a real sponger. He knew there was always something or other to eat in my bag, so he would waylay me, and walk backwards on his hind legs, trying to paw me with his front ones. I could see Kâmran coming towards me too, out of the trees, and I crouched down and seized the dog's dirty feet, which I didn't want to have all over me. The old fellow opened his mouth as if he were smiling, and hung out his tongue as I pressed his nose. In fact, we were having a game with one another. I only appeared to notice Kâmran when he had come right up to me, and then I said:

"Look at this ridiculous fellow. What a huge mouth! Doesn't he look just like a crocodile?"

However, he only looked at me with a rather bitter smile on his lips. I dropped the dog and brushed down my skirt, wiped my hand with my handkerchief, and stretched it out to my cousin.

"*Bonjour*, Kâmran. How's my aunt? I hope it's nothing serious."

He looked rather surprised, and said, "My mother, do you mean? There's nothing wrong with my mother. Did you hear she was ill?"

"Yes I did, and felt anxious: not having the patience to wait till Sunday, I got leave."

"Who said she was ill?"

There wasn't time to invent another lie; I said, "The doctor's daughter."

"She told you?"

"Yes. In the course of conversation she said: 'They've sent for my father; your aunt's probably ill.'"

Kâmran seemed very surprised. "There must be some mistake. In fact the doctor hasn't been to the house in the last few days, either for my mother or for anyone else."

Without prolonging this rather delicate topic, I said, "I'm very glad. I felt so anxious. . . . I suppose the others are indoors. . . ." I picked up my bag and wanted to go on. Kâmran took me by the hand.

"Why such a hurry, Feridé?" he asked. "One would think you were running away from me."

"What nonsense!" I said, "My shoes are hurting me. In any case, aren't we both going in?"

"Yes; but there, inevitably, we shall all be talking together. I want to talk to you alone."

To hide my emotion, I mocked him a little. "It's for you to command, sir."

"Thank you; in that case, if you will, we can take a stroll in the garden without anyone seeing us." As though he were afraid I should run away, he didn't drop my hand; and with his other hand he took up my bag. We began to walk side by side. It was the first time we had walked like this since our engagement began. My heart was beating like a bird's when it had just been caught; but I think that if he had let go my hand, I shouldn't have found the strength to run away. Without saying a word to each other, we walked to the end of the garden. Kâmran seemed much more disturbed and put out than I had expected. What had happened in those three months, what change had taken place between us, I don't know. But at that moment I felt guilty towards him; I repented of the savage way I'd treated him up to now. It was so beautiful and mild an evening that one forgot it was the middle of winter. The bare tops of the mountains all round us glowed in coral red. Was there some influence there, I wondered, that made me so easily admit my sins against Kâmran? I don't know. At that moment I had a longing to find some word that would give him pleasure. But I couldn't think of anything. Just when there seemed to be nothing to do but turn back, Kâmran said:

"Can we sit here for a bit, Feridé?"

"Just as you like," I said. (I called him 'thou,' for the first time since our trouble started.)

Without bothering about his trousers, Kâmran sat down on one of the rocks. I took him by the shoulder at once, and made him get up. "You're delicate," I said. "You mustn't sit on anything damp." And I took off my dark blue overcoat, and spread it where he was going to sit.

Kâmran couldn't believe his eyes; "What are you doing, Feridé?" he asked.

"To prevent your getting ill," I said. "It seems to me that it's my duty, from now on, to look after you."

This time my cousin probably couldn't believe his ears. "What's that you're saying, Feridé?" he persisted. "Are you saying that to me? It's the nicest thing I've heard from you since our engagement."

I bent my head, in silence. Kâmran had taken up my overcoat and was fondling the sleeves, the collar and the buttons. "I was going to reproach you a bit, Feridé," he said, "but now I've forgotten everything."

Without raising my eyes, I said, "I haven't done you any harm."

Fearing to come nearer me in case he drove me into one of my wild fits again, "I think you have, Feridé," he said, "indeed you've gone very far. Is it right to neglect a fiancé to that extent? All sorts of doubts have arisen within me. I hope Müjgan didn't make a mistake?"

Unintentionally I laughed, and Kâmran wanted to know why. At first, I didn't want to answer; but when he insisted, I looked away, and said: "If Müjgan had been wrong we shouldn't have been like this."

"What does 'like this' mean? Do you mean I shouldn't have been your fiancé?"

I shut my eyes and shook my head twice in succession.

"My Feridé!"

That voice, like a little cry, still rings in my ears. I opened my eyes, and I saw two large tears in those eyes of his, which seemed to have grown larger themselves.

"You've made me so happy at this moment, that if I remember it on my dying day, I shall weep. Don't look at me like that. You're still so young. You can't possibly understand this kind of thing. Well, I have forgotten everything." Kâmran had taken my wrists. I didn't struggle, but I began to sob. I was in such a state that Kâmran seemed almost frightened. As we returned along the same path, I kept sobbing and sighing at intervals. He didn't dare to touch me with his hand; but I knew he was happy, and I was content.

When we got near to the house, I said, "You must go first. I shall give my face a good bathe in the pool. What will they say if they see me like this?"

As if it had just come into my mind, I said to Kâmran, "Is there any question of a journey to Europe?"

"There is some idea of it," he replied. "But the fact is, it's not my own. It's a project of my uncle's in Madrid. Where did you hear about it?"

After a moment's hesitation, I said, "From the doctor's daughter."

"The doctor's daughter seems to tell you a good many things, Feridé?"

". . ."

Kâmran was looking at me attentively. "I hope my mother's illness wasn't just an excuse?"

". . ."

"Now tell me the truth, Feridé." Is that the reason why you came?" He had drawn near me. He wanted to stroke my hair, but he was afraid I should suddenly be frightened, and adopt some contrariness that would make trouble between us again. But no; I had begun to get used to him. He repeated his question.

"Is my guess right, Feridé?"

Knowing it would please him, I nodded.

"How lovely! What a change in my fortunes since yesterday." He leant his hands on the arms of the chair I was sitting in, and bent towards me. In this position I was enclosed on four sides. It was rather a clever way of approaching me without having to touch me with his hands. I was curling up in my seat like a hedgehog, and hunching my shoulders. I kept drawing further and further back, to avoid looking into his face, which was so close to mine. I was playing with my handkerchief; and I asked him:

"What is it your uncle has proposed?"

"Nothing very extraordinary. He wants me to go to him as secretary at the Embassy. He thinks it's a defect in a man not to have some definite office or profession. Of course, I'm only expressing his views, now. He says, 'Perhaps it would please Feridé to go to Europe with you, to some diplomatic post.' I don't know whether he's right, but that's what he says."

As the subject of our conversation had grown rather more serious, Kâmran straightened himself in his chair and raised his siege of me. I got up too, at once. We went on talking:

71

"Why did you say: 'Nothing very extraordinary' about this offer? Wouldn't you like to go to Europe?"

"From that point of view I've nothing to say against it. But from now on, I'm a man no longer quite free in his movements. I have to discuss everything affecting my life with you. Isn't that so?"

"In that case, you can go."

"You mean, Feridé, that you are quite willing for me to leave Istanbul?"

"Well, as it seems essential that every man should have a profession. . . ."

"If you were in my place, would you go?"

"Yes, I think I should. And I still think you ought to." I must admit I was speaking with my lips only. Otherwise, if I had expressed my real feelings at that moment, I should have spoken very differently. But justice is due to me. What other answer could I give to someone who asked me: "Shall I leave you and go?"

Kâmran, on the other hand, was distressed that I accepted a parting so easily. Without looking at me, he took a turn or two up and down the room; and then turned and asked me the same question again: "So do you think I'm right in accepting my uncle's offer?"

"Yes."

He sighed. "In that case, we'll think it over. There's still time before we need answer."

I gave up hope. When he said "We'll think it over," didn't it mean that the question wasn't yet settled in his own mind? I began to speak seriously, like a grown-up person, as I was always being asked to do. "I can't see what there still is to think about in the matter. Your uncle's offer is a nice one. A short journey wouldn't be at all a bad thing."

"Is an official post as brief a matter as all that, Feridé?"

"Well, you can't call it very long. One, two, three, four short years. It will pass in the twinkling of an eye. And of course, you will come back at intervals." I counted off those one, two, three four years on my fingers so easily. . . .

A month later, we put Kâmran on a steamer from the Galata Quay. All my relations were congratulating me on having urged him to go to Europe. Müjgan alone was not satisfied. In the letter she wrote me from Tekirdăgi, she said: "You have acted wrongly, Feridé. You ought to have stopped it. What's the point of spending your best years apart? Is four years a mere nothing?"

Nevertheless, those four years passed a good deal more quickly than Müjgan feared they would. When Kâmran returned to Istanbul for good with his uncle, who had retired, I had left school a month before.

Leaving school! During the time I had lived there, I had given that dark old building the name of "Dovecot." I used to say that the day I emerged, with a diploma of some kind or other, would be the day of my salvation. But one fine day the door of the dovecot opened, and I found myself in the street, in a new black veil as long as my whole body, and in fashionable shoes, and I wondered what had happened to me. Moreover, at home my aunt had begun preparations for my wedding. That made me furious. The house was choc-a-bloc with painters, carpenters, tailors and relations who came from a distance to spend the night with us. Every one had some job of his own; some were already writing the invitation cards, some were going round the bazaars to complete certain purchases, others were busy sewing. In my bewilderment, I was driven to every kind of foolishness. Far from doing anything useful myself, I put all sorts of obstacles in the way of the others. In the end, I was reduced to a state of lunacy. As of old, I put myself at the head of the children who were our guests, and turned the house upside down. The kitchen, as everywhere else, was being done up and painted: and so the new cook had transferred his pots and pans to a tent, which he had set up in the garden, and had begun to cook in the open.

One evening, I saw that he was cooking some sweet in front of the tent, and immediately a piece of devilry occurred to me.

"Children," I said, "you hide behind that heap of rubbish. Don't make a sound. I'm going to steal that sweet and bring it to you."

Before five minutes had elapsed I was back again with my young friends, with a dishful in my hands. The best thing to do would have been to give each child his share, and then to have sent them all to different parts of the garden, and hidden the dish in the rubbish heap. But this didn't occur to me, or rather I never thought that when the cook discovered the theft he would set up a chase all over the garden.

Almost at once there was a terrific row in front of the tent. The cook was shouting: "I swear to Allah I'll break his bones, whoever's done it!" The children were scared out of their wits and didn't listen to me; they started to run away, no doubt wisely. Because the cook was on our tracks a moment later, armed with a large stick, and he fell on us like a madman, wildly waving a skimmer. The shrewd fellow saw I was the biggest of the lot, and left the others to chase me. That instant, he tripped and fell full length on the ground: and his fury knew no bounds.

The cook was a stranger, and the situation was delicate. If I were caught, I should get a blow or two with the skimmer, and should be disgraced before I was able to explain who I was. As there was no chance of slipping round to the house, there was nothing for it but to run towards the street, yelling as I went. Mercifully the dressmaker, who had been at work since the morning, had gone to take a breath of fresh air in the garden, along with our old servant Dilber. I ran straight into them, flung myself upon them, and hid behind their backs, crying out: "He's coming!"

Dilber warded off the cook's skimmer with her hands, and shouted: "Here! What are you doing? Have you gone out of your mind? Don't you know that this is the young bride?"

At any other time, I should certainly have turned on Dilber for using that word. But I was so frightened that quite unconsciously I joined in with them, and shouted as well: "Cook, I swear I'm the bride!"

I have never seen anyone so crazed and so confounded as the cook. For a time he wouldn't believe the assurances of Dilber and the dressmaker. "No, no! A thief of that sort couldn't be a bride!" he insisted, and then growing a little calmer, continued: "Well, if it's really so, I offer the bride my congratulations. No doubt you'll buy me a new pair of trousers; look, you've gone and torn them at the knees." The poor man had knocked his nose and grazed the skin when he fell, but thank God he didn't add that to his claim for damages.

In spite of my insistence that it should be kept a secret, this comedy leaked out; and at every meal it became a habit to stare at me and laugh.

There were three days to the wedding. In the evening, while I was skipping with the children by that ill-fated door into the back garden, I was subjected to another attack. But this time the one who attacked me was the dressmaker who had saved me from the cook on the first occasion. This woman, who had done our sewing at the house for perhaps the last thirty years, was an old bespectacled spinster aged about sixty. Although she was one of the sweetest and dearest creatures in the world, on this particular evening she spat fire at me:

74

"I implore you, Mademoiselle!—in a few days' time we shall be calling you Madame. Is that the right way to behave? I've been looking for you for the last half-hour, to give your dress a final try on!"

Worse still, aunt Besimé was there too, and it was clear from the frown on her face that if the argument went on she would take sides against me. "I'm sorry," I said, "I was only here—I swear I didn't hear you."

My aunt could restrain herself no longer, and, stroking my cheek as she always did when she was about to scold me, she said, "Child, you make so much noise and laugh so much yourself that you can't hear anyone else. I've almost begun to be afraid that you'll go and do something of the same kind before all our guests in three days' time."

In spite of my appearing, during those days, to be more gauche and untamable than ever, it was a time when I was torn by very conflicting feelings, a time when I longed to be comforted and understood. Without withdrawing my face from my aunt's hands, I took the ends of my skirt in my fingers and made a slight curtsey, saying: "Don't worry, aunt; set your teeth for just three more brief days. Then your name and status will be aunt no longer. I can assure you that Feridé will not dare to behave like a cheeky spoilt child to her mother-in-law, as Çalıkuşu has done to her aunt!"

My aunt's eyes filled with tears, and she kissed me on both cheeks. "Feridé," she said, "I have always been a mother to you, and I shall continue to be one." I was so overcome that I suddenly took her round the waist and lifted her up, and kissed her on both cheeks, as she had kissed me.

My white dress was finished now, except for one or two small adjustments; when the dressmaker picked it up, I felt myself blushing deeply. I began to kiss everyone in the room one by one, and to beseech them: "What are you doing? Do leave the room! I won't dress in front of you all! Just think of it—Çalıkuşu with that long train behind her, just like a peacock. . . . Oh! The whole thing's so absurd. It makes even me laugh. What's the point of it? Can't the business be got over in ordinary clothes?" I asked imploringly. But no one would listen to me. When the dressmaker came up to me with the dress in her hands, I took refuge first in one corner of the room and then another, in a fit of trembling, just as though someone had come to arrest me. Those outside the door were making more noise and insisting on coming in: I begged them, "Just a little longer—please! One minute, and then I'll invite you all in." But they

75

wouldn't believe me. They leant on the door, calling, "She's deceiving us!" "She'll call us in when she's taken her dress off!" A lively struggle started, between the two parties. The children outside, and the grown-ups, pushed all together, and laughed, and tried to force the door, while I defended the position from inside with all the strength in my arms. And when the children began to stamp on the passage floor with their nailed shoes and shout, "Attack, attack! The war's begun!" the whole household ran upstairs. At my shoulder the dressmaker was crying out, "Don't do it! For God's sake, go away! The dress is being torn to pieces," but she was quite unable to make her voice heard.

Then for some reason, the noise seemed to stop for a moment or two, and I heard a footstep approaching the door. It was Kâmran. I heard him saying, "Open, Feridé; it's me. You won't keep me out? Let me in. I'll come and help you."

That drove me wild. "Let them all come!" I said beseechingly, "—it doesn't matter: but not you! For heaven's sake, go. I swear I shall cry."

But Kâmran took no notice of my supplications, and leaning hard against the door, he pushed it wide open. With a cry, I took refuge in a corner of the room; seizing an overcoat, I wrapped myself in it, and cowered down. The dressmaker was on the point of collapse: "Oh! The lovely dress is done for!" she cried, almost tearing her hair out in her despair.

Kâmran caught at the corner of the overcoat I was wearing, and said laughingly, "You'd better acknowledge your defeat, Feridé. Come now, open the coat: let's have a look at you!"

I could neither speak nor move. He waited a little, and then went on: "Feridé: I've just come in from the street; I'm very tired. Don't hurt me in this sort of way. I'm so curious to see your frock that if you persist in your obstinacy I shall have to resort to force. Look I'll count up to five. One, two, three, four, five."

Kâmran counted up to five as slowly as he could; then he drew aside the coat, and caught sight of my face, wet with tears.

He was very embarrassed; half forcibly, he sent the others out of the room, and shut the door. The dressmaker was dumb with incredulity, and Kâmran was in much the same state. A moment later he said, in a voice full of shame and emotion, "Forgive me, Feridé. It was only a little bit of a joke. I thought I had that much right, at any rate. But you're such a child . . . You forgive me, don't you?"

76

With my head still hidden in the coat I said: "All right; but you must go at once."

"On one condition; I'll wait for you by the big rock at the other end of the garden. Do you remember, four years ago, one evening, I made peace with you there? We'll do the same again now. Do you promise?"

After a slight hesitation I answered: "All right, I'll come. But you go now."

The poor dressmaker had no courage left to talk to a bride of so strange a character. She took off my dress without a word; and put on again my short pink frock, and on top of it my black school overall. Without so much as a glance at Müjgan, I ran off to my room and bathed my face in cold water, until my eyes were no longer red.

When I went into the garden it was dusk already. Now the main thing was to take refuge near him. Pretending to be wandering on my own, I passed at the back of the kitchen and had a word or two with the cook; and then I began to walk slowly towards the outside door. My object was, after covering my tracks, to descend on him from the far end of the garden wall.

But . . .

My eye caught sight of a tall woman in a black 'çarşaf,' in front of the street door, which always stood open. Her veil was down. Although she wanted to ask something at the house, she seemed to be afraid to enter. Kâmran had been waiting for me some time; I feared there was someone under that veil who knew me and would detain me in conversation, so I changed my direction and tried to make off among the trees. But the woman suddenly called out: "May I trouble you for a moment, young lady?"

There was nothing for it but to turn back and walk straight towards the door. "Come in, madame; can I do anything for you?"

"Is this the house of the late Seyfettin Pasha?"

"Yes, madame."

"You belong to the house?"

"Yes."

"In that case I have something to ask of you."

"I'm at your service, madame."

"I want to have a word with Feridé Hanim Efendi." I started slightly, and bent my head to avoid laughing. It was the first time I had heard "Hanim Efendi," and it sounded so strange. . . . I should never have the courage to tell her that *I* was "Feridé Hanim Efendi."

77

I bit my lip, and said: "All right, madam; do come in—if you ask at the house, they'll send for Feridé Hanim for you." The woman in the black çarşaf had entered the door and come right up to me.

"My meeting with you is lucky, my child," she said, "I want to ask you to do something for me. Please help me to have a word with Feridé Hanim alone, and if possible without anyone else knowing."

I looked at her with surprise; but as it was dark already, and she had not yet raised her veil, I could not distinguish her features. After a slight pause, I said: "Madame, I'm a bit oddly dressed, so I hadn't had the courage to tell you at once. But I am Feridé Hanim."

The woman made a slight gesture of astonishment. "The Feridé Hanim who is going to marry Kâmran Bey?"

"There is only one Feridé Hanim in the house," I said, smiling.

All at once the black-veiled woman paused. A moment before she had asked me to confront her with Feridé Hanim; why should she stand facing me now as though she were turned to stone? Was she still unwilling to believe that I was Feridé? Or was it something else she wanted? Trying to conceal my curiosity, I had to say again: "I am at your service, madame." Strange! The woman still could not open her mouth. I caught sight of a garden seat a little way off among the trees, and said: "If you like, let's go over there; we can talk there without anyone interrupting us."

The woman maintained her silence till after we had sat down. But finally she seemed to have made up her mind; and raising her veil brusquely, she disclosed the face of an intelligent, temperamental woman of about thirty. In spite of its being dark, it was apparent that her face had become alarmingly pale.

"Feridé Hanim," she said, "I have come here under pressure as the ambassador of an old friend of mine. But I never thought the task I had undertaken was going to be as difficult as this. A moment ago, I was insisting on seeing you, and now I feel as if I wanted to run away."

I felt a sudden trembling in my body. My heart was beating violently. But I felt that unless I showed courage, she would do as she had said, and run away. So I tried to appear as calm as I could, and said: "Duty is duty, madame. One must show courage. Does the friend you mentioned know me?"

"No. That's to say she's never actually seen you. All she knows is that you are Kâmran Bey's fiancée."

"Does she know Kâmran Bey?"

78

I really felt I had no strength left to ask further questions. Although at that moment I was almost beside myself with curiosity, I believe that if she had got up to go, I should not have been able to stop her.

"Listen to me, Feridé Hanim. You don't understand why I suddenly hesitated. I was expecting to meet a grown-up woman. But I see before me someone more like a school girl. I'm afraid of upsetting you too much; that's why I am hesitating." The strange woman looked as though she were really sorry for me. That hurt my pride, and completely restored my courage. I rose to my feet and leant against the seat under the tree; I folded my arms, and said in a quiet, serious voice:

"Hesitation doesn't do in these circumstances. I can see that the matter we have to talk about is important. So if we sacrifice our feelings and are quite open with one another, it will be better."

Faced with this evidence of my courage, the woman pulled herself together a little, and asked me: "Do you love Kâmran Bey very much?"

"I don't see what concern that is of yours."

"But it may be, Feridé Hanim."

"I've told you, madame, if you don't speak plainly, we shall get nowhere."

"All right, then. So be it. I'm forced to tell you that there's someone else who loves Kâmran Bey."

"That may be, madame. Kâmran is a young man with many attractions. I see nothing very extraordinary in the fact that someone else would like to possess him."

It was such an evening!—so calm, not even a leaf was stirring; but I knew too well that an unforeseen storm had broken. However, I found myself prepared to withstand it with a strength drawn from some source unknown to me. In the last sentence I had spoken to the woman, there was even a slight tone of mockery. From the way she drew herself up where she sat, and gripped the wooden seat, I could see that she had decided to bring the matter to a conclusion as briefly as possible.

In a mechanical, colourless voice, she said: "Although at first glance I looked on you as a child, I know now that I have before me a girl of breeding and education. Kâmran Bey, alas, has not realised your value as he should have done. Or maybe—who knows?—he did realise it, and merely succumbed to a passing weakness. The long and the short of it is, that two years ago, he and the friend I mentioned got to know each other. I don't know; would it be right, I wonder, to tell you more?"

79

I shook my head. "In order to prove that your words are true: yes."

"My friend's name is Münevver. She's the daughter of one of the old chamberlains. She married the man with whom she first fell in love, but they were not happy. Then she fell ill. The doctors advised her being sent to Europe. Just as she was about to come back, quite recovered, Kâmran Bey went for a visit to Switzerland, whether on leave or on duty I really don't know. And this happened. It was there they met. Kâmran Bey came to Switzerland for a week, and he stayed there nearly two months. Indeed, I think he probably got into trouble for it."

"Forgive me; I should like to ask you a question," I put in. "What is the point of this? Does your friend want me to know it all?"

This time the stranger felt compelled to rise; she twisted her gloved hands, and answered: "Well it's hard to say. Today, Münevver has become your enemy."

"I won't have that."

"But it's true, Feridé Hanim. Though she's not a bad person at all. She's very sensitive. Kâmran Bey is not a chance adventure for her. She hoped to marry him. If there's a fault anywhere, it is entirely with Kâmran Bey. Because he even concealed the fact that he had given his word to another. What compels me to take this unhappy duty upon me is this; I am afraid that this delicate woman may die."

"You mean, if she doesn't marry Kâmran?"

"Why should I tell lies? Yes, that's it. Münevver would certainly not survive that news."

"It's hard on her, poor soul."

"Or truer still, it's hard on both of you." I made a sign with my hand, as though to indicate that she had gone too far; and I laughed. "Don't bring me into it. At this moment you should only be thinking of her."

"Why, Feridé Hanim? It's true that Münevver has been my friend all these years. But you are a dear young girl, who's entirely innocent and blameless in the matter. That's why I feel sorry for you too."

I grew a little sterner now, and said with an arrogant gesture: "I can't allow that. Furthermore, I think there's really nothing left for us to talk about." I noticed that the stranger seemed to be looking for something. She kept opening and shutting her handbag. When she saw that I wanted to put an end to the conversation, she took out a crumpled piece of paper.

"Feridé Hanim, I couldn't help thinking that perhaps you would doubt my words. I brought with me one of Kâmran Bey's letters. I don't know—will it upset you to see it?"

80

At first I wanted to push the letter aside with my hand. And then, fearing I had done the wrong thing, I took it from her.

"If you like, I will leave it with you. You can read it later. After all, it's of no use to my friend."

Shrugging my shoulders, I said: "It won't be of any use to me either. It's a memento. It's better that she should keep it. Give me a moment. I'll have one look at it."

It had got darker. I moved out to the road between the trees and held the letter close to my eyes. I knew that writing! I began to read.

"My Golden Flower," it began, and then followed a row of compliments. Just as a dim light pervades the world, before the sun rises, so, before seeing the golden flower, a similar light had pervaded his heart. "I felt an inexpressible joy. I know I shall encounter something unbelievable," he seems to have said to himself; and then the unbelievable had happened. One evening when the lights were lit in the hotel garden, he saw his golden flower before him. . . .

I read what followed so quickly and was so little able to distinguish the words in the growing darkness, that I can hardly remember the rest; except, for some reason or other, the final phrases, which I read over several times, and which I can see before me to this day. "My heart is free. I need to love. When I see you with your tall and slender body and your violet eyes, the whole world changes colour."

The stranger came up to me slowly, and her voice trembled as she began to say: "Feridé Hanim, I am sorry for you—but believe me. . . ."

I gave myself a sudden shake, and interrupted her. Holding out the letter, I said: "Nonsense! There's nothing whatever to be sorry for. These are quite ordinary happenings. Indeed, I have to thank you. You have taught me a truth. And now, please, may I take my leave?" I bowed my head slightly and walked away. But she called after me again, "Feridé Hanim! One moment, I beg you. What am I to tell my friend?"

"Tell her you've done your duty. For the rest, she'll know what to do. That's all there is to it."

The stranger called me once more, but I didn't listen, and disappeared swiftly among the trees. I don't know how long Kâmran waited by the stone; it wasn't to witness peace between us again. But when he tired of waiting, and came to my room, he would have found, lying on the table, these few lines scribbled on a page of my ruled schoolbook; and they would have taken him by surprise indeed:

"Kâmran Bey Efendi: I have learnt the romance of the Golden Flower from beginning to end. We shall not meet one another again in this world. I despise you."

✎ PART TWO ✎

"Night and day, ever since you came, you've been writing and writing. You never stop writing! You can't call it a letter; letters aren't written in copy-books. You can't call it a book; everyone knows, books are written by learned men with long hair and long beards. You're a slip of a child. What is it you're writing, then, without ever stopping for a minute?" It's the old hotel porter, Hadji Kalfa, who's asking the question. He's been outside scrubbing the floors and singing away for more than an hour, and now he's tired: he's come to have a little talk with me, as he puts it. When my eyes fell on him, I couldn't contain myself, and started shaking with laughter. "What kind of get-up is this, Hadji Kalfa?" He generally goes about in a white apron, but today he was wearing an old-fashioned chemise, and clutching a great big stick in his hand, to prevent himself falling as he wiped the floor-boards with his bare feet.

"What else can I do? I'm doing women's work, so, of course, I dress like a woman," he retorted.

Hadji Kalfa has been the only person to enter my room, except for my unhappy neighbour, with whom I talk a little occasionally. During the early days he used to hang back rather. When he wanted to come into the room for something or other, he would knock, and call out, "Cover your face, teacher—I'm coming in." I used to tease him and say, "Come now, Hadji Kalfa, you've got a job to do, haven't you? Really, must there be all this ceremony between us?" He would screw up his withered face and scold me: "Oooh! It's not a question of what you think. It isn't the thing to do, to break in abruptly on Moslem 'muhadderat'" (using a rare expression). He must have meant "women," but I was a teacher, and too proud to demand the meaning of a word from Hadji Kalfa. All the same, I made fun of him, and pointed out the stupidity of all this deference. So now when it pleases him, he knocks at the door and comes in without any further delay.

83

Çalıkuşu

At first, Hadji Kalfa used to get annoyed at my inability to stop
laughing at him; but eventually he gave it up. "I know you do it to
provoke me, but I won't be provoked," he insisted. And then, with a
strange kind of sadness in his eyes, he would add: "You're like a bird in a
cage—so bored in this empty room; have your joke if you like and laugh:
it doesn't matter, if our friendship grows. Maybe I can be a bit of fun and
entertainment for you—eh?"

It was impossible to explain to Hadji Kalfa what I'd been writing. "My
writing's very uneven; so I'm writing copy-book style, Hadji Kalfa," I told
him. "Tomorrow or the day after I shall start lessons, and then the
children will be criticising me."

Hadji Kalfa leant on his stick as though he were posing for his
photograph, and there was a kindly smile in his eyes as he answered.
"You're taking the children in. Do you know how many times the spring
has come round with fresh yoghourt for Hadji Kalfa? These calligraphers
who write a large hand and scribble irregularly like spiders' legs—what
use are they? You don't know how tired I am of walking these offices, nor
what sort of officials I've seen in my day. You've no idea what a lot of
time's wasted in offices. You've got some kind of trouble, I know that;
but whatever it is, it's no business of mine. Only you must try not to cover
your fingers with ink when you're writing; that's what really disgraces
you in front of the children. Go on; you write what you like, and let me
sweep my floor."

After getting rid of Hadji Kalfa, I sat down again at my writing-table.
But I can't work; some of Hadji Kalfa's words keep haunting me. The
good man's right; because I'm a grown-up person and a teacher, who
starts work tomorrow or the next day, and I ought to try not to leave a
trace of my childishness by that time. Indeed, those inkstains on my
fingers, and on my lips, too, though Hadji Kalfa didn't say so, what of
them? Mightn't it be the inkstains that are responsible, when I'm writing
my diary at night, for my seeing myself so constantly back again at school;
and the feeling I have that those I shall never see again are quite near
me?

One thing that Hadji Kalfa said is still ringing in my head: "You're like
a bird in a cage, so bored in this empty room. . . ." It's not right that
anyone should call me a caged bird; today, especially, when I've escaped
from all cages. More than that, when he says 'bird,' it's as if he were trying
to pick up Çalıkuşu from the ground, as she lies there with her wing
broken and her beak closed. If Hadji Kalfa goes on talking like that, I'm

84

afraid he and I will fall out. However, I must make one more effort, so that I leave no gaps in my diary. I must go back once more to that hated world I've left behind.

That same evening, after learning all that there was to learn from the strange woman, I was making my way back to my room, and I ran into my aunt in the hall. I tried to hide myself in a corner in the darkness; but my aunt had seen me.

"Who's that?" she called out; "is it you, Feridé? Why are you hiding?"

I gave no answer, but stood there facing her. We couldn't distinguish each other's face.

"Why don't you go into the garden?"

No reply.

"I feel sure you've been up to some kind of mischief again."

My chest felt stifled, as though an unseen hand were pressing on it. "Aunt—!" I cried. At that moment, if my aunt had spoken one kind word to me, had lightly touched my cheek, had stroked my hair, I should have thrown myself into her arms, in tears; and perhaps I should have told her everything. But she didn't perceive my state of mind.

"What's the trouble now, Feridé?" she asked. It was the tone she used whenever I wanted anything from her. But to me, that evening, it seemed to signify, "Come now, haven't we had enough of this sort of thing?"

"It's nothing, Aunt," I said; "let me give you a kiss." After all, "aunt" meant "mother" to me; I couldn't bear to leave her without giving her one more kiss. Without waiting for her to answer, I took her hands, and kissed her in the darkness, on her cheeks and on her eyes.

My room was in a state of chaos. Clothes had been thrown on to the chairs; underclothing hung from the open drawers of the cupboard. What a disgrace, that someone who was daring to act as I was going to do, should leave her room as a careless schoolgirl would! But how could I help it?—there was so little time.

In the dark (because I feared they would see a light in my window and come in) I wrote a few sentences, feeling with my hand, for her to find. Then I opened the cupboard and filled my school suitcase with a few clothes that I valued as souvenirs, my diploma—tied up with a bit of red ribbon—and one or two simple pieces of jewellery, like the ring and the earrings my mother had left me. I remembered that it was just what children did when they ran away from home, and I laughed rather bitterly.

It was only when I got into the street that I began to wonder where I should go. Yes, where *was* I to go? If it were daylight it would have been easy; I had a vague kind of scheme in my mind. The chief problem was where to spend the night. Where could I take refuge at that hour? In spite of having thought everything out, I couldn't very well have walked the fields till morning with my suitcase in my hand. There would be a great to-do at home, before long. Perhaps they wouldn't have recourse to the police, to avoid a scandal; but it was quite certain that parties of searchers would be sent out in every direction. To travel by train or by steamer, or even by carriage was dangerous. They would soon have come upon my tracks. It's true there is no power that can force anyone to return home, when she wishes to live her life in her own way. But they would have looked on my decision as a piece of childish madness, the whim of a spoilt child, and would have given themselves a great deal of trouble in vain. I knew what sort of a letter I meant to write my aunt tomorrow, to dissuade them from this idea, and indeed to make them sorry to remember my name for the rest of their lives. But where was I to find shelter tonight?

At first, there came to my mind the names of a few of the friends who lived round about. They would certainly have given me a kind welcome. But the thing I had done was more or less a disgrace, and to take in a girl in my position, even for a brief night, might seem odd to them. Moreover, I should have to tell them something, to account for the unusual situation; and I felt I should find it very hard to give an account of my actions to strangers, or to listen to their advice. Finally the very names that first occurred to me were naturally the names that those at home would think of too, and they would begin to look for me there straight away. And is it likely that when my people came inquiring for me in a great state of mind, at midnight, that my friends' families would dare to tell them—just for my sake—"She's not here?"

I reflected that the high road to the station would be dangerous, and I turned down one of the roads at the back of the Içerenköy. It was getting darker and darker. Just as I was beginning to get alarmed and lose my courage, an idea suddenly came into my head. There was a refugee woman who had been wet nurse in a friend's house, eight or nine years ago. She used to live in Saharyicedit, and came to our home quite often. One day last year, as we came back from a rather long evening walk, we had called at her house and rested for half-an-hour in her garden. Our relationship was a good one; I always gave her my old clothes. I could

86

spend the night at her house, and it would never occur to anyone that I should be there.

A refugee cart was going down the street. At first I wanted to call it back, but that would have been risky, and moreover I had no small change on me. There was nothing left but to take the road to Saharyicedit on foot. I would pause, trembling, every time I saw a shadow in the dusk, or heard a footstep; who wouldn't have his doubts about a woman he found walking alone upon deserted country roads at night? Mercifully there wasn't a soul about. It was only as I was going along by the side of a vineyard that I avoided one slight danger. A handful of drunken men were coming in the opposite direction, singing songs. I cleared the low fence around the vineyard in one bound; and there I hid until they had passed. If there had been a dog in the vineyard I should have been in a bad way. Besides this escape, as I crossed the Saharyicedit road, I met a night watchman on the pavement, wearily dragging his stick. But as luck would have it, the good man turned into a side street without noticing me.

The nurse and her old husband were most surprised to see me. I told the tale I had learnt by heart as I came along; it ran something like this: "I'd been coming back from Üsküdar with my great-uncle, and the wheel of the carriage broke, at that very spot. We couldn't find any other carriage, at that hour, so we had to get home on foot. In the distance we saw your light, and my uncle said, 'Now then, Feridé, you stay the night with the nurse. They're no strangers. I've a friend near here who will put me up.'"

As a matter of fact, my tale wasn't a very easy one to believe, even for those simple folk. But the honour of entertaining the young lady for a night was so great an event, that they never doubted my word. Next morning, when the poor woman saw that the beautiful clean bed, fragrant with wild lavender, that she'd prepared for me, was empty and untouched, she would realise what had happened. But by then, the bird would have flown away; the caravan would have gone by.

That night, in the nurse's room, I put out the lamp, and sat staring into the darkness, as I worked out my plan for the future. My diploma lay in a corner of the cupboard, tied up with red ribbon. I'd thought it was fated to grow yellow with age; but it had suddenly acquired a new value. All my hopes rested in that piece of paper, which I'd been told was well worth having. With its help I was going to get a post as a teacher, in one of the provinces of Asia Minor, and spend my whole life happily and contentedly among children. Until I left Istanbul, I decided to hide in the house of Gülmisal Kalfa, in Eyüp-Sultan.

Gülmisal Kalfa had been my mother's nurse. When my mother married, she was married off to an old Customs official in Eyüp. They used to turn out apprentices. In contrast to her affection for my mother, she had quarreled with my aunts. While my grandmother was still alive, she used occasionally to come to our country house and bring me coloured toys from Eyüp, but after my grandmother's death, the old retainer stopped coming altogether, and my aunts forgot all about her. I don't know why; there must have been some disagreement between them. In any case, there was no safer place for me in Istanbul than Gülmisal Kalfa's home.

When my aunt got my letter, which had acquired more and more importance in my mind, she would do nothing but weep. As for that other creature, well, he was a human being. Even if he tracked me down, he would never have the face to present himself.

That morning, I found the old lady's street door half-open. There she was, wearing a shawl over her hennaed hair, and bath sandals on her bare feet, washing down the yard of the house. Without saying a word, I stood in front of the door, and began to watch her. My face was completely veiled, and she didn't recognise me, but stared at me confusedly with lustreless blue eyes.

"Do you want anything, Hanim?" she asked.

I swallowed once or twice, and then said, "Nurse, don't you recognise me?"

My voice made an extraordinary impression on her. She drew back as though she were afraid.

"Good God! Good God!" she exclaimed; "lift your veil, Hanim!"

I put my case down on the wet stones and raised my veil. The old woman gave a stifled cry. "Güzide, my Güzide has come! Oh, my child!" She threw her thin knotted arms around my neck, and the tears poured from her eyes. "Oh my child, my child!" she sobbed.

I knew why she felt so deeply moved. They always told me I was growing more and more like my mother. Indeed, one of her old friends who never forgot her used to say, "She's got a face and a voice exactly like Güzide's when she was twenty. I can't listen to Feridé without weeping." It was just the same now with Gülmisal Kalfa. The old Circassian servant was the first to show me what a beautiful thing weeping can be. I

88

remember my mother indistinctly, as a faint image, like those pictures one sees in deserted rooms, covered with dust, with their colour and outline dimmed by time. This vague picture had not, until today, aroused in me either much sadness or excessive love; but when Gülmisal Kalfa sobbed out "My Güzide!" and her old head couldn't distinguish between my mother and me, something curious happened inside me. My mother seemed to come before my eyes, and the bitterness of death into my heart; I, too, cried "Mother, little Mother!" and broke into stifled weeping. The old servant forgot her own trouble, and began to concern herself with me. I asked her through my tears, "Kalfa, was my mother very like me?"

"Very, my child. When I saw you I had quite a shock. I thought I was looking at her. May God preserve you, as long as the earth on her grave."

The old woman undressed me like a child in the room alongside the yard, and continued to weep silently. I shall never forget my impression of the first hours I spent in her little room, with its cambric blinds. After she had undressed me, she put me on a divan covered with some woven cloth; then she put my head on her knee and stroked my hair and my brow, as she began to tell me about my mother. One by one, she related all her memories, from the day she was born—the moment when, in her blue headband, she took her on her lap for the first time: up to the very last day, when they parted.

And when it was my turn, I told her all that had befallen me just as it had happened. The old woman listened to me with a smile on her face, as a child listens to a fairy tale; and now and again she said with a sigh, "Oh dear! My poor child." When I told her how I had escaped from the house the night before, and how I refused to return there as long as I lived, she got into a great state, and said, "Feridé, you've behaved like a child. And Kâmran Bey has shown he's got no sense. He'll repent of it: and he won't do it a second time," she added. It was impossible to explain my rebellion to Gülmisal Kalfa.

At the end of my story I told her, "Gülmisal Kalfa, don't you tire your poor old brain for nothing. After I've stayed two or three days with you, I shall go off somewhere else, and live by the work of my hands." As I spoke, the poor woman's eyes filled with tears: she stroked my hands, and pressed them to her cheeks and her lips, and asked me, "How can I let these lovely hands be sacrificed?" I sat the old woman on my knees, and jumped her about and pinched her furrowed cheeks. There was no great danger to those hands at all, I said; all they'd have to do was to pull the ears of a few mischievous children now and again. I explained how I was going to teach in Anatolia, and told her all the things I was going to do, with so much pleasure, that in the end she fell a victim to my enthusiasm. She took down from the wall her little Koran, wrapped in green crêpe, and swore upon it that as long as I was her guest she would never give me up to anyone. On the contrary, she'd turn away from her door anyone who came to look for me.

That day, I busied myself helping Gülmisal with the housework. Until now, I'd always had my food prepared for me. I had never even cooked an egg. All that would have to change. Where was I going to find a cook or a servant from now on? This was the moment, with Gülmisal Kalfa at hand, when it was my duty to learn from her how to cook, how to wash up, and launder my clothes, and how—if I may mention it—to mend my linen and darn my stockings.

I took off my shoes and stockings and started work at once. I took no notice of the old lady's objections and cries of protest. I drew buckets full of water from the well; I scrubbed the floor-boards and soaked them. And then, sitting with her beside the well, I cleaned the vegetables. "Cleaned the vegetables," I say lightly; but what delicate work it was! When the old lady saw the potatoes I'd been peeling, she cried out "My dear, you're throwing half of them away with the skins!"

Then I'd open my eyes wide, and say, "You're quite right, Kalfa. If I hadn't learnt that from you, I should have thrown away half the potatoes I'd laboured to buy, and been quite unaware of it to the end of my days."

I kept a little notebook by my side, so that I could record the things I learnt from her; and now and then I'd make her laugh by saying, "Nurse, what's the price of a potato?" or "How many centimetres of peel ought one to cut off the outside?" or "Nurse, how many buckets of water does it take to wash the floor?" and questions of that sort, till the tears would flow from the poor woman's eyes.

How can you explain modern educational methods to an ignorant Circassian? I took pleasure in doing all these things; and I felt as though they helped to numb a certain pain, of which I was somehow still conscious. After putting our saucepan on the fire, we would sit down on the spotless mat in the kitchen, and I would say, "Ah, dear Kalfa, who knows what beautiful places I shall be going to? I've a dim recollection of Arabia; and anyway, Anatolia must be far more beautiful than that. The people there are not like us, they say. They're said to be poor, but their hearts are generous, so that they don't grudge a kindness, even to an enemy, let alone to a poor orphaned relative! I shall have a small school; I shall decorate it with flowers from top to bottom. I shall have a whole regiment of children, and I shall make them call me 'Abla.' I shall sew black overalls for the poor ones, with my own hand. ('Which hand?' you'll say.) Don't laugh, don't mock me! I shall learn it all in time."

Kalfa, poor old thing, was laughing at one moment and blushing with shame at the next for having done so.

"Feridé, my child," she said with a sigh, "it's a very wrong road you're taking."

Well, we shall see which of us has taken the wrong road.

When that was all over, that dreadful letter was written to my aunt. At one place in the letter I wrote these words:

"Aunt, I shall speak openly with you. Kâmran never said anything to me, at any time. He never *meant* much to me at any time, either. He's never been more to me than a spoiled, insignificant stay-at-home, without soul or character; a delicate little bit of rubbish. Shall I say more? I never liked him, nor wanted him, ever. Nor did I have any other kind of feeling for him. 'If that's so, why did you consent to marry him?' you will ask. Çalıkuşu's well known for her caprices. I was just mad. But mercifully I pulled myself together in time. Do you realise what misfortune a girl with that attitude to your son could bring to the happiness of your home? Well, I have averted that disaster, by leaving you all, and breaking the bonds between us; and thereby repaying a little of all the kindness you've shown me for years past. After hearing this from me, I expect you'll save yourself the indignity of mentioning my name again. But believe me, if you ever come face to face with the ungrateful and disobedient girl who writes these unforgiveable things with so little compunction, you'll find her capable of making as good a row as any washerwoman. So the best thing we can do is to forget each other's names. Pretend that Çalıkuşu has gone to her death in some corner or other, just as her mother did. Shed a tear or two if you like. That's not my business. But I warn you, don't say, from a distance, 'I must help her somehow.' I shall reject such a thing with scorn. I'm twenty, and I've managed to save my own skin so far. I'm going to live as I please."

Whenever I remember that ill-mannered letter, I shall always weep with shame. But it was necessary. Nothing else would have prevented my aunt looking for me, and perhaps finding me too. My aunt may be as angry as she likes, but she needn't worry.

The next day, after posting the letter with my own hand, I went straight to the Ministry of Education. I had Gülmisal Kalfa's long çarşaf round my shoulders, and my face was covered with her small one. I had to go like that, both because I had to avoid being recognised in the street, and because I had heard that the Ministry of Education had no great confidence in women teachers who went about with their faces uncovered. Until I got to the door of the Ministry, I was happy and full of courage. I expected my business to be dealt with quite easily; a messenger would take me to the Minister, and as soon as he saw my diploma, he would say, "Welcome, young woman! We've been waiting for people like you." Then he would give me an appointment in one of the most prosperous parts of Anatolia. But no sooner past the door, than the atmosphere suddenly changed. I was seized with fear and disquiet. Corridors leading in and out of each other, the strangest of staircases from top to bottom of the building, and a swarm of people on those staircases, and in those corridors. I dared not ask any questions, but stared about me stupidly.

On my right, above a high door, a notice caught my eye, which read, 'the Office of the Ministry.' That would certainly be the Minster's room. In front of the door there sat a very magnificent office porter, his arms covered with gold braid, evidently bored with sitting in a shabby old armchair, whose springs were showing through the worn leather. From his appearance, you wondered whether he were Bey or Pasha, and from his manner when he spoke, you felt inclined to ask "Is this his Excellency the Minister himself?"

Full of awe, I approached him, and said, "I want to see the Minister."

The messenger moistened his fingers and twirled the ends of his long brown moustaches; he eyed me all over with a regal look, and enquired very slowly, "And what do you want, I wonder, with the Minister?"

"I'm going to apply for a teaching post," I replied.

He pursed his lips, to get a good view of his moustache, and announced, "The Minister is not to be bothered about a matter of that sort. Go and tell them in his office. You must follow the correct procedure."

I wanted to be told what the correct procedure was. But he didn't think it necessary to answer me, and turned his head in the opposite direction in the same haughty and lordly manner. Under my veil I put out my tongue, terrified. If this were how he behaved, what on earth would his master be like? Oh dear, what *was* going to happen to me, I asked myself.

They had ranged eight or nine buckets of water alongside the banisters, with a long plank across them such as we used for a see-saw at home, and had produced an odd kind of seat, on which a number of people, men and women, were sitting. Noticing an old woman with china-blue eyes and a black woollen çarşaf pinned under her chin, I went up to her and explained my position. She looked as though she were sorry for me, and said, "I can see you're a novice in the profession. Don't you know anyone in the Ministry?"

"No. There might be someone I know, but I can't tell. In any case, what use would that be?" I asked her.

From the way she spoke, it was clear that the woman with the blue eyes was a teacher of some intelligence. She smiled, and said, "You'll learn that later on, my dear. Come, let me take you to the Elementary Education Department. Just try to see the Director General."

The Director had a black beard, a dark complexion and heavy eyebrows; his head was large and his face marked with smallpox in places. When I entered his room, he was talking to two young women who were standing in front of his writing-table. One of the two was pulling some crumpled papers out of her bag with hands that trembled so much you couldn't help noticing them, and putting them one by one on the table. The Director just ran his eye over the papers and looked at the stamps and the signatures; then he said, "Go now, and register your name in the office."

Both women salaamed, and withdrew, walking backwards.

"What do you want, Hanim?"

The question was addressed to me. A little confused, and stammering slightly, I began to explain my position. But he suddenly interrupted me, and said sternly, "A teaching post, is it? Have you made out an application?"

I was more confused still. "You mean my diploma?", I asked.

The Director, with cynical impatience, pursed his lips and shook his head at a thin-looking fellow, a visitor, who was sitting in a corner. "Do you see? That's how it is with these people. How can one keep sane? They don't even know the difference between an application and a diploma. Then they go and ask for a job as a teacher, and it's not long before they're sticking their toes in and saying 'the pay is too little,' or 'the place is too remote.'"

93

The ceiling of the room swam round and round above my head; I was looking about me stupidly, at a loss what to say.

"What are you waiting for?" the Director asked in a harsh voice. "Come on; if you don't know what to do, ask someone who does know. Write out an application."

As I was trying to get out of the little room without knocking against anything in my dazed state, the young man sitting in the corner interposed: "Your Excellency permits me? Young woman, let me give you a little well-meaning advice. . . ." Heaven help me, what advice did he *not* give me? Women like myself should take to some trade or profession, rather than teaching. As his Excellency himself had just said, it was very doubtful whether anyone who (like myself) was unable to distinguish between an application and a diploma, could make a success as a teacher. But if I were to work hard, I might be able to earn my living—as a dressmaker, for instance.

As I came down the stairs everything looked black about me. Someone took my arm. I was in such a state of exasperation that I almost screamed.

"How did things go, my child?" It was the woman with the china-blue eyes asking the question. I set my teeth to stop myself weeping, out of anger and despair, and explained how things had gone. She gave me a kind smile and remarked, "I asked, my dear, because I wanted to know if you knew anyone here or not. All the same, don't give up hope. Perhaps we can still find some way out. Come, let me take you to an acquaintance of mine, a head of one of the departments. God save him! He's a good fellow."

We mounted the stairs again. The old school teacher pushed me into a tiny room divided off from the rest of a large office by a frosted glass partition. Today, evidently, I had *no* luck. Because there I met with a sight that offered me little encouragement: a gentleman whose beard was black on one side and almost white on the other was exploding with rage at an old messenger, and gesticulating as though he were going to strike him. The messenger was trembling from head to toe, in much the same condition as I had been in myself, not very long before. The gentleman took a cup of coffee that was standing before him, and emptied it out of the window into the street as though it were dirty water, and then pushed the messenger to the door and bundled him out.

I tugged my new friend gently by the skirt, and said, "For heaven's sake, let's get away from here!" But it was too late. The chief had seen us.

"Hullo, Naime Hodja," he exclaimed. It was the first time in my life that I'd seen an infuriated person calm down so quickly. *What* a variety of characters there is among these officials.

My blue-eyed teacher explained my situation in a few words. The chief addressed me with a charming smile: it would have taken a thousand witnesses to prove that this lamblike person was the same individual who so recently threw his coffee into the street and belaboured an old servant out of the room, shaking him as if he were a mulberry tree. "Uncover your face; let me have a look, my dear. Oh, you're still a child. How old are you?"

"Almost twenty, sir."

"Strange. All the same, however that may be, one thing's certain. You can't go into the interior. It would be dangerous."

"Why, sir?"

"Is there a why, my dear? The reason's obvious." The chief was laughing. He was making signs to Naime Hodja and pointing to my face with his hand; but he never said a word about the obvious reason. Finally, he winked at the blue-eyed teacher. "I can't say much more. You're a woman—you can explain better, Naime Hanim," he said. Then, wagging his beard from side to side as if talking to himself, he added, "Ah, you know what devils and sons of devils there are abroad in the world."

To which I replied with naive surprise, "Sir, I don't know who it is you're calling sons of devils; but you must find work for me, where they're not to be found."

At this the chief slapped his knees with his hands and laughed louder still. "Ah! That's really good. . . ."

Either I like a person the first time I see him, or I don't. And I don't remember that this feeling has ever proved wrong afterwards. However that might be, I'd taken to this good fellow at once. His beard, one side of which was white and one side black, gave him such a queer look: when he turned his head to the right you felt you were looking at a young man, but when he turned it to the left the young man disappeared, and an old one with a white beard began to smile at you instead.

"Did you 'come down' from the Teachers' College this year, young woman?"

"No sir. I am not a graduate of the Teachers' College; I have a diploma from the Dame de Sion School."

"What sort of school is that?"

I gave a lengthy explanation to the Director, and then handed him my diploma. I think it's probable that he knew no French, but in order not to give that away, he kept looking at one side of the paper and then the other, and turning it over and over. "Fine. Good. . . ."

The teacher Naime addressed him without formality. "My dear Bey Efendi," she said, "you like doing good turns. Don't send this child away empty-handed."

The Director knitted his brows and pulled at his beard; he was thinking hard. "That's all very fine; but maybe our people don't recognise a diploma from that school." And then as though something had just come into his head, he struck the table and declared: "My dear girl, you ask for a post as French teacher in one of the Istanbul grammar schools. Look: I'll show you how to do it. Go straight to the Istanbul Education Department."

I interrupted the Director. "There's no question of my remaining in Istanbul, sir. I absolutely must go to one of the provinces."

He was embarrassed. "That's the first time I've ever come across a woman teacher who wanted to go up to Anatolia of her own sweet will! We have the devil of a job to get our teachers to leave Istanbul. What do you say, Teacher Naime?" The Director had begun to have doubts about me; he interrogated me with considerable adroitness, and asked questions about my family. I had a dreadful time of it, before I was able to convince the good man. From where he was sitting, he called for Şahap Efendi, and in the doorway between the office and the portion screened off by glass a feeble-looking slip of a young fellow appeared.

"Look here, Şahap Efendi, take this young lady into your room. She wants a post as teacher in Anatolia. Write her out a draft application and bring it to me."

Well! I imagined my difficulties were almost over; I wanted to throw my arms round the Director's neck and kiss him on the white side of his beard. Şahap Efendi sat me down before an untidy desk in the office and began to ask me questions, in order to write the draft the Director had asked for, and to make notes of what I said on a sheet of paper. This shabby clerk looked rather ill, and his manner was nervous and apologetic; when he glanced at me to ask a question, his eyelashes seemed to quiver. Two oldish clerks who were sitting beside the window were muttering something to each other, and looking at us out of the corner of their eyes from time to time. One of them said, "Şahap, my son, you're very tired today. Let me write that application."

Nothing will stop this tongue of mine, especially when something pleases me. So without there being any occasion for it, I said, "How nice it is to see the way colleagues help one another in this department."

Şahap Efendi blushed a deep red and lowered his head. Had I made a *gaffe*, I wondered? It looked as if I had, because the others were laughing. I couldn't hear what they said; but I did catch the words of one of them: ". . . The teacher's experienced and pretty thick-skinned . . ." fell on my ears. What did the words mean? And what were the two gentlemen getting at?

The draft application was placed before the Director several times and came back again; and after it had been adorned very much with red ink, and stamped, a fair copy was made. "There you are, my dear," the Director announced, "God preserve you. I'll do all I can."

As there were other people with him I didn't dare say anything more. But I didn't know to whom I ought to take the paper, nor what I was to say. I hoped I might see Teacher Naime again; I looked around me, and my eye fell on Şahap Efendi. The little clerk was waiting for someone at the top of the stairs. On catching my eye he sheepishly lowered his head. One could see that he wanted to say something, but that he hadn't the courage. As I passed him, I said, "I gave you a lot of trouble today. Can you please tell me where I ought to take this?"

He still didn't dare raise his eyes: as though he were begging for some great favour, he said in a high trembling voice, "It's a difficult thing, comrade, to follow up this kind of procedure. If you'll allow me, I will take charge of your application. Don't worry. Just look in at the office now and again."

"When shall I come?" I asked.

"In two or three days."

I was annoyed that my business should be prolonged another two or three days. But a full month dragged on altogether while I was coming and going. Had it not been for the efforts of Şahap Efendi, perhaps it would have dragged on longer still. For all one may say, it is possible to find real humanity among human beings occasionally. I shall never forget the kindness of that young man. The moment he saw me through the door he would run along and wait for me at the top of the stairs. As he went from office to office with my papers in his hand, I felt full of compunction; and I didn't know how to thank him. One day the little clerk had his throat tied up in a bandage. He was coughing as though he were going to choke, and his voice was hoarse when he spoke.

"Are you ill? Why do you come to the office in that state?" I asked him.

"I knew that you would come today for an answer," he replied.

I laughed involuntarily. Was that a good reason? Şahap Efendi continued in a hoarse voice, "Of course, I have other work as well. As you know, new schools have been opened."

"Have you got good news for me?"

"I don't know. Your papers are with the Director General. He said you were to see him when you came."

The Director General had put on a pair of dark spectacles, which gave a still more dense expression to his wrinkled face. He was signing a pile of papers in front of him, throwing them, as he did so, one by one on the floor, while a white-moustached clerk was picking them up, bending down and drawing himself up as though he were saying his prayers.

Rather nervously, I said: "Sir, you gave orders that you wanted to see me."

Without looking at me, he said in a stern voice, "Have patience, woman; can't you see?"

The white-moustached clerk made a sign with his eyes and eyebrows that I should wait. I realised that I had disgraced myself, and drew back a few paces to wait beside the partition. When the Director had done with his papers, he took off his spectacles and wiped his lenses with his handkerchief.

"Your application has been refused," he said. "Your husband's service doesn't seem to have been as long as thirty years."

"Do you mean me, sir? There must be some mistake."

"Aren't you Hayriyr Hanim?"

"No sir. I am Feridé."

"What Feridé? Ah! I remember now. Alas, and your application has met the same fate. Your school is not one of those approved by the Ministry. A post cannot be given you with this diploma."

"Very well, then. What's to become of me?" I let out the senseless remark quite unintentionally. The Director put on his glasses again with an expression of amused indifference.

"That, after all—if you will allow me—is a matter for you to consider," he said. "If in addition to all the work I have to do I had to consider what was to happen to you as well, I should have a fine time of it."

That must have been one of the moments in my life the bitterness of which I shall never be able to forget. Yes. What *was* to happen to me? For good or bad, I had been working for years; and I was prepared to go to most of the out-of-the-way places, even at my age. And still they were turning me away. What was to become of me? To go back again to my aunt's house seemed worse than death. As a last resort I turned to the other Director. I bit my lip to prevent myself from crying.

"Bey Efendi," I said, "my diploma seems to be of no use; what am I to do now?"

Whether it was what I said, or the consternation with which I said it the good man seemed really concerned. "What can I do, my child? That was just what I said; but does anyone pay much attention to letters of recommendation?" His sympathy undid me completely. "Bey Efendi: I *must* find work. I will accept, cheerfully, the most remote village, the kind no one else will go to."

As though something had suddenly come into his mind, the Director said, "Wait! One more try. . . ."

There was a tall, pretty strongly-built gentleman reading the paper by the window. His face was turned towards the street, so I could only see a part of his beard and his hair, which was touched with grey. The Director called out, "Sir: may I disturb you a minute?" He turned and came up to us slowly, without saying a word. The Director pointed to me and said: "Sir, you're charitably disposed. This child is a graduate of a French school. One can tell from her manner and speech that she belongs to a good family. But—as you know—God alone enjoys security. This child is obliged to work. 'I'll go to the remotest village,' she says. But you know our people. You know what she is, too—a rose doesn't require any explanation! The thing's been dismissed by a mere 'can't be done.' It would get through, if only you'd be good enough to have a word with the Minister."

As he spoke, the Director patted his shoulders, which had begun to be a little bent with care before their time. From his dress and his bearing, I sensed that he was quite a different kind of man from any other I knew. He bent forward slightly as he listened to the Director, and put his hand behind his ear in order to hear better. His eyes were somewhat bloodshot, but calm and friendly, when he turned to me and began to

99

talk, in French, with a broken accent. He asked me questions about the
school where I had graduated, what work I had done, and what I wanted
to do. It was evident that he was satisfied with the replies I gave. While
we were talking the Director laughed good-humouredly. "She speaks
French like a nightingale. It's a matter for congratulation, really, in a
Turkish girl," he said.

Gülmisal Kalfa always used to say,

"If half the month is dark and drear,
The other half is daylight clear."

As that man looked at me (I learned afterwards that he was a great
poet), I felt as if this "daylight clear" was about to begin for me. I
recovered the happiness I had gradually lost a month ago. After speaking
the lovely words which I'd heard from no one else, up till now, the man
took me with him to the Minister's room. As he passed, messengers rose
to their feet and doors seemed to open of themselves. Half an hour later
I had been appointed to a vacancy as geography and drawing mistress in
the high school at the headquarters of the province of B.

Çalıkuşu returned to Eyüp that evening travelling as it were on wings
of joy. From now on she was a person earning her own living. No one
would dare to insult her now, with that insult they call pity and
protection.

Three days later, all the formalities were complete; I had received my
travelling allowance. One morning Gülmisal Kalfa took me down to the
steamer. Şahap Efendi had come down early to the quay and was waiting
for us. Never as long as I live shall I forget that young man's kindness.
He had occupied himself with all my affairs and neglected nothing, down
to the address of the hotel where I was to stay at the place I was going to.
And now, at this early hour, he had come to say goodbye to me, in the
wind and damp of the quay, his sore throat still swathed in bandages. He
put my trunk in the cabin with his own hands, together with a small box
he had brought along as a gift for the journey. He ran up and down again
and again, giving instructions to the crew and wearing himself out with
concern.

Till the steamer started we sat in one corner of the deck. At the hour
of parting one ought to talk all the time, oughtn't one? And say whatever
there is to say and be done with it. But in the space of that one hour,

Gülmisal Kalfa and I didn't exchange more than perhaps a dozen words. She gazed at the sea with her dull blue eyes and fondled my hands. But just as the steamer was about to leave, she couldn't bear it any longer. "I put your mother on board the steamer here, Feridé, and she wasn't alone like you. God grant that I shall embrace you again," she said; and began to sob desperately. In spite of the fact that Şahap Efendi was with us, perhaps I might have been unable to restrain myself either. But at that moment there was a commotion. "Come on, good woman, the gangway's being pulled up," they shouted, and took my poor old Kalfa by the shoulders, pushing her towards it.

The little clerk was still beside me. When I held out my hand to thank him, I saw that his face was blanched and that his eyes were full. For the first time he had the courage to look me straight in the face and call me by my name.

"Feridé Hanim: so it means you're going for good and all?"

In spite of the heaviness of the moment of parting, that was descending on me like a cloud, I couldn't help smiling. "Well, there can't be any doubt about it now, can there?" I asked.

He said nothing, poor fellow; but took his hand out of mine, and made off down the gangway.

I am very fond of journeys by sea. The pleasure of the journey I made as a little girl of six or seven, with my father's man, is still a lively memory; the steamer, the people on board, even the forgotten Hüseyin—I could just remember the sort of things that might linger in the memory of a bird, crossing a wide ocean: the wild delight of racing through that expanse of blue, with gleams of flickering light on every side. In spite of this wild effect of the sea upon me, I could not stand remaining on deck. As the steamer rounded Sarayburnu I went down to my cabin.

The box that Şahap Efendi had brought stood on my trunk. I opened it, wondering what it could be. A box of *fondants*—the very thing I love best in the world, I believe! I put one of the little clerk's gifts to my lips. But suddenly I burst out crying. I don't know why I cried at all. The more I tried to explain it to myself, the more my tears flowed and choked me. As though the poor sweets were the cause of this unreasonable grief, an impulse made me seize the box and throw it into the sea through the tiny porthole of the cabin. Yes, there can be nothing in the world more meaningless than these tears, I know that. But in spite of it, even now as I write these lines, tears are running off my eyelashes and blotching the pages of my diary. Is it because of the rain which is falling silently outside, I wonder? What's it like in Istanbul now? Is it raining there too? Or is the garden at Kozyatağı shining brightly in the light of the moon? Kâmran, the aversion I feel isn't only for you; it's for the places where you are, as well.

This morning when I awoke I found that the rain, which had been going on for days, had stopped. The clouds had scattered; and only here and there on the tops of the high mountains opposite my window, thin trails of clouds drifted. When I went to bed I had forgotten to close the window. A light morning breeze caught the sunlight and made it tremble and scatter in tiny yellow sequins on my counterpane and on my loosened hair. Five days in this small hotel room had got on my nerves considerably. At night, when I awoke for a moment, I used to find my cheeks damp, like leaves on which hoar frost has fallen; and my pillow was in the same state. It meant that I had wept in my sleep. Now, however, a little sun revived my gaiety and even my hopes again, and gave my body the lightness it had on those spring mornings when I used to wake in the school dormitory. Today was bound to bring me some good news. After all, I've nothing to be afraid of. I jumped out of bed full of enthusiasm and began to wash in front of an old fashioned wash-basin. I shook and splashed the water all round me and on to the glass of the mirror in front, as birds do, dipping their heads in and out of a clear pool of water.

There was a light knock at the door, and the voice of Hadji Kalfa was heard saying, "Good morning, teacher; you're about early again today."

In a cheerful voice I replied, "Bonjour, Hadji Kalfa. Yes, I am. How did you know I'd got up?"

Hadji Kalfa's voice laughed. "How do I know? You're whistling like a bird." Indeed I was beginning to believe too that there was something very bird-like about one side of me.

"Shall I bring breakfast?"

"Can't I go without today?"

This time the voice was angry: "No. It won't do. I don't want anything of that kind. You don't go out. You don't amuse yourself. You've stayed here shut in like a prisoner: and if you eat nothing, you'll get just like your neighbour opposite." Hadji Kalfa put his mouth to the keyhole and lowered his voice, so that my neighbour in the opposite room shouldn't hear this last bit. What good friends I've become with old Hadji Kalfa! The first morning, as soon as I woke, I had dressed, and started down the hotel stairs, jumping as I went, with my satchel under my arm. Hadji Kalfa, dressed once more in that white bath robe was cleaning a narghilé (hubble-bubble) by the side of the fountain.

"Hullo there, Feridé Hanim," he said when he saw me, as though he were a forty-year-old acquaintance, "what are you doing, getting up so early? I thought you would have slept till midday, tired out with your journey."

I laughed and said, "Would that do? Can a teacher with a sense of duty sleep on till midday?"

Hadji Kalfa set down his narghilé and put his hands on his hips; he began to laugh, and said, "Look at her—she's still a child herself, isn't she? And going to school with the dust on her shoes, to teach the other children!"

From the moment when I got my papers of appointment from the Ministry of Education, I swore not to behave irresponsibly; but faced with the child-like conversation of Hadji Kalfa, I suddenly became a child too. I threw my satchel into the air like a ball and caught it again. This action pleased Hadji Kalfa immensely. Clapping his hands, he said with a roar of laughter, "Was I wrong then? You *are* still a child!"

I don't know how far it is right to be as familiar as this with a hotel porter, but I began to laugh with him, and we started to talk about all kinds of things. Nothing would induce Hadji Kalfa to let me go to school without any breakfast. "You can't wrestle with a lot of strange brats all day long in a starving condition. I'm going to get you some cheese and some milk; and look here, this is only the first day: there's no need to be in such a hurry," he added, and made me sit down by the fountain. There was nobody in the hotel courtyard at that hour. Hadji Kalfa called out to one of the shops opposite, "Molla, bring our school teacher some milk— and some Istanbul rolls!" Then he turned to me and said, "The molla's milk *is* milk; your Istanbul milk is like narghilé water compared with it." According to Hadji Kalfa, the molla fed his cows on pears, summer and winter, and the milk had a flavour of pears in consequence. While the old Armenian was explaining this, he closed one eye and added jokingly, "There's just this about it. Molla smells a bit of pears, too!"

I had my breakfast sitting by the fountain, and Hadji Kalfa rinsed the narghilés and amused me at the same time with endless gossip of the town. Lord, what didn't he know? He knew all about the schoolteachers, down to the very dresses they wore. When I got up, he said, "Let me take you there; the school is quite near, but the road is rather difficult to find—

103

I'm afraid you'll lose your way," and setting off in front of me with his lame leg, he took me as far as the green-painted door of the Provincial Secondary School, which I should certainly not have found on my own. However wretched it might be in appearance, I was determined, that day, to like the school. But I must explain in detail what sort of disaster it was that awaited me there.

There was no one at the door-keeper's lodge. As I was walking through the garden, I met a woman whose face was covered with a double fold of veil, tightly wrapped in a woven çarşaf. She carried an old leather bag on her arm, and was evidently intending to go down the street. When she saw me she stood still, and began looking at me with great attention.

"Do you want something, madam?"

"I've come to see the Head Mistress."

"Have you got an appointment? I *am* the Head Mistress."

"Is that so, madam?" I asked. "I am Feridé, the new Geography and Drawing Mistress. I arrived from Istanbul yesterday."

The thickly-veiled Head Mistress had uncovered her face; she looked me over from top to toe. And then, "I hope there has been no mistake, my dear," she said. "We *had* a vacancy for a Geography and Drawing Mistress, and they sent a teacher from the Gallipoli School, a week ago."

I was much shaken by this. "It's not possible, madam!" I told her. "They've sent me from the Ministry of Education. I've got my instructions here in my handbag."

The Head Mistress raised her eyebrows, which ran into the middle of her narrow forehead, and looked into my face with surprise. "Heavens!" she said; "May I see your instructions?" The good woman read the paper several times over, looked at the date, and shook her head.

"This kind of mistake does occur sometimes," she said. "Without realising it, they must have appointed both of you to the same place. Oh dear, oh dear—Huriye Hanim!"

"Who is Huriye Hanim?"

"She's the *other* teacher, who's come from Gallipoli. She's a good sort of woman in her own way; it seems the climate there didn't suit her, so she asked to come here. It looks as though she's been unlucky."

"She's not the only one; it leaves *me* in a difficult position, madam," I said.

"It does, indeed. Don't let's upset the poor woman until the matter's been cleared up. I have some business with the Inspector of Education, and I'm going there; so you come with me. Let me see—perhaps we can find a way out."

The Director of Education was a clumsy, heavy kind of man who listened to questions with his eyes closed, as though he were asleep, and spoke in disjointed phrases, as though he were dreaming. After listening to us with some irritation, he said ponderously, "What am I to do? They've gone and done it, and there it is; we must write to Istanbul, and see what sort of answer we get."

A heavily-built clerk, looking from the red belt appearing below his short waistcoat, rather as if he were a carrier driver, interposed: "The date of this lady's order is quite recent; so she has really been accepted and properly appointed."

The Director pondered a little as though he were consulting an oracle. "No, that's certainly true. But we have no orders to dismiss the other one; we must write to the Ministry for an explanation. We shall get an answer in ten days' time. You must manage somehow or other till then, Headmistress," was the decision he gave.

I followed the Head Teacher again in her woven veil, through the same winding streets, and returned to the school forlornly. If only I had gone back to the hotel!

Huriye Hanim was a little bit of a woman about forty-five years of age, cross-looking, with a severe manner. She no sooner heard the news of what happened, than her face got a bit more clouded, her eyes opened wide, and two veins swelled in her thin neck. Then, with a cry like one of those shrill whistles the children blow when out of school, she exclaimed, "Oh, my dear friends—more trouble for me!" and went off in a faint on the floor.

The teachers' rooms were connected with one another. One old spectacled teacher had a regular struggle to drive out the students who were crowding round the door. Her colleagues laid Huriye Hanim flat on her back on the ground, sprinkled her with water and vinegar, loosened her openwork flannel shirt and rubbed her chest, which was discoloured with flea-bites. I was standing stock-still with my satchel on my arm in the corner of the room, uncertain what to do. The teacher who had driven the children out a short time before was looking at me crossly over her glasses.

"My girl," she remarked, "your solicitude surprises me; and you're laughing, what's more." She was right; unhappily, I was unable to contain myself, and had broken into a smile. But how was the good woman to understand that I was smiling, not at her, but at my own wretched position?

But I was not the only one to laugh. A tall young woman with sharp black eyes was laughing unrestrainedly. She came up to me and murmured quietly in my ear, "Anyone who didn't know better would think her husband had brought home another wife. There's no question of fainting; it's just spite." Huriye Hanim, whose face and nose were dripping with water, had opened her eyes. She was hiccupping with as much noise as though gunpowder had gone off inside her. Wagging her head from side to side and raising the pitch of her voice, she announced, "Ah, friends, what disasters have befallen me! Do I deserve all this, after all these years? But there! They say it's the nightingale that has to suffer for its song."

Here I went and put my foot in it again. There was no need to say anything, but I felt urged to show some civility, and asked, "I hope you are better?"

"*You*—asking after my health?" I can't describe the rage she got into. And the things she said! I wasn't content with making an attempt on her life; as if that weren't enough, I was enquiring after her health. The world had never seen such an exhibition of shamelessness and impudence and lack of manners. I hid myself in a corner and closed my eyes in shame. The teachers were quite unable to pacify Huriye Hanim. She kept lifting her voice and using language that wouldn't have been uttered in the meanest street, let alone a school. What sort of a person *I* was, was clear from my face. To rob *her* of her daily bread, who knew how many people in the Ministry I had . . . and so on. In the corner, my eyes darkened, my body had turned to ice, and my teeth were chattering. The worst of it all was that the other teachers were giving the impression that they'd taken her side of it, at once.

Suddenly, a fist came down on the table in the middle of the room. Glasses and carafes echoed with it. It was the sharp, black-eyed young woman who had laughed with me a little while before. She was much more like a wild animal now. She was shouting in a shrill voice, which improved as it got louder, "Head Teacher! What sort of a head teachership is this? How can you allow this woman to malign the honour of a teacher? Where do you think we are? If you let her say another word, I'll drag her—and not only her, but you too—off to the Courts. Where does the woman think she is?" And then the teacher with the black eyes stamped her foot on the ground, and challenged the other teachers. "I congratulate you, colleagues; admirable behaviour!   Here you are, listening and grinning while one of your own profession is insulted."

For a moment the storm abated. Teacher Huriye, perceiving that she was being left alone again, pulled herself together and began fainting and crying afresh. Time for lessons had presumably arrived. Teachers were taking up their exercise books, text books and work-baskets, and began to drift away one by one. The Head Mistress went out, remarking, "I shall be waiting for you in my room, my dear."

Soon afterwards I found myself alone with the colleague who had defended me. I felt bound to thank her. "Oh dear," I said, "you're in trouble too, on my account."

She shrugged her shoulders and laughed, as much as to say "that's of no importance." "I did it on purpose. It doesn't hurt to frighten people like that occasionally. If you don't, they only take advantage. What are you going to do? Can we have a talk after lessons?"

I went as far as the door of the Head Mistress's room but I couldn't bring myself to go in. The thought of renewing our conversation appalled me. I left the school, without being seen by anyone, and went back to the hotel. My arms hung at my sides; my satchel had grown heavier.

No sooner had Hadji Kalfa seen me than he raised his arms in horror. "Oh, teacher! Whatever's happened to you?" he began. He knew more about the affair than I did. How *could* he have heard it in such a short time? "Alas, child! Keep your eyes wide open, or they'll make a game of you by telling you they're going to write to Istanbul. If you know anybody at the Ministry, let's write there at once," he urged. I said I knew nobody except a middle-aged poet, who had recommended me to the Minister; as soon as Hadji Kalfa heard his name, he was as delighted as a child.

"Well, now! He's my patron!" he exclaimed. "At one time he was Director of the High School here. He's an angel, that man; write, my child—write; and if you love me, send my salaams: 'Your slave Hadji Kalfa kisses your blessed hands.'"

Poor Hadji Kalfa would come upstairs every now and again, dragging his game leg, to announce, "The Public Prosecutor says you're quite right—you mustn't be put off—you must press the District Director of Education about it." Or it would be: "The Municipal Engineer is going to Istanbul tomorrow. He's promised to drop in at the Ministry."

What a strange place! Within a few hours there wasn't a soul who hadn't heard of the scandal. All the talk in the hotel café was about it. "Hadji Kalfa," I said, "how's this? Everyone here knows everyone else."

The old man scratched the back of his neck and replied, "This place is only the size of the palm of your hand. Where will you find a place like Istanbul, whose every stone and inch I adore? No one would have known anything about it *there*. This place is full of chatter. Listen to me: let me give you some advice. Be wise; keep calm. Don't go about the market and the bazaars with your face uncovered. Now (curious how he pronounced that word 'now') if God be willing, everything will turn out all right for you. There's a woman teacher here, named Arife. She's got engaged, now, to a High Court Judge, and lives in the land of milk and honey. May your fate be the same. Was it on account of her beauty? Oh no; it was because of her morals—because she was serious-minded. Man hasn't a thing in the world more precious than honour."

As the days passed, Hadji Kalfa increased his confidence and his favours towards me. Every day he used to bring me small articles from his house to adorn my room; a lace cover for a tumbler, a hand-worked face towel, or a painted reed fan. Sometimes, while we were talking, a hard voice would call out from below, "Hadji Kalfa, in what hell have you gone and lost yourself?" This was Hadji Kalfa's employer, the hotel keeper. Every time, the old man would say slowly, as though he were intoning an old song, "Easy now, easy; may you be carried to your grave by Hadji Kalfa." And then he would shout, "Here we are, he we are! I've got a little job to do, up here. . . ."

I had another friend besides Hadji Kalfa in the hotel; a woman of thirty-five or forty years of age, from Monastir. Let me explain how our friendship started. I was putting my clothes away in my bedroom, on the first evening after arriving at the hotel; I heard the door creak slightly; I looked round; a woman, wearing a printed cotton dressing gown and a yellow crêpe covering on her head came into the room. She was no sooner inside than she asked after my health: "Welcome, young woman; please God you're well." Her thin painted face put me in mind of a dilapidated wall, full of holes stopped up with lime. She had pencilled eyebrows and pitch-black teeth, which made her face look dreadfully like a skull. I was somewhat embarrassed.

"Welcome to you too, madam," I said.

"Where is your mother?"

"What mother, madam?"

"The schoolteacher. Aren't you her daughter?"

108

I couldn't' help laughing. "I'm not the schoolteacher's daughter," I told her. "I'm the schoolteacher herself!"

The woman looked as though she would collapse at this; she slapped her knee and said, "So you're the teacher! I've never seen such a young one—a mere slip of a girl. I'd been thinking of you as a grown-up woman."

"You'll find them like this, sometimes, these days, madam."

"Yes. Yes. Anything can happen in this world. We live in the little room opposite. I've put the children to bed, and I came to give you a welcome. God preserve them, the children occupy me by day, and about this time they go to sleep. And then a depression comes over me. To be lonely is only good for the Almighty, don't you think so, my dear? I sit worrying, smoking one cigarette after another, till I see the daybreak. God sent you to me. Let's have a few words together." She had started by addressing me as a "young woman," but when she learnt that I was the teacher, she altered it into "little sister."

"Welcome to you," I said, "sit down," and sat down myself on the corner of the bed, swinging my legs.

"I'm not comfortable on a chair, sister," replied the woman from Monastir, and sat herself down on the floor, in a curious attitude at my feet, with her knees up. Then she took a tin of tobacco out of her dressing gown and began to roll some thick cigarettes. She offered me one.

"Thank you," I said, "I don't smoke."

"I don't smoke a great deal myself; only I'm so worried." My neighbour was really in trouble. In Monastir, it seems, she was the daughter of a man of considerable standing, who apparently owned vineyards, gardens, cows and oxen, as befitted his social position. Three or four people were fed daily at her father's door. A good many of the principal men of Monastir had asked for her in marriage, "but no doubt on account of my ignorance," she related, "nothing would satisfy me but that I should marry an officer with a sword." Would that her mother had given her a good beating, and made her marry one of the gentlemen of the locality. But how was the wretched woman to know what was going to happen to her only daughter? She went and gave her in marriage to a lieutenant with neither wealth nor substance, but for the sword about his waist. Up to the time of the Independence they managed more or less to get along. On the 31st of March, her husband went to Istanbul with the Army, and he was gone for good. He never came back again, and he never even wrote her a line. Finally, one day, she got news from a friend who had returned from Istanbul that her husband was at B., and had married one of the local women. "Ah yes; that happens according to our religious law. They can marry four wives." My poor neighbour was very distressed; after she'd wept a little, she took her three children and came here. Her husband, I may say, was not at all pleased with that. Nothing would make him see the wife he had married after so much importunity, nor even his children, the darlings of his heart; but he insisted on sending them back to Monastir, without more ado. She threw herself at his feet and grovelled like a dog; "don't torture me like this when I've been your wife all these years;" but nothing would induce him to have her here.

After listening to this long tale, I couldn't help saying, "Oh, my dear woman, why do you depend so much upon an individual who doesn't want you? If he kicks you out, you should do the same to him, and have done with it."

The woman from Monastir smiled as though she pitied her own simplicity, and said, "My sister, I opened my eyes and looked at him. All these years we've laid our heads on the same pillow. Is it easy as all that to part from your husband?" And with a tremble in her voice she quoted the verse:

"My mother I might leave one day,
But oh! My true love, never."

I asked rather angrily, "But how can one love a man who deceives one? I can't understand that."

She smiled bitterly (revealing the black teeth), and said, "Little sister, you're still a child. You've not had these bitter experiences, and you don't know. May God preserve you from them."

"I know a girl who discovered, two days before her marriage, that her fiancé had betrayed her with another woman. She threw her ring in the villain's face and fled to another part of the country."

"Then, sister, she'll have regretted it. I'm sorry for her. Her heart was rent with grief. Have you never heard what happens to people who are struck by a bullet? Some don't even know they've been hit; they run three or four paces, and think they're escaping. When the wound is still fresh there's no pain, but once let it begin to get cold! You watch and see how bitterly that girl will suffer."

I jumped up angrily from my bed and walked up and down the room as if I were losing my reason. Rain was beating on the windows; a dog could be heard howling in the street. The woman from Monastir gave a deep sigh and continued, "I'm a stranger in a strange land. My limbs are useless; my hand has no grasp; my strength fails me. If I'd been in Monastir, I could have rescued my husband in two days from the hands of that wicked woman; yes."

I opened my eyes in surprise. "What would you have done?" I asked.

"My rival here has used one spell after another," she said. "She has bewitched the wretched man. But the witches in Monastir are more cunning. If I sacrifice sixty piastres—no more than that—they'd save my husband from her clutches, and give him back to me." And the woman from Monastir began to give me details at great length about the witches in Rumelia. There was, it seemed, a certain Albanian, Arif Hodja by name, who had a way of fashioning a pair of field-glasses out of a pig's ear. No sooner did a woman look at her husband through these strange glasses, than he came to heel at once, no matter how refractory he'd been before. Because all the other women looked like pigs to him! Arif Hodja would sometimes stick a pin into a cake of soap, and when he'd said prayers over it, he'd bury it in the ground. As the soap melted in the ground, the enemy would melt away too, and turn to skin and bones.

The good woman went on telling me tales of the kind, describing similar sorceries, rolling cigarettes as she did so from the tin box, and then smoking them one after another. Oh, what miserable, futile talk. And that tale about a wound beginning to hurt when it had got cold . . . What nonsense: as if I should ever suffer for the sake of that other tyrant! Do I ever think of him?

My neighbour from Monastir used to arouse feelings of disgust in me, at first, because of the layers of cream on her face, the eyebrows blackened till they looked like horns, and the dreadful mascara round her deep-set eyes. But when I learnt that it was all so much guile and blandishment to win her husband back again I felt grieved. The poor woman was saying to herself, "To find favour in *his* eyes, I'd let my children go hungry, to get myself rouge and mascara, and adorn myself like a bride." But it's all no use; it's sorcery, as I said.

Ever since then, my door creaks, now and again, and I know who it is, without turning my head. "Are you busy, sister? May I come in for a minute?" I am so bored with being alone, that the voice really cheers me. I drop my pen and rub my aching fingers a little and prepare to listen again to my neighbour's wearisome love story; though by this time I really know it by heart.

Çalıkuşu

The view from my window, of the mountain rising sheer from the earth, pleased me in the early days. Then it began to weary me. What was the use of it, unless one could wander about its lower reaches, with one's hair blown about by the breezes from the misty slopes above, and amuse oneself by leaping like a young goat over its precipitous rocks? Where are they, those days when I was free to roam for hours about the countryside, and rouse the birds by hitting the fences along the garden borders, and throwing stones into the thick-leaved trees? However, the real reason why I wanted to go up country was this. Ever since I was a child I have loved to draw. It was almost the only lesson in which I took full marks in school. What a lot of scolding I had to listen to and what punishments I suffered, for the sake of the pictures I drew with pencil or paint, on the spotless walls at home and on the marble pedestals of the statues at school! On leaving Istanbul I had thrown a lot of drawing-paper and paintbrushes into my bag. On days when I was alone in the hotel and weary of my writing, I used to draw, and this was a pleasant solace for me. Indeed, I tried to produce two pictures of Hadji Kalfa; one in crayon, and the other in water colour. I don't know how far the portraits resembled him, but whether or not he perceived the peculiarities of his individual features, he did at any rate recognise himself from his bald head, his turned-up moustaches, and his white overall, and he much admired my skill.

The good man used to go round the bazaars tirelessly, buying cheap thick satins, and silk threads for velvet, and coloured beads to get his daughter to embroider a picture frame. At last, seeing how bored I was, he invited me to his home. Hadji Kalfa had a neat little house built, as a result of his wife's thriftiness: and when he had any spare time, he used to employ it in painting the house green, with the help of his children. The house was on the edge of a steep precipice, so steep that when you leant your elbows on the wooden railing, covered with white convolvulus, you felt slightly giddy. What happy hours I used to spend in that garden with Hadji Kalfa and his family! Nevrik Hanim came, I believe, from Samatya. She was a simple woman, and like her husband, a little rough, but good-hearted. When she saw me, she said, "You smell of Istanbul, young lady," and couldn't prevent herself from embracing me. At the mere mention of the name of Istanbul, her eyes would fill with tears, and her vast bosom would heave up and down with a deep sigh of longing, rather like a tinker's bellows.

Hadji Kalfa had a son of twelve and a daughter of fourteen. The girl's name was Hayganuş; she was a shy, ungainly Armenian girl, with heavy eyebrows and dark red cheeks, that were spotted with pimples, as though she had chicken pox. In contrast to his plump elder sister, Mirat was a tiny child, so white and bloodless that he looked like a little dried fish. Hadji Kalfa, it seems, could neither read nor write, but he appreciated the value of knowledge. One ought to know everything. Even pocket-picking might come in useful, given an opportunity. For two years Mirat went to the school for Armenian children, and for the following two years had been educated at the Ottoman school. According to Hadji Kalfa's programme, the child was to change his school every two years, and right up to his twentieth year he was to go on acquiring a complete knowledge of French, German, English and Italian, each in turn; and in this way become a fully educated man. Assuming, of course, that the rickety child (little earthworm that he was) didn't die before reaching that age, under the crushing weight of his burden!

One day, when referring to his son, Hadji Kalfa said, "You have, no doubt, noticed Mirat's name? What a cunning name it is: my head was nearly bursting for a week, just looking for it. It fits two languages. The Armenian version is 'Mirat'; the Ottoman version 'Murat.'" And then, to show that he was going to say something particularly clever, he winked one eye, and went on: "When Mirat does something wrong and makes me angry, I tell him he's neither Mirat nor Murat, but a plain nuisance!"

Once, at their house, I witnessed one of the old Armenian's outbursts of temper. It was something to be seen: the child's offence was that he didn't like some food his mother had cooked him. Hadji Kalfa started scolding him, quoting proverbs and rhymes.

"Just look at the creature—he just about comes up to your waist, and yet he's up to all kinds of bad habits. They gave a beggar a cucumber; he didn't like it; he said it was crooked, and threw it into the street. And what would a donkey make of a compôte of fruit? And you listen to what I say—anyone who doesn't improve when he's scolded is asking for a good hiding! Who are you to disdain the gifts of God?

'Know thyself is the charm
That will keep thee from harm.'"

As for Hayganuş, in spite of her being a girl, no less importance was attached to her education than to Mirat's. She used to go to the Catholic

School. One day, Hadji Kalfa wanted me to put his daughter through a stiff examination, in front of an old, paralysed woman and an aged Armenian lady, who were both neighbours of his. It was the most ludicrous situation. Hadji Kalfa insisted on putting the girl's books and exercise books on my knees: "Now then, let's see," he said, "Hayganuş, if you go and let me down before the teacher, may the bread I've fed you on come up and choke you!" After one or two additions and subtractions, I opened an illustrated "History of the Prophets." It dealt a little with Jesus, and baptism. The good girl began explaining what baptism was, and talked a lot of nonsense. As my head was full of the subject from my own schooldays, I corrected her, and gave a simple little explanation of the practice of baptism. Hadji Kalfa listened to me with his eyes getting wider and wider. He had no hair on his head, but the hair of his eyebrows was standing on end. My knowledge of Christianity seemed to him a real miracle.

"What's this?" he exclaimed, "A Moslem woman, and she knows my religion better than the priests! I thought I knew what sort of a woman you were: and now it looks as if you're really one of those learned people who have to have their hands kissed!" He made the sign of the cross as he spoke. Then he took his fat wife round the neck; and brought her to me; she moved from her seat rather like a barge moving off from a pier.

"Kiss the child for me in the middle of the forehead, do you understand?" he demanded; and thrust her at me. Poor old Hadji Kalfa; being a man, he made his wife discharge the obligation for him.

From that day on, the old porter began to tell everyone he met about my deep knowledge; so much so that when I went in and out of the hotel, the idlers in the café would peer through the windows. I said in annoyance, "Hadji Kalfa, for goodness sake do stop! Whatever's the point of it?"

He retaliated by saying, "I say it on purpose. I want it to get to the ears of those in authority. May they be ashamed of what they've done to you."

My acquaintance with the family of Hadji Kalfa was useful to me from another point of view. The good lady from Samatya knew how to make beautiful jam and sweets. This was surely a far more profitable science than my knowledge of the History of the Prophets. I got from her jam recipes that were both cheap and easy to make, and I wrote them down with scrupulous care in a note book in which I'd already put the recipes

114

of Gülmisal Kalfa's dishes. Who's going to remember to bother about providing for our greed in the future?

Please God, if things go well, and if I ever have a little house to which I can betake myself, I shall make myself a jam cupboard, like the one in Hadji Kalfa's house. I shall decorate my shelves with the sort of paper they use for making toy kites, cut into patterns, and arrange my pots in a row; coloured earthenware ones, that will shine like mother-of-pearl. How lovely! To be able to eat whenever it comes into my head, without having to ask anyone's permission or steal from the larder. Heaven grant that it may not make me ill.

Yes: red, yellow, white jam pots; only green missing. You, whom I could hardly bear to think of—Kâmran! It was your eyes that I so detested, that made green hateful to me. I remembered it so well, Kâmran; long ago even before I loathed you as I do, I always hated your eyes. I wasn't twelve when that hatred began; you won't have forgotten it, I know. Now and again I'd take a handful of salt and throw it in your face. Was that merely a childish prank, I wonder? No, it was to hurt your eyes, with the treacherous lights in them, like seaweed in green water.

Now, I've strayed from the point again; but it was only to record today's events. Where was I? Oh yes: the sun appeared for the first time for days, and aroused in me a child's feeling of joy; but Hadji Kalfa put it down to my having heard some good news, and he began to question me about it. Could *any* news relating to me ever reach my ears before he heard of it? Why, it was from this queer old porter that I used to learn when I was hungry or sleepy. "Now then, don't simper," Hadji Kalfa told me, "you're not laughing like that for nothing. You've heard something good, that's what it is."

To suggest that I had sharper ears than he, did something to soothe my vanity. I laughed significantly, half in fun and half in earnest. "Who knows," I said with a wink at him, "perhaps it's a secret that won't bear telling."

The sunshine was so bright, I couldn't think of wasting it. I crossed the bridge a little beyond the hotel, went up a steep incline confronting me, and over a field, a copse, and a second bridge. I wanted to wander further still, but there was a greater danger of losing myself beyond. In spite of my orthodox outdoor dress and veil and closely drawn face-covering, a number of rough-looking men had begun to trail behind and call after me. Remembering Hadji Kalfa's advice, I grew afraid, and turned back.

115

I felt sure that the chief clerk in the Education Department would greet me with the answer, "Not a word yet from Istanbul, comrade." But having started out, I felt I must call and see him. When the Director's messenger saw me on the stairs, he said, "It's lucky you've come, teacher. The Bey is looking for you. I was coming to the hotel in a few minutes." The Bey of whom he'd spoken was the Director of Education. Oh wonders! There he was again in front of his writing-table with its red cloth top, with his eyes half-closed, his collar loosened, and his hands and arms relaxed, as though in an attempt to relieve his perpetual weariness.

He yawned and stretched himself on seeing me, and began to speak laconically: "We've not yet had an answer from the Ministry, young woman. I can't foresee what they'll vouchsafe by way of a reply. But there's this to be said. Huriye Hanim is a teacher of some seniority, so I think they'll support her case. If an unfavourable answer comes, you will be in difficulties. A way out has occurred to me: there's a village called Zeyniler about two hours from here; its climate and water are splendid, its natural scenery most agreeable, and its population are by nature law-abiding and orderly; it's a paradise of a place. There's a pious foundation-school there. Last year we repaired and renovated it at considerable expense; and we succeeded in making good many of its educational defects. There's an apartment set aside for the teacher's residence in the school itself. What we want now is the co-operation of a self-sacrificing young teacher; one could wish that a distinguished woman like yourself would consider going there. It's a really good place. And at the same time you would be rendering a valuable service to the country. True, the pay would be less than what you would get here. On the other hand, the price of meat, milk, eggs and other things is unbelievably cheap, compared with prices in this district. If you like you will be able to save all your money. However, I will increase the present amount at the first opportunity. In that case you would be better off than the head of the preparatory school here."

I didn't know what to say to this offer; and held my tongue. The Director went on: "There's an old woman at the school. She carries on with the lessons, and looks after the school itself as well. She's a good woman who likes going her own way, and is very pious; but she knows nothing about the new methods of teaching. You'll undertake all that and change it. All the same, if you don't like Zeyniler and you write me a couple of lines, I'll put you into a good position here, at once; but after

116

seeing the place, you'd refuse an appointment to the district headquarters. Lovely climate, beautiful surroundings, inexpensive food and drink, and nice people. One way and another, rather like the villages of Switzerland; what more could one ask?"

I had a vision of sunny roads, shady gardens, streams and woodland; my heart was beating hard. All the same, I didn't dare say yes at once. I must at least consult Hadji Kalfa about it all. "If you'll permit me, I'll come back in a couple of hours, and give you my answer, sir."

The Director seemed to wake up a bit. "Oh my dear! The matter's urgent. There are other applicants too. If you miss this chance I shan't take any further steps."

"In that case, *one* hour, sir," I said.

As I was leaving the Director of Education, whom should I walk into but my colleague Huriye Hanim. I had learnt from Hadji Kalfa a few days ago that they had given us the name of two partners. The woman alarmed me so much that I felt quite nervous when I saw her, and tried to get away quickly, pretending not to see her. But she stood in my way and, like a bold street beggar, seized my sleeve, and began to speak to me.

"Young lady, I was rude to you recently. For God's sake, forgive me. It's the state of my nerves: I was very much upset, too . . . Ah, young lady, if you knew all that I'd been through, you'd be sorry for me. But forgive my rudeness, anyway."

"It was nothing, madam," I replied, and tried to pass her. But for some reason or other she had decided not to let go of me. First she complained of her circumstances. Five people dependent upon her were going to be left destitute in the streets. Huriye Hanim got more and more excited, and her voice got louder and louder. She kept beseeching me in a most unpleasant manner. I was at a loss what to say or what to do. Worse still, those who were witnessing this comedy came round us until there was a whole circle of messengers, and clerks, down to tradesmen's apprentices in aprons. My face and hands began to burn; I could have sunk into the ground with confusion. Now it was I who was beginning to plead.

"I beg you madam, do talk quietly. Everyone's looking at us." But her obstinacy increased, and she finally burst into tears; tearing her hair and pulling the buttons off her collar, she began to kiss my hands and embrace my knees. I saw with alarm that the crowd around us was gradually getting larger. You know how they press round merchants crying their wares in the streets of Istanbul, cheapjacks, street quacks and vendors of patent medicines? We were in the middle of just that sort of crowd. I began to hear people talking on all sides in the following strain: "It's a shame, poor thing." "Don't make her cry, young woman!" Suddenly a great big Hodja, with a green turban and a white beard, appeared at my shoulder. "My girl," he said, "it's a religious duty and an act of humanity to show respect to the old. Come, don't deprive this woman of her livelihood. Do what's pleasing to God and the Prophet. God protects the world: you may be sure He will make provision for you, from some invisible source of His bounty!"

Under my çarşaf I was trembling all over, and bathed in perspiration at the same time. From the other side, a café proprietor called out "Yes! And wherever God may be, *you* could pick up a living anywhere!" Part of the crowd began to laugh heartily. At that moment, the clerk with the red waistband appeared on the scene. He seized the café proprietor by the collar without a moment's pause, and flung him downstairs. "You mannerless fellow!" he shouted; "I'll stop your mouth for you!"

Why had they laughed? What the café proprietor had suggested was no more than the Hodja had said himself. Huriye Hanim cried so vehemently, and the gossip was spreading so fast, that if they had demanded it, I believe I'd have given my life to get out of the grotesque predicament. In the end I announced, "All right! All right! Just as you like; but for Heaven's sake let go my collar." I managed to drag my knees away, which she'd been trying to kiss as she knelt on the ground; and I went back to the Director of Education's room.

Not long after, a paper was signed, to say that I had resigned of my own accord from my position at the Central School and was a candidate for the post of teacher in the school at Zeyniler. Within an hour, all the procedure was completed, and the Director of Education—that very same Director, who was too lazy to move in his seat—went in his carriage to the office of the Governor, and got my orders signed. They could evidently deal with this procedure, which sometimes took months passing from office to office, quickly enough when they chose.

When I returned to the hotel, Hadji Kalfa met me at the door, and with a gesture that suggested pleasure and reproach, he said, "You kept it secret, but do you think I didn't get to know? May God bless you," he added.

"What have you heard?"

"Why that your orders have come!"

"What orders, Hadji Kalfa?"

"Bless my soul, that they've taken you on at the secondary school at Headquarters, and given Huriye Hanim her passport."

"You're wrong, Hadji Kalfa. I've come straight from the Director of Education, and that's not what happened at all."

The old man looked at me doubtfully. "No? The order came last night, and I heard it from a good quarter; that means to say then that the Director concealed it from you. I think there's some knavery going on, don't you? Come on now, explain to me."

Amused by Hadji Kalfa's naive suspicions, I related to him in one breath what had occurred; and taking my orders out of my bag, I waved them in my hand. "Long life to us, Hadji Kalfa! We're going to a place just like Switzerland."

As he heard me, Hadji Kalfa's big nose got as red as a cockscomb, and he began to beat his breast with his hands. "What have you gone and done, you foolish child? They've led you up the garden after all! Go to the Director at once and have it out with him."

I shrugged my shoulders. "It's not worth it, my dear Hadji Kalfa. Don't get so upset, or else you'll get ill, and *then* what shall we do?"

The good fellow had some right to be annoyed on my behalf, and work himself into a state of indignation. By the evening the whole thing became clear to the last detail. It seems the Director had protected Huriye Hanim, and had supported the point she had made in her letter to the Ministry, that she was the more senior teacher; and had asked that I should be removed to another place. But the Ministry, for some reason or other, saw fit to leave me where I was, and to direct my colleague to whatever vacancy might occur in the future. The Director of Education, the Head Mistress of the secondary school, and the Director of the Finance Department (who was probably a compatriot of Huriye Hanim from Rumelia) all met at a late hour to discuss the order, which had just come, and they planned to push me off to a village and keep Huriye Hanim in my place. The meeting between Huriye Hanim and myself in the corridor of the Education Department had all been arranged beforehand. In fact, they got hold of that white-bearded Hodja on purpose. As for Zeyniler, which I'd begun to look upon as an up-to-date European village from the account the Director of Education gave of it, it was apparently in an outlandish spot among the mountains. It had been vacant for a year, and even the most wretched teacher wouldn't look at it.

When these things dawned on me, I was amazed that a grown-up, high official should take me in with so much guile. I should never have believed it. Hadji Kalfa shook his head apprehensively.

"You don't know him," he said. "He's like a snake that's asleep. He goes on sleeping and sleeping, and suddenly he strikes one such a mortal blow, that you can't tell where it comes from. Do you see?"

What of it? As if one cared for such blows from a stranger, when one's own kindred can strike one so heartlessly! I shall know how to be happy at the village of Zeyniler. Up with the spirits!

Zeyniler, 28th October

Today, towards evening, in a four-wheeled carriage, I got to Zeyniler. It looks as though the Director of Education measures his distances by railway standards; because what he described as "a two-hour journey at most," took from exactly ten in the morning until late at night. But how could the blessed man do otherwise? He wasn't to blame: it was the fault of the people who didn't construct a funicular railway on the Zeyniler road, which follows the track of the mountain torrents in one place, and then climbs up the lower slopes of the hills.

Hadji Kalfa's family came as far as the spring—half an hour away from the town, to wish me God-speed. The whole family were dressed as though they were going to a wedding—or a funeral, rather! When he came to announce that the carriage was ready, I nearly didn't recognise Hadji Kalfa. He had taken off his towel and the heel-less slippers in which, with a rhythm peculiar to himself, he used to shuffle along the stairs and the corridors and the paved courtyards, and put on a long jacket made of faded cloth, buttoned up to the chin; on his feet he was wearing rubber boots—the kind worn by Imams. A great big fez, low-crowned in the Aziziye style, covered his bald head down to the ears. The toilettes of Hayganuş and Mirat and the lady from Samatya were as remarkable as his own.

I was sad to leave my little room, although I'd spent many bitter hours in it. At school they used to make us say by heart a bit of poetry that ran:

"A man is bound by threads, unseen but strong,
To those who dwell where he has lived for long—"

Times of parting will strain those ties, until they give a bitter sound, like the strings of a broken violin. How right he was that poet!

By a coincidence, my friend from Monastir left as well, on the same day as I did. But her departure took place in much sadder circumstances than mine. Last night, after packing my trunks, I had gone to bed. I was fast asleep, when I heard loud voices, though I couldn't rouse myself sufficiently to know what they meant. Suddenly there was a terrific noise, and I leapt out of bed. Something had fallen, and was being rolled over on the landing; children's cries, the sound of a box on the ears, and stifled groans mingled with the voices against the stillness of the night. I was still dulled with sleep, and the first thing that came into my mind was the thought of a fire. But people who tackle a fire don't beat *each other*, surely? With my hair loose and my feet bare, I rushed out of the room, and found a dreadful struggle going on—complete with sticks: an officer, an enormous giant of an officer with long moustaches, was dragging my neighbour from Monastir all over the place, and stamping on her with his boots. The children were all shouting at once, "Mother! Father's killing our mother!" The wretched woman moaned after each kick and each blow of the whip that descended on her with the hiss of a snake as she rolled on the floor; but suddenly, with unbelievable resilience, she got up again from the ground and clung to the officer's knees. "Let me be your slave—your victim! Dear sir, kill me! But don't leave me! Don't divorce me!"

I had hardly any clothes on, so I went back to my room again. What could I do, in any case? The people sleeping on the ground floor might have been roused; for the sound of footsteps and unintelligible voices could be heard from the bottom landing. A light began to move on the ceiling of the corridor. Hadji Kalfa's bald head gleamed through the banisters. The good fellow had wakened on hearing the noise, jumped out in his shirt and pants, and seized a tin lamp. The old porter tried to get between the two, and kept shouting "It's an outrage! It's a scandal! And in this hotel!" But the officer gave Hadji Kalfa such a kick in the stomach with the toe of his boot that the poor creature was hurled into the air, just like a great football, and rolled right into my room, on his back, through the half-open door, with his bare legs in the air. Fortunately, I acted pretty swiftly, and seized the poor man's head in my arms; otherwise his bald pate would have burst like a large pumpkin on striking the floor. My half-awakened state of fear and surprise, and Hadji Kalfa's situation on top of both, succeeded in upsetting me completely. The old man got on his feet, announcing, "The devil take the mule and its cursed shoes!" But by that time, I'd collapsed on the bed, stifled and choked by a paroxysm of laughter such as I'd never experienced in my life before. There I lay, rolling about and twisting the blankets in my hands. I couldn't make out what was happening outside. I wasn't able to collect myself again until the voices and the din had ceased, and quiet reigned in the hotel once more.

Later on, they explained to me what had happened. The senseless devotion of the woman from Monastir had touched her husband's heart at last. The officer had decided, at whatever cost, to send the woman and her children home; and last night he came to say that the tickets had been bought, and to tell her to be ready early the next morning. But would the woman from Monastir agree to part from him so easily? She began, inevitably, to beg him and importune him; and who knows what words and scenes ensued? In the end, the dreadful struggle had begun. It was perhaps two hours later, when I was getting ready to go to sleep again, that Hadji Kalfa knocked lightly at my door.

"Look here, teacher: there's no other woman in the hotel; that poor wretch of a woman is lying there in a fainting condition. It's no good laughing—see what you can do for her—you love your religion! It was my lot to be born a man, so I can't go in."

As I looked at Hadji Kalfa's face through the half-opened door, another paroxysm of laughter overcame me. I wanted to say "I do hope you will soon be better," but I couldn't get the words out. Hadji Kalfa looked at me and shook his head. "You laugh," he said rather sheepishly, "but that's all you do. You rascal! But come and look at that poor woman." He said "you laugh" so oddly, that even then I couldn't help laughing again.

I struggled over my wretched neighbour for more than an hour. The poor woman's body was covered with cuts and bruises; and every now and again she fainted. The pupils of her eyes disappeared, and her jaws were locked. It was the first time I had had anything to do with a fainting person, and I had no idea what to do. But when one is faced with a difficult situation, one gets enough strength to tackle it somehow. She kept fainting again, and every faint lasted at least five minutes. I rubbed the good woman's arms and body till I made her cry out; I moistened her face with water which I made her girl pour out of a carafe. Her forehead, her cheeks and her lips were bruised in several places, and the blood from the cuts mingled with her rouge and cream and dripped from her chin on to her chest in dirty black drops. Oh! What a lot of paint she must have had on that face: for all the water I spilt, I never got to the end of it.

This morning, when I woke, I found the room opposite was empty. The officer had flung her and the children into a carriage, very early, and had taken them off. Before she went, my neighbour had wanted to see me, to ask my forgiveness; but as it was still night, and she knew I had been sleepless on her account, she decided to spare me. She left her salaams with Hadji Kalfa and kissed my eyes once more.

From my carriage, I caught sight of Hadji Kalfa's face, and began to laugh. He knew the reason for this unseemly amusement, and shook his head with an angry smile, scolding me. "Ah, you laugh, and go on laughing!" and then he started talking of the awful kick he'd had the previous night. "That wretched, spiteful mule gave me such a kick, my entrails were in a dreadful state. Mirat, let me give you some fatherly advice. Keep your mind on your own affairs; there are strong bonds uniting husband and wife, and it's only an ass who comes between them!"

The whole family came with me, one on top of the other in the four-wheeled carriage, as far as a little spring beyond the town. This was the parting place. Hadji Kalfa put some fresh water from the spring into two corked bottles he had provided, and started giving instructions to the old "jarvey" at great length. His lady from Samatya, with her eyes full of tears, filled my basket with little rolls she had made for me a few days before, and the impulsive Hayganuş (whom I'd thought quite indifferent to me), suddenly began to weep as though she had hurt herself; and what weeping! I was wearing two pearl earrings; I took them off and fastened them in Hayganuş' ears. Hadji Kalfa felt abashed by my present: "Oh, teacher—what you call a present ought not to be anything that costs money; these are valuable pearls!"

I laughed again. How was I to explain to the simple man that compared with the pearls that his daughter had shed for me, mine were not worth two pence?

After Hadji Kalfa had put me back in the carriage, he sighed deeply, and struck himself on the breast: "To tell you the truth, this parting is more painful to me than last night's kicking." This put me in mind again of last night's incident and made me laugh once more; the old man was still shaking his finger at me as I moved away, saying "Ah, you rascal! You laugh and you laugh. . . ." Dear old Hadji Kalfa! You wouldn't have said that if we hadn't moved a good way off and you could have seen my eyes.

The carriage had got as far as the up-and-down mountain roads. At one moment it would be dried-up watersheds we were passing through, and the next, following the borders of deserted fields and neglected vineyards. We kept coming upon solitary villages at distant intervals, and barefooted women carrying baskets of brushwood on their heads; or two-wheeled carts which seemed, from the sound they emitted, to be groaning with weariness. Along one narrow vineyard road, two be-whiskered gendarmes came towards us, dressed so like brigands that they were quite alarming. As they passed alongside of us, they said good-evening to the jarvey, and looked closely at me. Hadji Kalfa had said, "The roads, thank God, are safe enough, but whatever happens, draw down your veil; yours is not the kind of face to go uncovered in that sort of country. Do you understand, miss?" The minute I saw anyone in the distance, I remembered Hadji Kalfa's injunctions, and veiled my face.

As the hours passed, the road plunged into a gloomy, solitary district.

These four-wheeled carriages make a thin, mournful sound; and their inventors contrived wisely. The distant echo they awaken on the mountain-side and in the valleys comes to one like a voice of consolation. Particularly in a rocky place; it seemed to me that in the distance, on the other side of a mound of blackened stones which bore the appearance of being burnt, there was an invisible road, and that on this road, running behind us, a woman was weeping, with a plaintive voice. Evening was coming on, and as the sunlight slowly faded from the hill-tops, darkness began to descend upon the mountain passes; and still the road went endlessly on. Now there wasn't a village in sight, nor even the sign of a tree. Fear slowly began to rise within me; supposing I couldn't reach the village of Zeyniler before nightfall? Supposing I remained alone on these mountain-tops?

From time to time the jarvey stopped his horses and rested them, and talked to them as if he were talking to a human being. In the middle of a rocky district, I took advantage of one of these pauses to ask him, "Is it much further?"

He shook his head slowly: "We've got there," he answered.

Had he not been a sober person of some age, I should have assumed he was joking. "What do you mean?" I asked. "We are at the back of beyond! There's no village—not a thing to be seen!"

The old man was trying to get my luggage out of the carriage. "We're going down this path," he said. "Zeyniler is about five minutes from here. There's no carriage road."

In between the rocks, we began to descend as steep as the stairs of a minaret. Below, in the darkness of the evening, was a pitch-black clump of cypresses, surrounded by a fence, and among some deserted gardens a solitary cottage or two, and some wooden houses appeared. At the first glance, Zeyniler looked to me like the ruins of a fire, whose smoke was still smouldering. As I said the word "village," there came before my eyes a vision of lovely cottages, charmingly set among green surroundings, like the dovecots of summer residences on the Bosphorus. But these houses looked like they were tumbling down; they were no more than blackened ruins. In front of a broken-down mill we met an old man in a turban and a greatcoat. He was dragging along by the rope a wretched-looking donkey with staring ribs, which he was trying to take into one of the houses. When he saw us, he stopped, and began to look at us attentively. This old hodja was, it seems, the village "muhtar" or headman; the jarvey knew him, and explained who I was, in a few words. With my full çarşaf and the closely-drawn veil, no one could tell I was young. That being so, the headman must have found me a bit too well-dressed, because he looked at me curiously, and then handed the donkey over to a bare-footed child, and set off in front of us.

We were now in the narrow streets of the village. I could see the houses more clearly. Do you know those ruined fishermen's cottages at Kauaklar, battered on one side by the winds of the Bosphorus, blackened and perished by the rains, with their nets spread out in front of them? The houses here reminded me of them at the very first glance. Below them were stables, consisting of four posts, and above these, one or two rooms reached by a hanging ladder. Anyway, Zeyniler seemed quite unlike any village I'd ever seen or heard of until now.

We stopped at the red gate of a garden surrounded by wooden fences. This red wood was the first bit of colour I'd seen in this village which seemed to be black all over, right down to the leaves on the trees. The muhtar began to knock on the door with his fist. At every blow the door shook as though it would break. Daring for the first time to open my mouth, I suggested "Perhaps there's no one there?"

The headman shook his head and replied, "Hatije Hanim must be saying her evening prayers. We'll wait a little."

The jarvey, however, had no time to wait; he put my baggage down in front of the door and left us. The headman gathered up the skirts of his cloak and squatted on the ground. I sat down on the edge of my suitcase, and we began to talk. It seemed that this Hatije Hanim was very devout; apparently she belonged to a religious order. It was she who cared for the living and the dead of the village. It was also she who read the chants for the dead. It was she who poured the last drop of holy water from Mecca into the mouths of the sick in their agony. It was she who bathed the bodies of the dead women and wrapped them in a shroud. The muhtar appeared to be a man who had evidently had some schooling. I understood that he wanted to seize this opportunity to give me some advice. He was not an opponent of the new methods of education, but he complained that the new schools neglected religious instruction. Up to now, several teachers had been there and gone away again. It was no use; not one of them had sufficient knowledge of the Koran and the Catechism.

The Muhtar thought the world of Hatije Hanim. If I were to continue to leave the teaching to this good woman, so pious, so intelligent, so religious and so devoted, I should be likely to give more satisfaction to the village. As I listened to this advice, the clatter of shoes began to make itself heard from within. An iron bar clattered behind the door, and a hoarse voice called out, "Who's that?"

"It's not a stranger, Hatije Hanim; the teacher's arrived."

Hatije Hanim was a powerfully built, large-faced, somewhat hunchbacked old woman in her seventies. She had a green muslin covering over her hennaed hair, and on her shoulders a heavy cloak, like the mantle worn by Turkish ladies in days gone by. Between the wrinkles of her brown face, which was as hard as leather, was a pair of unbelievably bright and lively eyes, and her teeth were pure white. She peered at my face and tried to distinguish my features beneath my veil: "Welcome, teacher: come in," she said.

Rather as though it were forbidden to leave the garden and go into the street, she leaned one hand against the door, and took up my kit with the other; then bolted the door again, and led the way in. We passed through the garden, she in front and I behind. The school building which the Director of Education had renovated at such great cost, was exactly the same as the other houses. Only they had surrounded the supporting beams with boards, which hadn't yet time to get black, and made the place into a classroom.

As I was about to enter, Hatije Hanim seized my arm. "Wait a minute, my dear," she said. I drew back at once. She muttered a short prayer. "Now then, dear," she told me, "don't forget to say 'In the name of God,' and enter with your right foot first."

The ground floor was as dark as a prison. The old woman took me by the hand, led me across a narrow yard, and up a dark staircase, whose steps swayed with age. The floor above consisted of a broken-down corridor, and a great big room, in which the wooden frames of the windows were tightly closed. This was the teachers' quarters, whose existence the Director of Education had announced with such pride. Hatije Hanim put down my trunk and took a lamp out of the fireplace, which served as a cupboard, and lit it.

"The room's been empty this last year, so it's dirty. I shall clean it tomorrow morning, please God." The poor woman was, it seemed, the previous teacher at the school. When the Education Department repaired the school, pity for her prevented their putting her into the street, and so they had kept her on there, at two hundred piastres. She was, as it were, half teacher, half servant. Well, she would do whatever work I gave her.

I realised that the good woman was afraid of me. Officially, I was her superior. After making it clear that I was not the sort of girl who would knowingly do anyone any harm, I began to look round my room. Dirty floor-boards, so old they were full of holes, a blackened ceiling whose sagging beams had yielded to the weather; they had put a broken tumble-down fireplace in one corner, and on the other side an uneven bedstead.

So from now on, my life was going to be spent in a room like this? I felt stifled, as though I had fallen into some airless cave. My hands and feet turned cold. "Dear Hatije Hanim, help me," I said. "Let's open one of these windows. I don't expect I can do it alone." The old woman wasn't going to let me have a hand in this. After a struggle, she managed to move one of the shutters. When I saw the view, my hair stood on end.

Facing me was a fearful-looking cemetery. The evening light had not yet died away from the tops of its rows of gravestones; and beyond them were dun-coloured puddles, surrounded by reeds. I heard the old woman draw a deep breath. "One should get used to it when one's alive, my dear," she said. "That's the place we all get to in the end." Were the words mere coincidence, or had I unwittingly given a sign of fear and apprehension? But I pulled myself together immediately: courage was essential.

With an indifference that was almost cheerful, I remarked, "So there's a cemetery here? I didn't know."

"Yes, my dear. The cemetery of Zeyniler. A relic of old times, people are buried elsewhere now. This is a historical kind of place. I am going to light Zeyni Baba's lamp: I'll be back directly."

"Who is Zeyni Baba, Hatije Hanim?"

"May his help be always with us. He is a holy man; his body lies here under the cypress tree."

Hatije Hanim walked straight to the staircase, slowly whispering a prayer. I don't know whether I had been afraid of this kind of thing hitherto; but at that moment, to be left alone in a dark room with the smell of cypress trees filled me with terror. I ran after the old woman, and asked "May I come with you?"

"Yes, come. It will be better. If you pay a visit to Zeyni Baba immediately after you arrive, it will be all the more appreciated."

We went into the cemetery from the back door of the school and began to walk through the gravestones. On the eves of certain feasts and Ramazans (the Moslem month of fasting) my aunts used to take me to the family cemetery at Eyüp. But it was in this dark Zeyniler cemetery that I felt for the first time that death was a melancholy and terrifying thing. The tombstones were of quite a different shape from those I had seen elsewhere. With smooth tops and coal-black surfaces, these stones stood tall, upright, and ranged in order, line upon line, like ranks of soldiers. The carving on them was illegible. But on the top of each one the words "Oh God . . ." could be distinguished.

I remember listening to a fairy tale when I was a child. The story goes that an old-fashioned army was coming from the far side of a distant mountain, to seize and carry off some unimportant sultan. The troops hid in caves by day, and travelled on by night. In order not to be seen in the darkness, they wrapped themselves from head to foot in shrouds of black. After they had travelled like this for months on end, on the very night when they were going to seize the town, God had pity on the little sultan, and turned the whole army into stone, just as it was making its treacherous advance by night, in its black shrouds. As I looked upon these dark stones ranged row upon row, I recalled that old tale to mind, and thought to myself, "I wonder now whether this was the very place in the story where those terrifying soldiers of death were turned into stone?"

"Who were these Zeyniler, Hatije Hanim?"

"I don't know, my dear, any more than you. This village seems to have been theirs long ago. Now nothing remains but the minarets. Zeyni is the biggest of them. May his help always be forthcoming! He must have been one of the saints. They bring sick people here whom no one can cure. I knew a paralytic woman whom they brought here on her back, and she went away walking on her own feet."

The tomb of Zeyni Baba was under a big cypress tree at the very end of the cemetery. Hatije Hanim used to light three lamps on it every night, one on the branch of the cypress tree, one on the inside of the door, and the other at the head of the coffin. The tomb was a cave dug in the ground. Zeyni Baba seems to have suffered a term of severe trial in this cave, without seeing the sunlight for seven years. When he died, no one could touch his corpse; they erected a sarcophagus over it. Hatije Hanim lit two of the lamps, then entered the cave, and pointing to the stair, which had several steps, announced, "Come along, dear, let's go in."

I didn't dare go down those steps. My companion turned. "Come along, my dear. You've come so far it would be a shame not to go in. Ask Zeyni Baba whatever request you have in your heart."

My heart was fluttering like a falling leaf. I went down the steps. If the dead could feel as they are lowered into their tombs, their sensations would resemble mine at that moment. The smell of cold damp earth filled my lungs. Zeyni Baba's coffin was covered with green-coloured zinc; as Hatije Hanim explained later, Zeyni Baba had spent the whole of his life in contentment and poverty, and didn't wish any fine covering to be laid upon him after his death. Sometimes, evidently, the coverings that were sent down from one place or another didn't last a week, but fell to pieces and rotted away.

The old woman, still muttering her prayers, placed some oil in the lamp at the head of the coffin, and then turned to me and said, "When anyone in the village is going to die, the angel Gabriel (blessings upon him) will come and visit Zeyni Baba, and after that, his lamp will go out of its own accord. Now, my dear," she added, "make your request to Zeyni Baba."

My knees were giving way; I no longer had the strength to stand. I put my forehead, which was burning like fire, against the cool covering over Zeyni Baba; and speaking with my aching heart rather than with my lips, I said very slowly, "Dear Zeyni Baba, I am only a small and ignorant Çalıkuşu. I don't know how I ought to entreat you; please forgive me: they never taught me any of the things that would please you. I have heard that you endured your great trial here for seven years, without seeing the sun. I hope it wasn't because you too had to run away from the cruelty and faithlessness of human beings. Dear Father, I'm going to ask you for something important. There must certainly have been times during those seven years when you regretted the sun and the wind; give me a little of the patience of that spirit that made you resign yourself to the bitterness of those moments, without complaining and without tears."

I am alone in my room. Hatije Hanim left me early, and withdrew to her cave-like little room on the ground floor. There she'll be, I expect, praying and telling her beads till midnight. I have been writing these lines for the last two hours, by the light of my lamp. A distant sound comes from without, and now and again there are little noises in the ceiling above. I listen, with a slight tremor running down my spine. Then I begin to hear other voices too, in the tumbledown building. The stair creaks slowly, and there are secret murmurs, as if people were whispering in the corridor.

Come now, Çalıkuşu; go to bed. Don't be afraid of those voices speaking to each other in the street. No matter how cruel they may be, they cannot hurt you like those other lips, maligning their cousins to their "golden flowers."

Zeyniler, 20th November

I made a calculation today. About a month has elapsed since I came to Zeyniler. But that one month seems longer than ten years to me. Up to now, I haven't cared to write anything in my diary. Or to be honest, I haven't dared. Who knows what I might have descended to, in the cruel despair of those first days? But now I've begun to get used to the place; as Sister Alexei was never tired of saying, "My girls, incurable sickness and unavoidable disaster have only one remedy: resignation and endurance." It is as though grief had a secret majesty of its own. Such things are less cruel to those who do not complain; to those who greet them with cheerful faces. Çalıkuşu always listened to those words with a smile; but now I find that they are true, and I can't smile at them ever again.

This last month some of the hours I've spent in Zeyniler made me feel I was going to be suffocated. "It's useless to try and deal with the situation; I can't stand any more," I used to say. Well, at those very times, Sister Alexei's prophetic words used to come to my aid. Although I was weeping tears of blood, I'd begin to laugh; I'd sing and I'd whistle. So much so that in the end, my heart would begin to believe in my assumed cheerfulness, and quiver slowly into life again, like thirsty flowers put in water.

And then I set myself to find consolation in the things that lived around me. I would take a fresh leaf in my hand, and rub my cheek and my lips against it; I pressed to my heart a miserable little kitten I found in the garden, and warmed it with my breath. And if I did nothing else, I said to myself, "Feridé, there's no use just being stupid. Make a little effort. After all, you know quite well that in order to live, you've no assets left but courage and a smiling face." Obviously, my cheerfulness was a fleeting thing; an effort towards adjustment. So let it be. A little gleam of light in a closed cave, a sickly flower growing between the stones of a ruined wall, is still, in spite of everything, a possession, a consolation.

Today is Friday; no school. The rain which has been falling for some days has stopped. Outside, Autumn seems to be staging a farewell display. The range of mountains in the distance looks as if it is smiling at the sun, in the water with the reeds around it. The cypress trees and the tombstones seem to have lost their fearful severity. I examine myself scrupulously; I see that I have begun to get accustomed to this somber and depressing place, have even begun, indeed, to make it my own, and to love it.

The morning after my arrival, I began lessons. That first day will live as one of the most unforgettable days of my life. In the morning, I was able to see the classroom, which the Director of Education had restored at such great expense. The place must surely have been an old stable. Only they have put down floor-boards along the ground, broadened the windows, and fixed in window-frames. On the panels of the walls, which looked as sooty black as the chimney of the stove, there hung a map, a chart of a skeleton, a picture of a farm, and another one of a snake. These, evidently, were the new educational equipment. At the bottom of the wall on the garden side of the classroom—a relic of the time when the place was a stable—there was a manger, which they hadn't thought worth removing. They had made it into a kind of cupboard, by nailing a wooden cover over it. Here the children put away their food, and their books, and the firewood they brought to burn in the school. Hatije Hanim told me this cupboard served another purpose once. For a long time they had shut up mischievous children there, to bring them to their senses, when a beating wouldn't make them behave. The headman had a small boy named Vehbi, who, it seemed, spent nearly all his time in this box. When the child did something naughty, he would go into the place on his own, lie flat on his back, like a corpse in a coffin, and close up the lid again with his own hands. I was much surprised to hear this and asked whether the

131

headman hadn't something to say about it. Hatije Hanim shook her head, and said, "The headman is very glad. 'Well done, Hatije Hanim,' he says, 'that was a bright idea. We have a cupboard at home. If God be willing, I'll shut the young rascal up there, when he misbehaves himself.'"

"A fine system of discipline! Are there boys in the school?"

"Yes, there are one or two. When they grow up, we send them to the boys' school at the village of Gariplar."

"Where's that?"

"Behind those rocks that are beginning to catch the light."

"Isn't that hard on these children? How do they come and go as far as that in the snow and wet of winter?"

"They're used to the journey. When it's not muddy, it hardly takes them an hour. It's only in rainy, muddy, wintry weather that they have a little difficulty."

"But why don't we teach them here?"

"Can men and women be taught together?"

"Have we got to call them men?"

"Of course, my dear; great big young men of twelve or thirteen years of age!" Hatije Hanim paused a moment. She had something on the tip of her tongue that she was reluctant to say. Finally, she took courage. "Consider: it would never do, *now*."

"Why not?"

"Because you're a very young teacher, that's why, my dear." In Stambul there's a saying that 'a woman of good repute even runs away from a cock.' Our Hatije Hanim herself must have been just such a woman. I saw no need to reply, and occupied myself with other things.

A large part of the equipment which had been produced at so much sacrifice consisted of five large old-fashioned school benches. But the strange thing was that they had pushed them into a corner of the classroom, as if they weren't worth using. "Why have you done that, Hatije Hanim?" I asked.

"I didn't do it; it was the last teacher, my dear," she replied. "The children always sit on the floor. The teacher was afraid to throw them away, in case an inspector or someone came. When the children come to school, we make them sit there, at first; then when they're going to begin reading their lessons, we let them sit on the mat. The ones who are well-to-do have cushions of their own."

I asked the old woman to help me, and I took up the mat. After having cleaned the place, I put the benches out in a row, and made it look more like a classroom. It was clear that Hatije Hanim wasn't a bit pleased, but she didn't dare oppose me; she did whatever I asked.

While I was trying to get the job finished, with my hands covered with dirt, my pupils began to crowd in one by one. The little creatures' clothes were so poor and miserable that hardly one of them had any shoes or stockings. Their heads were tightly wrapped in very old bits of cloth, and they came clattering up to the classroom door in the sandals they wore on their bare feet. There they took them off and put them all in a row.

As soon as the children caught sight of me, they drew back at once in fear. They looked shyly through the doorway, and when I called them, they covered their faces with their arms, or hid behind the door. So I had to take some of them by the wrist and pull them into the classroom. When they came near me, they closed their eyes tight, and gave me such kisses on the hand that I found it hard not to laugh. Every one of the kisses—evidently a custom in the village—resounded with a noise that amused me, and left my hand slightly damp. To ingratiate myself with the little people, I said a word of welcome to each one. But they left my questions unanswered, with a determined silence that quite abashed one; and they only agreed to give their names after a great deal of coaxing.

"Zehra, Ayşe . . . Zehra, Ayşe . . . Zehra, Ayşe . . ." Heavens! What a lot of Zehras and Ayşes there are in this village! And although I was in no mood for laughter, very odd thoughts came into my head. If an inspector were to come, for instance, and want to get to know my pupils, I should be able to settle the matter very briefly, by saying, "I have nine Ayşes and twelve Zehras." Or I could simplify things by seating all the Ayşes on one side of the classroom and all the Zehras on the other; or, while they were playing ball in the garden (because I had every intention of making the children play games during the intervals) we could pick teams by having all the Ayşes on one side, and all the Zehras on the other. It began to amuse me, and I couldn't wholly conceal it. I used to say to the new girls, "My child, are you Zehra or Ayşe?" and very often I got the expected answer. One plump-faced little girl turned out to be the bravest of them all. Raising her dark eyes to my face, she asked with surprise, "How do you know my name?"

One by one, I made my pupils sit on the benches, and warned them to remember their places. The little creatures' state was worth seeing; they found the greatest difficulty in getting accustomed to the benches, and took up the strangest positions, as though they were sitting on the branch of a tree, or a vine trellis. When I left their sides, they would watch

133

me out of the corner of an eye, and then, slowly drawing back their dirty legs, which hung down very oddly, they would tuck them underneath them, like snails retiring into their shells. What was I to do? Perhaps I'd get used to it all in time.

One thing tickled me very much. The very children who came up to me abashed and embarrassed, who kissed my hand with tight-shut eyes, whose mouths would only utter monosyllables, with the simpering of a village bride, would no sooner open their lesson-books than they began to read aloud from them at the tops of their voices. As the class got more crowded, the noise began to increase, and my head began to swim. I asked Hatije Hanim whether they always did lessons at the top of their voices in that way. "Can one stand it?" I asked.

She looked at me with some surprise, and answered, "Of course, my dear. That's what school means. 'Can the tree be pruned without the help of an axe?' The more they raise their voices, the more the lesson gets into their heads."

The class was now nearly full. I struck the teacher's desk—the only nice new piece of furniture—as hard as I could with my hand. I was going to address them, and urge them to work quietly. But no one took any notice of the noise I made, nor even looked up. On the contrary, the clamour grew, as though one had thrown a stone at a bee-hive. It was quite clear that I was going to have a good deal of trouble to bring these children into line. But in the end no doubt I would succeed.

"Hatije Hanim," I said, "You take the class today, in your own way. Until I've got them in some kind of order, I shan't be able to start teaching."

The old woman said somewhat hesitatingly, "I teach in the way I've always seen it done, my dear. I haven't got all your knowledge. But what of that? I didn't go to school." I understood later what the woman meant; Hatije Hanim thought I was putting her through an examination. She was afraid of losing her two hundred piastres a month. . . .

Although the weather was fine, several of the girls had come to school with their heads covered with old cloths. I asked Hatije Hanim why they did this. She answered with surprise, as she did to most of my questions, "Why, dear, they're girls big enough to be brides. They can't go about the streets with bare heads."

Heaven help them! These children of ten or twelve years old, with their anemic, colourless faces, these bloodless little creatures—'grown-up girls'! I had indeed struck a strange place. All the same, I was glad in a way. Those who looked on these children as potential brides would certainly regard me as an old maid; and no one would make fun of me now by calling me a child.

The last to come to school were the boys. These lads had work to do at home, like grown men—fetching water from the well, milking the cows, and carrying firewood from the mountains. Hatije Hanim told them to stay outside for a while; and then, rather diffidently, she suggested, "I think you must have forgotten your veil, my dear."

"Is it necessary?"

"Oh, indeed it is. I won't interfere, of course, but isn't it a sin to teach with your head bare?"

I was ashamed to say "I don't know," so I said with some irritation "I forgot to bring my veil when I came," and told a lie.

"That's all right," said Hatije Hanim. "I'll give you a clean piece of gauze," and taking a bit of green embroidery out of a box that creaked when it opened, she gave it to me. There was nothing to be done but to put up with my lot. I threw the piece of embroidery over my hair, and fastened the two ends under my chin, like fortune-telling gypsy girls in the streets of Istanbul. The closed casement of one of the windows was rather like a long mirror. Without calling attention to myself, I went to the window and began to survey my reflection. I'd thought out a dress for myself, after becoming a schoolteacher. In my opinion a teacher shouldn't be dressed like other women while she's at work; my invention was very simple, a black silk tunic down to the knees, a leather belt round the waist, and below the belt two little pockets for a handkerchief and a notebook. But to give a little relief to the black dress, it was to have a white linen collar. I don't like long hair: when I'd become a teacher, I couldn't leave my hair as it was. For the last month, although I'd begun to let my hair grow, it had so far only got to my shoulders. For my first class I'd dressed as I've just described, and had brushed my hair neatly back, in case it fell over my forehead in an unruly way. This green veil looked so odd with my shiny black tunic and my short hair (which had no sooner been released from the brush that it began to curl) that I had to bite my lips to keep from laughing.

Let me present my boy pupils, for whose sake I'd covered my head with Hatije Hanim's green veil. First of all there was little Vehbi, who used to spend his time like a mouse in the cupboard. He was an amusing imp, indeed. His bright eyes, black as two beads, his shrewd little face

and his sharp chin identified him as the little devil of the school. As
round as a ball, with clear whites to his eyes, shining teeth, and a bright
red mouth, was a very dark Arab, Jafer Ağa; if you addressed him as Jafer
only, he didn't content himself with giving no reply, but would throw
stones after you in the street. Then there was Asur, with a melancholy,
dirty face and small teeth; ten years old, as withered as a skeleton, and
marked with smallpox. And finally, the most important figure in the
class: Hafiz Nuri, who must have been ten years old, but whose face was
as wrinkled as that of an old man of seventy. Under his chin he had a
scrofula scar, recently healed, which made his throat look like a new-
peeled twig. His eyes were hollow, with no eyelashes, and his head was
egg-shaped, under a white turban; in fact, the sort of creature you might
see on show at a fair.

Hatije Hanim put down beside her some long sticks freshly cut from
the cemetery that morning, and began to call the children to her side one
by one, to teach them their lessons. While she did this, the noise in the
classroom continued. When Sister Alexei was disturbed by the noise we
made in class, she would put her waxen fingers together, with all the
simplicity of a portrait of the Virgin Mary, and say, "Children, you are
making me suffer the miseries of Calvary." Well, it's Çalıkuşu, who was
leader of all the mischief and disturbance in that class, who's got to suffer
now the very torments she endured. I tried for two weeks to overcome
the tumult, which was enough to make your head swim, by making my
pupils work more quietly, to accustom them to listening together to a
lesson given in class. On those first days, in spite of all my efforts, I could
do nothing with the children. After Hatije Hanim's freshly cut stick,
which hissed down like a snake in the classroom, my voice made very
little impression on them.

Sometimes I would give in. "Come in, Hatije Hanim," I'd call out to
her. And her coming into the classroom in a fury, like the flying witch in
the fairy tales, did a lot to help me. In the end, the noise would be
gradually abated, and the class would be quieter. The children began to
understand what was said to them and even Hatije Hanim, who believed
that the more they shouted the more the lesson was implanted in their
minds, was satisfied at last. Now and again she would say, "Thanks be to
God, my dear, my head's rested." But it wasn't merely that I was after;
what I wanted was to give them a little life and a little joy. It looked
almost beyond the bounds of possibility. The somber cheerlessness that
one found in the streets and the houses and the tombstones of the village

was to be seen in the children as well. Their lips didn't know what it was to laugh; their tired eyes, heavy with care, looked as though they were thinking of death.

And wasn't I slowly beginning to be like them? Before, I used to think of death very differently: for fifty or sixty years, indeed as long as one chooses, one runs here and there and amuses oneself, until one falls exhausted with weariness. And then one's eyes become heavy with longing for a sweet sleep, and one stretches oneself out to rest on a clean white bed. Bunches of flowers are placed on white marble, shining in the sun; and a few birds come to drink from the small trough of water standing on the marble. That was the kind of picture that presented itself to my eyes, when one spoke of death: beautiful, and almost happy. But now my lungs seem to breathe and my tongue seem to taste its bitter savour, in the scent of the soil, and the aloe-wood, and the cypress.

Hatije Hanim was responsible to some extent for the children's being so heavy and joyless. This good woman believed it was a teacher's duty to extinguish in the heart all worldly desires. At every opportunity she brought the little things face to face with death. She believed that it was for this reason that certain charts of natural history had been sent to the school. She taught them, for example, a dreadful prayer in the following style:

"The fleeting world moves on; it waits for none.
Roll on, O world! Your course will soon be run."

And then she would hang the chart of a skeleton in the middle of the room, and say, "Tomorrow, when we die, our flesh will perish like this, and our bones will dry up till they look like that," and go on to describe the terror of death and the miseries of the tomb. According to the old woman, the other charts more or less illustrated the same thing. While showing a picture of the farm, for instance, she would say something of this kind: "God created these sheep, saying, 'Let my servants eat and worship Me.' But tomorrow, when we are in the grave, and the questioning angel takes his redoubtable stand with his flaming sword—let's see what answer we shall give then!"—and again pass on to a description of death. As for the chart of the serpent, Hatije Hanim introduced it as Shahmeran. By inscribing the names of sick villagers on the serpent's stomach, you help to cure them. Yes; I employed endless devices to amuse those wretched children, and make them laugh; but my labours were all in vain.

We made a rule in the school regarding the intervals. I send the children into a garden for an hour or half an hour, and try to teach them amusing and interesting games. All the same, they have no taste at all for any of them. So, out of necessity, I leave them to their own devices and withdraw into a corner. The most popular game among the dull-eyed, weary-faced little girls (who are more like suffering grown-up people) is to gather in one corner of the garden and say prayers, full of dreadful words like death, and coffin, and bier. Ah! And there's one game that makes one's hair stand on end. They howl, all together, making their voices tremble, and chant:

"They come like robbers,
They strip you bare,
They put you in a coffin,
And leave you there;
Death, the oppressor,
Claims you forever.
You cannot escape him,
Never—never!"

Funeral processions, row upon row, pass before my eyes. One of the games the children love most is the corpse game. This, which they generally perform in the long midday interval is a kind of play, and the chief actors are Hafiz Nuri and the Arab, Jafer Ağa. The latter falls sick, and the little girls collect round him, read the extracts from the Koran, and pour water from Mecca into his mouth. Rolling his small beady eyes, he breathes his last breath; then girls lament with loud voices, and bind up his chin. Afterwards they wash Jafer Ağa, on the table on which the dead are laid out. The coffin, which the children bring out and decorate by ornamenting a broken wooden door with their green headdresses, is exactly like a dreadful, real one. The recitation by Hafiz Nuri of the prayer, in an ominous funereal voice, his reading of the invocation, and the whole manner of conducting the service, is something to make one's hair stand on end: and at the head of the tomb there's an inscription that breaks in upon my dreams at night—"Zehra, daughter of Jafer."

As I've said, one can, so to speak, smell death in the very air of the place. Ah, and the nights!—the nights that drag on and on as though the hours would never pass. To face the terrors and fantasies of the night is harder still. One night the jackals began to howl in the mountain. I was terribly afraid; whatever happened, I wanted to go down to Hatije Hanim's room. But when I opened the door of that vault-like room, that smelt of mildew, the sight which met my eyes was a thousand times more dreadful than the howlings of any jackals. The old woman, swathed in white from head to foot, was on her prayer mat, reading something or other in a hoarse voice as though she had passed beyond herself, and swaying from side to side as she told her beads.

However, there are three things that I've begun to like. First, the running stream below my window, which seems, when I'm alone at night, to be a sort of companion to me, with its ceaseless sound. Secondly, little Vehbi, the child who used to spend his life, during Hatije Hanim's reign, being punished by having to lie on his back at the bottom of the chest. I've pretty well fallen in love with the rascal. He is unlike any of the other children here. He pronounces his K's like J's; and his conversation is cheerful and unafraid.

One day in the garden Vehbi was looking at me very attentively with his bright eyes.

"What are you looking at, Vehbi?" I asked.

"You seem to be a pretty girl," he answered, without the least hesitation. "Won't you marry my elder brother? Come and be our bride. My brother will give you slippers and chemises and combs."

Vehbi's every attitude was good and pleasant, but he paid no heed to what I said; even when I scolded him or pulled his little ear, he took no notice. But perhaps it was for that reason that I loved him so much. And now, when Vehbi behaved in this improper manner, I frowned and said, "Is that the way to talk to one's teacher? If anyone else heard you say that, they'd make you eat your words!"

The child answered, as though amused by my naïveté, "Don't be silly: as if I'd say it to anyone else!" Mercy on us! This slip of a village child, what didn't he know? He continued with the same unconcern, "I shall call you my Istanbul sister-in-law. I shall bring you chestnuts. My brother will hang gold round your neck."

"Haven't you got a sister-in-law?"

"I have; but she's so dark. We're giving her to Hasan the shepherd."

"What does your brother do?"

"He's a gendarme."

"What does a gendarme do?"

Vehbi scratched his head and thought hard. Then he said, "He kills the infidel."

Another characteristic of Vehbi's is that he's proud and obstinate. He knows how to act like a grown-up man. When I catch him out making mistakes at his lessons, he's angry and ashamed. He's most reluctant to correct his error. If I press him further, he rebels, and looks at me with scorn.

"You're a woman; you don't understand," he says.

The third thing I love is the little orphan girl. It was perhaps the fifth morning after I'd started lessons. Running my eye over the class, my heart suddenly jumped with surprise and pleasure. At the end of the last row was a little girl, with a face as lovely as an angel's, faded golden hair that was almost white, and clear, fair skin; and she was smiling at me, with teeth like pearls. Who was the child? Where had she suddenly come from? I motioned to her with my hand. "Come over here," I said.

She leapt from her seat with the lightness of a bird, and came hopping to my side, just as I used to do at school. The mite was very poor; her feet were bare, and her hair all over the place. Her delicate white skin could be seen through the rents in her print frock, which had lost its colour. I took the little hands. "Look at me, child," I said.

She raised her head, fearfully. Two dark blue eyes shone through the curly lashes. The sorrow I'd endured at Zeyniler had not made me cry; but the beautiful eyes of this half-naked child, and her teeth smiling like two rows of pearls in her red mouth, would have made me sob, if I hadn't taken a firm hold of myself at that moment. I stroked her chin lightly and said to her as I did to all the girls, "Is your name Zehra, child, or Ayşe?"

She replied with a pure Istanbul accent and an unbelievably sweet voice, "My name's Munisé, teacher."

"Do you belong to this school?"

"Yes, teacher."

"How is it you haven't been for some days?"

"My elder sister didn't send me, teacher. We had work to do. I shall come now."

"Have you no mother?"

The little girl lowered her eyes and was silent. It seemed to me that I had unwittingly touched a secret wound in the child's heart. Not insisting any further, I asked her something else.

"Was it you who was singing yesterday evening, Munisé?" The day before, in one of the neighbouring gardens, I had heard a child's treble voice singing a song. The voice was so sweet and so different from any other voices I had heard here, that I leant my head out of the window and closed my eyes; I pictured myself for a few moments far away, in a place whose name I didn't want to remember; a land of insincerity. The singer of the song couldn't have been anyone but this small child.

Munisé nodded her head, shyly. "It was me, teacher," she said.

After sending the child back to her place, I started lessons. But I felt something extraordinary within me. That small child had affected me like warm spring sunshine. It was as if a bright ray of light had fallen upon a bird's nest buried in the snow; sick at heart, trembling and unsatisfied, her head hidden under her wings in the cold misery of her nest, Çalıkuşu was slowly beginning to revive, and recover her old cheerfulness. A curious lightness came into my movements, and a glowing harmony into my voice and words. As I taught, my eyes would inadvertently keep turning towards her. And she kept looking at me too, a sweet smile on the pearl-like teeth, and love in her azure eyes, which I felt to be almost touching my lips. I knew the feeling of motherhood for the first time in my life. I had to live alone: but if only I had at least, a little girl like that! What sorrow that it can't be granted me!

I was able to learn very little about Munisé from Hatije Hanim. The woman she called her elder sister seems to have been her stepmother, and her father, a former forestry official, who, having taken his second wife from this village, remained bound to the place when he was pensioned off. Thanks to his wife's house and meadow and his own five or ten piastres a month pension, he got along somehow. I told Hatije Hanim that according to her description, the family wasn't in too bad a way: then why didn't they look after the child?

The old woman frowned. "Thanks be to God that she's looked after at all!—anyone else would have thrown her into the street!"

"Why?"

"That child's mother was a bad woman, my dear. I don't very clearly remember; was it five years ago?—She made off with a gendarmerie lieutenant. The child was very small then. Afterwards, the officer deserted her, and went to another part of the country. When the woman lost her reputation, the young men took her with them off to the mountains. In a word, she went to the bad."

"That may be, Hatije Hanim. But what fault is that of the child's?"

The old woman shook her head with the same crude fanaticism. "What more can they do? They're in no position to dress the child of a woman like that in silk clothing," she replied.

Munisé didn't come to school every day. When I asked her why, she used to give some reason such as that her elder sister had made her do the washing, or scrub the floor, or gather firewood for her from the mountain. Her companions didn't look on the child very kindly. In class they always kept her at a distance from them, and whenever they got an opportunity they would bully her and make her cry. I was a little to blame there. I hadn't been able to conceal the love I felt for the little girl; and those who saw me caressing her in class and keeping her by my side in the garden to talk to, looked on with resentment.

I heard Munisé crying in the school garden one day, and begging someone, "What harm am I doing to you? Don't do it!" Keeping myself out of sight, I looked out of the window. The other girls were filling their mouths from the fountain, and pursuing Munisé to squirt the water over her. The child was weeping and running from one corner of the garden to another, trying to cover her face and neck with her hands. Those girls, so heavy and frightened in their demeanour, so downcast in their looks, had turned into hounds chasing a wounded deer. They were leaping about with rough agility, on their dirty legs, and circling round her like birds of prey, uttering wild cries. They were forcing the little girl into a corner, rolling her on the ground, and squirting the water that swelled their cheeks into her face and on to her chest, which her torn frock had left half uncovered.

I lost my head. I flew out of the room like a madman. I ran so fast that my right foot went through one of the rotten stair-boards. When I got out into the garden, the nature of the battle had changed. A champion, as small as Munisé, but somewhat tougher, had appeared— little Vehbi. I shall never forget the heroism of that nine-year-old little urchin. Vehbi had gone into the muddy pool that lay a little beyond the water flowing from the fountain, and he was splashing about in it like a duck, subjecting Munisé's attackers to a dreadful shower of mud. Their arms, feet, and faces were getting black with it. His thin voice sounded like a sharp whistle in the midst of the girls' cries: "You daughters of infidels, leave the girl alone! I'll kill you all." The girls had to retreat before this attack. Munisé was half fainting; I took her in my arms and carried her to my room.

It is impossible to express what I felt as I pressed that beautiful little girl in my arms. It was as though a hot spring was boiling in the depths of my heart. There was a kind of fire in my breast, bringing the tears to my eyes and making me catch my breath. A faint glow of warmth began to penetrate my whole being. It seems to me that I have had this feeling of elation before. Yes, but where?—and when? It can be nothing but the memory of an old dream. Because there are things about this dim and shadowy sensation that the mind can't grasp, as there are in a dream. I see myself flying in the empty spaces of the air, with a torrent of leaves rushing all round me, beating against my face and my hair with a harsh rustling sound. Where was that, I wonder? No, no! It's a lie. I'm feeling the sensation for the first time in my life.

I neglected my pupils that day, and busied myself with Munisé. I washed her beautiful body, like a lily beaten by storms, and her bright fair hair, which was almost white. The poor child went on weeping for nearly ten minutes. Ah, those tears! It seemed to me that the teardrops were falling drop by drop, not on the small girl's face, but into my heart. I was slowly gaining the child's confidence. While I was hastily shortening one of my old dresses for her and sewing it up, she was hiding herself in my skirts like a kitten, and looking earnestly into my face with wet eyes. Like all children who have suffered an untimely and unmerited misfortune, Munisé had all the character of a grown-up person. Certain things that I had only begun to understand in the last month or two she had learnt long ago. Yes, she had borne all the afflictions of her three small brothers and sisters; even so she couldn't satisfy her elder sister, and was beaten every day. A week before, a neighbour's cow had come into the garden; and while Munisé was trying to drive it out, her youngest brother fell off the swing. After her elder sister had given her a good beating, she shut her up in the stable, and gave her nothing but scraps of dry bread for two days. Munisé showed me the violet bruises and sores on her ivory skin. They were all traces of those blows. I couldn't stand it.

"Well, Munisé," I said, "Isn't your father sorry for you?"

She gave me a profound look, as though sorry for my ignorance, and said with a smile, "He's sorry for me, and I'm sorry for him. But there's no help for either of us." As she said it, there was such hopelessness in her sigh, and in the gesture she made with her open hands, that my heart was melted.

I dressed Munisé lovingly and gladly, as though I were playing with a doll. When I showed the child to herself in a looking-glass, she went a deep red with sheer pleasure. She looked fearfully at her hair, tied up on both sides with a rosy ribbon, at her short dark blue wool frock and her long black stockings. I heard later that Munisé's smart appearance was the subject of gossip for the village of Zeyniler for days after. Some were pleased with my kindness; but a great many were not. Such a degree of pity for the child of a creature who had wandered about the mountains was too much, it seems. Then there were others who considered that so much emphasis on dress was a sin, and an incentive to the child to follow the road her mother had taken. Poor Munisé derived no pleasure from her rosy ribbons, her short dark blue frock and her black stockings. Her stepmother put the clothes away in a box—who knows why?—and two days later the child came to school again in the same torn dress. Munisé rarely comes to school. She's not appeared now for three days. We'll see tomorrow: I shall ask little Vehbi for news of her.

Zeyniler, 30th November
I get a little fonder of the school every day. The tumbledown classroom has really begun to take quite a clean and attractive appearance. Indeed, I've succeeded in decorating it a little bit. The children whom I found so wild and strange in the early days are much more approachable now. Is it that I have got used to them, or is it that, thanks to my tireless efforts, they are slowly beginning to come into line?—I don't know. But I think both influences are at work. I am working very hard. For my own sake rather than for theirs, and to prevent myself going out of my mind with the perpetual ennui of inertia and loneliness, I struggle on day and night. When I seem to fail, I'm not downhearted. When I feel that I have been able to awaken a little glow of life in these spiritless children with their careworn eyes, I rejoice. Some of the village neighbours call on me now and again. They don't take much pleasure in conversation, and don't seem to know how to laugh. Perhaps they go away a little embarrassed. In the early days, although I tried to dress as simply as possible, they still considered me too smart, I believe, and didn't approve of my appearance. Indeed, the muhtar's wife made remarks, too, on a few occasions. I tried to be as pleasant and as friendly as I could to them; I even did some of them little services, like writing letters for them, and cutting out and sewing their dresses. And now I have a feeling that their ideas about me have changed a little.

144

The other day the muhtar's wife came in again. She brought me greetings from her husband. The muhtar, it seems, had told her, "The first time I saw her I wasn't very taken with her; but God knows she's a good girl. She stays in school like a good housewife. If there's anything I can do for her, let me know."

Of course I thanked him for this expression of goodwill. There's another important personage here who likes me and visits me constantly, and that is the village midwife, Nazife Molla. Seeing that her name is neither Zehra nor Ayşe, she must belong somewhere else, and the fact that she's a great chatterer indicates it too. I daren't ask too many questions, lest people say that I'm a gossip, but she tells me curious and amusing things about the village. According to her, there is very little understanding or refinement. For instance although we were quite alone in the room one day, she put her mouth very close to my ear as though afraid others would overhear, and said a number of things about Munisé's mother, that were full of pity and tolerance. At the end of it she shook her head, and added: "The fault lies with that monkish husband of hers. The sin be on his head. But mercy on us, my girl, don't go and tell other people what I say. They would stone one into one's grave."

It seems that the midwife has a son who knows the Koran by heart. This Ramazan he has gone to B., to beg alms; he must have found it fairly lucrative, because he still hasn't come back. If God be willing, she means to get him married this year. The good woman praises her son now and again. She closes one eye in a significant manner, and thereby gives me hope. If I submit to certain rules and conditions, I understand I shall be regarded as worthy to become the wife of Hafiz Efendi. The truth is, this woman is an endless source of amusement to me.

The midwife came again this morning. She asked me if I knew how to chant the Prophet's nativity hymn. It seems there is to be a wedding in the near future, and that at weddings in this village they chant the Prophet's nativity hymn instead of playing music. I bit my lip to prevent myself from laughing.

"I do know," I said, "but I've no voice, midwife." The midwife regretted it. One of the previous teachers read the hymn beautifully, and earned a good deal of money by it. However, that was not really the object of today's visit; they were making one poor girl a bride. The neighbours, as an act of grace, had provided one or two cooking utensils and a bed; and they wanted an old dress from me, in order to dress up the bride. In point of fact, the girl was no stranger to me; she was one of

145

my pupils. When I heard the news I was amazed: "But there aren't any girls fit to be brides among my children, midwife," I said. "The oldest is twelve."

Nazife Molla laughed. "What, my dear? Do you call twelve young? I was fifteen when they dressed me up as a bride, and they called me an old maid. True, the old customs have changed, but this orphan has no belongings, and she was stranded. There's a shepherd, Mehmet, here: we're giving her to him. At least he'll give her a slice or two of bread."

"Who is this girl, midwife?"

"Zehra."

There are seven or eight Zehras in my class, so I couldn't place her very readily. Then the midwife told me which it was, and I was frozen with surprise. The Zehra who was to marry Mehmet the shepherd was a creature strange enough to frighten one, even if she were only seen in a dream; she was, I suppose, mentally defective. She had wild hair, as coarse as brushwood and the colour of henna, patches of the same colour in her waxen face, and alarming eyes on a level with her narrow forehead. At the first encounter I had taken it for granted that the child was sick. She never spoke in class except when there was something to be explained or a lesson to be read aloud; then she'd begin to shout in a dreadful voice. The point I couldn't understand was that Zehra was the best pupil in the class when it came to doing sums or learning by heart. In the playground, she kept away from everyone, just as she did in class. She didn't take part in that charming coffin game, nor in the game of saying prayers for the corpse when it was laid out, nor even the more cheerful funeral games; but she had a game of her own, which she played now and again, that shocked me more than all the others. Zehra would stand in the middle of the garden; and after behaving as though she heard a voice coming from the air, she would roll her eyes, as she stood there, and begin to make a murmuring sound, like an urn boiling, and other very curious noises. Then this state of ecstasy would increase, her red hair would stand on end, she would foam at the mouth and start going round and round, with loud cries. No doubt it was a game. But somehow, as I witnessed it, I would begin to tremble. And while the midwife was explaining to me that the girl was to be a bride, I was saying to myself, "Oh dear, if Mehmet the shepherd sees her playing that game, I'm sorry for her."

After my neighbour had gone, I unpicked one of my old dresses and began to fashion a bridal gown for Zehra. What is one to do? One must at least try and give the poor girl a little semblance of style. Mehmet the shepherd mustn't leave her and run away the first night, at any rate.

Zeyniler, 1ˢᵗ December

Zehra was made a bride last night in the muhtar's house. To prevent Mehmet the shepherd from feeling low-spirited, they played a drum and a horn on the village green and had one or two wrestling contests. Among the women, too, eve-of-the-wedding festivities were held. The Prophet's nativity hymn was chanted. My gift of the bridal dress seemed to be too European for some of the older people of the village. Such phrases as the following reached my ears: "Tomorrow on the day of Judgement . . .", "Munkir . . . Nekir . . ." (the names of the two angels who question the dead in their graves), "Red hot mace . . ." (with which sinners are beaten). Some of the younger ones, on the other hand, were full of envy, and probably some of them even envied the bride. I enjoyed myself a great deal that night. The muhtar's wife had prepared a magnificent spread; I understood from what was said around me that this sacrifice was incurred to make a show for the teacher from Istanbul, rather than for the sake of Zehra herself.

Before they handed over the bride to Mehmet the shepherd, a preposterous ceremony of hand-kissing was performed. Among the hands in the town to be kissed by the shy young men with their eyes shut, were my own. That seemed to be necessary, presumably on the grounds that a teacher was a kind of mother. A secret comedy took place at this hand-kissing ceremony which I shall never forget. The muhtar's wife and the midwife, as the leaders, sat at the head of the row, on a mattress; as I could not manage to sit with my legs crossed as they did, I settled myself on the corner of a laundry basket, alongside the fireplace. Mehmet the shepherd didn't dare raise his eyes from the ground, and had not seen me at first. The midwife pointed me out to him from her corner, and said, "Mehmet, my son, kiss the teacher's hand;" and the young man came up to me covered with confusion. I put out my hand quite seriously; but the shepherd had no sooner taken it than he dropped it again. He looked like some idiot who didn't believe it was a hand! I tried my hardest not to show that I was laughing, and said "Kiss my hand." After the good fellow had taken my hand again he couldn't stand it; he threw off his embarrassment and looked straight at me: our eyes met. And the worst of it was that just at that moment, a tough resinous log burnt up brightly in the fire, and lit up my face so that he saw I was laughing. I don't remember in all my life seeing anything as funny as the dismay of the shepherd at that moment.

After the hand-kissing ceremony they took the bridegroom to the room where the bride was. Zehra looked almost pretty, with her hair dressed and combed by me, with my own hands, not long before. But according to local custom, instead of a bride's veil, she was swathed in a kind of sack made of green satin; so I couldn't see what impression she made on the shepherd.

Zeyniler, 15th December

When I awoke this morning, it seemed to me that there was something lacking. As I looked around, I discovered the reason. The stream, which flowed at night with the sound of a mournful lullaby, had stopped. I got up to open the window; the wooden shutters offered a great deal of resistance, and as I pushed them hard, I saw that snow had begun to filter in between them. This, then, was the night when the snow began to fall. Zeyniler had almost completely changed in appearance. I had heard from Hatije Hanim that once the snow began to fall here, it lies till April. How excellent! For it means that this dark and depressing place, whose very leaves look black, begins its true springtime in the months of winter. For me, snow has always been something more beautiful than freshly-opened almond blossom. No feast-day gives me the joy and the pleasure that I find in rolling in the garden in this soft, clean, white substance. And then what lovely means it gives of taking revenge on people one dislikes! I had an enemy at one time, who was very much afraid of snow. Without giving him any warning, I'd put snow down the thick collar that enveloped his delicate throat, and go wild with joy to see him getting purple in the face with the cold, while his teeth chattered.

Zeyniler, 17th December

The snow increases, and roads are closed; so that a lot of the children don't come to school. Today was the bitterest and most painful day of my life. In the morning, my pupils brought me bad news. Munisé did something wrong last night. Her stepmother set upon her, to beat her with a stick; and the child threw herself out of the window into the garden. They thought she wouldn't stay long in the snow and the dark, and would soon come to the door and beg to be let in. But although hours had passed, the child had not been seen again. Finally they told the neighbours, and the young men of the village tumbled out into the streets with torches in their hands; but the wretched child could nowhere be found. Even those of her companions who liked Munisé least felt sorry for her. They searched everywhere for her, till evening; and as they knew how interested I was in the little girl, the muhtar kept sending news to me by Vehbi.

Vehbi, today, was as serious and concerned as a grown-up man. To indicate that Munisé hadn't been found yet, he showed the palms of his hands, blue with the cold, and said with his teeth chattering, "Poor little girl; the wolves must have eaten her."

Towards evening this fear of Vehbi's began to spread to the grown-ups, and some of them said, "The child cannot have gone to another village in this storm: she'll either be frozen to death somewhere from the cold, or else wild beasts have devoured her." The evening of that day descended like a black cloud; that day of blinding storm, during which you could not see your own hand. A wild sense of hopelessness descended on me. For the first time I believed those who say that life is cruel and evil and ignorant of law: and I rebelled against it. My voice and my breathing were stifled; my head was on fire; I went early to bed, for the light hurt my eyes that night. The storm raged louder and louder outside, and shook the shutters of the window with its blows. Who knew where the poor little girl was buried? Who could tell in what corner of the darkness something still flickered, like a glimmer of light?

I don't know how many hours had passed. On occasions like that, one loses all sense of time. I was suddenly conscious of a noise, as though something was knocking on the door on the cemetery side. What could it have been except the wind? No, this was something other than the buffeting of the wind. I sat up in bed, and I listened. And in the heart of the night I seemed to hear a stifled human cry. I jumped out of bed at once, and put something over my shoulders; and started to run downstairs. I meant to look in at Hatije Hanim's room and wake her up; but she had heard the voice too, and had gone out into the yard with a candle in her hand.

We didn't dare to open the door straight away; moreover the noise had now ceased. Hatije Hanim, her voice as gruff as a man's, called out, "Who's there?"

There was no answer. Once again the old woman called out, and this time, in the sound of the wind, we heard a voice wailing. Hatije Hanim called, "Who are you?" But I had recognised the voice: it was Munisé! I cried out and flung my weight upon the iron bar of the door. No sooner was the door opened than a gust of wind, snow-laden, filled the place. The old woman's candle suddenly went out. In the darkness there fell into my arms a small body frozen as stiff as ice. While Hatije Hanim was trying to light her candle again, I pressed her to my heart and wept bitterly. Munisé had clearly come to the end of her strength; she had fainted in my arms. Her face was blue and her hair dishevelled, and snow had soaked her clothing through.

When I'd undressed the child I put her into my own bed and began to rub her body with pieces of flannel that Hatije Hanim had warmed over the stove. The first thing Munisé did when she came to herself was to beg for "a piece of bread." The Lord be praised, we had a little milk; and with Hatije Hanim's help it was warmed, and we began giving it to the child in spoonfuls. As minutes passed, Munisé's face began to glow and the light came into her eyes. Now and then she sighed in my arms; who knows what pain it was that made her weep? Oh, the gratitude in the eyes of that child! What is there in the whole world more beautiful than the power to do even a little bit of good? That miserable gloomy room, swaying like the keel of a sinking ship in the middle of the storm, suddenly, in the warm glow of the stove, became an intimate and happy home, so that I felt ashamed of the mistrust of life that I had shown a little while ago.

By this time the child had begun to talk; with her arms around my neck and her fair hair falling over my wrists, she looked into my eyes and slowly replied to the questions I asked. Yesterday evening she had grown very much afraid of her stepmother, and had run away to a barn at the other end of the village, and hidden herself in the straw. Straw keeps one as warm as a bed; but today she had got very hungry, and she knew if she went out they would catch her and take her home again. So she had no other course but to wait for another night. It seems I was the greatest ray of hope for the poor child; she diverted herself that whole day with one illusion: "Teacher will give me bread."

Shortly afterwards I noticed that a shadow had fallen on the child's bright eyes, and that her joy had begun to grow less. There was no need to ask the reason; the same fear had possessed me. Tomorrow morning Munisé would have to be sent home again. I was not without one faint hope; but it was the kind of hopeless hope that we feel for things hardly to be realised because they are so beautiful. I said to Hatije Hanim in a low voice, fearful of rousing a fruitless dream in Munisé: "If they really don't want this child, I wonder if they would agree, if I asked to adopt her? I've no belongings, but I swear I would look after the child as if she were my own. I wonder if they would let me have her?" I put out my hand, trembling, and bent my head, as though fulfilment of this crazy wish depended on a word from Hatije Hanim.

The old woman had her eyes on the stove, and was thinking hard. She nodded her head slowly, "It wouldn't be a bad thing: let's have a word with the muhtar tomorrow; if he says it's all right we can deal with her father. That would be excellent," she said.

In all my life I don't think I'd ever heard words that filled me with so much hope. Without answering, I pressed Munisé to my breast. The child kissed my hand and began to cry; "Mother, little mother!" she said.

As I write these lines, Munisé is sleeping on my bed, the cheerful glow of the fire quivering on her golden hair. Now and again she sighs deeply and gives a deep cough. Oh, if they give this child to me, how much happiness it will give me! Then I shall fear neither night nor storm, nor misery, nor anything in the world. I shall care for her with my own hands and make her happy. Once, I was mad enough to hope that for other children; but they died, those other children; they died, one evening, in each other's arms, in my heart.

But now I have made peace with life again, and everything delights me. Kâmran, it was you, one evening, who destroyed those unhappy children that I'd kept buried in my heart. Even so, tonight I feel less resentment for you than I did.

Zeyniler, 18th December

I shall probably not sleep tonight. For those who are happy, the nights are so long, just as they are for those who are sick. . . .

In the morning I went to the muhtar's house with Munisé. The old man thought I had come to ask for news of her. He began to comfort me: "She hasn't been found yet. But I still have hopes of one or two places." I recounted to him the events of last night; when I came to the end of my story, my heart was beating, my eyes were misty. I clasped my hands, as if I were going to ask for the most impossible thing in the world. "Give me this small child," I said. "Let me adopt her; let me take her to my heart. You can see that the poor child will be lost if she's left in their hands."

The muhtar closed his eyes and pondered for some time, pulling at his beard. Then he said, "Very well, my dear. You'll be doing a good deed."

"You mean you'll give me Munisé?"

"Her father's unable to look after the other children, anyhow. If he doesn't give her up, what's he going to do? If he's at all reluctant, we'll give him a few piastres."

I don't know how it was that I didn't go mad with joy at that moment. Had I ever imagined I'd get her so easily? I had thought the matter over for hours, since the evening before. I'd found answers to any objections they might make, and had, so to speak, prepared speeches in my mind, in order to move their hearts to pity. And if more were needed, I was going to give them a few odds and ends of jewels that had been left me by my mother. Could I possibly use them to better purpose, than by saving that poor little victim? But there was no need for any of it. Munisé was being left in my arms, like a toy that has come to life. I am not like other people. When I am very pleased and happy, I can't express my feelings in words. I feel I want to throw my arms round the neck of my companion, to rumple him and kiss him. That was the kind of danger the muhtar ran at the moment; and he only escaped it by simply having his wrinkled hand kissed by me.

Two hours later the muhtar arrived at the school, accompanied by Munisé's father. I had thought of the man as someone with an evil face, a frightening, oppressive kind of person. But, on the contrary, he was a little bit of an old fellow, sick and sorry. He told me he came from Istanbul, but for nearly forty years now he had not been home. He spoke of Aksaray and Sariyer hesitatingly, as though recounting a confused dream. He was willing to let me have Munisé; but I felt that he was really sorry for her. I promised I should do all I possibly could to make the child happy, and that I would always let him see her.

Zeyniler's poor dark school had never seen such a merrymaking and so much rejoicing in its life. I'm sure of that. The rooms and corridors couldn't contain the fun I had with Munisé. There came a cheerful twittering from the roofs, as though our laughter had aroused the birds that were sleeping in the eaves. Munisé adopted the character of a spoilt young lady in a few hours. There was a red woollen dress of mine that I could no longer wear; by shortening it slightly and taking it in, I made her a chic little suit. The sight of the child in that dress was like a draught of fresh water to me, or a sweet that melts in your mouth.

Although it was not snowing quite as heavily as it had done a day or so ago, it hadn't stopped. Before dusk, I had taken the child by the hand into the garden, and we had walked there, and run after one another, and played ball among the tombstones, until Hatije Hanim had come to light Zeyni Baba's lamps. Our happiness brought a smile even to the old woman's puckered face. "Come on now, get inside," she said; "you'll catch cold and be ill." But she beamed kindly at us all the same. Catch cold?—as though one could catch cold, with fires burning inside one!

This evening's sky looked to me like a tree that has spread its branches from west to east: a great jasmine tree that swayed slowly and dropped its white flowers over us.

Zeyniler, 30th December

I've become such friends with Munisé that the child takes all the time I have that's left over from lessons. I want to teach her all I know. Every day I give her one or two hours' French lesson, and indeed occasionally (with doors and windows shut) I teach her a little dancing—if they were to hear of it in the village, they would stone us! Now and then I feel inclined to laugh at myself; "Çalıkuşu, you're going to teach her everything. But Heaven protect her: you'll turn her into a Mirat—Hadji Kalfa's son," I say. This poor village child suddenly began to reveal the characteristics of the daughter of a good family. There was a pleasing refinement in her speech and in her manner. I'd been surprised at it at first; but now I begin to understand the reason. Munisé's mother was certainly not as common a creature as they had led me to believe. The child was extremely grateful to me. Sometimes, for no apparent reason, she would draw up to me and take my hands, and begin to touch my cheeks and my lips. Then I would take her delicate wrists in my hands, and kiss her small fingers one by one. The poor child didn't know that it was really she who was conferring a benefit on me; she thought it was a sacrifice on my part to have taken her in.

The child would say the most unexpected things. . . . On the second day after her arrival I told her, "Munisé, if you like, you can call me mother; that will be better."

She looked at me with a charming smile. "That would never do; I shall call you 'abla.'"

"Why not?"

"You're a child! How can I call you mother?"

Her words wounded my vanity. I warned her with one finger: "You're a little demon. Why should you call me young? I'm a grown-up woman, over twenty!"

Munisé looked at me with her tongue between her teeth without saying anything.

"Isn't it true? I'm a great big grown-up woman," I repeated.

She set her lips, like a grown-up person herself. "You're not so much older than I am, abla; only fourteen or fifteen."

I gave in, and began to laugh. Munisé was discomfited, and said shyly, "You will still be a bride, abla. I shall put ribbons in my hair, each side; I shall be beautiful like you. . . ."

I shut the child's mouth with my hand. "If you talk like that again, I shall cut off your tongue," I told her.

One of the child's characteristics was her delight in dress: she was very vain. I have never liked girls of that nature, but Munisé's way of dressing in front of a mirror and smiling at herself with pleasure was not without its charm. Yesterday, indeed, I caught her with the end of a burnt match in her hand. She was trying to blacken her eyes, in secret; the rascal! I wonder whom she learnt that from? It doesn't matter now: but in a few years' time, when she is a young girl, if she falls in love with someone and wants to marry him, it wouldn't do at all. When these thoughts come to my mind, I suffer the anxiety that all mothers feel over all girls; and yet I am pleased as well. Yesterday, Munisé asked me something, with a good deal of confusion. She wanted to have her hair done like mine. Here was the very thing I had begged of Heaven—that I should be able to play with Munisé as though I were playing with a doll. I took the small girl between my knees, loosened the tresses of her hair, and combed and brushed them as she wanted.

She took a small looking-glass that lay on the shelf: "Dear abla," she said, "come—let's both look at the mirror side by side." Like two sisters who were having their photograph taken, we put our heads together and laughed into the glass and stuck out our tongues at each other. With her dark blue eyes, her clear fair complexion and her sweet delicate face, Munisé was as lovely as an angel. But she didn't seem pleased. She tried to touch out my nose and my lips in the mirror.

"It's no good, abla," she said, "I can't look like you."

"All the better, child," I replied.

"I'm not beautiful like you, abla." She put her head nearer to mine, and with her small hand on my throat, this time she rubbed my cheek, and said, "Abla, you're like velvet: and one can see oneself in your face like a looking-glass."

I laughed at the silly child's nonsense, and rumpled her hair, which I'd taken so much trouble to arrange. But why should I conceal it? No one will read this diary but myself. I found myself prettier than I'd realised, and felt inclined to concede the truth to those who told me, "Feridé, there's something about you that's different from anyone else."

What am I saying? Oh, that little girl!—while I'm trying to bring her up to be a sensible child, she'll make me as vain as she is herself.

Zeyniler, 29ᵗʰ January

I've not touched my diary for a month. I have had more useful things to do than to write; besides, what is there to be written about days that are full of happiness? For a month now I have been living in a deep peace of soul. The pity is that it did not last.

Two days ago the mail van passed here and left four letters for me. No sooner had I seen them than a great conflict began in me. Without knowing from whom they were or what they contained, I said to myself, "I wish they had been lost on the way without my seeing them." I was not wrong in my first guess. I recognised the writing. The letters came from him.

The envelopes had passed from hand to hand before reaching me, and they were covered with blue and red writing and stamp marks. Before daring to stretch out my hand, I read the address on one of them: "To Feridé Hanim, teaching in the secondary school at the Headquarters at B. . . ." I crumpled the envelopes in the palm of my hand and threw them on to the shelf near the stove. Munisé saw me with my head leaning against the window, looking into the distance, plunged in thought.

"Abla," she said, "where have you got a pain? Your face is as white as a sheet."

I did my best to recover myself, and smiled at her. "There's nothing the matter with me, child. I've got a little headache. I'll come out into the garden with you for a while; it will soon go."

That night I lay sleepless for hours, with my eyes gazing into the darkness. I am weighed down by a great lack of decision; that heartless brute; who knows what he has dared to write me in those cruel, insolent letters? I lit my lamp more than once, in an impulse to read them. But I checked myself. To read them would be a degradation for me; an indignity.

Two days passed in the interval. The letters were still there. They were wearing me out in secret, and seemed to poison the air of the room. My persistent sadness had conveyed itself to Munisé. The poor girl knew where my grief came from, and she would look at the letters that were making me ill, with hatred and loathing.

This evening, I was sitting by the window, deep in thought. Munisé came up to me with some trepidation, and said with a nervous gesture, "Abla, I've done something: but I don't know—will you be angry?"

I turned round at once, and involuntarily my eyes went to the shelf near the stove. The letters were not there. Feeling choked me. "Where are they, Munisé?" I exclaimed.

The child hung her head, "I burnt them, abla. What could I do? You were so worried."

I gave a little cry, "What have you done, Munisé?" I demanded.

The child expected me to be very angry with her and to shake her by the shoulders, and she was trembling. I put my face in my hands and slowly began to cry.

"Don't cry, abla: I haven't burnt them. I spoke as I did on purpose. Then, if you hadn't minded, I should have burnt them after. Here they are: take them." The child was stroking my head with one hand, and trying, with the other, to make me take the letters. "Take them, abla. Perhaps they come from someone you love?"

I roused myself suddenly. "You naughty child!" I exclaimed, "What are you saying?"

"How am I to know, abla? Would you cry like that unless they were from someone you loved?"

I was ashamed of what the scrap of a child was saying, and I was ashamed of my tears as well. It was essential to put an end to the situation; after all, I had made my decision. "Child, I wish you hadn't spoken like that. But as you've said it, look here: I'll give you proof. The letters didn't come from anyone I loved. Come along: let's burn them together."

The room was dark; only a twig of brushwood which had begun to go out burnt more brightly at intervals. I threw one of the letters into the fire. The envelope began to curl up and burn. As it finished I threw in the second, and then the third. Munisé snuggled up to me with a feeling I couldn't understand. As the letters burnt one by one, we were silent, as

156

though confronted by someone about to die. When the turn came for the fourth, an unbearable pang of remorse overwhelmed me. But once the others were burnt I couldn't have left that one. As though I were tearing out a piece of my very heart, I threw in that one too, with deep disquiet. The last letter didn't catch fire immediately, as the others had; it emitted a thin smoke from one end, and began to burn invisibly. And then I saw the envelope had given way and opened, and that a page covered with fine writing had slowly begun to burn. I could bear it no longer; Munisé suddenly bent down, as though she knew what was going on in my heart, and, putting her hand into the fire, she saved a portion of the last letter.

It was only after I had put the child to bed that I dared to read it. Only these lines remained: "My mother began to cry the other morning, as she was looking at me. 'What's the matter, mother?' I asked. 'Why are you crying?' At first she didn't know what to say. 'It's nothing; I had a dream,' she said. I begged her and insisted, and in the end she had to tell me. Crying quietly, she gave me this explanation. 'I saw her in my dream; she was wandering in some dark place, and I said to the person I met 'Is Feridé there? For God's sake tell me.' A woman with her face veiled took me by the hand and made me go down into some dark place, rather like a chapel of the Dervishes. 'Here you are,' she said, 'Feridé lies here. She died of consumption.' I looked: and there my child lay, with her eyes closed. The colour of her cheeks had not even faded. And with the pain of it I woke up in tears. They say that if you dream of someone dead, you are bound to see that person in the flesh. Isn't that true? I shall soon see Feridé, shan't I, Kâmran?' I have written you my mother's actual words. Leave me on one side; but is it right to make this old woman weep still more? Your aunt's dream has been my dream since that day. Whenever I shut my eyes, it is you, in some remote country place—you, with your eyes closed, your dark hair and your fresh face. . . ." Here the piece of letter ended. It was just a description of my aunt's mourning for me. Kâmran, you can see that everything divides you and me. We are no longer even enemies; we are two strangers, who will never meet again.

Zeyniler, 5th February

Last night, very late, sounds of firing began to come from the direction of the swamp. I was afraid, but Munisé wasn't in the least disturbed. "It's always happening; gendarmes are chasing the brigands," she said. After the shooting had gone on at wide intervals for about ten minutes, it stopped. This morning we learnt the news. Munisé's guess had been right. An incident had taken place between a few ruffians who had been robbing the mail, and the gendarmes. One of the gendarmes had been killed; the other, severely wounded, had been brought to the guest room at Zeyniler.

It was towards midday when little Vehbi came to school, all out of breath. He seized my hand, and said "Teacher, put your çarşaf on quickly, and come along. They want you in the village guest room."

"Who wants me?"

"The doctor. Father said so."

I put on my çarşaf at once, and with Vehbi in front and I following, we went to the guest room. This was a ruined endowment consisting of two low rooms and a twisted corridor with some stone stairs. They provided shelter for those who couldn't continue their journey on account of darkness, or snow, or indisposition, and a little food as well, out of charity. I stroked the nose of a fine horse that was pawing the ground and breathing steamy clouds into the cold air; and went inside. The yard was so dark that they had a lamp burning. A stout military doctor with a thick overcoat and great big boots was seated on one of the steps, writing something down, and talking to several people in the yard whose faces I couldn't distinguish. I saw his face in profile. He had full white moustaches, and thick eyebrows, and a lively, likeable face. But Heavens! When the man spoke, what rough, even coarse, language he came out with! So much so, that it occurred to me for a moment to turn round and go back. He gave a loud laugh, which was a sure sign he was going to use bad language again, and then turned his head and saw me, and suddenly stopped.

"Ha, Captain!" he said to one of them, whose large black beard I could see against his brown jacket; "you must forgive me, but those who called you 'Clumsy' were a thousand times right. There's a woman with us; why don't you make me talk decently?" He turned to me: "Forgive me," he said, "I didn't see that you'd come. Go on up. But wait a moment: let me come down. These stairs are unsafe. They don't look as if they'd bear both of us at the same time. Here you are now, up you go. I'm coming."

I went up, two steps at a time. I could hear the old doctor going on teasing the man he'd called the Captain. "That teacher's from Istanbul, Captain. You wonder how I know, don't you? Ah, my dear Captain, have you never looked at anything in the world except with the vacant gaze of a sheep? I knew it by the way she went up those steps; did you notice how she hopped up?—like a partridge. And now, if you like, I'll tell you her age. The good woman isn't more than forty, whatever happens." That kind of crazy conversation has always amused me; I laughed to myself and said, "Ah! There you're wrong, doctor." Five minutes later the old doctor came up, making the stairs creak beneath him, and he began to talk, without looking directly at me.

"Madam, you know what's happened. We have a wounded man here. It's not serious; but it needs attention. I have to go directly—what's wanted is nothing but rest, but I'm afraid of contagion of the mouth and face. Confidence in doctors is slight, too; if they get an opportunity, people have recourse at once to some old wives' medicine. They stick all kinds of rubbish on the wound. You have been to school and college: I will explain to you what there is to be done. Until the good fellow gets on his feet again, you will look after him: but I don't know—can you stand it?"

"I can stand it, doctor. My nerves are good. I'm afraid of nothing, sir."

The doctor raised his head in surprise. "Come now, let's have a look at your face," he suggested.

There was so strange a sincerity in these direct words, that I raised my veil without any concern. Indeed, I laughed a little. The old doctor raised his arms; he started to laugh, with comic surprise in his simple face, and gusts of laughter. . . .

"What on earth are you doing in this place?"

Now I was embarrassed. I wondered if the man had seen me before somewhere. All the same, I wasn't afraid to get a little fun out of the situation. He had the sort of face that gave one a feeling of confidence and intimacy. "I don't think you can claim to know me, doctor."

"I don't know you personally, my dear, but I know the type. Yes, I know the type. Indeed, it's a type that's dying out in the world, I'm sorry to say."

"Like mammoths, you mean, sir?" The mischief that I'd had, perforce, to suppress in me for five months began to bubble up in me again. As Sister Alexei always said, it doesn't do to give me any encouragement. I get spoilt at once, and play the fool, mincing and slurring my words as small children do. The doctor, in any case, was a man who had seen a bit of the world and was a decent fellow. With the same loud laugh, he replied, "The very opposite of those large ugly elephantine monsters!—a slip of a girl: a cheerful, frank, nicely-dressed,

159

and I'm old enough to add—pretty—child! Tell me now, where have you tumbled here from?"

Under the rough talk and noisy laughter of this military doctor from town, I began to sense a delicate compassion. At last, trying to look serious, I answered, "I am a teacher, doctor. I wanted to be of service, and they sent me here. I don't mind where I go. I'll work wherever they want me to."

He was looking at me attentively as I spoke. "You mean you came here 'to render service'?—merely to serve education and the children of the country—is that so?"

"Yes, that's my purpose."

"At your age, and with your figure? Come, tell me the truth. Look me straight in the eyes; ah, that's right! Do you think I'm going to swallow all that?" He went on as though he could see right into my heart, with those white-lashed eyes smiling so sweetly above his plump cheeks. "No, that's not so. The real reason is elsewhere. And indeed it isn't a question of bread and butter. The more you try to conceal it, the more clearly I see. If I were to ask you who you are, your family, home, and so on, you wouldn't tell me, would you? I know, you see. There's a mystery here. I shan't go into it too deeply; a sign between us is enough."

We were both silent. The old doctor, after a few moments' thought, asked, "Will you allow me to do you a small service? Are you willing for me to get them to send you to a better place? I know a few people in the Education Department."

"No thank you. I'm quite content with my position."

He laughed again and shrugged his shoulders; and then said a little dryly, "All right; all right. But sacrifices of this kind can't be kept up by force. One of these days, if you've had enough of it, write me a couple of lines: let me give you my address. That's bare humanity."

"Thank you."

"Well that's done. Now let's see to our work. Let me explain what you have to do." He opened the door of one of the rooms. On a broken-down couch a poor fellow was lying; his body and face were covered with a military raincoat. "How are you, Professor—a bit more cheerful?" he asked.

The wounded man lifted the raincoat with his hand, and tried to move. "Don't stir: lie down. Have you got any pain?"

"No, thank God. Only my cheekbone hurts."

The doctor laughed again. "Ah, my beloved bears! He thinks his kneecap is his cheekbone. He imagines his stomach to be in the sole of this foot; but he terrorises those who confront him. It will pass, Professor. You'll feel nothing. Thank God that bullet didn't go a bit more to the left. Do you want to stand upright on your feet again within a week? If you say 'No, I'm comfortable here, let me rest a bit,' that's different. If that's how it is, you will do what this young lady tells you, do you understand? She's your doctor now; she'll change your dressing. If I hear that you've made a blunder, with the excuse that it's homemade medicine—it will be the worse for you, I can tell you. I shall come again, and cut your leg off—*gradually!*" He had begun to loosen the bandages. He probed the wound a good deal and made the poor fellow shout out "Help, help!" "Stop your noise, man. Aren't you ashamed, and you a man? A great big moustached fellow, aren't you ashamed to shout out in front of a slip of a girl? This isn't a wound, it's a pin-prick. If I knew that I should fall into the hands of a nurse like this, I'd get a harmless cut on some part of my body too."

The old doctor left the village an hour later with the bearded Captain. You can hardly imagine a more ordinary event, can you? And yet I don't know that I've ever been as inwardly moved by so strange and deep a feeling.

Zeyniler, 24th February

They say summer will be early this year. For a week now the weather has been clear. The world is full of light and sunshine. But for the snow on the hills, it might be May.

Today was Friday. After lunch I busied myself in my room with a watercolour drawing of Munisé. Suddenly there was a knock at the door: Hatije Hanim came in with her limbs trembling and her veil fallen on to her shoulders. I had never seen her in such a state of emotion and excitement.

"Oh God! Teacher—two gentlemen have come, downstairs. One seems to be the Director of Education; he's come to inspect. Do come down quickly! I'm afraid to talk to them."

I put on my çarşaf quickly, laughing to myself: "Those idle creatures who were too lazy to move hand or foot in their own rooms—so *they've* taken the trouble to come here! Unbelievable." Down below I was confronted by two men in front of the classroom door; one very tall, the other very short. While I was looking round for him, the short man

161

walked up to me. An eyeglass shone in his face, which I couldn't easily distinguish in the dark.

"Are you the teacher? I am honoured. I am Reşit Nâzim, Director of Education. What a dark place this is; it's not a school, it's really a kind of stable."

I opened the classroom door: "It's a bit lighter inside, sir."

He strutted in—such an arrogant walk for such a short figure. He took one step inside, and stopped short, waving his hand as though making a speech, to announce, "Mon cher, look at this. Quelle misère, quelle misère! You'd need a thousand witnesses to convince anyone that this was a school. We shall have to be ruthless. Once again you'll have to concede that I was right to say so. 'All or nothing.'"

I could see them better now. The Director of Education, whom I'd thought a youngster at first glance, a dandy, freshly turned-out, was really a clean-shaven man close on his fifties. His eye and eyebrow twitched incessantly; with every word he spoke he gave a new significance to his wrinkled face. As for the other, he was an unbelievably tall dark man, rather dry, with a slight moustache: so tall he seemed almost hunchbacked. The Director of Education turned to me again and said, "Madam, let me present my colleague, Mumtaz Bey, Public Works Engineer of the Province."

For the sake of something to say, I replied, "Really, sir? I'm delighted." The Director of Education was walking about, stamping his heels to test the power of resistance of the classroom and touching the benches and charts with the tip of his stick. "My dear, I have extensive plans. I shall pull everything down and rebuild entirely. Brand new establishments. If they don't give me the allocation I need, all the worse for them! I came fully prepared. The Istanbul Press is exactly in the state of a battery ready to open fire at the slightest sign from me. 'Bang, bang!' a dreadful bombardment. You understand?—either the world will materialise in this head of mine, or I'll give up my post."

I've no doubt that all this fine talk was to throw dust in my eyes, the poor village schoolmistress. He adjusted his eyeglass again and enquired, "How many pupils have you?"

"Thirteen girls and four boys, sir."

"A school for seventeen children! Amazing indulgence. Are you going to look at the building, Mumtaz?"

"No need; the evil's there for all to see." I noticed that while the Director of Education was speaking of his grandiose schemes, the

162

Engineer was looking at me out of the corner of his eye. Finally, so that I shouldn't understand, he said in very broken French, "I beg you, my dear, find a pretext to make this girl show us her face; its colour glows like fire under her veil. Where's she come from?"

The Director of Education wasn't what he seemed to be. He was annoyed at what his colleague had said, and answered him in still worse French: "I beg you, my dear, remember we're in school; be serious." He pulled the shrivelled skin under his chin like a piece of elastic, and considered. Suddenly coming to a decision, he turned to me. "Madam, I shall close the school."

I was much taken aback. "Why, sir, has something happened?"

"Madam, children cannot be taught in a vile building like this. And then the pupils are so few. As long as I remain in this province, I shall exert all my energies and do my best to put a great many of the villages in possession of a cheap, but well-equipped, sanitary, modern—in fact, a *new*—school. Now please give me a little information." He took a rather elegant notebook out of the pocket of his morning coat, asked for some details regarding the school, and made a note of them. Then, "As for you, Madam," he said, "I shall post you to another suitable place. When you get notice to close the school, you will come to Headquarters, and we'll do all that is necessary. Will you kindly tell me your name?"

"Feridé."

"Madam, there's an excellent practice in Europe, under which they add one's father's name. It makes a name more distinct. You teachers must make use of these innovations. For example, instead of inscribing your pupils in the register like this: 'Melâhat, *father* Ali Hodja,'—you will call them Melâhat Ali, and there you are. Do you understand, Madam?— And *your* father's name?"

"Nizamettin."

"We shall call you Feridé Nizamettin, Madam. The form will seem strange to you at first, but you'll get used to it. Where were you educated?"

I refrained from mentioning the name of the school, because if it became apparent that I knew French, perhaps the Engineer would be upset, on account of what he'd just said. So I simply said, "I was educated privately, sir."

"Well, as I said, when you come to Headquarters you will come and see me. We'll find a suitable post for you. Come on Mumtaz, we've still two villages on our programme."

163

Seated on one of the children's benches, swinging his long thin legs, the Engineer pestered him again in that beautiful French of his. "This is an exceptional little creature. You go and leave me. Whatever happens, I must find some way of getting her to uncover her face."

The Director of Education got into a state again; and in order not to convey anything to me, he said in Turkish, "We haven't time. You can write your report later. Come on." And he started off. The Engineer stood at the street door, and looked as though he were examining the roof and windows of the building; but he was waiting for me to come out into the daylight. I turned my head away obstinately, and pretended to be busy with something. As he crossed the garden, the good fellow turned his head once or twice, and when he was through the street door he kept to the wooden partition and raised himself on tiptoe now and again to look inside.

The news soon spread in the village. In spite of its being Friday, the children and their mothers ran to the school, and seemed very distressed at the proposal to close it. I was much touched that the children who, I'd thought, were strange and without feeling towards the school or myself, should weep and kiss my hands. Hatije Hanim wound a great band round her head and withdrew to her room. I, too, was going to find myself in a difficult situation, but to tell the truth it was she, poor soul, who was to be the real sufferer.

Towards evening the muhtar's wife and the midwife came to the school again. Both were distressed. As for the midwife, she looked significantly at me and sighed, adding "I had other hopes; but the good God didn't see fit to further them." I had to reciprocate these sentiments, with an assumed grief. "What can we do, midwife?" I replied, lowering my eyes, "it looks as though it wasn't to be my fate."

The fact is, that small gentleman with a monocle had turned Zeyniler upside down with one word. It was no good expecting the villagers to open their mouths. Although I knew that it wasn't possible to stumble on a worse village than Zeyniler, the prevailing emotion spread to me as well. Munisé was the only exception. That little villain flew about full of joy. "When shall we go, abla? Shall we go in two days' time?" she kept asking, hopping about with excitement.

Zeyniler, 3rd March
Tomorrow we take the road. Munisé was very delighted about it during the first days; but since yesterday, a strange absence of

cheerfulness has begun to show itself, and she now fixes her eyes on the distance, deep in thought, and answers my questions pensively. "Munisé, if you don't want to come with me, let me leave you behind," I suggested.

"God forbid, abla," she said at once. "I'd throw myself into the well."

"Is it that you're sad at parting from the others?"

"I'm not sad."

"In that case, do you want to see your father?"

"I'm sorry for my father, but I'm not so fond of him as all that, abla."

"Very well; then what's the trouble?"

She lowered her eyes and said nothing. If I insisted further, she'd pretend to laugh and put her arms round my neck. But I didn't believe in this false cheerfulness. As if I didn't know when she was really happy! All the same, I had always found a little melancholy in those bright child's eyes. I had tried so hard to make her tell me, but all my efforts had been in vain. Today, chance taught me the child's secret trouble. Munisé had disappeared for a short time, towards dusk. She knew, however, that I'd want her at that particular time. She was to help me with the preparations for the journey. I called her several times: no answer came. She was in the garden, no doubt. I opened the window and called out, "Munisé, Munisé!"

Her answer came faintly from a distance, from the direction of the tomb of Zeyni Baba: "Yes—coming."

When she reached me, I asked her what she had been doing, walking about alone there. She was embarrassed as she answered, and tried to take me in by producing meaningless excuses. I looked closely at her face. Her eyes were as red as could be: there were traces of freshly-dried tears on her cheeks, which were a little pale. I got impatient suddenly, and began to insist, to make her tell me what she'd been doing there, and why she was crying. With her hands in mine, she turned her head to keep her face hidden, and kept silent, with a slight trembling of the lips. I was determined to make her speak, at all costs; if she concealed the truth from me, I should leave her here, I said. She couldn't bear that. As though confessing a great sin, she said with her head bent, in shame, "My mother came to see me. She had heard I was leaving. Don't be angry, abla." And as she divulged this great sin, her whole body trembled, and her eyes filled with tears.

I understood; I understood the grief of that little heart so much better than the child had expected. I smoothed the hair that had fallen over her face, and slowly stroked her chin. In a low, steady voice I asked, "What is there to be afraid of and cry over in that? Isn't she your mother? Of course you want to see her." The poor little child still couldn't believe it, and looked fearfully into my eyes. She was searching for childish reasons to induce me to believe that she didn't love this woman of whom everyone spoke with malice and contempt. But she loved her so much, so closely. . . .

"Child," I said, "if you didn't love your mother, I should reproach you. Does one ever not love one's mother? Run off and bring her back. Say, 'My abla's very anxious to see you.' I'm coming to the tomb."

Munisé wound her arms round my knees, and kissed my skirt; then she ran off hard into the garden. I knew that what I had done was very incautious. If they hear that I have talked to that woman, they will say cruel things, and perhaps remember my name with malediction. Well, let them. . . .

I waited a long time for them, beyond the little sepulchre in a group of trees. The woman must have gone some distance. Munisé must have had to run to the other side of the reeds to turn her back. At last they appeared. To see them coming along together, mother and child, was so sad a thing—so sad. . . . They were walking apart, as though they were withdrawing from one another, out of shame, and came along slowly, making out that the mud was hindering them. I had prepared myself to say something full of love and compassion to the woman. But I don't know how it was, when we confronted each other I found nothing to say.

She was a tall, elegantly made woman. On her shoulders she had an old mended çarşaf, and over her face instead of a veil a piece of dark violet muslin. The shoes on her feet were soaked and torn, with the heels scratched. I could see that she was trembling, as though she were afraid of someone. Trying as far as possible to appear calm and unembarrassed, I said, "Do unveil your face." After a slight hesitation, she lifted her veil. It was clear that she was young, at the most thirty or thirty-five. But her fair face was so tired and so worn. . . . I had always known women of that kind being very much painted. But there wasn't a trace of paint on her face. The thing that touched me most was her resemblance to Munisé. It suddenly dawned on me: when Munisé grows up and reaches the same age . . . then. . . . With an involuntary movement I took the child by the shoulders and drew her to my knees. I took a deep breath: my eyes filled. I had taken a great responsibility upon myself. But I would go through with it, and bring Munisé up to be a woman of good moral character. This shall be the greatest consolation of my life.

As though she were thinking too of the things that were passing through my mind, I said to her, "I know that fortune hasn't seen fit to give you the pleasure of bringing up this little girl yourself. What are we to do? The world is like that. I want to tell you this—that you may feel content. I've taken her to my heart. I shall bring her up as though she were my own child. I shall deprive her of nothing."

She had the courage, now, to speak for the first time. "I know it, lady. Munisé has told me. I used to come and see her, now and again when I came this way. May God reward you."

"You mean you've been seeing Munisé?" I could feel that Munisé had begun to tremble again; her small arms were around my waist. She had been taken in a fresh offence. This meant that she'd been seeing her mother secretly. And what was sadder, for some reason she had been ashamed to tell the woman that she had concealed the meetings from me. "If we had remained here, I should have let you see the child at any time you wanted," I told her. "However, tomorrow we are going to B. After that I don't know where I shall go. Set your heart at rest: I don't say I shall be a mother to her, because nothing can take the place of a real mother. But I shall try to be a good elder sister." We saw that a man was walking about in the reeds below; it was the father of my pupil Jafer Ağa. He used to come to the swamps constantly, for duck shooting. Munisé's mother was suddenly upset.

"Let me go, young lady," she exclaimed, "they mustn't see me with you." The words showed that the unhappy woman had a sensitive spirit. In fact, I'd already discerned that, from her condition, her attitude, and the expression on her face. My first guess was right. It was from her mother that Munisé had inherited the delicacy and good breeding both of her face and of her nature. The concern shown by the woman to protect me from talk touched my pride. I didn't want to part from her without leaving her with a good impression. To show that I attached no importance to gossip, I asked, "Why are you hurrying away? Won't you stay a little longer?" The poor woman looked at my hands with gratitude; her lips were trembling to kiss them. But it was obvious that she didn't dare to touch me. We sat on the trunk of a frail poplar which the last storm had uprooted; and we took Munisé between us.

Now it was the other's turn to speak. Poor soul! She spoke with so much urgency and in such a seemly way, it was as if she were seeking relief by explaining her life to me. . . . The woman had a simple but tragic life story. She was born at Istanbul, in Rumelikavak. Her father, a minor official, and her mother, died one after the other, and she was given to a good family in Bakirkoy, as an adopted child. She grew up with the children of the house and was treated almost as a young lady. When she reached the age of fifteen or sixteen, good opportunities of marriage began to come her way; but she didn't accept any of them, and found some excuse every time; because she had a lover—the young master of the house, a young man whose moustaches were hardly visible, who was attending the military college. True, she had no hope; come what may, she knew she was only a little foster-child. But she was glad enough, at the time, to see his face and to hear his voice at the beginning of the week. Just at that time the master of the house was appointed Treasurer at B., and the family migrated there, with all their belongings, leaving only the boy at the military college at Istanbul. The four months she spent without seeing the young man drove her nearly out of her mind, as though it were four years of separation; and finally, when he joined his family for the summer holidays . . . After a short time, the affair became known. The master of the house and his wife and the young ladies rose against her together, and, unwilling to have her in the house any longer, sent her to an old woman in a nearby village. Munisé's elder sister, who died of diphtheria when she was four, was born there. In the circumstances, who would be likely to take in such a girl, with a child on her hands? At last, wretched with misery, she consented to marry an old forestry official. She said nothing about the early days; she seems to have been content with her fate. But after her husband had settled down at Zeyniler, she was oppressed with an unbearable weight of boredom. She felt stifled in her dark surroundings, and grew paler and wasted away from day to day. While the poor woman was relating all this, a weariness came over her body and her eyes, as though she could still see herself in that heavy darkness. Well, it was just at that time that a gendarmerie patrol came to the village in pursuit of some brigands. For two or three weeks the young officer of the gendarmes, who had pitched his tent on the opposite side of the reeds, began to pursue her. The devil tempted the woman: she left her husband and children, and went off with the officer.

This simple tale somehow affected me deeply. Evening was approaching; I began to walk towards the school, leaving Munisé alone with her mother. At the moment of parting, these two beings who would never see each other again, might have something to say to each other. They couldn't embrace each other and weep while I looked on, and the pain of parting would have been with them forever. As I clambered over the gravestones and returned to the school, I pondered deeply: "Munisé, I always pitied you and loved you because of your being left alone in the world. All the same, at this moment, I envy you. I envy your mother, a wretched fallen woman, but for all that a mother. When you leave the place where you were born and grew up, you will carry with you the memory of a mother's glance in your eyes, and the bitter joy of a mother's tears on your lips."

B., 5ᵗʰ March

I filled my case this morning with the papers I had brought with me from the village of Zeyniler, and went to the Education Department. I left Munisé asleep. It was early: the offices were just being opened. The officials, who came in by ones and twos, were drinking coffee and smoking their hookahs rather sleepily. In place of the chief clerk with the red belt, there was now a gentleman sitting there with a black curly beard and a greasy collar. I asked one of the messengers: he said that the Director of Education and the chief clerk were now changed, and it would be necessary for me to see the bearded gentleman.

I approached him and made my salaams. I told him I was the teacher of the school at Zeyniler which had been closed on the Director's orders, and that I had come to hand over the school records. The chief clerk thought a bit. "Ah, yes," he said, "Very well. Wait a little while outside till the Director comes."

I had to wait for the Director exactly three hours, in the dark low vestibule of the office. Those who go to and fro in such places look closely at one, and there were some of them, indeed, who made remarks as well. A broken ladder was leaning against the edge of one of the windows; I made a temporary seat of one of the steps of it and began to wait. The window looked out on to the yard of a tumbledown seminary. A theological student with blue baggy trousers and sleeves rolled up was cleaning vegetables by the side of the fountain; sparrows were playing about in a great plane tree whose branches came right into the window at which I was sitting. With my elbows on my knees and my chin in my hands, I was deep in thought. Yesterday morning at that hour, I hadn't yet left Zeyniler. Big and little, all my pupils had come as far as the carriage road over the steep rocks, to wish me God-speed. What a shameless heart I have. How quickly I get to love the people around me! My uncle would take me by the hands now and then, and say, "Ah, my

169

importunate girl: first you look on one as a stranger and run away; then you stick to one like the resin of a tree." The good man was right. I loved all those children, some for their beauty, some for their ugliness, and some because they were poor. Now if I could leave a bit of my heart in every place I left behind, how satisfactory! Poor little wretches: each one kissed my hand. Mehmet the shepherd and Zehra sent me a newly-born kid. The kind fellow's present touched my heart. The dear little creature still hadn't got its eyes open: I put it into Munisé's arms. To the doleful bells of the carriage, we left Zeyniler further and further away. Munisé and I waved our handkerchiefs to the children behind us until they were lost to sight among the blackened rocks.

The carriage drew up at the door of the hotel at a moment when Hadji Kalfa was rather curiously engaged. The old man was driving off a great cat, that flew out of the door with a piece of liver in its mouth. He had the stem of a hookah in his hand as if it were a stick, and was shouting out, "You wait—you villain of a cat—I'll have the skin off you!" I called out "Hadji Kalfa!" as he passed me. He didn't grasp, at first, where the voice came from: he stopped, and no sooner did he see me in the carriage than he raised his arms and shouted as loud as his voice could carry, "Ah, my little teacher—bless her two eyes!"

The old fellow's pleasure was worth seeing. To the cat which was trying to climb the wall of a ruined building opposite, he called out cheerfully, "Go ahead and take your fill of it. Don't hurry—you're welcome to it!" And then he came up to me. Hadji Kalfa was so delighted, that it was only on the second floor of the hotel that he noticed Munisé, who was following me with the kid in her arms. "Hullo teacher—and who is this? Where does she come from?" he asked.

"My little girl, Hadji Kalfa," I said. "You hadn't heard that I married in Zeyniler, and now I've got a little girl?"

Hadji Kalfa stroked Munisé's chin and retorted, "'Never consider what a man says: consider what makes him say it.' That too may happen, with the help of God. What a girl, though! She's worthy of what you say. She's wonderful."

By a happy chance my blue bird room was empty again. I was very glad. In the evening Hadji Kalfa took me off to his home, by force; I made an excuse that I was tired and didn't want to go, but the old man pretty nearly ordered me. "Look here, you could walk for six months, and not even harm your complexion. Make up your mind to it."

All this was delightful and very satisfactory. But there was another matter that made me thoughtful. Last night before going to bed I made a calculation, with the strangest result. I couldn't believe it: I did the sum again on my fingers. Unfortunately, it was true; but although the result was a most unpleasant one, I couldn't help laughing. Up to now, thanks to my efforts and my work, I thought I'd managed to make both ends meet. In fact, however, I'd done nothing but spend the little money I had in my possession. My poor old servant Gülmisal had told me I shouldn't go to a strange part of the country without having a substantial sum of money by me, and she had sold one of my mother's diamonds and handed the money over to me in a separate purse. Since then I had had many expenses. Yes, it was a fact; I'd remained unemployed so long, and then my travelling expenses had amounted to a great deal. In addition, I hadn't borne in mind that I was only a poor village schoolteacher: whenever I came across someone hungry or miserable, I felt it my duty to give him some little help. But men are really very merciless creatures: taking courage from my soft-hearted appearance, the open hands around me had increased very much lately. . . . Of course my monthly salary (the amount of which I don't know even today) couldn't have met all my needs. Worse still, I hadn't yet succeeded in getting the last two months of it. Confronted, then, with these unusual expenses, I had dipped into the purse whenever I was in difficulty. But now the poor little bag had got so light that I didn't dare count what remained in it. This meant that in spite of all my five months' adventures and all my weariness, it was still the help of my family that had kept me alive. I fingered the leaves of the plane tree that came in through the window, and felt like laughing and crying at the same time, as I thought it over. But once again I managed to discover some consolation for myself. "Don't worry, Çalıkuşu. Even if you've earned nothing, haven't you learnt, anyway, what it is to be independent, and to live and to suffer? Isn't that of some value? Come! From now on you'll give up your childishness and become a grown-up woman," I told myself.

While I was meditating in this way, there was a sudden stir in the dark corridor. An old servant with an overcoat in one hand and a walking-stick in the other was hurrying towards the Director of Education's room. A few minutes later I saw the little form of the Director himself, erect and arrogant, with his monocle gleaming, come up the stairs. I was about to enter the room after him; but the servant who had been carrying the Director's hat and stick just before, planted himself in front of me.

171

"Wait a minute, woman! Let the Director get his breath. What's your hurry? How did you manage to wait nine months in your mother's womb?" he scolded me. I had gradually got used to this kind of treatment, so I wasn't upset. On the contrary, I urged him in a quiet voice, "Now, old dear, when your master's had his coffee, let him know: say 'the teacher you were expecting has come.'"

The Director of Education was *not* expecting me. But if I were to say that, I thought the old servant would perhaps get even more exercised. What is one to do?—one has to learn duplicity of this kind. The old servant came out of the room again in a few minutes; he didn't distinguish me at once in my black çarşaf, and began to call out, "Where's that woman? Good God, she rushes a man off his feet and then she clears off!"

"Don't be angry; here I am. Shall I go in?"

"Come on; go inside. Good luck to you."

The Director, with his head bare, was seated at his desk with a great big cigar at his lips, and was saying something in a sharp aggressive tone that one would hardly have expected from his small frame, to an individual who was buried in an armchair in a corner. "Sir, what a country, what a country! They spend a fortune, and don't have a single visiting-card printed for themselves. The servant comes to the door, and brings you news that eighty people want to see you. The messenger can't pronounce their names correctly, and confusion arises. In an office, I'm in favour of the system of mad Peter. One should pursue officials not only in their official lives but in their private lives too. One should have a say in what they eat and drink, the places where they sit or walk about, and the clothes they wear. No sooner had I come than I sent a circular to the schools. They were not to shave at a mirror less than once in two days; and I said that teachers whose trousers were not pressed and whose shirts were without collars should be dismissed. Yesterday I was going to inspect one of the schools; in front of the door I ran into a teacher: I pretended not to recognise him. 'Go and tell the teacher that the Director of Education has come,' I said; 'Sir I am the teacher,' he answered. 'No: you must be a servant. You can't be a teacher dressed like that. If I were to come across a teacher dressed as you are, I would take him by the arm and throw him into the street.' The fellow stood there frozen to stone; I didn't look behind me; I went straight in. Now tomorrow I shall go to the school again. If I see that man in the same condition, I shall dismiss him at once."

I was waiting for the Director to stop, so that I could begin my story. But he had no such intention. He continued to let off steam irrepressibly. "Yes, sir. I recently sent a circular to the school; 'Men and women teachers must have visiting-cards printed at all costs. Applications to the Department without a card will not be accepted' I said. But who takes any notice?" And suddenly he turned to me with a stern demeanour. "I mention it because this teacher too has received that circular. But in spite of that, she makes her application again without a card. The messenger's voice breaks in again with the same refrain: 'I think you sent for a woman: she's come.' *Who* has come? An unknown character."

I was petrified. Evidently all these expostulations and all this anger were directed at me, because I'd elected to come in without a card! "I never received any orders from you, sir," I managed to say.

"How's that? Where were you, teacher?"

"You came last week—I'm the mistress of the school at Zeyniler. You ordered the school to be closed."

The Director of Education raised one eyebrow in thought. "Ah, yes. I remember now. What have you done? Is all the procedure completed?"

"As you ordered, sir, and I've brought you the records you asked for."

"Good. Hand them over to the chief clerk; let him examine them."

The chief clerk with the dirty collar interrogated me for exactly two hours. He cast his eyes over the papers time after time; sundry vouchers, documents of evidence, demand notes. He asked a whole number of things I didn't know, and objected to the reports I had brought from the village Council of Elders. And when I expressed my surprise, now and then, he started abusing them and saying, "Do you call those people Hodjas?"

He nearly reduced me to tears over the stamp of a document which had been cancelled by mistake. Then he brought up another question. I don't know how many years ago, they had sent two-hundred-and-fifty piastres to the schoolmistress, to have the roof mended. Apparently her receipt was not there. "Why was the account for this sum not presented? Where's the receipt? If you can't find it you'll be taken to Court," he said, and got very agitated. "Sir, don't say that; not even six months have passed since *I* went there," I said, almost in tears. But I couldn't make him understand. In the end he exclaimed, "Oh, God! I can't put up with a mess like this. I haven't the time to lose my reason over it," and took the papers in to the Director of Education.

173

Çalıkuşu

In the room where I was, there were still two other clerks; one of them had not yet grown a moustache; the other wore a turban. They appeared to be very busy at their writing-tables with their work, and to be taking no notice of us. But when the chief clerk went out of the room in a rage, the two young men jumped up from their places at once, and put their ears to the door that led to the Director's room, and began to listen. But they might have saved themselves the trouble. Two minutes later, the Director could be heard beginning to shout in a voice that was audible not only from our room, but probably from the street as well. The turbaned clerk clapped the other one on the back with delight. "Heaven bless you, Director! Go on, give him a good scolding. A swine like that needs bullying."

The Director was saying to the chief clerk, "I'm sick of you, sir! What sort of a love of formalism is this? What sort of a stuffy bureaucrat's mentality is this? The woman is right, the woman is right! These vouchers cover years: after all, she can't have been responsible for *them*. If you don't understand, go! Leave the place and go. You can go as far as you like. If you don't go of your own accord, I shall send you. Ah—! Write out your resignation at once. If you don't, you're not a man worth the name."

I felt I was going to have a stroke. "Oh dear!" I exclaimed. "Oh dear, gentlemen," I said to the clerks, "without intending it, perhaps I am the cause of this disaster. Let me go—don't let him see me when he's in a rage. Perhaps he will do something dreadful."

The turbaned clerk was ready to jump for joy. "No, no, comrade," he said, "don't take any notice—the wretched fellow deserves it all. If only a more insolent fellow than himself would come along now and then, and give him a good lesson! There's no pleasing him—he's a swine, with the hide of an elephant! Bless you, after this scolding, he'll calm down for a day or two and sit back a bit—and give himself a bit of peace, and us too."

The voices had ceased. The clerks ran back to their desks at once. Hafiz Efendi was muttering something to himself: "There's a saying—'It takes a man without religion to deal with a man without faith.'" The chief clerk entered, his legs and his beard quivering; without turning his head, he scanned the two clerks with a sidelong glance, like a girl looking at someone out of the corner of an eye. But they were working so peacefully and quietly that he was reassured, and sat down at his desk again. But he couldn't work. After puffing and panting several times, he slowly began to speak: ". . . Worthless fellow—fifty years of age, and he's been in

174

so many different posts that he hasn't the sense of our head messenger. He'll be out of here tomorrow. . . . Yes; mark my words, one of these days we'll have an inspector upon us, running his eye over the accounts and saying, 'Oh, these fellows! Are you all idiots? Why hasn't a receipt been made out for this two-hundred-and-fifty piastres? Why haven't you spotted this error in the accounts with your own eyes?'—if the fellow brought us all up before the Court, he'd be right. Can one play fast and loose with the Imperial Treasury? By God, if we were to die and disappear, they'd get this money out of our dependents in a hundred years' time, if necessary!"

The clerks had raised their heads from their registers and were listening to these deep sayings with respectful attention. The chief clerk, finding the atmosphere a favourable one, inquired, "Did you hear the nonsense that fellow was talking?"

Hafiz looked up in astonishment: "Oh, we heard a voice, but we didn't know it was addressed to you."

"Partly to me; an intolerably pedantic fellow."

"Never mind," said Hafiz, "they know nothing about office procedure in there. If it were not for your Excellency, this office would be upside down in three days." It was Hafiz who was speaking—Hafiz, who had been pleased as a child, a few minutes back, at the way the chief clerk was being insulted. What strange creatures they are! All the same, the turbaned clerk's suggestion proved fairly effective. The chief clerk seemed to be considerably softened, and much calmer after the storm. He lit a cigarette, and puffed the smoke on either side of him. "Well, there it is," he said, "has anyone served this country and ever been thanked for it?" After which, without worrying me further, he took over the documents at once.

Soon after, I entered the Director's room for the second time to complete my business; my knees were trembling with weariness, and my eyes were heavy. The Director was now defending a fresh cause. With considerable display of bad temper, he was making the messenger remove the dust in the room, altering the place of the pictures on the walls, and every now and again examining his hair and his tie in a small hand mirror. The few words which passed between him and the old gentleman in the corner explained to me the reason for all these preparations. Pierre Fort, a French journalist, had come to the town. The Director of Education had made his acquaintance and that of his wife at a dinner party given by the Governor of the Province the night before.

175

Çalıkuşu

Pierre Fort seemed to be a very interesting man. In his paper, he had written a series of articles under the title of "A Few Days in green B." The Director was explaining with enthusiasm, "Today at three o'clock, husband and wife promised to call on me. I shall show them a few of our schools. True, we haven't got a single school about which we can boast much to a European; we shall have to do a little window-dressing. I'm hoping we shall get a good write-up, anyway. Thank God I am here; if the visit had taken place in my predecessor's time, we should have been put to shame before this European, and he'd have cleared off."

I was still waiting by the door in a fold of the screen. "What do you want again, woman?" he demanded.

"The accounts are finished, sir," I replied.

"Good. Thank you."

A pause.

"Thank you; you can go."

"You will have further orders for me? About a new post?"

"Yes; but at the moment I have no vacancies. When a vacancy occurs we'll do something. Have your name registered in the office." The Director of Education spoke quickly, in a sharp voice; he was waiting for me to withdraw at once, and go. "When a vacancy occurs. . . ." I had heard those words very often in the Ministry of Education in Istanbul, and knew them well, alas. The Director's irritable voice aroused a strange feeling of rebellion in me. I made one step towards the door, in order to go, but at that moment a vision came before my eyes—the vision of Munisé playing with her kid, and waiting for me, in our room at the hotel. Yes, I was the old Feridé no longer. I was almost a mother, with serious responsibilities. I turned round again, and bowed my head like some poor person putting out his hand in the rain to people passing in the street. With a frightened supplicating note in my voice, I said, "Sir, I can't afford to wait. I'm afraid to mention it, but I'm in difficult circumstances. If you don't find work for me at once. . . ." I couldn't say anything more. My throat was choking with despair and shame, and my eyes filled with tears.

With the same capricious and excited gesture, he replied "I've told you woman; I've no vacancy. There's only a village school at Çadirli—but that's not my affair. They say it's a dreadful place. The children seem to be taught in the village café. There's nowhere for the teacher to stay, either. If it suits your purpose, I'll appoint you, but if you want anything better, you'll have to wait. . . . Come on, now, madam, I'm waiting for your answer."

I had heard myself that this Çadirli was a worse place than Zeyniler. But to accept would be better than to drag on an existence here for months, and be subject to all kinds of insults. I nodded my head and said in a whisper, "All right: I must accept."

But the Director of Education didn't hear my answer. Because at that moment the door suddenly opened, and someone outside called out, "They're coming." The Director of Education buttoned up his frock-coat and dashed through the doorway. Nothing remained for me to do but to withdraw and go; but just as I was about to pass through the door, I heard him say in French, "Come in, I beg you."

First, in came a young woman dressed in a thick overcoat. When I saw her face, I couldn't restrain a slight cry of surprise: the journalist's wife was one of my old school friends, Christine Varez. Christine, one holiday, had gone to France with her family, and there she had married one of her cousins, a young journalist; and she hadn't returned. My friend had changed almost beyond recognition, in a few years. She was now a serious-looking grown-up woman. When she heard my voice, she turned her head, and in spite of the thick veil over my face she recognised me at once.

"Çalıkuşu, my little Çalıkuşu—you here! Oh, what luck!" Christine had been one of the friends who loved me most. She took me by the hands and drew me into the middle of the room, and then insisted on drawing up my veil, and began to kiss me on the cheeks. I don't know what impression this made on her husband, whom I'd not yet succeeded in seeing, and still more on the Director of Education. My back was turned to them: I hid my face on my friend's shoulder, not to show the tears in my eyes. "Ah, Çalıkuşu, I might have thought of anything else, but I should never have expected to find you here, with a black Turkish çarşaf and tears in your eyes!"

I pulled myself together slowly; I wanted to lower my veil again with a discreet gesture, but she prevented it. Forcing me round to look at her husband, she said, "Pierre, let me introduce you to Çalıkuşu." Pierre Fort was a tall man, fairly good-looking, with light chestnut hair; but a bit free-and-easy—or was it that by dint of living so long among correct people who weighed their words that he gave me that impression? The journalist kissed my hand as though talking to an old friend: "Mademoiselle, I am very pleased to make your acquaintance; you know

177

we're not strangers at all—Christine has talked so much about you. . . .
Indeed, I should have recognised Çalıkuşu, even if she hadn't introduced
us. There's a group photograph of you all, pupils and teachers together.
You've got your chin on Christine's shoulder. You see how well I know
you?"

They seemed to have entirely forgotten the Director, and had begun
to talk to me instead. For a moment I happened to turn my head: what I
saw would have made me shout with laughter, if I'd been anywhere else.
A few strangers had come in, as well as the guests. They formed a semi-
circle around us, with the Director in front, in the middle; their mouths
were inches open with surprise, like villagers intent on an interesting
conjuring trick, as they watched me talking in French. Funnier still,
amongst them was the Municipal Engineer. I gathered afterwards that
this gentleman was acting as a guide to the visitors. The poor fellow had
got his wish at last!—he'd seen my face. All the same, if he happened to
recall the words he'd said about me in French to the Director of
Education in the village, he must have felt a little bit embarrassed.

Anyway, there it was. It had hurt my pride to reveal myself to one of
my old school friends in such a condition; but unwilling to add to it an
impression of moral ignomiy as well I went on talking in a clear voice,
with my customary assurance and cheerfulness. The Director of
Education saw the humour of the situation. Inclining his little body in
an ironic bow, he said, "I beg you, do sit down; don't disturb yourself."
There was no longer any question of my going away. I said slowly to
Christine "I'm going to beg you to let me go now;" but she stuck to me
like glue, and nothing would make her let go of me. The Director of
Education noticed my friend's insistence. This man who had treated me
so coldly and ruthlessly such a little while ago, was now bowing to me
and offering me an armchair. "Madam, don't remain standing, I beg of
you," he insisted. I had no alternative, and sat down.

Christine still couldn't make out how she'd found me here with an
old-fashioned çarşaf on my shoulders. "You don't know, Pierre," she told
her husband, "what an interesting girl Feridé is. She belongs to one of
the most aristocratic families of Istanbul, and she has so fine an
intelligence, and such a lovely character . . . ! I'm so surprised to see her
here."

I felt both pleased and confused to hear her praise me. Now and
again my eyes met the Director's; the poor man hadn't yet got over it.
And that impertinent Engineer! He had ensconced himself in a corner of

the room, and was staring at me. Of course I didn't look at him: but just as one sometimes has a sort of creepy feeling, as though an insect were walking over one's face, I had the feeling, without looking at him, that his eyes were straying over my face like an insect. In order to allay Christine's curiosity, I had to give some kind of explanation.

"There's not really anything to be surprised at. Everyone's keen about something, and I'm keen about teaching. It was my own choice—I wanted to work in this province and serve the children of the place. I'm content with my lot, and in any case it's not such a dangerous enterprise as starting on a journey round the world in a sailing-boat. I'm surprised you can't bring yourself to look on it as something quite natural."

"I understand, mademoiselle," said M. Pierre Fort loudly with a gesture of comprehension. "And no doubt Christine too can understand very well such fine impulses of the soul. But she hasn't been able to get over it all at once. The conclusion I draw from this is that there is in Istanbul a set of modern young girls who have had a good European education: they belong to an entirely different generation from the generation which destroyed itself with useless melancholy like 'Les désenchantées' of Pierre Loti. They prefer action to empty dreams, and they'll give up their prosperity and happiness in Istanbul, to come and arouse Anatolia, on their own initiative. What a beautiful and lofty example of renunciation!—and for me, what an exceptionally good subject for an article! I shall, with your permission, mention your name in connection with 'the Awakening of the Turks,' Mlle. Feridé Çalıkuşu!"

"Christine," I said in alarm, "If you let your husband insert my name in the paper, my friendship with you is over."

Pierre Fort misunderstood my desire to conceal myself. "This modesty is very beautiful, mademoiselle," he said, "the wishes of a young lady like yourself must be obeyed. May I ask which of the schools here has been fortunate enough to have you for a teacher?"

Didn't I say so? Now the worst had happened! I turned to the Director of Education and said in Turkish, "Where was the school you offered me? Was it Çadirli Village?"

Pierre Fort had a look at his notebook. "Wait a minute, please, what did you call it? Çagirla or Çanirli? Mademoiselle, if we get an opportunity in the course of our tour of the Province, we shall visit you in your lovely village among your pupils."

The Director of Education got up from his seat, scarlet in the face. "Mademoiselle Feridé insists on a post as a village teacher. But I'm convinced that she can render greater services as French teacher in the Teachers' College here at Headquarters." I looked at him, not understanding what he said. He gave me his explanation in Turkish. "You hadn't told me you were a graduate of a French school and knew French. That being so, the situation is quite altered. I shall now notify the ministry about you; and until your order of appointment comes, you will work in a supernumerary capacity. You should begin work tomorrow morning; is that all right?"

I was not unaware of the fact that life always gives some joy after a disaster, and that, as the beautiful proverb says, "if the first fifteen days of the month are unlucky, the remaining fifteen are sure to be lucky." But I should never have believed that the moon would rise like this after so profound a darkness, and after a moment so devoid of hope. Munisé came before my eyes once more; but this time, not like a poor child playing with her little kid in the room of a hotel, but as an elegant young thing turning cartwheels in the flower-garden of some superb house.

When we were about to part, Christine drew me into a corner: "Feridé, I was going to ask you—why didn't you get married?"

No reply.

"You don't answer. Where is your fiancé now?"

I bent my head and said very slowly "I lost him last Autumn."

Christine was much affected by this answer. "What, Feridé? Are you telling the truth?" she asked. "Oh poor Çalıkuşu . . . ! Now I know what wind it was that blew you here." Her hands were trembling as they held my wrists. "Feridé, you loved him very much, didn't you? Don't conceal it from me, child—you never would admit it, but everyone knew that." Her eyes thoughtful, and her voice full of warmth, as though she were pursuing a far-off dream, Christine continued: "You're right—it wasn't possible not to love him. He came several times to see you, and I remember seeing him then. He had an expression that was unlike anyone else's. How tragic! I'm very sorry for you, Feridé: I think there's no greater disaster for a young girl than to see the death of the fiancé she loves."

When you said it, I lowered my eyes and closed them, and said "You are quite right." In the circumstances, what else *could* I say? I told you a lie, Christine. I know a tragedy still greater for a young girl. Young girls who see their lovers die are not so much to be pitied as you believe. They have one great consolation; after months and years have passed, when they are alone at night in a dark, cold room in some unknown place, they can still call their lover's face to mind. They have the right to say, "The last glance of those pitiful eyes was mine." They can kiss the face of his image in their hearts. But I am denied that right, Christine.

B., 9ᵗʰ *March*

I began work this morning in the Teachers' College at B. I believe I shall soon get fond of this place. But after Zeyniler it would be a shame to say I didn't like it. My new colleagues don't look too bad; and my pupils are very near to me in age. Indeed, I should think some of them are older than I am, grown-up women. Ah! And there's a turbaned Director named Rejep Efendi who is amusing. When I came to the school the assistant mistress took me straight to the Director's room, and begged me to wait, saying that Rejep Efendi had gone to the Department, and would come soon. I waited nearly half-an-hour for him, partly looking out of the window at the recreation ground, and partly trying to read the confused writing in the charts on the walls. At last he came. He had been caught in a shower on the way, and his long black coat was wet through. When he saw me in the room, he said, "Welcome, my dear. I've just been notified by the Department. May God have favour on us all." His round face was encircled by a round beard, beginning to go white, and his cheeks were red as apples; his eyes squinted, so that he looked everywhere at once. He studied the water that was running off him.

"Dear, dear," he said, "may God punish me—I forgot to take my umbrella. You see what's befallen me. 'The feet have to bear the miseries of a thoughtless head,' they say, but this time it's my coat that has suffered. Excuse me, my dear. I'll dry myself a bit." He had begun to take off his overcoat; I got up and said, "Sir, don't let me inconvenience you: I'll come later," and prepared to leave. But he urged me to sit down again, with a wave of his hand. "No, no. What formality need there be between us? I might be your father." He was wearing a yellow satin shirt or waistcoat. (If you looked at the collar you'd call it a shirt; at the pockets, a waistcoat.) He drew a chair up to the stove and sat down; and as he warmed the soles of his big leather boots, which had nails in them like those in a horse's hoof, he began to talk to me. He had a strange voice, that sounded to the ear like some metal struck with a hammer, and pronounced all his K's like G's.

Çalıkuşu

"You're a mere child, my dear." (This was the remark I heard on all sides, and it had begun to annoy me.) "Yesterday, too, your affairs went so well. All the same, it's more difficult to retain a post than it is to acquire one. And you will work with that in mind. My woman teachers are practically like my own daughters, at any rate so long as they're discreet. One of them tried a bit of impertinence recently; never again! Without consulting the Director of Education, I gave her her passport and turned her out. Isn't that so, Şehnaze Hanim? Did she regret having opened her mouth?"

Şehnaze Hanim was the Assistant Director of the School, a middle-aged, frail, sickly-faced woman who couldn't utter a word without coughing. As I said just now, I noticed that she wanted to say something, and she nervously replied, "Yes, yes—that's what happened," and then, as though she didn't want to lose the opportunity of putting a word in, she added, "I can't agree to give the porters less than two dollars; what are we to do?"

The Director leapt from his seat, as though the nailed soles of his wet boots, which were beginning to steam beside the stove, had caught fire. "Listen to the scoundrels! I swear I'll take the rope over my back and carry the luggage myself. I'm a mad kind of fellow: I'm crazy enough to do it! You go and tell them so." Then he turned to me again. "Do you see these squinting eyes of mine? By Heaven, I wouldn't sell their side glance for a thousand pounds. If I look like this, all sense goes out of their heads. People must be sensible, intelligent and well-behaved. They mustn't make mistakes while they're on duty, and they must preserve the dignity of a teacher when they're outside. Assistant Director, did you say it was time for school?"

"Yes, sir. The students are in class."

"Come on, my dear. Let me present you to the students. But go and give your face a good wash first." The Director pronounced the words with some embarrassment, and lowered his voice. I was thoroughly taken aback. Was there a smudge on my face, I wondered? The Assistant Teacher and I exchanged glances. She was as much surprised as I was.

"Is there something on my face, sir?" I asked.

"I tell you as a daughter, my dear: indulgence in finery and ornament is innate in womenfolk. But for teachers in particular, it isn't seemly that they should go into a classroom with their eyes and faces painted. I'm warning you today in a fatherly spirit."

182

I was more embarrassed than he. "But I never paint, Director. I'm one of the last people in the world to paint my face."

Rejep Efendi was looking at my complexion obstinately. "But you've done so; you've certainly done so," he insisted.

I suddenly understood, and couldn't help laughing. "Director," I said, "I object to that paint, too; but what can I do? God put it on. There's no hope of getting it off with water." The Assistant Director had begun to laugh with me: "It's her natural colour, sir," she pointed out. Now the laughter communicated itself to the Director. But his laugh was unlike anyone else's; he began to laugh "Ha ha ha," but he let fall the H's as if he were teaching the alphabet to children who had just come to school.

"But that's amusing—ha!—from God—he!—from God—ha! So God gave it to you? Assistant Director, have you ever seen such a bright face? My dear, your mother must have nursed you with rose syrup instead of milk. My God!" I could see that Rejep Efendi was going to turn out to be a very nice fellow. I felt drawn to him at once.

The Director put on his overcoat, still slightly steaming, and prepared to take me to the class. As soon as I caught sight of my pupils through a window in the passage, my heart came into my mouth. Oh Heavens, what a crowd of them! There were perhaps fifty children in the classroom, nearly all of them young girls of my age. I almost melted away before the mass of eyes suddenly fixed on me. If the Director had withdrawn at that moment and gone away, I should have been hard put to it to find a thing to say. But thank goodness, he was tremendously keen on making people listen to him. "Get up, my dear, let's see you in your place," he said, and after having pretty well forced me into the teacher's chair, he started on a long speech. Oh dear, and the things he talked about! Europeans, he said, had acquired from the Arabs medicine, chemistry, astronomy, and mathematics; and if they had borrowed mathematics from the Arabs, why couldn't we do the same with the great European sciences? It was a lawful privilege to gain honourable access to the scientific and cultural treasures of Europe, and to profit by them within one's capacity. And such profit, it seemed, wasn't to be had by means of the French language only. The Director thoroughly let himself go. "Aaah!" he shouted in that metallic voice of his, calling attention to me, "the keys of knowledge of those countries are in the hands of this slip of a girl. Don't look at her outward appearance. She looks no bigger than your finger, but within she's a jewel, believe me. Hang on to her, make her talk, take in wisdom

183

from her mouth, and suck her dry like a lemon!" I felt he was going to be seized with one of those infernal fits of laughter.

Oh Heaven! I was going to be disgraced. For the first time I dared to look directly at the class. They were laughing too. That's how it happened that my first exchange of glances with my pupils was a delightful smile. I believe it was that look, that surreptitious smile, that endeared us to each other from that moment. The growing laughter in class at last attracted the attention of the Director. He suddenly struck his fist on the table. With one of those fearful side glances from his squint eyes, which he'd said he wouldn't sell for a thousand pounds, he looked over the class and shouted: "Ah—what's going on now? What's going on? Give you an inch, and you'll take an ell. It's never any good spoiling womenfolk: I'll pay you out for it. Quiet, this moment; and remove that senseless grin from your faces!"

The girls didn't take so very much notice. Indeed I was more taken aback than they were. The speech lasted for anything up to fifteen minutes. Now and again, when the laughing tended to increase, Rejep Efendi struck the table with his fist and threatened them, half in jest and half in earnest: "What are you grinning at? I wish I had some pincers!" He finished up by saying for the last time, "Hold on to her; don't let her out of your clutches. If you don't imbibe wisdom from her lips as you were sucking a lemon, the worse for you. May the very bread you receive from your mothers—your fathers—the state—the nation!—taste bitter to you," he shouted; and then rose and went out.

I never imagined that first moment would prove so difficult. Çalıkuşu, the little wren who used to chirp from morning till night, without stopping, had turned into a nightingale that had eaten its fill of mulberries. My head felt vacant, and I couldn't think of a word to say. It was more than I could do to prevent myself from giving a little laugh, involuntarily. Thank goodness, my pupils thought I was still laughing at the Director's speech. They took a look at my face and began to smile. Suddenly courage came to me. I'd pulled myself together.

"Young ladies," I began, "I know a little French; if that's of any use to you, I shall be delighted." From that moment the spell was broken. My tongue was set free; I spoke without any difficulty, and felt that my girls were gradually warming to me. To be able to say "my girls," in front of great young things like these—what bliss! Except that they laughed a little too much now and again, the atmosphere suited me admirably. But if Rejep Efendi were to look through the window with his side glance worth a thousand pounds—horrors! So I thought it advisable to give my pupils a further warning. "Mesdemoiselles, your laughter should not exceed the limits of a smile. I have nothing in my hand like the Director's pincers to threaten you with; but I shall be angry with you," I said.

In a word, my first lesson went off very well.

B., 28th March

I was pleased—very pleased, really—with my girls. They liked me so much that they wouldn't leave off following me round, even in the intervals. As for my colleagues, I couldn't find much wrong with them. There were not lacking some who adopted a more than usually cold attitude towards me, and others who whispered unflattering things about me in a corner of the room. But do we all love one another, even at home?

It was two lovable young people from Istanbul, called Nezihe and Vasfiye, whom I liked best among them. They were inseparable; but Assistant Director Şehnaze Hanim warned me not to be too intimate with them. What the reason was, I don't know. Besides those, there were two old acquaintances: one, the tall woman with the piercing black eyes who had taken my part a little while ago in the central secondary school. It seems she gave one lesson a week here. She was the only one of my colleagues who was not afraid of the Director's side glance. On the contrary, Rejep Efendi would avoid her; covertly wiping the collar of his blue overcoat, he'd say, "God, what a spiteful creature! If I could only get this over, I'd know better another time."

The other old acquaintance was a large bespectacled, gap-toothed old schoolteacher who had in days gone by been my travelling companion. She was a teacher in the neighbourhood of Göztepe. She fixed her eyes on me and looked attentively into my face, exclaiming, "Good God!—I've never seen such a likeness! Some time ago I used to meet a mischievous schoolgirl in the train: *so* like you. . . . But I think she was probably French, or something of the kind. She was up to every kind of trick, and used to make a carriage full of people die of laughter."

I looked down, and said "Probably."

And there were several men teachers at the school; Zâhit Efendi, an old teacher of theology; Ömer Bey, the geography master, a retired colonel, with a grey moustache; a writing-master, whose name I don't know, and finally the music master, Sheikh Yusuf Efendi, the most significant person not only in the school, but in the whole of B. It seemed that Yusuf Efendi was a Mevlevi dervish, who fell ill some years ago. The poor fellow was probably tubercular; the doctors decided that if he stayed where he was, he would die. So two years ago he came to B. with his widowed sister, and the two lived together in a small quiet house. Those who knew the little house say it was like a small music museum; there was every kind of instrument and music there. As a matter of fact, the Sheikh was a distinguished composer, and had compositions one couldn't listen to without weeping. I saw him for the first time on a cold rainy day: I had been out in the garden during the interval with the children, and had played with them on the pretext of teaching them a new ball game. I had enjoyed myself; and when I came in, my black tunic was quite wet. Let me say in passing that the dress which I had invented myself evidently began to spread through the school, indeed even among my pupils. The Director objected to its colour: "It's not seemly for Moslems to wear black. It ought to be green," he said. But we made out that it would stain, and took no notice. A great tiled stove was burning in the teachers' room. I got into the space between the corner of two walls and the stove, and was standing with my hands in the pockets of my tunic, drying myself; the door opened, and a tall thin man about thirty-five years old, came in. He was in civilian dress; so I knew that this must be Sheikh Yusuf Efendi, of whom they had told me. They were very fond of him in the school. My colleagues surrounded him at once, and took off his overcoat.

Concealing myself behind the chimney of the stove, I began to study him. He was a gentle, kindly man; in his faded face there was that delicate, transparent whiteness that is generally found in the faces of people doomed to die. And there was that subtle plaintiveness in his voice that you hear in the voices of sick children. He was complaining to my colleagues of the rain, which wouldn't stop, and said he was waiting with bitter impatience for the clearer weather.

For an instant our eyes met. He screwed up his eyes a little to see me better in the darkness of the corner, and asked, "Who is that young lady?—one of our pupils?"

My colleagues turned towards me all together, and Vasfiye said with a laugh, "I beg your pardon, sir. I forgot to introduce you: our new French teacher, Feridé Hanim."

I acknowledged him from where I was, with an inclination of the head. "I am very pleased to make the acquaintance of a great composer, sir," I said.

Artists are very sensitive about expressions of that kind. A pink flush spread across his white face. He rubbed his hands together and bowed. "I am not convinced that I have produced a work worthy of the standard of a composer. If there be a little virtue in a few of my pieces, it is no more than an attempt to express with a sincere voice that same divine melancholy that is to be found in the works of some of the great poets, such as Hamit and Fikret."

To be truthful, I like Yusuf Efendi as I would an elder brother.

B., 7ᵗʰ April

I've been granted one more of my greatest wishes. Since yesterday, I have acquired a lovely little clean house. It was Hadji Kalfa, thank Heaven, who found it for me. It is two minutes from his own house, and on the bank of the same ravine. It has three rooms, and is a dear little place, very small, and with a garden of its own. And better still, they let it to me furnished. Munisé and I felt very happy indeed yesterday. As a matter of fact we were going to do a little cleaning and put our things straight. But not a bit of it: what with laughing, romping, and chasing one another, we didn't get a minute to spare. Oh, poor little Munisé couldn't believe her eyes. She felt she'd walked into a palace. Only Mazlum (we had named the kid that Mehmet the shepherd gave us "Mazlum") somewhat alarmed us. The little rascal escaped though the open door of the kitchen into the garden, and thence to the hill that sloped down, as deep as a minaret, to the bottom. Heaven forbid—but if his hoof slipped the slightest bit, he would be into the ravine. But those wily creatures know better than I do where to plant their feet! Anyway, until we got him in again, we had a good many heart-burnings.

Yes; we are very pleased with our house. Munisé slides her feet over the green tiles in the hall, and fingers the flower pictures on the walls very lovingly. But in the evening we grow rather downcast when it gets dark. Fathers and brothers are returning to the neighbouring houses, with their handkerchiefs in their hands; no one ever knocks at our own door at such a time, and that's how it will always be.

This place has such a beautiful springtime. . . . It's green as green everywhere. Flowers of every colour are blossoming in my garden, and ivy climbs though the windows of my room. Ah, and the steep hill opposite our garden is like an emerald waterfall. In those waves of green, the poppies show blood-red, like fresh wounds. I spend all my free days in the garden with Munisé, playing "catch-as-catch-can," and skipping.

Çalıkuşu

When we get tired, I begin to paint, and Munisé lies full length on the lawn with her kid. Interest in painting has been aroused in me again. For the last few days I've been struggling with a watercolour painting of Munisé. But that wretch of a girl can't sit still long; she gets tired of posing. She finds it hard to sit quietly in front of me with a garland of wild flowers on her head, and the kid in her bare arms. Now and again Mazlum starts being obstinate, and struggles with his long thin legs. Then Munisé says, "Abla, I swear *I* want to sit still, but Mazlum won't. What am I to do?" And she runs off. "Do you think I don't understand your devilry?" I say. "You're tickling the little beast on purpose."

My school lessons don't go too badly, I think. The Director is very pleased with me, only he gets angry now and then because I am too fond of laughing. "I'll get the pincers to you too," he says. I pretend to look surly. "What am I to do, sir?" I tell him; "my upper lip is a bit short, so that you think I'm laughing even when I'm serious." For some reason the Director is interested in the language lessons; he has even found an old alphabet, and spells it out. He asks me the words, and writes out the meaning in pencil in the margin of the book.

My friendship with Yusuf Efendi has grown very much: I am very much taken with this frail and tragic sufferer. He says such beautiful delicate things with his rather plaintive voice. . . . Something happened ten days ago. The school has a deserted room full of articles no longer used. That day I'd gone into this room to get a chart for a lesson; the shutters were closed, and it was almost as dark as evening. As I was looking around me, an old organ covered with dust caught my eye, in one of the corners, and I was suddenly stirred by a feeling that was partly sweet and partly sad. The happy days of my childhood had been passed among the deep, sonorous hymns played on such an organ. Like one approaching the grave of an old forgotten friend, I went up to the organ with faltering steps. I had forgotten why I had entered the room, or where I was. Slowly I pressed down my foot: I put my finger on one of the notes. The organ emitted a deep and echoing sound, as though from a wounded heart. Oh, that sound! Without thinking what I was doing, I drew up a chair and sat down at the instrument; and slowly, very slowly, I began to play one of the canticles I loved best. As the sound of it swelled, I gradually lost myself, and began to fall into a deep dream. The dark corridors of our convent school came before my eyes again, and troops of my school friends passed through the vestibule, with their black overalls and their short hair. I don't know how long I stayed there or what I

188

played. I was wholly absorbed in the old dream of my early days. Behind me, I heard a deep "Ah!"—in a voice that was like wind among the leaves. I turned my head, trembling a little: in the darkness, the fair face of Sheikh Yusuf Efendi was visible. He was leaning against a broken cupboard with his head bowed; and there was great weariness in his blue eyes, as he listened to me.

"Go on, my child," he said, seeing that I had stopped; "go on, I beg you." I gave no answer. Bending my head still lower over the organ, I played on until the tears that had begun to flow, had dried again. And then I stopped, with breath choking in my breast, weary and exhausted. "How deep a feeling for music you have; and how sensitive a heart, Feridé Hanim. I am amazed that a child's spirit should be acquainted with such an ocean of melancholy."

I answered with an attempt to sound indifferent, "These are hymns called canticles, which are essentially sad things. The melancholy is in them, not in me." Yusuf Efendi didn't believe me; he shook his head slightly. "I don't call myself a master of the art, but I am equal to distinguishing between the virtues of a piece of music from a real artist and those of one who is simply fond of music. As it is with voices, so it is with fingers; they have certain vibrations which flow only from the unrest of a sensitive heart. Can you give me the notes of some of those hymns you call canticles?"

"These are things I play by ear, sir. What do I know about their notes?"

"No matter. One day, at a time convenient to yourself, perhaps you will kindly play them on the organ again, and I will take them down in my notebook. One of the old religious brotherhood who died recently left me an organ. I am interested in musical instruments, too. I put it in a corner of my house. I should like to play those pieces."

We went out of the room together, still talking. When we parted, the Sheikh promised me something: "I have a few pieces I have played to no one—the real fruit of that same unrest; I am sure people wouldn't understand them. Please God, one day I will play them to you. Are you willing, little lady?"

This incident strengthened my friendship with the Sheikh still further. I haven't yet heard the pieces he promised to play, but I'm sure they would be very beautiful; because I believe this frail and sensitive Sheikh could bring sounds from a mere block of wood. A few days ago, one of the children brought him a lute that she wanted to buy, for him to examine it. He ran his fingertips over the strings, and I had a feeling that those delicate fingers were not touching the lute at all, but the strings of my own heart.

B., 5ᵗʰ May

I committed a great crime yesterday. My heart beats when I think that it may become known: but there! I felt compelled to act as I did. One night every week, the teachers stay late on duty at the school. It was my turn yesterday. During the evening preparation I was making a round of the school with the Assistant Director Şehnaze Hanim. In one of the classrooms we noticed that a gas lamp was not burning properly, and went in. The Assistant Director is a very practical woman. She can do almost anything. She got on to a chair, and was examining the lamp, when an old maidservant came in. She had a letter in her hand, and began to approach one of the students sitting in a row at the back. Just as she was going to give her the letter, the Assistant Director suddenly said, "Stop, Ayşe; what's that?"

"Nothing: someone left a letter with the porter for Jemile Hanim."

"Bring it to me. How often have I told you that I am to see the letters for the students first? What a forgetful woman you are!"

At that moment an odd thing happened; Jemile jumped up from her seat and seized the letter out of the servant's hand. The Assistant Director didn't lose her composure. "Come here, Jemile; why don't you obey?" She was a delicate woman without much apparent strength, but her tone was so commanding that even I trembled. A deep silence had descended on the class; a fly could have been heard on the wing. Jemile came slowly up to us with bowed head; she was a girl of sixteen or seventeen with a pretty face. I noticed that she always escaped from her companions and walked in quiet corners of the garden, deep in thought. In class, too, she was pensive and abstracted. When I saw her face closely, I understood that she was much upset. There wasn't a touch of colour in her face. As she bent her head before us, her lips were blanched and her eyelids quivered.

"Jemile, give me that letter." No answer. The Assistant Director stamped her foot on the ground insistently. "Come, what are you waiting for?"

"Why, Director?" There was a whole despairing revolt in the little word. The Assistant Director put out her hand with a sharp movement, seized the girl's wrist, and snatched the letter from her. "Now, go back to your seat."

Şehnaze Hanim scanned the envelope and knitted her brows slightly. But she quickly recovered herself. Amid deep silence, she addressed the class, which was now tense with excitement. "The letter is from Jemile's brother in Syria. But I shall not give it to her till tomorrow, because she didn't obey me immediately," she announced. The students bent their heads over their books again. I stole a secret glance round the class as I went off with the Assistant Director. In the back row, several girls had put their heads together and were whispering something. As for Jemile, she had hidden her head on her desk and her shoulders were shaking.

As we walked along the corridor, I said to the Assistant Director, "Your punishment was a heavy one. How can she wait till tomorrow? Who knows how impatient she is!"

"Don't worry, my dear. She understood: she'll never read that letter."

"But why, Director? You won't give her a letter from her own brother?"

"No, my dear."

"Why not?"

"Because it's not from her brother at all." The Assistant Director lowered her voice still more, and went on, "Jemile is the daughter of a fairly well-to-do man. She fell in love, this year, with a young lieutenant; nothing will induce her father to agree. The girl is watched both at home and at school. They sent the lieutenant to Bandirma, and we are slowly trying to cure the child. But every now and then he reopens the poor creature's wound afresh. This is the third letter that has fallen into my hands." We had reached the Assistant's room as we talked. Şehnaze Hanim crumpled the letter up with an impatient gesture, lifted the lid of the stove and threw it in.

It was nearly midnight. I hadn't yet gone to sleep in my bed in the room reserved for the teacher on duty. At last I made my decision. Finding an excuse to send the maidservant on duty in the corridor downstairs, I went into the Assistant Director's empty room. Through a window, whose blinds had remained undrawn, a pale streak of moonlight entered. Trembling like a thief in the night, I opened the lid of the stove, and there among a heap of torn and crumpled paper, I found and rescued Jemile's poor little letter.

On my nights of duty, I very much enjoy going round the silent dark dormitories and empty corridors after everyone has gone to sleep. Here

I cover up a small girl whose counterpane has fallen off; there I straighten the blanket of some little sick child coughing in her bed and put my hand gently on her hot forehead. Further on, a young girl is asleep upon a cloud of chestnut hair, and I ask myself what hope it is that makes her smile with those little parted lips. In the dark, still, bedrooms, where a great many of the girls are sleeping, a heavy dream cloud seems to have gathered. Rather than dispel it, rather than rouse the poor dears from the dream they are bound to wake from sooner or later, I tread on tiptoe and walk with a beating heart. When I found Jemile's bed that night, the poor child had just gone off to sleep. This I could tell, because there were teardrops on her lashes, still not yet dry. Slowly I bent over her.

"Fortunate girl," I said, "I wonder how glad you'll be when you find the letter from your lover in the pocket of your school overall? You'll ask yourself what invisible fairy came in the night and left you what you'd lost. Jemile, it's not a fairy; it's only a poor creature—a luckless person always condemned to burn her own letters, and part of her heart with them, because they come from someone she hates."

B., 20th May

Lessons stopped yesterday. In three days' time we start exams. All the girls' schools in B. have been celebrating the May festival on the banks of a river, an hour away from the town. I don't enjoy that kind of outing in a crowd, so it was my intention not to go, but to spend the day in my garden. But Munisé, who saw the girls' schools going by, singing songs, began to fidget. Just as I was trying to amuse her, there was a knocking at the door. I looked up and saw Vasfiye, one of my colleagues, and with her a few students of the senior class. Vasfiye had been sent by the Director to fetch me at any cost. Rejep Efendi was shouting, "I had the lamb specially stuffed for her, and had some halva made as well. It's a shame, and it won't do at all," he'd said. As for my pupils, they too begged me to come, for the honour of the senior class. "If the 'Silkworm' doesn't come, nothing will induce us to go," they insisted. 'Silkworm' was my new name. Çalıkuşu was done with. Now 'Silkworm' had made its appearance, and the worst of it was that my older pupils didn't hesitate to call me 'Silkworm' to my face. It's a severe blow to my pride and my dignity as a teacher. If the name were confined to the school I shouldn't complain: but the other day I was going past one of the cafés, and there was a rough sort of a fellow in the dress of a villager, a silk merchant, they said; and what should he do but shout out from one end of the café to another: "I've got a garden with eight mulberry trees; but I'd give all eight of them for one like that!" I felt so ashamed that I'd have been glad if the earth had opened and swallowed me. I didn't go near that street again.

I was in a difficulty now. If I were to persist in not going, they would say, "She gives herself airs," and would only tease me. And so, against my will, I had to put on my çarşaf and follow them.

The children had all been dressed in white. The banks of the stream were transformed into fields of camomile flowers. What a lot of girls' schools there must be in this place! There was no end to the stream of girls, singing songs as they came along the roads that twisted like serpents between the green gardens. The men teachers had withdrawn to a bunch of trees on the far side of the stream. It was only Rejep Efendi, with his blue overcoat and big black umbrella, who was going about among us, and shouting orders to the cooks as they built their fireplaces from the stones, away in a corner. The teachers and grown-up students, with great difficulty, persuaded the Director to let them discard their çarşafs and run about free, and they sent him away to join the men teachers. I don't know why, but I couldn't enjoy myself a bit today. The pleasure and delight of these hundreds of small girls induced in me only a sad and passive melancholy. Here an elementary school was playing a march; there a troop of young girls were pushing each other and shouting at the tops of their voices, as they played at ball games or "prisoners." And still further off, a big crowd of all ages applauded a child who was reading a poem or making a speech. Munisé was lost in the crowd. Was the young rascal likely to sit still beside me? In the distance on the edge of a high embankment, there was a row of chestnut trees. Some of the young teachers, together with the older scholars, had put up swing ropes on the branches; skirts of all colours were flying between the patches of foliage, and there were waves of cries and laughter. I had slowly separated myself from the crowd, and seated myself in the shade of a large rock on the bank of a mountain stream. I was picking little yellow flowers from the crannies in the rock, and throwing them into the water under my feet, absorbed in thought.

Suddenly I heard a shrill voice shouting, "I have found her! Here's the Silkworm!" It seems they'd been looking for me, to go on the swings, and they took me off there half by force. "I don't want to go; I'm tired, and I don't know how to swing," I protested. But it was no good saying anything to colleagues or students. Mürüvvet Hanim, the woman with the sharp black eyes who had taken my part a little while ago at the secondary school in the town insisted on swinging with me. We jumped on to one of the swings. All in vain; my arms shook, and my knees gave way, as though they wouldn't support the weight of my body. Poor Mürüvvet tried hard, but gave up at last.

"No good, Silkworm. You really are afraid of a swing. You've gone the colour of ashes: you'll fall," she told me.

The Director had lunch with us. He too had noticed my apathy today. "Come now, why aren't you laughing?" he'd say occasionally. "What a contrary child you are. When I say 'Don't laugh,' you laugh; and here you sulk." The good fellow continued to tack himself on to me after lunch. He had brought a samovar from school, especially, and wanted to make me some tea himself. One of the teachers beckoned me from a distance, and called out, "We've sent one of the servants to get Sheikh Yusuf Efendi a guitar. We're going to get him to play, a little way off. Get out of the clutches of that talker and come too," she suggested.

This was indeed an opportunity not to be missed. Yusuf Efendi's playing absorbed me more and more. The unhappy composer had been ill for some time, and had been unable to come to school in consequence. We had heard a day or two ago that he was better. He had waited to come to today's school outing.

The women teachers had separated Yusuf Efendi from the men, on some pretext. A little band of nine or ten of us began to follow a narrow path along the edge of the stream, doing our best to conceal ourselves. The Sheikh was very lively and cheerful today. There was some way to go, and he was laughing at those who feared he would get tired. "If this narrow path goes on to eternity, I still shan't get tired. I feel so strong today." One of my colleagues murmured in my ear that some of the men teachers were drinking 'raki' in a corner, and that they'd given Sheikh Yusuf Efendi a glass or two. It may be that a little of his cheerfulness was due to this. After walking for five or ten minutes along the stream, we reached a broken-down water mill. Here, at a place called "Hot Springs," the bed of the stream gradually got narrower and became a kind of ravine. The rocks along the edge of the stream were so high that the sun could not penetrate, and the water ran as though in the light of dawn. It was impossible for anyone to hear us here. They sat Yusuf Efendi down under a thick-leaved walnut tree, and gave him his guitar. I had crouched down a little distance away, on a rock against which the waters foamed. Once more my colleagues wouldn't leave me alone. "That won't do, that won't do. Come here; you've got to come," they insisted, and sat me down opposite the player.

The guitar began. I think I shall hear his music all my life. My colleagues were half stretched out on the green grass. Even in those who had seemed most insensitive, lips trembled and eyes grew full. I whispered to Vasfiye, who had let her chestnut hair fall on to my shoulder, "I first heard the Sheikh at school. Of course, it was very beautiful, but it wasn't like this." "Yes," said Vasfiye with a mysterious smile in her dreamy eyes, "because Yusuf Efendi has never been so happy as he is today, and at the same time so unhappy."

"Why?" I asked.

She looked attentively into my face, and let her head fall on to my shoulder again. "Hush, lets listen," she said. The Sheikh today was playing old melodies. I hadn't heard one of them before. At the end of each piece my heart missed a beat, and I said to myself, "Now he's bound to stop." But his eyes were closed, and his temples seemed to grow paler, with a fine moisture visible on them; finishing one piece, he went on to another. I couldn't look away from those half-closed eyes. For an instant I saw that there was a trace of tears on his pale cheeks. Suddenly my heart began to beat hard. It was a sin to tire a sick man so much. I could stand it no longer. I waited till he had finished one of the songs, and then said, "Won't you rest for a little? You seem overwrought. What is the matter?"

He gave no answer. With those innocent child's eyes, with their wet lashes, he looked deeply at me; then he put his head to the guitar again and began another song:

"I burn: O ask me not to tell
The secret that you surely know!
How can your tyrant will compel
Words from a heart so full of woe?"

While Yusuf was finishing the song, his head dropped on to the guitar: he had fainted. It was only a slight faint, but the teachers were all in a great state.

"It's all our fault," I said. "We oughtn't to have tired him so much." I jumped swiftly over the rocks and went down to the stream to wet my handkerchief. It was only a slight faint. Indeed it was no more than

195

giddiness. When I returned to his side with the handkerchief, which I'd dipped in water, he had opened his yes.

"You alarmed us, sir," I said.

"It's nothing," he replied with a wan smile. "It happens now and again."

I was conscious of something strange among my colleagues; they were looking at me significantly, and saying something quietly to each other. We were returning by the same road; I had stayed right behind with Vasfiye.

"There's something about Sheikh Efendi," I said. "He looks as though he's secretly unhappy about something."

My companion looked searchingly at me again with the significant look she had given before. "Are you being honest, Feridé? Don't be annoyed, but I can hardly believe you. You mean you know nothing?" Vasfiye fixed her eyes on me curiously.

"If I knew, what reason should I have to conceal it?" I asked. She still refused to believe me.

"How is it you don't know what the whole town's aware of?"

I shrugged my shoulders, smiling at her incredulity. "You know I live very much shut away and alone in the town. I am not interested in anyone else's affairs."

My companion took my hands. "Yusuf Efendi loves you to death, Feridé," she said.

Involuntarily, I covered my face with my hands. The joyful voices of the children could still be heard on the banks of the river. I slipped away from the rest, without anyone noticing it, and turning down a road between the gardens, went home alone.

B., 25th July

The summer months lengthened and lengthened. The heat was unbearable; everything was faded. There was nothing remaining that you could call green. The hills opposite, once dark green, were now faded and burnt out in colour. They looked lifeless and meaningless in the distance, like great heaps of ashes in the dazzling light of the sun. I was weary to the point of extinction. The place was quite empty now. Pupils had scattered, and many of the teachers had gone elsewhere to spend the summer months. Nezihe and Vasfiye wrote to me now and again from Istanbul. Istanbul was very beautiful this year, they said. They couldn't stop talking about the seaside and the islands. If they could possibly manage it they were going to remain there. To tell the truth, I had no intention of remaining here myself. The affair of Sheikh Yusuf Efendi had upset me very much. I felt ashamed to mix with other people; when the schools reopened, I would ask for a post in another district. I should be content with a more remote and indeed a more unpleasant place—a place of the kind that would wear me out, and make me work hard. Never mind that, as long as I were left alone.

B., 5ᵗʰ August

It's the second time since I became a teacher that I've seen one of my pupils made a bride. But this time it's not as it was with poor little Zehra. It was at this very hour that Jemile lay awake, with the teardrops still wet on her lashes; tonight, at the same hour, Jemile's lovely head had a new resting place: the breast of the young lieutenant she loved. These two young people had been so persistent in their love that their fathers had bowed to the inevitable at last. I dressed Jemile, as I had Zehra, with my own hands. For some time I had declined to go anywhere where there was a crowd; but Jemile came especially to my house, and begged me, kissing my hands. I wonder if she knew the service I had rendered her one night in the dark? I don't know. But on the day that she got the consent of her mother and father, I was the first to whom she brought the news. It's probable that she had her suspicions.

Yes, I dressed her myself. I put on her bridal veil with my own hands. There is a custom in this place: all the young girls, no matter who, tie up their hair with bridal ribbon for luck. In spite of my resistance, I couldn't prevent Jemile's mother from fastening a tiny piece of ribbon on one side of my hair. I was very curious about the lieutenant. I wouldn't believe in their happiness till I had seen Jemile on his arm. But there was no possibility of that. I had to go home early. Here, as everywhere else, I saw that all the women were covertly looking at me and whispering something to one another. The word 'Silkworm' could be heard again on everyone's lips. One stout woman, covered with gold and jewels, who was said to be the wife of the Mayor, looked attentively at my face, and said to those around her in a voice that I could hear, "That Silkworm is a real beauty, indeed. The poor man's got every right to be in love."

Well, I couldn't stay on after that. I begged leave of Jemile's mother. I told her I was unwell and that it was impossible for me to stay. Some of my colleagues were with the bride. The old lady pointed them out to me:

"Her teachers are giving Jemile some advice; you go and say something to her, teacher."

I smiled, and accepted this innocent suggestion. Drawing my pupil into a corner, I said, "Jemile, in my capacity as your teacher, your mother has asked me to give you some advice. You gave *yourself* the best advice; but I've a word of warning for you, my child. If someone tells you, before your young officer reaches you, that a strange woman has come in from the street and wants to tell you something in confidence, don't listen, my dear. Run away from her and hide your pretty head on the sturdy breast of your lieutenant."

Jemile must have been surprised; and rightly, because I was astonished too. Why had I said it, I wondered? I seemed to hear it from a strange voice. And I can't help wondering what I meant.

B., 27ᵗʰ August

There was a feast tonight in our tiny garden. Munisé and I had invited Hadji Kalfa's family to supper. In our anxiety to make a little ceremony of it, we bought in the street, three or four red paper lanterns, and hung them on the branches of a slender almond tree that spread above the table. Hadji Kalfa was delighted when he saw them. "Ha, ha! This isn't an ordinary party; it's a tenth of July public fête!"

I laughed. "Tonight is *my* tenth of July, Hadji Kalfa," I said. Yes, tonight was my festival of liberty. Exactly a year had passed since Çalıkuşu had escaped from her cage. One year: three hundred and sixty-five days! What a time! At first I was very cheerful; I laughed and talked all the time. I behaved so foolishly that the lady from Samatya was choking with laughter, and Hayganuş's red face with the pimples took on the colour of the red lanterns. Hadji Kalfa slapped his knees with his hands. "What have you done to make yourself so entertaining, my dear girl?"

We sat in the garden till late; and then, giving one of the lanterns to Mirat and one to Hayganuş, I said farewell to my guests. Munisé was very tired after her day, and began to doze in her chair while we were still talking. I sent her to bed, and stayed on in the garden alone.

It was a calm, starry night. The lights had been put out in the houses on the terrace opposite. The mountains rose up in the starry sky in an impressive mass of shadow. I leant my wrists and forehead against the cold metal of the railings along the bank. There was neither sound nor life around me. Only at the bottom of the ravine there was a little water flowing, and the reflections of a few stars in the stream, which was still not dry, in spite of the unbearable heat. The candles of the paper lanterns were giving out at last; I felt that the joy within me was fading as their colour died, and that a deep, helpless darkness had begun to invade my heart. One by one the days of this first year passed through my mind— some dark, some bright; oh God, how long? How long? I have a strong body that can stand up uncomplainingly to cold and suffering and pain. Maybe I shall live another forty or fifty years. Perhaps it will take almost fifty years to celebrate the anniversary of this sad victory. Oh how long life is, how long! Probably even Munisé won't be left to me. Slowly my hair will turn white. "Let me hope, let me endure. . . ." Very well; I'm ready to do that. But wait for what? In the course of this last year I'd been unable, several times, to control myself, and had dissolved into tears. But never had my tears burned so bitterly as tonight. Before, it was only my eyes that wept: tonight my heart is weeping too.

B., 1st October

Two weeks have passed since lessons began. A great many of my teacher colleagues came back to B. Even Vasfiye, who wanted so much to stay at Istanbul; the poor thing couldn't find a place anywhere. Nezihe has had something very lucky happen to her. One Friday she met a young officer on the water, and he followed them from the Bosphorus as far as Fatih. Like every other man who'd met my two friends, he too seems to have preferred Vasfiye. Indeed they made an assignation in one of the parks. But as bad luck would have it, Vasfiye had visitors that day. Reluctant to leave the officer wondering what had happened, she begged Nezihe to go. "My dear Nezihe, you take my place; say I shan't be able to come today. Make an appointment for another day instead." When Nezihe reached home in the evening she said she hadn't seen the young man. But there was something strange about the girl's behaviour. The reason came out a few days later. It seems that whatever Nezihe did that day, she caught the fancy of that young man; and the treacherous girl got engaged to him a week later. Vasfiye was very unhappy. She was upset on the one hand at being deceived by a close friend; and on the other she complained of being left alone. Now and then she sighed: "Ah, Feridé Hanim, what good friends you and I might have been. But—how shall I put it? Cheerful, good, friendly girl that you are, you don't understand 'joie-de-vivre.' Just think what a happy new life is awakened when young chickens come out of the shell—that's how it is at school!"

199

Ah! Violent rain began a few days ago, with thunder and lightning. It dispelled the chronic sadness which the hot still summer had brought me, and that intolerable weariness of life, so difficult to understand. I felt so light, so cheerful. . . .

B., 17th October
It has been raining for ten days, and with what violence! On the first days the few remaining flowers were destroyed; those that had been, like me, rejoicing, and whose fading colour had been renewed with life. The poor things bow their heads in the garden under the ceaseless rain. They shrink and tremble as though they were saying, 'Come, that's enough!' When I returned from school this evening, I was more or less in their own condition. I was soaked through; my çarşaf clung to my body and my veil to my face. It made those who met me in the streets laugh at the state I was in.

Munisé's complexion was a little pale this evening—evidence that she had caught cold; and I made her go to bed early, and brewed her some lime-blossom tea. The little wretch complained in bed and joked at my precautions: "Abla, a cold can't do anyone any harm; have you forgotten the night last year, when I lay in the straw in the snow?" she asked.

Tonight I couldn't sleep at all. After putting Munisé to bed, I took a book and stretched myself out on the couch. I began to listen to the noise the rain made on the roof and in the gutters; it was like a funeral that had gone on and on for a fortnight.

I don't know how much time had elapsed, but suddenly there was a violent knocking at the door. Who could it be at that hour? I did not dare to open the door; I leant over the balcony of the guest room and saw a shadow in the darkness—the shadow of a tall woman trying to protect herself from the rain, beneath the balcony, with an umbrella in her hand. The light of the hurricane lamp she held was dancing, reflected in the puddles of the street.

"Who is that?" I demanded.

A trembling voice answered me, "Open the door, please; I have come to see Feridé Hanim," it said. I was trembling myself as I opened the door. I have been afraid of strange women ever since that evening; and when one came asking for me in this way, I was prepared for bad news. The visitor who had come at this strange hour raised her lantern to see my face. I could distinguish two sad blue eyes and a face that looked unhappy.

"Will you let me come in, teacher?" That face and that voice both gave me confidence. I saw no need to ask who she was or why she had come. "Come in," I said. I opened the door of the living room, near which I was standing; the woman was looking around her, as if she were afraid of making the room wet. She did not dare sit down. "What rain, what rain!" she said, for the sake of something to say. "It seems overwhelming." I was looking intently at her face, because it was clear that her wretchedness was due to some reason other than the weather; and I gathered that she did not want to talk until she could explain her real object. So I didn't ask her what she wanted, all at once. My first feeling had not misled me. The woman had a kindly face and an aristocratic bearing. I said at last, "To whom am I talking, madam?"

She bowed her head as though she were afraid of me. "Feridé Hanim, I am no stranger; it is true that up to now we've not met one another, but I know you from a distance." She paused a little, and then, gathering courage, she added: "I am the sister of a colleague of yours at the school, the music master, Sheikh Yusuf Efendi."

My heart suddenly came into my mouth; but I had to keep up my courage and not let her sense anything. "Really, madam?" I said; "I am very pleased to have you here. I hope the Sheikh is a little better?" It was hardly the remark to make to a visitor who had called at such an hour and in such a state, but what else could I say? She could find no answer, and was silent. I lowered my eyes to the ground, not daring to look her in the face. I heard her give a little sob, and prepared myself for a tragedy from which there was no escape. I bent my head still lower, and waited. She was clasping her breast and her throat to keep from weeping.

"Friend," she said, "he is dying. Tonight, towards nightfall he suddenly grew worse. He has been unconscious for six hours: he will not live till morning."

I did not answer.

"My dear," she went on, "Yusuf is three years younger than I am; but I look upon him as my child. When our mother died Yusuf was a little fellow, and I was not much bigger myself. So I acted as mother to him. I bound my life to his. I had barely reached your own age when I was left a widow; I might have married again, but I did not want to. My little Yusuf, I thought, must not be left alone. However, now it is he who is leaving me behind. Why do I tell you all this, my dear? Don't be annoyed with me—don't put me out for the sake of what I am going to beg of you, or for my intrusion at this hour."

I could see that her weary body had suddenly given way, at this point in her story; I felt that something serious had happened. I wanted to take her by the shoulders, but she was now embracing my knees, and sinking to the ground, distraught with tears. I withdrew with a slight movement. With as steady a voice as I could assume at such a moment, I said, "Madam, I understand your misfortune. If there's anything I can do. . . ."

A ray of hope shone in the woman's faded blue eyes, swollen with crying. The poor soul was trying to control with her hands the sobs that shook her body. "Yusuf has been ill for ten years. I struggled so hard; I did all I could. But the dreadful disease got no better. It was consuming my brother in secret, until it did for him. At last something happened: he saw you. He is a very sensitive man, really; and he began to waste away before my eyes."

At this point in her story I could not restrain a faint cry of protest. "Madam I swear I have done nothing to your brother. I'm nothing but an afflicted person myself!"

She wound her arms around my knees again: "My child: perhaps you have a lover. Don't be angry with me. I swear I'm not telling you these things with any sense of reproach. I'm not the uncouth woman I seem to be. After all, I am Yusuf's sister. For years I have lived among his music. I'm not reproaching you or even complaining of that chance meeting. I could see that Yusuf was melting away like a candle, where he lay. But I could see too, that he was dying happy. He uttered no complaint, no bitter words, no indication of distress. Sometimes he used to lose consciousness; and then his eyelids would tremble a little, and his pale lips used to say your name slowly, with a secret smile. Yesterday he took my hands, and kissed my fingers one by one, and said to me: "Sister, show her to me once more." He began to implore me, as a child does. I was ready to make every kind of sacrifice for Yusuf. But I saw no way of doing what he asked. My heart was torn with grief for him. 'Get well, Yusuf, get well quickly; of course you'll see her again one day,' I said, and smoothed his forehead and hair. Ah, Feridé Hanım—if you had seen how that sick man grew angry with me, without saying a word, and how he turned his head away and closed his eyes in despair! It is impossible to tell you. . . . Today, towards evening, he closed his eyes for the last time. I knew that they would never be opened again. I had denied him nothing; I had dedicated my life to him, and all my happiness. To see him close his eyes in grief without seeing the one thing he wanted—it's not possible to explain that sorrow to you, Feridé Hanim; it's not possible. It would be a pious deed, like giving a drop of water to a desperate man. . . ."

Well, she was unable to continue. She hid her face in my skirt, and sobbed like a child.

I shall remember tonight's events like a dream. In the pouring rain, following the dull glow of the lantern in front of me, I passed though many dark, narrow streets. I felt nothing, I was sensible of nothing; like a leaf fallen into the flood, I was being borne along without my will.

They took me up to a spacious room full of shadows; lutes, guitars and violins hung on the walls, and the untidy shelves were littered with rubbish, the accumulations of years. The composer, in a wide iron bed in a corner of this room full of instruments, lay dying. Treading on tiptoe, we approached the bedside. The calm of death was already perceptible on the waxen face of the dying man; darkness filled the hollows of the closed eyes. Only on his lips, on his parted lips showing his pure white teeth, a little of the colour of life remained.

The poor woman who had seemed so distraught and wretched a little while ago, was now displaying a most surprising endurance and composure. Oh God, what miracles there are, in this thing they call love and compassion! Rather as a mother wakes her child to get him up for school, she put her hand upon the sick man's head. "Yusuf, lad—look! Your colleague Feridé Hanim has come to ask after you. Open your eyes, Yusuf," she said. The sick man neither saw nor heard. The chance of his dying without opening his eyes once more, was making the poor woman gradually lose her calmness. She had begun to weep again and her voice was stifled. "Yusuf, lad! Open your eyes once again! If you die without seeing her, I shall grieve all the more."

My heart was melting with compassion; my knees felt ready to yield beneath the weight of my body. I had been leaning at the head of the bed, against some dark thing like a table, and now I perceived that it was an organ. I trembled. My heart spoke to me; it told me that the only miracle that could open those sad eyes, might be the organ itself. What I was contemplating was perhaps a crime, or perhaps an even greater sin than that: but like a chasm that draws in those standing on its brink, that organ compelled me. Instinctively, I placed my fingers on one of the notes, and pressed with my feet. The organ gave a deep sound, as if its heart was broken. In the dark corner of the room, the pipes, whose shadows lengthened on the walls trembled as if they were secretly lamenting. I can't say whether it was fact or fancy; my eyes were veiled with tears. But it seemed to me that the sick man opened his blue eyes for the last time, at the sound.

His sister had hidden her face in the pillow; she was sobbing. As though I were performing some pious rite, I bent over the sick man, and touched his eyes with my lips. They seemed to flicker with the last vestige of life.

So it happened that I was to give my first kiss to the eyes of a dying man.

B., 2nd November

This is the last evening in my house in B. I'm off early tomorrow. After what had happened, I couldn't, of course, have stayed on here. Everyone was talking about me in the town. Everyone was curious about me. On the way to school and back, people follow me, interrupt my walk to peer into my face under my veil; so that I've begun to wear it doubled. I hear ill-mannered fellows, who don't even think it necessary to lower their voices, say "Ah! That's the Silkworm. The poor Sheikh!" I was too diffident to talk to my colleagues, and when I went into class, I felt myself growing scarlet. This couldn't have gone on. There was nothing else for it, and I went to the Director of Education. I said I was unable to stand the climate of the place, and I begged him to find me a post elsewhere.

Perhaps he had heard the talk. Because he acceded to my request at once. Only it was difficult to find an opening that would suit me, in another place. I said I would accept it, if the pay were less or if the school were smaller—all I wanted was a place some distance away. Two days ago, they appointed me to the High School at C.

Poor Çalıkuşu!—she returned with the autumn leaves, blown by the wind.

∾ PART THREE ∾

23ʳᵈ April

Today is the feast of St. George. I am alone in the house; indeed, not only in the house, I'm almost alone in the town. Houses are empty, shops are closed. The people have all gone off early, with their lunch-baskets, to the Willows, for the Feast of Lambs. An old paralysed beggar always sits at the corner of the street; and even he didn't want to be left out of the fun. He jumped triumphantly on to the back of a porter, just as if he were getting into his carriage, and joined the procession. But it was the dogs that pleased me most. The wily creatures had got wind of the feast, and a few of them tacked themselves on to the tail of each party as it set out with bags, coats, and baskets.

I sent Munisé along with the wife of Hafiz Kurban Efendi, the regimental padre, one of our neighbours. She made a great fuss about going without me, but I tied a scarf round my head and told her, "If I feel well, I'll come along later." I took them all in by saying I was not well; I'm not really ill at all, and feel, if anything, happier than usual. It was just that I didn't want to go: I don't care for crowded places.

As soon as I was alone in the house, I pulled off the scarf and started my housework, singing a little and whistling to myself. After a man's job for days on end at school, work in the house rather pleases me. When that was done, it was time for my birds. I cleaned the cage for the little things, gave them fresh water, and put them out in the garden to get some sun. There are a dozen of them now. When we came here, we had to leave Mazlum with Hadji Kalfa's boy. Munisé was very much upset, and cried over it; so to prevent the child worrying about Mazlum I bought her the birds. Then I got interested in them myself. But our neighbour's sandy cat gives the little things no peace; whenever I put their cages out in the garden, she will come and sit opposite them. She looks such a quiet, good-tempered cat, watching the birds softly with her half-closed green eyes. She licks her lips and makes little sounds, as though she were talking to them. Today just to see what would happen, I let one of the birds out of the cage and put it close to her face. Her fur stood on end as if the wind had blown it: the green eyes shone, her claws showed in the soft paws, and she all but sprang at him. The unhappy bird pressed its wings close to its little body, which was trembling all over. I held the cat by her head with my free hand, and said to her: "Anyone looking into your mild eyes would think you were an angel from heaven, but you really want to devour this little bird, don't you? So now I'm going to have my revenge." And I opened the hand that held the bird. It trembled, but it never moved. It couldn't believe that it was free. Then with a shrill chirp it flew off and I laughed. The cat's green eyes followed it with a look of astonished regret; I turned them back towards my face, saying, "So you did swallow up the little bird, did you, you yellow tyrant?" And I laughed again. I had a feeling of deep happiness, as if I had taken revenge, not only on the sandy cat, but on all the yellow creatures that attack small birds. The only thing that spoilt my pleasure was the thought of the other birds; for they seemed to be saying, "Why don't you make us happy in the same way?" And moved by one of those imperative and irresistible demands of conscience, I went straight up to the cages, and would have let the whole lot out, when suddenly I thought of Munisé. Leaning my cheek against the bars of one of the cages, I said to them: "It's all very well, but if I let you out, what shall I have to say to that other yellow tyrant, Munisé? What can we do, my little friends? It doesn't matter how hard we try, we never quite escape these yellow tyrants. . . ."

After the birds, it was my turn. Whenever the day is sunny, I wash my hair in cold water, and then have the great pleasure of drying it slowly in the sun. That is what I did today. I climbed up into the cherry tree that stands opposite the birdcages, and let loose my wet hair to the little spring breeze. My hair has grown at last, and very nearly reaches my waist. When I was in B. I was ashamed to tell the others why my hair was short, because they think it rather shameful for a woman to have short hair: a sin, in fact. Everyone, even Hadji Kalfa, had given me all kinds of hair tonic, and when they saw how quickly my hair grew, they took all the credit themselves, and quoted my abundant hair as evidence of the value of their remedies.

The cherry tree is right opposite the birdcages, and the birds were all singing. Their little eyes, looking into the sun, gleamed like pearls. I was imitating them by whistling, as I swung on a branch, when I happened to glance at the window of the house alongside ours. Whom should I see but Hafiz Kurban, our neighbour and regimental padre, looking at me with round blear eyes, which shone like two mosque candles in his moon-shaped face.

I can't describe how I felt. I must have looked like nothing on earth; my feet were bare, and I had on an open-necked white shirt. The first thing I did was to wind up the heavy coil of hair that hung down my shoulders, and to cover my throat. Then I dropped to the ground in a heap. Thank goodness, the branch wasn't very high. I heard a voice say: "Lord have mercy on us!" The one to get hurt was the one who fell; but the one who cried out was my neighbour Hafiz Kurban.

This Hafiz Kurban Efendi, whose name I can't mention without laughing, is a regimental padre in his fifties, and he is said to be very rich. His wife is a slip of a Circassian girl, pretty, black-eyed, and very unspoiled, barely thirty. We are very good friends; it is she who has taken Munisé today. She hasn't a child, and she is as fond of mine as if she were her own. But the cherry tree incident did not please me, and I felt really ashamed of myself in front of the padre. Who knows how shocked he was? Even now as I write the words, my cheeks are burning over it. Oh dear!—here I am, a schoolteacher, and I still persist in my crazy ways. No wonder Rejep Efendi, the Director, used to say to me: "Heaven grant you a long life: but even when you die and get carried to the cemetery, you'll still upset the priest while he's conducting the funeral."

The afternoon part of my day's programme was to write the events of the last six months in my diary, which I hadn't taken out of my box since I came here. I went to the window from which I could see the gulf and part of the fortifications. As a matter of fact, the very reason I came to this house was that I so loved the view from that window. Otherwise there is nothing very much to be said for the house. I had accepted the first post I was offered, in order to get away from B. I never stopped to think whether I should like this place or not; nor did I pay much attention to the smallness of my salary. However, by good luck, the place is pleasant enough. It is quiet and healthy—"soldiers' country;" every person you speak to, native or stranger, has a father, brother, son or husband who is a soldier, either an officer or a private. And some of the teachers, and even the Battalion padres and the regimental mufti, have some connection with the Army. My neighbour Kurban puts on uniform now and then, turban as well, and he has even been seen with a sword.

I like the women especially. They are such honest, hardworking, friendly people; so simple, and on such good terms with life; and they seem to like work as much as play. There is a wedding every week, and every wedding lasts a week itself, with all sorts of celebrations and ceremonies, so that they have some kind of entertainment every night. At first I wondered how they made their money last out, but in time I discovered the secret. A woman can wear a costly bridal dress at every wedding for ten or twelve years, and then do it up and pass it on to her daughter. But their pleasures are very simple; the musician is an old Armenian woman who will play a concertina for a few coppers or a piece of cloth. Yes, simple pleasures; but the women are happy enough. I wish I had been born here among them, and had dabs of henna as large as dates stained on my fingers and the palms of my hands.

My neighbours took to me at once, and the only thing that hurt them was that I didn't mix with them enough, or share their amusements. I didn't want them to think me proud; so I went out of my way to please them, and practised politeness, as schoolchildren do.

Of all the places here, the one I am most fond of is called the Willows. On days when it's crowded I haven't the courage to go there, but on quiet evenings I often go with Munisé, on the way back from school. It is a coppice of willow and plane trees; who knows how many years old? The lower branches of the willows have been pollarded, and only those at the top of the trunks are left. If you go there about sunset, you have the feeling of entering an endless ruined grotto; the shafts of sunlight turn the old, gnarled tree trunks into broken columns, reaching as far as the eye can see. On the far bank of the stream there are rows and rows of gardens, with hedges around them, and between the gardens are narrow paths, steeped in shadow. When I see those paths, they look to me as if they led to other, unknown, worlds; and would bring you, in the end, to your heart's desire.

The rich people here live in a quarter called "Hastalar Tepesi," Invalids' Hill. The name is not a happy one, but the place is where all the most fortunate people live. When I came here, I was shown a very charming house there, but I couldn't very well take it, because I am not as well off now as I was at B., and have to live more simply, in a little house. However, the house I have is not badly situated. It looks on to an open square, with a café and shops, and it is in a busy part of the town. This morning, for instance, everyone from C. who went off to the Willows passed my door, and now, though it is still early, they are beginning to return. A little while ago a group of officers passed on the way back. They stopped for a word with a lieutenant who was hurrying the other way. "What are you coming back for?" asked the lieutenant. "I haven't been yet; I've just come off duty." A stout middle-aged major, with his tunic unbuttoned (whom I'm always meeting) replied: "Don't bother to go: there's nothing down there today. We've looked everywhere, but there was no Gülbeşeker." I suppose the officers here are very fond of Gülbeşeker. The word is always on everyone's lips, young or old. As far as I can make out, it is a kind of sweet rose-juice; but to look for it at this outing on the feast of St. George and then to be upset because they couldn't find it, seems to me childish.

Gülbeşeker! How often I've heard the word. For instance I was coming home from school the other evening, and there in front of me were some young people, rather poorly dressed, offering something to one of their number, and he was declining it. He kept saying, "It won't do—I swear it; I've just had a meal—I can't eat a thing, not even fruit. I won't have it, whatever it is." To which one of the others replied, shaking him by the shoulder: "Not a thing?—not *Gülbeşeker*?" The first one gave in at once, and said with a grin, "Oh well, I haven't the face to refuse *that*."

Sometimes, too, the men sitting in front of the café will have a joke with a cheerful urchin who often goes past, carrying water. "Hello, Suleyman," they will call out; "when are we going to celebrate your wedding?" "Whenever you like. I'm quite ready," says the child. "You're so poor, Suleyman: how will you manage?" "I shall spread Gülbeşeker on my dry bread, and eat it," he will say.

This joke gets repeated every day. But strangest of all, our neighbour Kurban Efendi accosted Munisé at the front door, three days ago, and insisted on kissing her. Then he said: "Just like her teacher. She smells of Gülbeşeker."

The groups in the street returning from the Willows are beginning to increase in number. Now I can hear a light laugh; it is Munisé's laugh, and here she comes. Although it's only four hours, I feel as if I hadn't seen her for four months.

23rd April. (Two hours later.) I've learnt what Gülbeşeker means. Munisé told some of the teachers she met at the Willows that I was not well, and they felt anxious about me, and called to ask how I was. I insisted on their coming in for a few minutes, and for a joke I said to one of them, "Well, were *you* able to get any Gülbeşeker? Because the officers going down the street have been complaining that they couldn't."

My colleague said with a laugh, "We had none either, as you know well enough."

"What do you mean?"

"I mean that *you* didn't come."

I stared at her in surprise, and said "I don't understand." Then they all began to laugh, and she said with some hesitation: "Don't you really know?"

"I swear I don't."

"My poor little Feridé, how stupid you are. Gülbeşeker is the name the men here have given you because of your lovely colour."

Stammering with surprise, I said: "What—me? So *that* is what they meant by Gülbeşeker? And that's what the street lads meant by spreading it on their bread and eating it? Oh, mercy!"

I covered my face with both hands, in confusion: "This means I've been the talk of the whole town. Oh! How *ashamed* I feel!"

My companion pulled my hands away from my face, and said, half seriously and half in fun, "Why complain? You've attracted the attention of all the men in the place; how many other women have done that?"

What a wretched lot men are. I shall get no peace here. Oh dear! How can I ever move among decent people? How can I look my neighbours in the face?

1st May. I was correcting some of the children's work when there was a knock at the door, and Munisé called out from below, "Abla, there's a visitor." A woman with a black çarşaf was walking about in the hall; but as her face was veiled I couldn't recognise her. So I asked rather hesitantly, "Who are you?"

There was a sudden peal of laughter, and she leapt on to my back like a cat! It was Munisé. The young sinner seized me by the waist, danced me round the hall and started kissing me all over my cheeks and throat.

The veil had made her look quite grown-up. Indeed, the child has grown a great deal these last two years. She is very slender now, and nearly as tall as I am; imperceptibly, she has become a gracious and delicate girl, whose beauty grows as a flower's does, from day to day. But one never notices such things, when they're right under one's noise. I should have been happy to see it; but no! It made me sad, somehow.

Munisé noticed my sadness. "Abla, what's happened to you? It was a joke. Don't be angry."

I was gazing at the poor child, and she began to wonder if she had done something wrong. "Munisé," I said, "I shan't be able to keep you with me always; because I can see that you won't stay. You are already adorning your head like a bride, and trembling with excitement. I know how it is—you'll set your heart on being a bride, and then you'll leave me."

My eyes filled with tears, as though I felt the pain of loneliness beginning. With a look and a gesture I begged Munisé to give me a word or two of comfort; but the faithless child pursed her lips and answered: "What can I do, abla? That's the custom."

"You mean to say you'll leave me, to become the wife of a stranger?"

Munisé didn't reply; she only laughed. But what a laugh! The wretch: she loves that stranger more than me, already.

So I took back what I'd just said. "Even if you do marry," I told her, "there's plenty of time before you are twenty."

"Isn't twenty rather old, abla?"

"Nineteen, then. Oh well!—if you like—eighteen. You don't answer, but you're laughing. You're laughing very cunningly, as though you wanted to be able to say, 'I know.' But I swear it shan't be before you're eighteen."

The wretch was laughing again, amused at my bargaining. If I hadn't felt too ashamed to do it, I should have sobbed. All blond people are heartless; one way or another they'll always hurt you.

10th May. Among my students is the thirteen-year-old daughter of a rich pasha. She looks as if she has grown up and then shrunk again; her teeth are bad and she is much too small. But in spite of all this she gives herself airs. "Hanim Efendi Nadidé"—I called her that for fun, and from then on they called her that at school—lives in the finest house in Hasta Tepesi, and every day she goes backwards and forwards to school in her father's landau, with an orderly who has long moustaches like a ram's horn. It's my belief that this young lady comes to school not so much to learn as to give herself airs in front of her teachers and her less wealthy schoolfellows. The other children are her slaves, and the teachers know their place too well not to put up with the airs and graces. Now and again her lady mother will invite some of the teachers to a meal at the house, and my poor colleagues just cannot stop talking of Madame's toilettes, the food they have had there and the pomp and circumstance they have been shown. Their attitude amuses and repels me. I know quite well what kind of people these Abdurahman Pashas are—a lot of vain and foolish people who delight in attracting the attention of the uneducated and commonplace. The others have tried several times to take me with them to the house, but I always pretend to be insulted, and shrug my shoulders with distaste. Among the poorer children, I would think nothing of tying up shoelaces or taking the mud off their boots, but I've little use for this vain young thing—indeed I've even scolded her in school. But perversely enough, she pesters me more than any of the others, and never leaves me alone. This morning towards noon, a carriage drew up at my door, and what should I see but Abdurahman's landau! The orderly with the long moustaches opened the carriage door, and my pupil Nadidé Hanim came into the house as proud as a princess, surrounded by all the children in the quarter. The whole place was alive: you could see the women's heads behind all the lattice windows. Nadidé Hanim was bringing a letter from her mother. "Mademoiselle," she announced, "my father the pasha, and my mother and I, invite you to our house today, and we place this carriage at your disposal." I saw at once what they wanted. They think they can beguile me with their luxury and wealth, as they have the others. My first thought was to dismiss the young lady, and the orderly, and the carriage, with a frigid acknowledgement. But another idea came into my head, and I resolved that these nouveaux riches should learn a lesson. I had seen better examples of these pashas at Istanbul; indeed I had a fair amount to do with them there, and it used to be Çalıkuşu's greatest amusement to remove their masks, and reveal the baseness and degeneracy that was hidden beneath them. I can't explain what made me want to—I was born that way. I'm not an ill-natured girl; I love children, and people of no importance; but I'm always up against those who boast of wealth.

After behaving like a lady for two whole years, I thought I had a right to a little fun. I dressed myself smartly but simply, for the occasion. Thank heaven I had a dark blue dress which my uncle had sent me from Paris. I didn't hesitate to make Nadidé Hanim wait a little downstairs. I found a cutting from a fashion book which I had cut out of a magazine and kept, and I fixed it into the corner of the mirror. It had taken my fancy while I was in B., and I used all my skill and energy to copy it, though the style was fantastic and out-of-date. What did I care? I was looking for effect, like an actress. Today I was considering the impression I was going to make on these suburban beauties.

I didn't leave the young thing downstairs merely to make myself smart; I kept her waiting so that I could have a good look at the poorly-dressed young person who smiled at me from the mirror of my dreary room. I looked at her a little shyly, as though I were looking at a stranger. After all, no one else will read my diary, so why shouldn't I tell it everything? I found her beautiful, with a beauty that entranced me; the eyes were eyes that shone like stars; the eyes of the happy, carefree Çalıkuşu whom I had known in Istanbul. But when they began to laugh it was all changed—a pity there were all those delicate lines in a face that was beautiful enough to make me want to cry. I saw something likeable even in its faults. My aunt in Tekirdăgi used to say, "Your eyebrows are like your conversation; they begin so nicely and delicately, and then they lose their way." And then there's that lip of mine, which, being short, is always slightly parted, showing my teeth a little. This is the lip that the Hodja in Bursa said would take me smiling even to my grave. I heard the young lady downstairs stamping noisily, on purpose, as she walked up and down, but I still could not tear myself away from the young woman in the looking-glass. How disconcerted and amazed I used to be at B. when they called me "silkworm;" and now at C. it was "Gülbeşeker." All the same, I could give those very names to the girl in the mirror—to this creature bright as morning, lovely as April roses touched with hoar-frost.

For a moment I looked round in fear of being observed, and then I leaned towards the looking-glass and kissed myself—my eyes, my cheeks, my chin. My heart beat like a small bird's: my moist lips trembled.

What a pity these mirrors are only invented by man! However hard you try, you can't kiss your hair or your eyes. No matter what you do, you're confined to kissing your lips and your mouth.

What *am* I saying? Sister Alexei would tell me: "Dress as a priest, and you will have the soul of a priest." I wonder if I dress like a coquette, shall I become one, at heart? What absurd, what shameful, talk is this for a schoolteacher! But after sitting soberly for two whole years I feel I deserve a little fun today.

When I saw the ladies in their drawing room posing before me like a lot of strange actresses, I laughed to myself and said, "Wait a bit and see what happens." They were considerably surprised to see that I didn't emulate the other teachers and kiss the skirt of the lady of the house, or the younger ones, but contented myself with a very simple and natural greeting. They exchanged glances. An old woman from Pera whom I took to be the governess put on her gold spectacles and looked me over from top to toe. There was so much assurance and lack of embarrassment in my speech, such freedom in my movements and gestures, that the drawing room became as disturbed as a ship in a storm. The drawing room itself was a kind of bargain shop window, which money, rather than taste or breeding, had filled with a thousand varied objects. The so-called ladies had sat here for years, like so many lifeless mannequins, taking pleasure in astonishing the poor and inexperienced women of C.

With a rather mischievous courage, I gradually asserted myself in the drawing room, so that they were confronted by a strange and unconventional visitor; and while I was playing this rather low but amusing comedy, I did my best to behave quite naturally and not to show my hand. I made them feel that I disapproved of everything they showed me, everything they said and did, until I arrived at making them deeply and bitterly conscious of their gaucheries and inexperience. The eldest daughter, for instance, was showing me the pictures. After saying, in politely veiled language, that they were very ordinary, I found a miniature in a corner, and asked why this beautiful thing—the only real work of art in the room—had been left there. In a word, I fell for none of their fineries, tacitly criticising everything they had. As for the meal, didn't I torment them? Who knows how many people had choked at these rich and elaborate meals, how many guests had secretly sweated because they didn't know how to handle the knives and forks, and how many unhappy people had declined a dish because they didn't know how to eat it? So today I avenged them. But I behaved with so much circumspection and discretion that the ladies could not refrain from watching me with astonishment out of the corners of their eyes. Now and again I looked at them. But my looks made the spoons in their fingers tremble.

And as for the stupid old governess from Pera, who (boasting of her ridiculous friends) tried to show off before ignorant people, I made her wish she had never been born. As I was a teacher, she looked on herself as my colleague, and thought it her professional duty to argue with me. But I wouldn't stand for that! She tried to get out of it by saying that she couldn't put her case in Turkish: "I can't explain myself properly in Turkish," she maintained.   Whereupon I replied: "Never mind, mademoiselle; let's talk French." If she had tried to talk French I should soon have discomfited her.

While discussing etiquette in high society she was unable to find the right word for something she wanted to say; but she was determined to impress me, and insisted: "All the same, I have moved in high society a great deal, and I've seen these things with my own eyes." I looked at her with some contempt, and said laughingly, "Yes but it's not enough to move in society; one must be at one's ease there." This remark of mine (admittedly not very polite) thoroughly upset the poor woman, and with the excuse that it was time to give a lesson to one of the pasha's small children, she left hurriedly. The other ladies were now as quiet as lambs. As the masks of their false finery and pride were abandoned, their real selves began to appear; and, in fact, they didn't prove a bad sort of people, so that I was ready to revert once more to my true position, as the plain and humble primary teacher who was aware of her place and appreciated her unimportance.

The lady of the house, and the younger ones, kept begging me to come often. "I'll come now and again," I told them, "but I can't always come, or what would the others say? If they see me coming often, they'll think I'm trying to get something out of you." Madame was very anxious to know who I was, and did her utmost to make me tell her. "I am the poor daughter of the family of some standing," was all I would say.

"My dear child," she said, "with your beauty and attractions you could marry into a really good family."

"That may be, madam," I replied, "there might be some harmless fellow who would be glad to have me. But I prefer to earn my living by the sweat of my brow—one needn't be ashamed to work."

"What would you say if you were asked by a nice young man of good family?"

"Of course I should be grateful for the honour he'd done me, but I don't think I'd accept," I said.

Later on I understood the real object of my visit. I hadn't been invited to their home merely to be dazzled by their finery. The pasha's eldest daughter offered to show me the garden, in which were displayed, or

215

rather in which were laid out, a thousand varieties of flowers, grasses, shrubs and flower pots. In one part of it was a group of eight or ten pine trees, three or four years old;—but to explain what follows, I must go back to an incident of twelve days ago. Next door to our school playground there was a big garden, and the children had torn up the dividing fence, so that the two gardens were really all one. For some time past, three or four labourers, with red kerchiefs round their heads, had been digging it up, and during the school intervals I used to go along and watch them sweating away at work. On the day in question I had noticed a young workman among them. He was dressed as the others were, but I detected something different about his face and general appearance. Under his bronze skin, for instance, there was a certain transparency, and the look in his eyes was different; while as for his hands, they were as small and delicate as a woman's. Because he wasn't an old man like the other workmen, I didn't go near him; all the same, he had the courage to approach me, and ask me to get one of the children to bring him some water, as the heat had made him very thirsty. I have no liking for the prudery that will make a woman run away from every male, so I didn't draw back; and remembering that, after all, I was a schoolmistress, I announced, "Very well, young man: wait a moment, and I'll tell one of the children," thinking to myself as I did so, "This must be some young man of good family who has fallen on bad days." This workman was shy and bold at the same time. As he spoke, he was confused enough to mix up his words, but he kept asking questions, and rather inappropriate questions at that. "I've only recently come here," he said. "They say living is cheap, but what is it like in winter? Are there plenty of pears and apples?" While he was drinking his water, I smiled and thought to myself, "It's quite clear the poor fellow isn't quite all there."

And now here I was meeting this poor workman again, among the trees of the pasha's garden. But this time he was dressed very differently. His well-brushed hair, his sword, his buttons, his decorations, his collar, his face, his teeth, everything about him proclaimed the captain on the General Staff, bright as a new pin. He stood there between two plane trees with his gaitered legs together, his head held high and his body erect, just as though he were having his photograph taken. His teeth gleamed, under a slight moustache and parted lips; his eyes sparkled with confidence. In fact, his stance and his dress were such that one expected him to draw his sword with his white-gloved hands, and call the men on parade to attention.

Nerimé Hanim, the pasha's eldest daughter, said in a tone of surprise, "Ihsan!—you here? Where on earth have you come from?" But the poor girl was playing her part so awkwardly, that when she said in a surprised voice, "Ihsan, where have you sprung from?" it was clear that she was not being honest. Yes, we were to play an absurd part in a ridiculous comic opera. I was to learn this later, but at the moment I had to pretend to notice nothing, and to be calm and unmoved. Evidently these pashas like to give one surprises. But my obstinacy was uppermost today; let them do what they would, I was trying not to seem disturbed. Perhaps they expected me to be ashamed and run away, but I remained composed and said nothing.

"Feridé Hanim," said Nerimé Hanim, "you come from Istanbul too. You'll let me introduce my cousin and foster brother, won't you?"

I said at once, "Of course—I shall be delighted," and without giving him a chance to speak, I introduced myself: "Feridé Nizamettin, one of the non-commissioned officers of the *education* army."

The young officer could not preserve that fine, bold silence of his. Here was the teacher, confronted by a handsome young warrior, tall, gallant, smartly-dressed, shining as bright as the sun; the very individual she had seen a few days ago dressed in workmen's clothes—and it didn't astound her! Would you believe it? Indeed, it was he who showed surprise; it was he who seemed quite ignorant of the famous ceremony of salutation which they had meticulously taught us at school for years, as if it were something of great importance. He half lowered the hand he had raised, probably with the intention of giving a military salute, and seemed to prefer to stretch it out and take my hand. But when he realised he was wearing a glove, he pulled his hand away, as if the wretched glove had suddenly caught fire. I talked to him quite composedly for three or four minutes. Face to face with me, the poor young man remembered how he had asked me for water, dressed quite obviously in the clothes of a workman, and he lowered his eyes in confusion. But I behaved as if I had never been there, and was seeing him for the first time. A minute or two later I went indoors with Nerimé Hanim. That young person said with some hesitation, "Feridé Hanim, of course you recognise Ihsan?" That meant she too was aware of the incident at school. I said "Yes," quite simply.

217

"I believe you're displeased; so let me tell you the truth. Ihsan made a bet with his brother officers—What of it? You know what young men are."

I caught my lip in astonishment, and couldn't help asking, "What was it about?"

Nerimé Hanim blushed, and gave a laugh to conceal her embarrassment. "Some of the officers had met you on your way home from school and said that you were very pretty. We Istanbul people don't look on that as an insult, like the local people here, do we, my dear? Then Ihsan interrupted them, and said 'I shall certainly find some way of talking to the schoolteacher, if she's so pretty." And that very day, without wasting time, he put on one of the workman's clothes, and won his bet. Amusing, wasn't it?"

I didn't answer. Her words were met with a chilly response, and poor Nerimé Hanim couldn't have failed to notice it.

In the drawing room, the curtain went up on the last scene of the day's strange comedy. The news that I had met Ihsan Bey had reached them before we got upstairs. They all revealed it by their expressions; and on a secret sign from Madame, everyone left the drawing room except Nerimé. Madame, after a little pause, began to talk.

"What did you think of Ihsan, my dear?"

Again I answered very simply, "He seems a nice young man, Madame."

She agreed. "He's good-looking; he's had a good education, and he's been appointed to Beyrout on promotion."

"That's splendid," I said. "He really is a nice, likeable young man; and he seems intelligent, as you say."

Mother and daughter exchanged glances; my words seemed to surprise them and please them too. Madame laughed cheerfully and announced: "God bless you, my dear. You've made my task easy. I'm Ihsan's foster-mother, and I brought him up as though he were my own son. Well, my dear, it's not usual to discuss these things with young girls in person, but you're wise and sensible. I want you for Ihsan. That's God's will; he's been very much taken with you, and since you like him too, pray heaven you'll be happy. We'll get a month's leave for him, and your wedding shall take place here; then you can go off together to Beyrout."

I felt things were already moving in that direction; it was amusing enough as a situation; but somehow, to be wanted for a wife in a strange country gave me a feeling of sadness. However, I gave no more sign of sorrow than I did of joy. "Madam," I said, "this is a great honour for me. I thank you and Ihsan Bey with all my heart, but it can't be."

"Why not, my dear girl?" Madame asked with astonishment. "Didn't you say just now that you liked him, and found him very nice?"

I laughed, and replied: "Madame, I'll say again—Ihsan Bey is a fine and worthy young man. But if the possibility of marriage between us had crossed my mind, or heart, could I have praised him to you quite so openly? Wouldn't that have been a little forward in a girl of my age?"

Mother and daughter exchanged glances again; and a brief silence ensued. Then Nerimé Hanim took me by the hands and said, "Feridé Hanim, surely this isn't your final answer?—because Ihsan will be very upset."

"I tell you, Ihsan Bey is a very nice young man; anyone would be glad to have him for a husband."

"Yes, but it's you he wants. Just now I had to tell you that he made a bet about you with his friends; does that sort of thing happen every day? The poor boy was in such a state of mind for ten days that he kept saying, 'I'll die before I give her up. I *must* have her, come what may.'"

I felt that Nerimé Hanim would go on with this conversation, and say all kinds of things to win me over. So I said politely but firmly that it was impossible, and begged leave to go. Nerimé Hanim seemed quite distressed. She said to her mother in a disheartened voice, "Mother dear, you tell Ihsan, it's more than I dare. It never occurred to him that Feridé Hanim would refuse him. He'll be terribly distressed."

Oh! These men. The same pride, the same conceit in all of them! It never enters their heads that we women have hearts as well, and that there may be things for us too which we "*must* have, come what may."

When the pasha's landau left me at my house, Munisé was with our neighbours. Before taking off my best clothes, I thought I would have one more look at myself. The room was rather dark, and I could only just make myself out in the looking-glass, which looked like a gleam of moonlight on the wall. The light played strange tricks. My short blue dress looked white to me, and the skirt of it was like white silk, lost in the darkness. I suddenly covered my face with my hands.

At that moment Munisé came into the room. "Abla!" she said.

I put out my hands, as if to ask her for help, and I was going to answer "Munisé!" But I made a mistake; and another name crossed my lips—the name of my great and hated enemy.

C., 11ᵗʰ May

This week was a lucky one. With yesterday's comedy still fresh in my mind, I became the subject of another. But this one was a thousand times more fantastic than yesterday's, a comedy that made me more of a rebel than ever. I'm writing it down just as it happened.

The scene was our reception room downstairs. Hafiz Kurban Efendi's wife came in, wearing the old-fashioned scarf in which she goes to weddings, and lots of chains of gold coins round her neck. Still, there was something curious about her appearance. To judge by her eyes, she had been crying. We began to talk.

I: "Are you invited to some important party?"

She: "No, my dear. I've come specially to see you."

I: "Then why are you so smart today? Is *that* specially for me?"

She: "Yes, my dear, it's for you."

I couldn't help pursuing the joke a little further, and said, "In that case . . . perhaps you're paying a visit to a prospective bride?"

A look of innocent surprise came into her face. "How did you know?" she exclaimed.

I asked her frankly, "What have you come for? Are you a marriage agent?"

She (with a sigh): "Yes, my dear."

I: "For whom?"

She (as if she were saying the most ordinary thing in the world): "For my husband."

That so simple a woman should joke with this apparent unconcern amused me, needless to say, and I burst out laughing. But she wasn't laughing herself; on the contrary, there were tears in her eyes.

"My dear," she said, "my husband has fallen in love with you; and he wants to divorce me. I begged and implored him, and said, 'It doesn't matter; take this other woman; only don't divorce me. We'll get on very well together. I'll cook your food and I'll be your servant.' My dear friend, have pity on me!"

"But if Kurban Efendi leaves you, is he sure he'll get me?"

She replied with a simplicity that really annoyed me, "Yes, he is. 'I'm prepared to give a five pound piece,' says he."

"My poor friend," I said, "come now! Set your mind at rest. There's not the slightest chance of anything of the kind happening."

The wretched woman thanked heaven; and the curtain dropped.

C., 15th May

This evening, when school was over, the headmistress asked me to come to her room; and this is what she said:

"Feridé Hanim, my dear, I am very pleased with your keenness and the serious way in which you do your work. But you have one fault. You still believe yourself to be in Istanbul. There's a well-known proverb that says 'Beauty always brings trouble.' You're both pretty and young, so you ought to look after yourself better; but you've been guilty of several indiscretions. Now, don't get into a state, my dear; I'm not saying it's your fault, but I do say that you've been incautious. For instance, this place is not so much behind the times that women can't go about smartly dressed, and that applies to our teachers as well. But what may seem quite natural to others, has attracted attention in you; because, my dear girl, your youth and beauty have turned the head of every man you meet, to such an extent that there has begun to be talk in the town. I sit here as if I knew nothing, but I get news of all that's going on. From the officers in Barracks and the business men in the cafés, right down to the older students in the secondary school, there's not a soul that doesn't recognise you at a distance; not one that doesn't talk about you.

"And now you might ask by what right I speak to you about these things, and why I do so; and there are two reasons, my dear. The first is that you're a really good child, but after all, very inexperienced. I've become something of an expert in human nature, and so I want to be a kind of mother, or aunt, to you. And the second reason is that there is the good name of the school to be considered. Isn't that so, my dear?"

Without looking me in the face, she continued rather diffidently, "The school is a sacred place, like the Mosque. It's my most important duty to protect it from gossip, scandal, and every other kind of evil. Isn't it? But all this talk has, unfortunately, drawn attention to the school. Do you notice how many fathers and brothers have come to fetch their daughters and sisters? It may be you haven't noticed it, but I have. They come to see you, not to fetch the children. It seems that one day you tied up one of the poorer children's hair with a bit of ribbon; I don't know how the news got about, but an impertinent young subaltern met the child in the street, gave her some money, took the ribbon, and went off with it. And now, from time to time, he sticks it in his buttonhole, and makes his friends laugh by saying, 'now you've got to look up to me. I've been given a decoration by Gülbeşeker.' And yesterday our doorkeeper Mehmet brought me some strange news. Some drunk men coming back from the public house the night before stopped in front of the school door, and one of them made a speech, in which he said, 'I saw Gülbeşeker touch a black stone in the wall. For God's sake let us worship.' So you see, my dear, these goings-on are neither good for you nor for the school. But as if all this was not enough, you've committed another indiscretion; you seem to have had a talk with Captain Ihsan in Abdurahman's house. If you had accepted Madame's proposal no harm would have been done, but to meet a young man and then refuse so good an offer has attracted attention. 'Ah, she refuses Ihsan Bey, it means she loves someone else; who is it, I wonder?' That's the kind of talk going around now."

I listened to all she had to say without answering or moving. The headmistress, who was afraid at first that I should object and protest, began at last to be uneasy at my silence. With some show of hesitation she said, "What have you got to say to all this, Feridé Hanim?"

I sighed deeply, and said, "It's all true, headmistress. I was beginning to be aware of it myself. I'm sorry to have to leave this lovely place, but what can I do? Write to the Department and make some excuse for having me sent somewhere else. Your greatest generosity and kindness would be not to give the real reason but to find some other excuse. You can say, 'She lacks knowledge of administration,' or 'She won't work, she is idle,' or 'insubordinate.' Say what you like, I shan't complain. But don't say, 'She's become the talk of the town!'"

The headmistress said nothing, but she thought hard. I turned to the window, in order not to show that my eyes had filled with tears. I looked at the mountains opposite; they seemed like clouds slowly fading away in the darkening sky. Ah! Çalıkuşu was beginning to feel the wind of exile again, from those mountains. The wind of exile! It's a phrase without meaning for those who have never really experienced it. In my mind's eye, there spread out before me roads growing narrower and narrower, and more and more dreary, that seemed to have no end to them. And in

my ear I could hear the distant echo of bells. Oh, how long, how long?
And why? To what end?

C., 5th June

My birds had their revenge. During these long holiday months I have
been imprisoned, as they were. The headmistress said there was no
chance of a transfer for me before September. For the present, then, I
tried to let myself be forgotten. I hardly ever went out, and my
neighbours no longer sought me out as they had before. Maybe they were
frightened by the gossip. But now and again I had a talk with a middle-
aged woman very like my aunt in appearance, and with a voice so like
hers, that, with some diffidence, I asked her a favour. "My good friend,"
I said, "don't call me 'teacher.' Can't you just call me 'Feridé'?" My
neighbour was a little surprised, but she didn't refuse. While she was
talking, I would shut my eyes. I imagined myself in the garden at
Kozyataği. . . .

But what am I saying? Perhaps I'm on the verge of a nervous
breakdown. I feel a lack of strength and decision. I laugh again, just as
in the old days; I romp with Munisé and the porters' children; I whistle
to the birds. But I am full of sorrow and anxiety. On the way to this place
I couldn't sleep, on board the ship; one passenger with a plaintive voice
was singing a song with the words "My vagrant heart is set on you," and
what I heard that night I can't forget. Months after, as I stood in my
garden on an April day, with the flowers beginning to blossom, I slowly
began to sing that song. What an enigma man's mind is! How had I
managed to remember the air and the words of a song I had heard only
once? From that day onwards, as I worked, as I watered my birds, as I
looked at the glimpse of sea I had from my window, that song hung on
my lips; and yesterday, towards evening, singing over the last line, "My
vagrant heart is set on you," for no particular reason I began to cry. There
was really nothing in the words or the tune of the very ordinary song to
make one cry, so I decided it was "nerves." I won't sing that song again.

C., 20th June

I have a friend at school called Nazmiye. She is twenty-four or
twenty-five, a pretty, bright, merry sort of girl. She talks well and plays
the lute; the result is, everyone likes her, and she is in close touch with
the best families of the place, and invited somewhere every night. My

colleagues at school don't care much for her, and I hear a certain amount of gossip. It may be that she dresses a bit conspicuously, and they don't like that, or perhaps they are jealous; how can I tell? Nazmiye has a young man—a captain, who is in love with her. He sounds a very nice young fellow, but his family don't agree to their being married at present, and they are keeping their relationship secret. Nazmiye told me about it as a great confidence, and wanted me not to tell anyone else. Yesterday, when I was at home and feeling father bored, Nazmiye came in.

"Feridé Hanim," she said, "I've come to fetch you. Tonight we are invited to Feridun's aunt; they're giving a party at their country home in Subaşi. Although she doesn't know you, she sends you her love, and specially begs you to come."

"What! How can I go to a strange place that I don't know?" I asked.

"How can my young man's aunt be a stranger to you?" she replied. "And I have another idea, too; you'll have an opportunity to meet him. If you don't go, I swear I won't."

I made all kinds of excuses, but she found an answer to them all. The truth is, my excuses were all rather childish. As I've said already, Nazmiye was such a little demon that she could get round anyone, and she used so much persuasion and begged so hard, that I could resist no longer, and accepted her invitation. But there was one thing that struck me at the time. As I began to dress Munisé, Nazmiye said with a little frown, "Are you going to bring that child?"

"Of course," I said. "How can I leave Munisé alone in the house? Does it matter?"

"No, why should it? All the better. But you do sometimes leave her at home. . . ."

"Yes; but so far I've never slept away from the house." I'm not generally considered to be a fool, and in the last two years I had seen a good many things going on and heard a good deal, too, so I don't know how it happened that I came to be taken in, until Nazmiye's last words awakened my suspicions. I can't understand it at all. Probably boredom and the need for fresh air had really made me rather stupid.

A small country carriage took us across the stream, and in half an hour or so, going along one of the narrow roads between the gardens overhung with trees, we came to the country house. On the way we met a flock of sheep and goats. An old shepherd was drawing a wooden bucket out of a garden-well and watering his flock at the stone trough, and it reminded Munisé and me of Mazlum. Full of excitement we jumped out of the carriage; and with tears coming to our eyes, we seized on one of the kids and kissed its long ears and fine muzzle, all dripping with water. For a moment I thought of buying one of them from the shepherd. But what use would it have been, since we would have to leave soon? Hadn't we enough burdens, without adding to them?

The house to which we were invited was an old building in the middle of a garden that seemed to have neither beginning nor end; it was surrounded by pergolas covered with foliage. Feridun Bey's aunt was a middle-aged woman whose dress and appearance did not, I must say, much attract me. So much adornment doesn't really suit an old woman. Her hair was dyed yellow; she had henna on her temples, and dabs of rouge on her cheeks; in fact, she was a queer sight.

She received us in a room on the first floor. She took off my veil, and then, with an excess of familiarity, she kissed my cheeks as though she were savouring them.

"I'm so pleased to meet you, my little pearl," she said. "Gülbeşeker, and what a Gülbeşeker! I declare, one feels inclined to eat you! No wonder everyone falls for you. . . ."

I felt upset; but I had to hide my feelings. There are some ill-mannered folk who really don't know what they are saying; she must have been one of them. Munisé and I were left alone in a room for quite a long time. The sun had set; the rosy glow of evening was fading slowly in the mass of thick leaves that covered the pergola. I was trying to pass the time by joking with the child; but the worm of anxiety was gnawing at my heart. All this disturbed me. From the garden there arose voices of men and women, talk and laughter, and I could hear a violin being tuned up. I leaned out of the window; but I could see nothing, because of the thick vine leaves. At last I began to hear noisy steps coming up the stairs. The door opened; the mistress of the house came in with a big lamp.

"My pearl," she said, "I've neglected you sadly. But I left you in the dark on purpose: one never tires of the garden when the sun is going down." The old lady declared as she trimmed the lamp, that on moonlit nights the garden was "a veritable paradise." Then Nazmiye came in. Outside the door, two tall officers in uniform caught my eye; my head was uncovered, and quite involuntarily I drew back. I wanted to cover my hair with my arm.

Nazmiye was laughing. "My dear, yow rustic you've grown! Surely you're not going to run away from my young man? Take your arm away; I'm ashamed of you," she said.

She was right. There was no reason to run away like that. The officers had come, rather diffidently into the room, and Nazmiye introduced one of them: "My fiancé, Feridun Bey—my friend, Feridé Hanim. What luck that my two friends' names should be so much alike!" The young officer laughed broadly at this. When I was a child, my grandmother used to buy some queer matchboxes, on the top of which was the picture of a clown at a fair, with a Kaiser moustache, round shoulders, and a lock of curly hair falling down into his eyes. Well, Feridun looked just as if he had jumped right out of one of those matchboxes! He took my hand unceremoniously in his rough palm, and gave it a good squeeze and shake, saying, "Mademoiselle, we are both thankful and grateful to you for having honoured our party. Your good health!" Then he introduced the officer behind him. "If you will allow me," he said, "your servant would like to introduce a very close friend and benefactor, Major Burhaneddin Bey. He's a major, but not the ordinary kind of major. He's the younger son of the famous family of Solakzade."

The younger son of the Solakzade family was a man of over forty-five; his hair and moustache were turning grey already. It was evident from his looks that he came of a good family. In his dress, his deportment, and the way he spoke, he was quite different from Feridun, and he almost effaced the bad impression, not unmixed with fear, that his friend had given me. I regained confidence a little.

Burhaneddin Bey talked with ease and fluency. He saluted me from a distance with a polite inclination of the head, and with a slight bow, he said: "Your servant, Burhaneddin. Mademoiselle, my father used to love this garden better than any other part of his property; he used to say, 'This place is lucky; whatever happiness I've had has come to me from this garden.' Now that you have condescended to visit us, I see that my father's words were prophetic."

This was evidently to be counted as a compliment. But what was Burhaneddin's connection with the garden? I looked inquiringly at Nazmiye, and waited for the answer; but she was not looking at me, and persisted in averting her eyes from mine. The lady who, until now, I had thought was the owner of the property, had taken Munisé by the hand and had led her away. The four of us sat together for more than half-an-hour in the room, and talked about anything and everything. Or rather they talked, for I no longer had the power to talk, or even to understand what was being said. My heart seemed to be in an iron vice; I breathed with difficulty; my brain had stopped working, and I could neither think nor feel. I withdrew, and tried to efface myself in my corner, with the irrational fear of a young animal exposed to danger in its home. Below, they were playing a violin sonata, and this was followed by a recital of oriental songs, with a number of bass and treble voices. Sitting on a sofa, Nazmiye and her young man kept pressing closer and closer to one another; and I slowly turned my back on them. They really were a very common couple; not ashamed to behave before two strangers as if they were in one of the vulgar love scenes you see at the pictures. Yes, these were both bad and vulgar people.

A little while before, the stout lady had put a tray covered with plates and glasses on the table. Burhaneddin Bey, with his hands in his pockets, was strolling up and down the room, stopping now and again in front of the table with his back to us. After one of these turns I noticed that he had stopped in front of me; and, bending slightly over me, was saying "Will you condescend to have something, young lady?"

I looked up in surprise. In his hand he held a small cup, with a glowing ruby-coloured drink in it. I shook my head, and said very slowly, "I don't want anything."

He bent over me still further, and I felt his warm breath on my cheek. "This won't do you any harm, young lady; it's the world's finest and most harmless liqueur. Isn't it, Nazmiye Hanim?"

Nazmiye nodded. "Don't insist, Burhaneddin Bey—Feridé must be treated as if she were in our home here. Let her do as she likes."

Up to that moment, Burhaneddin, with his greying hair and his courtly manner, had inspired me with a vague confidence, but now I was beginning to be afraid of him too. What was happening to me? What sort of a place had I fallen upon? How was I to save myself? The lights of the room were slowly going out, and I could see little sparks in the darkness that surrounded me. The sound of singing was coming from far away, like the sound of the sea.

"My pearl, dinner is ready. We have a few guests, and they're waiting for you." The stout lady had spoken, and I pulled myself together a little.

"Thank you, I'm not very well. Please let me stay here," I was able to say.

Then Nazmiye came up to me. "Feridé, dear," she said, "they're not strangers, only one or two friends of Feridun's and Burhaneddin's and some of them have their sweethearts and their wives—yes, their wives— with them. If you don't come, it'll be so rude. They've come specially for you."

I tried to snatch my wrist away from Nazmiye's hands, and moving to the far end of the settee, I withdrew into my corner. I couldn't speak. I had to clench my teeth to prevent them from chattering. Burhaneddin Bey said, "It's for our guest to command. It's our duty to act as she wishes. You go down to the guests and say that Feridé Hanim is not well; and you, Binnaz Hanim, bring us our food here. It's my duty not to leave our guest alone."

At that moment I nearly went mad. To stay and eat in that room alone with Burhaneddin! Not knowing what I was doing, and quite without thinking, I jumped up and said, with such strength as I could muster, "Very well; as you choose." Nazmiye and her young man went down in front of us, arm in arm, and Burhaneddin followed a few steps behind. At the end of the dark corridor a door was open. I found myself suddenly blinded by the light, and stumbled a step or two in the flood of light that fell from the candelabras, and dazzled me. I walked forward a little, swaying from side to side under the brightness. The long mirrors gleamed on the walls, and made the room seem endless; the reflection of the chandeliers was repeated in them far into the distance, like torches on a dark road. A great many eyes and faces came indistinctly into view, and I felt as if I were in a dream. . . .

And then there was a deafening burst of applause. Voices were drowned in the music, but not extinguished by it; the noise was like the roaring of the wind in the mountains. "Long live Burhaneddin Bey, long live Gülbeşeker—long live Gülbeşeker. . ."

When I opened my eyes I found myself in Munisé's arms. She was rubbing her face against mine, weeping and saying, "My poor dear!" She was sobbing and pressing her face against mine and kissing my eyes, which were smarting with eau de cologne; and my hair was wet. I was wet from top to toe. In the half light of the room I felt that a great many people were looking at me, and my first movement was to cover my bare neck with my arms. A voice I didn't recognise kept shouting, "Leave the room, I beg you; leave the room!" I tried to struggle and get up; a hand

228

took me by the shoulder and the same voice said, "Don't be afraid, my dear; it's nothing. Don't be afraid." Between my eyelashes I looked into the face of the speaker. It was the fat old eunuch, the one who always had his jacket unbuttoned. He looked at me; and then turning to those standing by, he said, "Poor thing! She's only a child." Nazmiye was kneeling down and rubbing my palms, and saying, "Feridé, are you feeling a bit better? You've quite upset us." I turned my head away and shut my eyes, so that I shouldn't see her. I learnt afterwards that the fainting fit had lasted more than a quarter of an hour; neither eau de cologne nor burnt cotton-wool had the least effect in bringing me to, so that they gave up hope, and got a carriage ready to fetch the doctor. When I came to, I asked them to take me back to town in the same carriage. If they wouldn't consent, I said, I wasn't afraid to go off alone, although it was very late. They had no choice to but to agree. The fat eunuch put on his coat, and jumped up beside the driver.

As we were about to start, Burhaneddin Bey nervously approached me. Without daring to look in my face, he said, "Feridé Hanim, you have quite misunderstood us. You can be sure no one wanted to do you any harm. We only wanted to entertain you and show you a little country fun. You've been brought up in Istanbul; how could we guess that a young woman who saw no harm, a few days ago, in conversing with one of our colleagues, would behave in this strange way? Let me say again—no one meant you any harm. Anyway, I beg you to forgive me for having upset you so much."

The carriage plunged into the gloom of the narrow vineyard roads. Sitting back in one corner and shivering with cold, I closed my eyes, and slowly the picture of another night came before me—the night when I ran away from home in Kozyatak; the night when, without knowing what I did, I set off alone on the dark roads. . . .

Now and again the branches of the heavily-scented carob trees came through the windows of the carriage, and touched my eyes and face, till they woke me from my dreams. I heard Munisé sigh deeply, as she leant against the other window of the carriage; and I turned to her slowly and said, "Are you awake, Munisé?"

She didn't answer, but bent her head still lower; and then I saw that my dear child was crying, and doing her best, as a grown-up person would, to hide her tears.

I took her hands, and asked, "What's the matter, dear?"

As though she were an older and more experienced person than I, she took me in her arms, and bending down, she whispered in my ear, "Abla, how I've cried tonight, how frightened I've been! I know why they invited you there, abla. Don't let's go to that kind of place again. Need we? Not you? May God take care of you as he would my mother—because what would happen to me if anything happened to you?"

Oh, what shame, what misery! I felt ashamed before that child as if I were a fallen woman; I hadn't the courage to look her in the face. I put my head on her little knees, and wept like a child in its mother's lap, until we reached home.

When I went to the headmistress's house, the sun had just risen. The old lady was surprised to see my eyes swollen with crying, and my face pale at this time of the morning.

"Nothing's wrong, I hope, Feridé Hanim?" she said. "What has happened to you, my dear? I've never seen you like this. Are you ill?"

The old lady's serious manner and somewhat stern face always slightly alarmed me, and prevented me from opening my heart to her; but at that moment, and in that strange land there was no one else to whom I could tell my trouble. My duty and my profession as well both led me to her. Confused and trembling, I told her all about the incident of the previous night. The old lady listened and frowned a little, without saying a word. At the end of the story I leant forward, stretched out my hands, and begged with wet eyes for a few words of comfort. "Madam," I said, "you're older and far more experienced than I am. For heaven's sake tell me the truth. Tell me, must I be looked on now as a wicked woman?"

This question aroused quite an unexpected emotion in the headmistress. Taking me by the chin, she raised my face and looked straight into my eyes; not, as was generally the case with her, with the look of a headmistress and stranger, but with the love and understanding of a mother. Then stroking my face and fondling my hands in her lap, she said with a stammer in her words, "Feridé, it isn't until today that I have realised what an innocent, honest girl you are. Had I known, I might have kept you closer to me, and I might have been able to protect you better. What a pity! Ah, that Nazmiye! My dear, I know a great deal, and I understand it all. But the world is of such a kind that one's obliged to conceal much of what one knows. Nazmiye's a bad creature. I've made many attempts, and tried hard to save the school from her evil ways; it isn't possible to get her moved, because she has innumerable protectors, from the Governor and the officer commanding the regiment, down to the battalion padre. If Nazmiye went away, who would be left to run after the aristocratic families? Who would play the guitar? Who would provide the fun at the secret parties of the higher officials? There are a number of rich heirs like Burhaneddin who would get hold of simple pretty innocents like you, if they could. Feridé, I'm well aware of the plan they had in store for you. Burhaneddin Bey is an old rascal who has squandered the wealth he inherited from his father, to deceive a great many wretched women, and ruin a great many homes. To get hold of a girl about whose beauty all C. is talking has become a matter of vanity with him. The more so, as he heard that you talked to Ihsan Bey. So they approached Nazmiye, and who knows what they promised her, to play this trick on you? Be thankful you've got off as cheaply as you have, my dear. All the same, I have to tell you that you cannot stay here. In a day or two, you may be sure, the incident will be all over town. You must leave by the first boat. Do you know anywhere you can go? Have you relations, or anyone you know, Feridé?"

"I've no one, madam."

"Then go to Smyrna. There are one or two people I know there. One is a school colleague, and the other is the chief clerk in the Education Department. I'll give you a letter. I believe he'll spare no pains to find you a post." Her sympathy quite overwhelmed me. I snuggled up to her like a kitten saved from death in the rain and snow; I rubbed my cheek against her hands as she stroked my hair, and then I kissed her palms.

The old lady sighed a little and went on: "You can't go home in this state, Feridé; and it wouldn't be right, either. Come along, my child. I'll put you to bed upstairs. Have a little sleep; I shall send for your things, and for Munisé. You must stay here till you go."

I slept and slept and slept until evening, upstairs in the headmistress's room. As I opened my eyes I saw the old lady; she came to my side, put her hand on my forehead, and kissed my hair, which I'd done up in two plaits, just like the girls of C.

"Are you ill, Feridé? Have you any pain, my dear?" she asked.

There was nothing wrong with me; I wasn't ill; but I didn't raise my head from the pillow. It seemed to me that I would find consolation here, like faint perfume in a handkerchief, as I grew to know the increasing love of this new mother that I'd found in these days of loneliness and distress.

The Steamer *Prençipeza Maraya, 2nd July*

I wrapped myself up in my greatcoat against the wind. I had sat up on deck until the moon rose and the deck was deserted, except for one tall passenger, who hadn't once changed his position throughout the evening, and was leaning against the rail of the steamer, whistling sad little tunes into the face of the wind. I had always loved the living sea— the smiling, moaning, wrathful sea; but tonight the waters gave me a feeling of loneliness, without hope or consolation. I went below, shivering as if the damp of the night had penetrated to my very bones. Munisé was asleep in the berth of the cabin. I opened my diary and began to write, burdened with a feeling of great loneliness, and listening to the tremors that came from the deep about us.

Today the headmistress came to the pier with me. I didn't say goodbye to any of my friends. The only person I happened to see was the large woman who was so like my aunt; and once again I seemed to hear her calling me by name. We had left Mazlum at B., and now, again, we had to leave our birds behind. I entrusted them to the headmistress, and made her promise not to forget to feed them and give them water. She said, "Feridé, you're so fond of them; let them go with your own hand. It will be a far greater kindness to them. They'll be better that way."

I gave a sad laugh, and said, "No, madam; I used to think that too, but now I've changed my mind. Birds are poor creatures without any sense; they don't know what they want. Until they escape from their cages they struggle and suffer. But do you think they'd be any happier outside? No, not a bit of it. I believe these little creatures get used to their cages, in spite of everything, and when they do regain the open air and spend the night on the bough of a tree with their heads under their wings, they remember their cage, and fix their little eyes on the light of the windows, and long to be back in it. One has to keep birds in their cages by force—yes, by *force*."

The old lady stroked my cheek and said, "Feridé, what a strange child you are! Why cry about anything as unimportant as that?"

There were a few passengers who had boarded the ship at C. I overheard a conversation between two officers among them; the younger officer was saying to his companion, "Ihsan Bey was to have left four days ago. I told him to wait a day or two, and then we'd go to Beyrout together. But without meaning to do so, I drove the poor wretch to disaster. If he'd gone four days ago, he wouldn't have got into all this trouble."

The elder of the two replied, "Yes, it's really a most regrettable affair. Ihsan is a difficult fellow; I don't know how the thing happened. Do you know any details?"

"Yes, I was an eyewitness. We were together, yesterday, in the Municipal Casino; Burhaneddin Bey was playing billiards. Suddenly Ihsan came in, drew the major into a corner, and began to say something to him. I don't know what passed between them, but they seemed to be talking quite amicably and politely to one another. Then all at once I saw Ihsan step back a pace, and strike Burhan Bey a tremendous blow. The major tried to draw his revolver, but Ihsan had already drawn his sword; and if people hadn't thrown themselves between them, there would have been bloodshed, sure as anything. Ihsan will be brought before a Court Martial tomorrow."

"If one of us had done it, we should have been in a pretty bad way. But I think Ihsan has some influence with the pasha. He is his nephew, and his wife's adopted son. All the same, it's a good thing this happened to that fellow Burhan. He had got completely out of control."

"If that's so, he'll get off lightly."

"I wonder what the trouble was about?"

"They say it was a political quarrel; politics haven't been stamped out of this army of ours yet."

"Well, if you ask me, I believe it was some trouble over a woman again. Don't we know our Burhan?"

The officers strolled away, talking. I understood, now, who had sent the bunch of roses that an old sailor had brought and left in my cabin. Ihsan Bey, I may never come across you again, and if I do I shall have to pretend not to recognise you. But the day you go before the Court Martial for my sake, I shan't forget that you remembered me. I shall keep one small petal from these roses in my Diary—these roses, that so delicately concealed the name of their giver. And I'll keep your memory in my heart as something very precious.

Up on the deck the lonely passenger was still whistling his sad little tunes. I looked out of the open porthole of the cabin; the dawn seemed to be rising out of the sea. Come now, Çalıkuşu; go to bed! The late hour and your weariness have made your eyes heavy. What have you to do

Çalıkuşu

with the dawn? That is the time for "Golden Flowers" that have been lapped in sleep (and more than sleep) far, far away, to open their eyes to happiness.

❧ PART FOUR ❧

Smyrna, 20ᵗʰ September

I've been in Smyrna for nearly three months; and my affairs are not going well. I have one last hope. If that, too, disappears tomorrow, I do not know what will happen to me. I dare not even think. The man to whom the headmistress in C. recommended me went sick a month before my arrival, and has gone to Istanbul for six months' change of air. There was nothing for it but for me to go to the Director of Education on my own. And whom do you think I found? Why, the worthless creature I came across in B., who sat there as though he were asleep, and spoke to one as though he were in a dream. Of course those beautiful dreamy eyes, which the Creator fashioned for sleep rather than for sight, didn't recognise me. "Look in in a few days, and we'll see," he told me; "We'll find something." With him, a few days meant one or two months; and in fact, that was how it turned out. Today, I went there again. He was good enough to receive me fairly well, and began telling me, in that soft, subdued voice of his, "My dear, there's a village school about two hours away from here. The climate's pleasant and the scenery delightful. . ."

It was the very speech he had made to me when he was sending me to Zeyniler. I was seized with folly suddenly. I found my tongue, and took the words out of his mouth with a laugh. "Don't give yourself all this trouble, sir," I interrupted; "Let me tell you the Ministry has expended a lot of money and energy and has produced a new school there. Now all that is needed is the effort and sacrifice of a young teacher like me. Thank you! I saw something of your kindness once before, when I went to Zeyniler."

Of course, having said it, I quite expected to be thrown out. But oddly enough, he was not in the least angry. On the contrary, he laughed hard, and said philosophically, "What are you going to do, my dear? This is a matter of administrative necessity. Someone has to go, if you don't."

The office of a Director of Education is never in want of visitors. From an armchair in the corner, a voice was heard, stuttering slightly, "B-But what a delightful little girl!"

I turned round sharply. At last I had caught one of those disrespectful people who called me names; who persisted, moreover, in calling me names that suggested sweets or silkworms. I would teach him a good lesson and pay him out for all the others. But he gave me no chance to say anything; he turned to the Director of Education, and said in a very authoritative voice, "For god's sake give the young woman what she wants: don't torment the child."

The Director replied deferentially, "Your order shall be obeyed, Reşit Bey Efendi; but really we have no vacancies at present. There's only the post of French Mistress in the secondary school, and of course that won't suit this young woman."

"Why not?" I inquired. "As a matter of fact, your servant was French Teacher at the Teachers' College at B."

The Director hesitated. "Yes. But we have advertised the entrance examination. And it's tomorrow," he pointed out.

"Good," said Reşit Bey, "what harm would there be in this young lady taking the examination? Actually, I shall be there, too. Providence will look after us. Now mind you don't let the examination start before I arrive."

Evidently Reşit Bey was a man of some importance; but Oh God!— how unimaginably ugly! As I looked at him, I had to bite my lip till it bled, to prevent myself laughing. People are either dark or fair, surely? But in this fellow's face, there was a wide range of colours, from the white of a freshly healed wound to dusty black. He had so dirty a complexion that I was surprised to find it had not stained his collar. You would really think that someone had shoved his hand into coal dust for a joke, and blackened his face all over. He had two baboon's eyes very close to one another, under cover of hairless eyelids, red as an open wound. He had a strange nose that hung over his white moustache to the edge of his lip, and the heaviest jowl you ever saw. There were two pouches, one on each side of his face, just like the pouches in which monkeys store their nuts and other treasures. All the same, I was getting on. The good turn he had done me, with the help of a few words, was no small thing. In any case, the Almighty, when he'd fashioned the gentleman's face, must have seen that he'd gone too far, and made up for the injustice by giving him a warm heart. To my mind, goodness of heart is something better than beauty of eye or face; what else can heartless beauty do but break the spirit of some poor girl and kill the love she feels?

Smyrna, 22ⁿᵈ September

Today I sat for the examination. The history exam went badly; then they asked us to conjugate in writing the imperative and the indefinite tense of nine or ten verbs like 'over-estimate,' 'exploit' and 'implore.' I didn't even know the Turkish version, let alone the French. But the oral test went well. Reşit Bey talked French to me, and said a few words that made me hope I should be successful. May heaven help Munisé.

Smyrna, 25ᵗʰ September

The results are out. I didn't get through. One of the clerks told me "If Reşit Bey had wanted it, you'd certainly have passed. Who would have the nerve to vote against him? He must have some other idea in his head."

My situation was very bad now. In a couple of days' time it would be the first of the month; I should have to pay my rent. The last medallion— a thing I'd inherited from my mother—came to my assistance. I gave it to one of my neighbours today, and she agreed to get her husband to sell it and give me the money. I didn't want to lose this relic, because it held the photograph that my father and mother had taken the year they were married. And now all I had was the poor picture, out of its frame. But I found some consolation here too; for I said to myself, "I know my father and mother would rather be at rest in the heart of the daughter they left, than in gold itself."

Smyrna, 27ᵗʰ September

Today I got a note from Reşit Bey. He seems to have found me a job; he invites me to his house in Karşiyaka for a talk. The clerk in the Education Office had suggested that this man had been hostile to me: apparently he was wrong. Well, let's see. Tomorrow will show.

Smyrna, 28ᵗʰ September

I have come back from Reşit Bey's house in Karşiyaka. It's a real palace. Now I know why they attach so much importance to this gentleman! Reşit Bey received me courteously; he explained that he had

237

liked my French, but that he'd not been able to prevent his colleagues doing me an injustice. The job about which he had written in his letter was that of French tutor to his own daughters. "Your qualifications and your manner have both pleased me," he said. "What is the point of hanging about in one of the schools? Wouldn't it be better to give my girls French lessons and live with us? We could give you a nice room. . . ."

That really meant a post as a governess; it would be an easier and better-paid job than anything I could get as a teacher. I've never liked that profession, and always looked upon it as a kind of servant's job; but that couldn't be helped. It wouldn't do to disappoint Reşit Bey. I thanked him for his confidence and his courtesy; but making Munisé my excuse, I explained that I could not accept. Reşit Bey, however, saw nothing in that. "We've plenty of room for her," he maintained. "Is a child likely to be a burden in a house like this?" But I could not give any definite answer. I asked for three days' grace; I would have one more try. If I found an official post as a teacher, well and good: if not—well, then. . . .

Karşiyaka, 3rd October

They've given Munisé and me a room on the top floor of the house, facing the sea. It's small, but it's a nice little room, like a birdcage. From my window I gazed out on to the sea and the quayside until it was quite late. The whole gulf can be seen from my window: opposite me is Smyrna. But to be truthful, the quay at Karşiyaka entertains me more. What a lovely, gay life goes on here! The trams run till midnight; endless crowds of young people parade up and down in the light of the street lamps. In the distance is a Casino, whose red and green lights are reflected in the sea, and you can hear songs being played on guitars, sometimes lively and sometimes plaintive. I don't know—but this is what I seemed to see: all I could distinguish in that light were the flecks of black and white that were the clothes of people—couples betrothed, in love with one another. Moreover every unseen corner, and the top of every pile of rocks, whose dark shadows were discernible in the sea—all seemed to be full of lovers hidden from sight. Whispers and secret kisses came from the sea; clandestine love-making, lip to lip. The cool breath of the night, that weighed on my heart and stopped my breathing, came from the lips of girls like those, their heads on the shoulders of their lovers, their eyes looking into green eyes, like the dark hues of the night sea.

They've been good enough to accept me as a young lady in this house. My burdens have never seemed heavy to me; so I felt grateful to the old servant who would not let me carry my box up to my room, but insisted on taking it out of my hand. Munisé was not yet of an age to understand such things. The splendour of the house blinded the poor child's eyes. As we were going upstairs, she wanted to repeat a joke we were always playing in our own house, and halfway up the staircase she suddenly seized my skirt and tried to pull me down a stair. I took her by the arm, and bending down, whispered into her ear, "Munisé, child, we're in someone else's house. Let's hope we'll have our own house again; then we can play that game again, darling." The child left off at once; she understood my meaning. When we got to our room the joy in her small face had disappeared. How delicately the child understands me! She put her arms round my neck and hugged me closer than she had ever done before, covering my face with little kisses.

As I shut the window I had one more look. Everyone had disappeared; the lamps had been put out, and the sea that had sparkled just now in the light of the shore lamps had receded, leaving a bare beach of sand; and now laid its head on the white pillow of the rocks like a child gradually falling asleep.

On my way here today—Oh! Stop. I dare not write that down.

Karşiyaka, 7th October

Life doesn't pass too badly in this house of Reşit Bey's. One of my two pupils is my own age, and the other one younger. The name of the elder one is Ferhunde. Her style of beauty is a replica of her father's; so she's ill tempered. Little Sabahat is just the opposite. She is as pretty as a doll, a bright, plump child. One of the women servants screwed up her eyes one day in a significant way, and said "Our late mistress was ill about this time, and a young Army doctor used to keep coming and going. It's evident that the mistress must have kept on looking into that doctor's face, and that was how the child was so pretty."

My greatest fear was from the servants. Why should I conceal the truth; am I not more or less one of them? But I've acted very circumspectly; I've not ordered any of them about, and so they respect me. Nevertheless I think Reşit Bey's influence is to be seen there. The greatest drawback of the house is that it hums like a bee-hive. What's worse, Ferhunde and Sabahat insist on coming down whenever a guest comes. And a worse drawback still is Reşit Bey's grown-up son, Jemil Bey. He is a young man of about thirty, unprepossessing and lacking in sense. He seems to spend ten months of the year in Europe, getting rid of his father's money. Two months he spends in Smyrna. Thank goodness we have got to the last days of those two months. Had it not been so, I should have left the house three days ago. "What's it got to do with you?" I shall be asked; that's what I said to myself, but I reckoned wrongly. Three days ago, Ferhunde and Sabahat had kept me in the downstairs drawing room till it was late. After I left them, I went upstairs in the dark; at the head of the stairs on the third floor I ran into a man's shadow. I gave a start and tried to go back. Then I heard Jemil Bey's voice say "Don't be afraid, my dear; it's not a stranger." A ray of light from one of the side windows lit up his face. "I'm sorry, sir," I said; "I didn't recognise you at first. I want to go by." Jemil Bey stepped to the right; but as the head of the stairs was narrow, there was no room to pass him. "I couldn't sleep," he said, "so I got up to wait for the full moon."

I understood his purpose. I wanted to escape quite naturally, and as if I were unaware of it. None the less, to give him some answer, I said "It's not time for the full moon, sir."

He answered me very slowly, "What do you mean by that, Mademoiselle, when there's a rosy moon that's suddenly appeared at the top of these very stairs? Does any moon in the world shine as seductively as this one?" Jemil Bey took hold of my wrists, with a sudden movement, and I felt his warm breath in my face; I pulled myself violently away. If I hadn't grasped one of the banisters, I should have fallen to the bottom. I bruised my head badly, and couldn't restrain a slight cry of pain. Without making any noise, Jemil Bey came down to where I was. Although I could not see his face, I knew that he was agitated. "Feridé Hanim," he said, "forgive me. Have you hurt yourself?"

I was going to say no, that it was nothing, and beg him to let me go; but I couldn't answer, and nothing but a stifled sob escaped me. To suppress it, I tried to cover my mouth with my handkerchief; and then I saw that a little blood was flowing from my lip, where it had been hurt slightly. We were standing by the staircase window: in the dim light that came through the open shutter, Jemil Bey could see the blood as well. His voice was distressed and trembling as he said "Feridé Hanim: I've behaved like the commonest of men. Be generous enough to say you have forgiven me, Feridé Hanim."

240

After his abominable behaviour, this cool politeness fairly made my hair stand on end, and gave me back my courage completely. I replied in a stern voice "There's nothing extraordinary in what you've done, sir. It's usual enough to treat women servants this way, as though they were adopted children. By taking a position in your house so like theirs, I've provoked the situation myself. You needn't be afraid: I'll find some excuse or other, and leave tomorrow, without any talk." Then I went upstairs, quietly and naturally, straight to my room.

With my bag in one hand and Munisé in the other, it was easy enough to go. But where to? Three days have gone by and I still haven't carried out my decision. I'm still here, because the time has come to admit what I was ashamed to write in my diary on the night I came here. I'd come one evening when it was getting dark: wouldn't it have been better to wait until the following morning? Of course it would. But there was no chance of doing that. On that hopeless evening when I came here, the house was full of guests. Reşit Bey showed me to his guests as if I'd been some new ornament he had purchased. Everyone had looked at me admiringly, but with a suggestion of pity. While I was trying to please each one of them separately, with the rather shy politeness forced on me by my situation, I fainted, and lost consciousness for a moment. I sat down suddenly on the edge of a chair, and closed my eyes for half a minute, perhaps even less, without even trying to efface a rather bewildered smile. Reşit Bey and the young ladies' guests were very much upset. Sabahat ran up to me with a glass, and made me swallow a little water, while we both laughed as if it were a joke. One of the guests, an elderly lady, smiled and said "It's nothing; it's the effect of the south wind. Ah—these neurotic, delicate, modern girls! The slightest change in weather, and they wither away like roses." They all took me for a frail and delicate girl, a young lady who could stand no fatigue; and I confirmed them in their opinion, and showed my gratitude to them for thinking as they did. I had told them lies. But the true cause of the faint was a very different one: that day, for the first time in her life, Çalıkuşu was starving.

Karşiyaka, 11th October
Ferhunde and Sabahat had guests from Smyrna again today; four girls between fifteen and twenty years old. In the afternoon we were to have a walk along the sea shore, and go across to Kayrakli and back by boat. We returned, unwillingly, to the drawing room, with our çarşafs on

our shoulders. The girls played the piano and chatted a little; and they made off into the corner in twos or threes, and told each other secrets. It was quite obvious what they were talking about, with their heads close together, smiling as if they were tickling each other. Sabahat was a dear, mischievous girl, and she liked inventing tricks to amuse her guests; there were some albums on the shelf full of photographs of members of the family, and friends. She took down one of these, and collected her friends about her at the top of the table, to show them the pictures. The fun was not so much in the photographs themselves, as in what Sabahat said about them. She had a joke for every one, and said such outrageous things about the life and character of each, that we laughed inordinately. An imposing-looking pasha, for instance, his breast covered with decorations, looked as though the whole world were at his feet; but she revealed that his wife used to beat him with a broom. And again there was a certain relative of theirs, a grown-up woman, but rather countrified; one day as she was getting out of the steamer at Korkaryala, she fell into the sea, by accident, and into her local jargon, so to speak, at the same time, calling out "Save me, save me!—my sweet life is going." Reşit Bey had a wet nurse from Konia who gave you a feeling, when you saw her for the first time, such as you'd never had before. Then there was a man dressed as a hodja, in a turban and baggy trousers; but opposite the photograph was another of him, taken in a tail coat, with an eyeglass, after he had become a member of Parliament. The hodja was looking at the member of Parliament with indignation, his eyes wide open; and the member of Parliament was pursing his lips and regarding the hodja with amused contempt. The result was so funny that I took Sabahat's hand to stop her turning over the page, and laughed helplessly at it. Ferhunde was trying to make fun of me. "Feridé Hanim," she said, "if you like, we'll marry you off to this nice-looking fellow; he isn't attached at the moment. He's divorced his first wife, and he's looking for a modern woman, who'd be worthy of a member of Parliament." I was still laughing as I left the table, and said to Ferhunde "Write off at once; I'm ready enough. If one can find no other happiness, at least one can spend one's life laughing."

Sabahat had turned another page, and beckoned to me again. "Feridé Hanim," she said, "if you look at *this* picture, I'm afraid you'll give up your member of Parliament." And all the visitors cried out together "*Oh, how nice!*" and called me across with a wave of their hands. "It's quite useless," I said, as I went towards the table; "whatever happens I shan't give up my member of Parliament." I bent over the album, among the curly heads already mingled there; and I couldn't help giving a little cry, as they had done. The photograph that was looking into my eyes and smiling at me from the pages of the album was a picture of Kâmran. Sabahat didn't make fun of the original, this time; on the contrary, she started telling her companions about him with much interest and enthusiasm. "This Bey," she told them "is my aunt Münevver's husband. Their wedding took place last spring, when I was in Istanbul. If you were to see him, you would think nothing of the photograph. You never saw such eyes as he's got—and such a nose! And let me tell you something stranger still. He used to be in love with the daughter of one of his aunts. A little bit of a thing she must have been, very smart and full of mischief. Indeed that's why she was called 'Çalıkuşu.' But Çalıkuşu had no use for Kâmran Bey: that's how it is with love. . . . In the end, within a day of their being married, she left the house on her own, and went off into the blue. Kâmran Bey would neither eat nor drink for months; he was waiting for that faithless girl. But if she'd had any intention of returning, would she have gone off the very night before she was to be a bride? I was present when my aunt Münevver kissed the hand of her new mother-in-law; the old lady must have been remembering the strange little wren, who wouldn't stay on her perch; she wept like a child."

I listened to all the details, leaning against the piano, without a word or a movement. Kâmran was still smiling at me from the album. "Heartless," I said in a very deliberate voice.

Sabahat turned to me and agreed: "What you've said is very true, Feridé Hanim. What can you call her but heartless?—a girl who wouldn't keep faith with a young man as charming and good-looking as this one!"

Kâmran, I hate you. If it weren't true, shouldn't I have wept, shouldn't I have fainted, shouldn't I have gone into mourning, when I heard that piece of news? But I've never laughed in all my life as I did today, nor plunged into enjoyment and pleasure so readily. Indeed, if one unfortunate accident hadn't befallen me, I should have called it the happiest day in my life. Towards evening the weather cleared, and enabled us to have a fairly long country walk. We were passing along the edge of the river; one of our visitors saw a kasunpat flower on the other bank. "Oh, how lovely!" she exclaimed. "If only I could pick it!" I laughed. "Would you like me to make you a present of it?" I suggested. The decline was dangerously deep and broad. The girls laughed too, and one of them said in fun "Now if we'd only got a bridge. . . ." I replied casually, "I think it can be crossed without one," and jumped, without more hesitation. There was a cry behind me; I'd succeeded in getting across to the other side. But as bad luck would have it, I was unable to pick the kasunpat and take it back as I'd promised, because my feet had struck the very edge of the bank, and I'd seized a branch of thorn to stop myself falling, and torn my hands. Yes, if the accident hadn't befallen me, if the pain of the thorns piercing my palms hadn't made me cry, right up to the time when we got home at night in the dark, I could have called today the happiest and most amusing day in my life. Kâmran, it was because I hated you that I ran away to strange places. And now my hatred is so deep that I'm still not far enough away. I want to go away as far as I can from the world in which you live and breathe.

More and more have I made up my mind that I can't stay in this house. Every two or three days I've been going down to Smyrna and calling at the Education Office. Yesterday I chanced to meet one of my former teachers, Sister Bérénice, on the steamer. I had seen her once before, two months ago, and as we'd been very fond of each other at school, I explained my situation to her a little. Sister Bérénice said yesterday "Feridé, I've been looking out for you for the last few days. They want a Turkish language and drawing mistress in our own school. I've recommended you to the Headmistress. There's no need to take a house of your own; you can live at the school. After all, you're used to the life we lead."

My heart began to beat. I believe that if I were to find myself there again, among those deep organ voices, and the fragrance of those days, I might recover some of my childhood's dreams once more. I didn't even have to consider. "All right, Sister," I said. "I'll come. And thank you!"

Before going there today I called in at the Education Office, with the object of getting my papers back. They told me the Director had been asking for me for the last three days. Wondering what he wanted, I went in to see him. When the Director of Education saw me, he said "You've had a long time to wait, my dear, but you're in luck. A good post has turned up. I'm going to send you to the school at Kuşadasi."

Kuşadasi: what a lovely name! My own name. I had a feeling that it must be a pleasant place. But what about the promise I had given to the Sisters' school? I waited and thought for a minute or two before replying. On the one hand there was a whole new life; on the other, perhaps, poverty and wretchedness—but wasn't there something to attract, as well, and to console? There came before my eyes the little children of our own schools, neglected, the victims of rough treatment. The poor little wretches were like flowers waiting for a little sun, a little sympathetic understanding, that they might blossom. They showed all the gratitude and affection in their hearts to anyone who was willing to give them sympathy and love. I realized that in spite of everything, I'd begun to love the pathetic little creatures very deeply. Wasn't it from among them that Munisé has come to me? Besides, there had been one or two experiences in the last two years of my life; just as the light can hurt sore eyes, so happiness can hurt sick souls. And for sick souls, as much as for sore eyes, there's no better medicine than darkness. I'd accepted the position of teacher so that I might not die of starvation; my calculations had turned out badly. This profession certainly could starve you any day; but what of it, when it could satisfy the hunger my heart felt for sympathy, and give me the consolation of dedicating my life to the happiness of others? In any case, it was impossible to reawaken the lost dreams of those vanished days. The oppressive dreams of those days, their ancient fragrance, the soft moan of the organs, were gradually fading from my mind. "All right, sir," I told him. "I'll take it."

Until I got my orders I did not wish to say anything to anyone in the house. But a fresh incident forced me to do so. The old maidservant had been saying curious things to me for some time; the other day, for instance, she said for no particular reason, "My dear, I get fonder of you every day. And not only I—everyone else as well. Ferhunde and Sabahat, they are children, but they don't give the house a sense of sweetness. It's been quite different since you came. You've such a nice nature and disposition; when you're with the grown-ups you're a grown-up, and when you're with the young, you're young as well." She said a great many more things like that. I could only regard her words as expressing the kindliness of one fellow-worker to another; but the old woman came out with it last night. "What can we do, my dear? Can we keep you here by force, I wonder? I've thought of a way: but don't you be suspicious. I swear no one has said a thing!"

I realised, by now, that she was really speaking for someone else. But I pretended not to understand, and went on listening. When she was afraid to finish a sentence, she'd pass on to something else; and now she began to tell me: "Our Bey is not old. I knew him as a child. He isn't good-looking, but he has dignity and distinction. Yes, and his character isn't too bad, either. My dear, this house can't be left without a mistress. Tomorrow or the next day, Ferhunde and Sabahat will get married. God forbid that we should be landed with someone impossible. Feridé Hanim, anyone can marry one of those young men with twirled moustaches, but it's a very different thing to find distinction of this sort. Oh! If only we could find the master the right kind of girl! What do you think?"

I said nothing, but smiled rather bitterly. I considered; so this was the meaning of all the respect that Reşit Bey has shown me, all the importance he has attached to Ferhunde's and Sabahat's lessons, all the hours he's spent joking with us—yes, and even playing ball; all of it. I remembered the words of the clerk in the Education Office: "If Reşit Bey had wished, he could have appointed you to the post of French Mistress." A few years ago I would have revolted against a suggestion of this sort; but now, to dismiss it, I answered the Kalfa with indifference, and replied, "Yes; I could have gone with you to choose him a bride. We should have looked out a good little wife for Reşit Bey. What a pity—I'm going to Kuşadasi in a day or two. The young man I'm engaged to is coming there too; we're going to be married in a month or so." And as the old woman looked at me with astonishment, "Sleep well, my dear Kalfa," I added, "I'm going to bed early," and withdrew to my room.

Kuşadasi, 25th November

When they said to me "Would you like to go to Kuşadasi?" I was delighted at once, and said to myself "I feel sure I shall find the happiness and tranquility I've been seeking for so long, when I get to Kuşadasi—my namesake!" I wasn't wrong, either. I liked this place better than any other. Was it because the country was so lovely? No. Kuşadasi did not turn out to be, as I had thought, a Robinson Crusoe island where I was to spend a lonely wandering life with my little butterfly, Munisé. Or was it that I was particularly comfortable there? No, it wasn't that. On the contrary, I've never worked so hard. What was it, then? My real reason may provoke a smile; but what can I do? I must be truthful. And I love Kuşadasi because it is *not* beautiful, and not a peaceful place. It's my opinion that the Almighty created beautiful countries and beautiful seas as he did beautiful faces—to bring pain to man's heart in secret.

When I came here a month ago, the headmistress of the school took me on one side. She is a delicate, worn out woman about fifty years of age; "My dear," she told me, "I've just buried my two sturdy sons, in the space of exactly three months. I am lost to the world. They have sent you here with the status of deputy headmistress; you are young, you seem well-informed. I'm going to leave the school to you. Run it as you think best. We have two other teachers, two elderly women: we can expect nothing from them."

I promised to work as hard as I could, and I kept my word. "Feridé Hanim," the headmistress said to me yesterday, "my dear, I cannot thank you enough. You have worked ten times harder than you promised. Within a month, both the school and our children have flourished. God bless you! From your colleagues down to the youngest child, everyone loves you. Even I forget my troubles and the bitterness of my heart, at times; and when you laugh, I begin to laugh too."

The poor woman thought I was working for love of her dark eyes, and was grateful. But what a lovely thing it is to work: to give yourself to others, with all your heart! Çalıkuşu was the old Çalıkuşu again. There was none of the weariness of life that I'd had at C., nor the rebellious moods of Smyrna. It had all vanished, like a passing cloud that once darkened a summer sky. The idea of devoting myself to the children of others and to their happiness, till my hair turned white, doesn't alarm me in the least. That place in my heart, left empty by the little ones destroyed there, I gave to the children of others, two years ago.

Kuşadasi, 1ˢᵗ December
For some time now, there's been talk of war, on all sides. I had dedicated my life to the school, and I didn't even listen to it. But today the town was alive with excitement: the war had begun!

Kuşadasi, 15ᵗʰ December
The war started fifteen days ago. Every day crowds of the wounded come to the hospital. Sadness has fallen on the school; a great many of my children have fathers or brothers in the Army. Poor little things!—of course, they don't understand the danger. But the sadness has fallen upon them too, as upon their elders.

Kuşadasi, 15ᵗʰ December

What wretched luck—oh dear, what wretched luck! They occupied the school today, by order of the Commander. It's rumoured that they are going to turn it into a temporary hospital. Let them do what they choose: I don't care.

But how am I going to spend my time now, until the school's started again?

Kuşadasi, 24ᵗʰ December

Today I had gone to fetch a few books that had been left at the school. There was so much confusion, that far from finding the books, one ran the risk of getting lost oneself. Believing it to be hopeless, I was turning back, when one of the nurses opened a door, and said, "Let's have one more try, and ask the senior medical officer. Very likely he's carried off some of the books himself." The room was full of bottles, bandages and chemicals; the chief medical officer had thrown off his jacket and, moaning and groaning, was trying to straighten out the mess.

As his back was turned I could only see his neck, his white hair and his bare wrists. To worry a man in that state about books would have been inconsiderate: so I pulled the nurse by the skirt and said, "No, don't do it." But she noticed nothing and said, "Didn't you find some French picture books, sir?—where are they?"

The old doctor flared up at once; without turning his head, he made a reply so wicked and so outrageous, that I covered my face with my hands involuntarily, and tried to escape. But just at that moment he turned. "Hullo, my little one," he shouted immediately, "it's you again, is it?"

I'd no sooner seen his face than I called out impulsively, "Doctor Bey—the doctor from Zeyniler!" I'm not exaggerating: I positively shouted. He came towards me, knocking over the glasses, and he took my hands. He pulled down my head and kissed the hair over my çarşaf. We had only met for a single day—indeed, it wasn't even a day, only a few hours; what kind of secret connection was it that could bind us one to another and throw us into each other's arms two years later, like friends of forty years' standing, or father and daughter, rather? Who can say?— so incomprehensible is the human heart.

Hayrullah Bey asked me, just as he did at Zeyniler, "Tell me now, you little good-for-nothing, what are you doing here?" His blue eyes, bright as a child's, twinkled between his white eyelashes with an indescribable benevolence. I smiled back at him, just as I'd done at Zeyniler, and said "You know, Doctor, I'm a schoolteacher. I go from place to place; and now I've been appointed here." With the greatest concern, as though he understood my whole life and all my feelings, he asked me, "Still no news, little one?"

I drew back at once, as if someone had splashed water in my face, and winced involuntarily. And with an attempt to look surprised, I said "From whom, Doctor?"

He threatened me with his finger as if annoyed. "What lie are you going to tell me, child? Your lips have learnt to lie, but your eyes and your whole demeanour still preserve their simplicity. Whom did I mean? Why, whoever it is that sends you about like this from one place to another."

I shrugged my shoulders and laughed. "You mean the Ministry of Education?—and then, of course the wish to serve my country's children?"

The doctor repeated once more the challenge he had put to me at Zeyniler. As his words had affected me considerably, they'd remained in my memory word for word: "At your age, as you are now, with this face of yours? Very well; so be it, my good-for-nothing, as long as you don't behave like a savage." He had forgotten his medicines, and I my books. He went on talking: "So you're a teacher in this school, are you?"

"I was worried that you'd taken over the school, Doctor."

"Wait—there's another thing. What was the name of that wretched village?—where I made you a nurse; you remember? Will you help me here too? There's not much difference after all. It's either your little monkeys or my dear little bears. They're so alike in spirit . . . the same response, the same child-like heart; and to help these folk of mine who have suffered in the last few months, is a more worthwhile job, my little girl. . . ."

My face lit up immediately, and I was as happy as a child. Let me have an occupation on which I could expend my strength and my devotion, come what may. "Very well, Doctor. I'll begin work whenever you like."

"Now, at once. Look here: see what a mess they've made of this, for instance. It's not a hand, it's almost a . . ." and again he used what would be considered bad language. I interrupted him, in some confusion: "On one condition, Doctor. Not too much soldier's talk when you're with me."

He gave a great laugh, and replied "I'll to my best; but if there's an accident now and again, you must forgive me."

We worked together until evening; there would be wounded coming tomorrow, we heard, and we were ready for them.

Kuşadasi, 26th December

I've been working as a nurse with Hayrullah Bey for the last month. The war continues: there is no end to the troops of wounded arriving at the hospital. There is so much to do. . . . Some nights I don't even go home. Last night I had to look after an old captain who had been severely wounded; towards morning, utterly tired out, I was dozing in an armchair in the dispensary. I felt a light hand touch my shoulders, and I opened my eyes. It was Doctor Hayrullah Bey: he was afraid I might be cold, and wanted to cover me with a thin blanket without waking me. "Sleep on, child—don't disturb yourself," he said, smiling with those blue eyes, which looked dull and tired in the light of the early dawn. His kindness at that moment so touched me, that I wanted to say something to express my gratitude; but weariness and sleep defeated me, and I fell asleep again, smiling.

In spite of two great faults of his, I love the old doctor very much. One of his faults is his use of bad language. It's true that those around him do the kind of stupid thing that's enough to justify it; but that's not what prompts him to use language that makes me fly from him. For days I don't look at him. But he's conscious of it too. "Don't take any notice, my child," he says, "these words have no place in the dictionary. It's soldiers' language." Hayrullah Bey puts one in mind of small children, whose faults one cheerfully forgives for the sake of their lovable contrition. His second fault is a more serious one. There's a most incomprehensible delicacy in this rough man. He understands with the most uncanny insight things one hardly dares admit even to oneself. He knows, for instance, a great part of my adventures that I've tried hard to avoid telling other people. How is it that I've told him? I've not even been aware of having done it. All I did was give short dry answers to the occasional questions that he has put to me. However, he has fitted together all I've told him, and reproduced my whole story.

It seems that the Doctor has no people of his own. He married twenty years ago, and his wife died of typhus nine months later. Since then he has lived as a bachelor. He says he comes from Rhodes, but he has a little property in Kuşadasi. In any case, he must be a man in no actual need of his pay as a Colonel; for he spends several times that amount upon the sick. As an instance of this, I read a letter, a day or two ago, which a wounded soldier had received from home. The man's old mother wrote to say that she was in the last stages of destitution, and that the children were begging in the streets for want of food. The wounded man listened to the letter, and moaned wretchedly. Hayrullah Bey was examining a soldier in the bed next to ours. He suddenly turned to this poor fellow and said, "I should like to know what resources you have, on which to bring up such a tribe of children?" This rather cruel gibe went straight to my heart like an arrow. Given an opportunity, I should certainly tell the old doctor what I thought of him. But he mentioned the matter to me before I could. "My child, don't say anything to him; but take down the address of that bear's mother, and let's send her ten pounds or so," he told me. As far as I can see, this old doctor is soldiering neither for the sake of his pay nor because he thinks it his duty to do so. He has one passion—his love for the poor soldiers he calls his beloved bears. He's always trying to conceal this love, all the same, for some reason, as if it were something to be ashamed of.

Kuşadasi, 28th January

When I came to hospital this morning, I heard that four officers had been brought in seriously wounded. I was told that the nurses and Hayrullah Bey were looking for me: whenever he is going to do a difficult operation he always likes to have me beside him. "One oughtn't to show you this sort of thing, my child; but no one else can do it. All the others annoy me and make me swear: so I'm lost as to what to do," he explains.

I threw off my çarşaf and hastily put on my overall. But by the time I was ready the operation had been done. They were sending the wounded man upstairs on a stretcher. Hayrullah Bey sent for me, and said, "We've got through an important bit of tailoring (his name for an operation). It's a young staff-officer, a major. A bomb has played the devil with his right arm and one side of this face. I've given him my room; I want you to look after him. He needs very great care."

Talking as we went, we entered the room. A man was lying on the bed, very still, with his arm and his face in bandages. I went up to him with the doctor. Only part of the left side of his face was visible; and the face didn't seem strange to me. But it was impossible to identify him in his present condition. Hayrullah Bey felt the pulse of his left arm and bent over him: "Ihsan Bey—Ihsan Bey!" he repeated.

A thought suddenly flashed upon me like lightning. It was the staff-major I had met in the Abdurahman's house at C. I drew back a step, and was going to leave at once, and beg the doctor not to send me to this particular wounded officer again. But the sick man opened his eyes and saw me.

He recognised me, but couldn't believe it was I. Who knows what wild dreams his illness and his fever had given him—how often his reason had deserted him, perhaps—since the day he was wounded? Yes, I could see from the look in his clouded eyes that he could not believe that it was myself; and he closed his eyes again with a little smile on his pallid lips. Ihsan Bey! It was such a little time ago, that they took advantage of my want of a father or brother or any acquaintance to defend me, and dragged me off to their night orgies. In my heart, it was as though I'd left that town with my face buried in my hands, degraded, like an ordinary woman of the streets. That day, when I looked out on to the world like a miserable creature forced to bow its head to absolute tyranny, it was you who defended me. You showed such magnanimity as to risk your profession and your future, and perhaps even life itself. Unhappy chance has brought us together again today; and I shan't run away from you. I shall dedicate myself to your service as a younger sister, in the bitter hopeless days that lie before you.

Kuşadasi, 7th February

It seems that Ihsan Bey's wound was not dangerous, and that he would recover within a month. But from above his right eyebrow as far as his chin, the wound covered the whole of his cheek, and disfigured him terribly. I was not present when Hayrullah Bey changed his bandages—not because I could not stand it: I was seeing worse wounds than this every day—but because I saw that my look gave him more pain than if a knife had touched his frightful injury. The wretched man!—he knew what sort of countenance he would take away with him from hospital. So he said nothing; he was in a state of bitter hopelessness. When Hayrullah

Bey urged him "Make a bit more effort, young man; you'll be plumb on your feet again in about three weeks' time," he was thoroughly upset. I exerted all the sympathy my heart could offer to enable the wounded man to spend his days happily. Sometimes I sat at his bedside reading a book, and I even told him fairy tales. Yes, though the poor fellow said nothing, it was clear that he couldn't rid himself for one moment of the thought of remaining disfigured for life. Sometimes I tried to think of some indirect form of consolation; in a talk ostensibly about something quite different, I would suggest that there was nothing in the world so worthless as beauty of face, and nothing more harmful, and that one should seek beauty in the soul and in the heart.

Kuşadasi, 15th February

Ihsan Bey recovered even more quickly than we had hoped. This morning, when I took him his tea, I found him up and dressed. Involuntarily there came before my eyes the good-looking staff-captain with the smart uniform and the proud bearing, whom I'd met by chance a year ago in Abdurahman Pasha's garden. And was this the proud staff-officer?—this invalid soldier so ashamed of the wound in his face, turning away his head on its thin neck in the collar of his major's uniform? It may be that I revealed a little of what I felt; I tried to divert his attention by pretending to be angry.

"Ihsan Bey," I said, "this is childish. Why have you dressed before you're completely well?"

He lowered his eyes. "Because I feel less well when I'm lying down; that's why," he replied. We were both silent. And then, trying to conceal his nervousness and irritation, he added "Well, I want to go. There's nothing wrong with me. I'm quite all right again."

My heart was melting with pity. I fell to joking, not to give myself away. "Ihsan Bey, I see that you don't intend to listen to me. Your soldier's obstinacy is aroused again. But let me tell you this: I shall give you away—I shall tell the doctor everything. He will put you in your place, you see," I told him. I put the tray down quickly and went out; but I did not go see the doctor.

25th *February, towards evening*

I have had a tremendous battle with Hayrullah Bey. It wasn't about work; it was because he had carried the impropriety of interfering in other people's business a little too far. That was the reason. . . .

We were just talking about Ihsan Bey. I observed that the question of his face troubled him very much. Hayrullah Bey pursed his lips and said "He's right. If I were he, I should go and throw myself into the sea; and as quickly as possible. What's he good for now, except as food for fishes?"

I got really angry. "I believed you to be quite a different sort of person, Doctor," I retorted. "What beauty of face can be compared with beauty of soul?"

Hayrullah Bey began to laugh at me and tease me. "That's all talk, my child," he said. "At that rate no one would give a penny for a man. Are there no girls of your age then?" He was dusting his collar, as though dissatisfied with it.

I turned on him. "You know a little about my life. You've stolen some of my secrets, almost by force. I did have a good-looking lover; a very good-looking one indeed. I got to know that he'd deceived me, and I cast him out of my heart. I hated him."

Again Hayrullah Bey gave a laugh, and pierced me to the heart with his blue eyes, which got smaller and smaller as they laughed at me from between his white lashes. "Look here, my child," he said, "that's not so. Look me straight in the eyes. Do you love him?"

"I *hate* him."

He took my chin, and still looking into my eyes, he said, "Oh, unhappy child. You've been burning away like firewood with love of him for years now. That beast has wasted himself as well as you. He'll not be able to find such love in another."

My voice was choking with anger as I answered him. "Why do you calumniate me like this? How do you know it all?"

"You will remember; I knew it the day I saw you in that village. It's useless to try to conceal it. Love shows itself, like sleep in a child's eyes." My own eyes darkened; there was a buzzing in my ears. But he continued, "Meanwhile, you live for others; and you've so strange a way with everyone and everything, so heartbreaking a smile—the kind that belongs to those who see dreams—that my heart burns for you, my child. As a creature, you're different from others. Legends tell of fairies born of a kiss, who've grown up nourished by kisses; that shouldn't be set down to mere imagination. There are instances of them in the world. You, my little Feridé, are one of them. You're a creature made to love and be loved. Senseless child, you've made a great mistake, whatever comes of it. You shouldn't have let that young fellow go. I know you would have been happy."

I wrenched myself away with a cry of resentment, stamping my foot on the ground. "Why did you say that? What did you want of me?" I demanded, and began to cry.

It was then that the doctor came to his senses, "You're right, my child, you're right. I shouldn't have said such things to you. I've made a fool of myself; forgive me, child," he tried to console me.

Well, I was angry; I couldn't look him in the face. "You shall see—I'll *prove* to you that I didn't love him," I insisted. And I went out and slammed the door.

Again 25ᵗʰ February, night

When I took Ihsan Bey his lamp, he hadn't yet undressed. He was standing in front of the window, looking at the last red glow of evening reflected in the sea.

"How you've longed to see your uniform, sir," I remarked, for the sake of saying something. The darkness of evening had fallen upon the room. As though he were taking courage from the darkness, Ihsan Bey shook his head with an enigmatic smile, and expressed himself openly for the first time.

"My uniform, you say. Yes: that's my only hope now. That's what brought my face to its present state. I see there the only chance of repairing the damage I've suffered."

I didn't understand what he meant, and looked at him in astonishment. He continued with a little sigh: "It's very simple, Feridé Hanim. There's nothing difficult to understand about it. I shall go back as a regimental officer. The bomb left half its job unfinished; let it be completed. Then I shall be saved as well." The young major spoke with the grief and the directness of a child.

Unwittingly, I blew out the match I had struck, and bent down as though to adjust the wick. Very slowly I said "Don't talk like that, Ihsan Bey; if you want to, you can be happy. You can marry a nice girl, for

255

instance; you could have a happy family life, and children. You would forget all that."

Although my head was turned away, I felt he was not looking at me, but still gazing out of the window at the sea. "Feridé Hanim, if I didn't know what a true heart you have, I should say you were making fun of me. Who'd have me, in my present state? Before I was like this, women could at least look at me without laughing, and even then I didn't please them. And now that I'm such a wreck . . ." He didn't want to finish his sentence, but tried to pull himself together. "Feridé Hanim," he said, "all this talk is useless. Excuse me, will you? Please light the lamp."

I struck another match, but my hand refused to approach the lamp. I fastened my hand on the flickering light, and thought hard, waiting for it to go out. When the room was dark again, I spoke. "Ihsan Bey: when you had all that success, you were a proud and selfish man. Grief and despair hadn't given your heart the softness it has now. Even then, regardless of your profession and perhaps even of your life, you defended a young girl, a poor little secondary school teacher. And then, more important than any of that, you weren't as wretched—don't try to conceal it: I know your trouble—you weren't as wretched as you are today. Why shouldn't that school teacher dedicate her life to your happiness?"

The wounded major answered me in a voice that choked a little. "Feridé Hanim, I beg you not to make me absolutely desperate, by putting impossible dreams of that kind before me."

But I'd made up my mind. I turned to him; and bending my head, I said to him "Ihsan Bey, I beg you to marry me. Accept me. You'll see how happy I shall make you—how happy we both shall be."

I couldn't see the major's dark face through my lashes, because they were screened with tears. He simply lifted my outstretched hands to his lips, and rather fearfully kissed the tips of my fingers.

Everything was over. From now on, no one would dare to say that I didn't love him deeply.

Kuşadasi, 26th February

From today, you're to be a stranger. You were nothing but an enemy to me, Kâmran. I knew that we should never again come face to face, never again look at one another with the eyes of this world, never again hear each other's voice. But in spite of that, I couldn't free my heart of the feeling that I was betrothed to you. No matter what I say or do, I can't

256

help regarding myself as one who belongs to you. Yes: why should I tell a lie? In spite of all my dislike of you, my revolts against you, in spite of all that has passed, I'm still a part of you. I felt it this morning, when I woke for the first time the betrothed of someone else. After waking for so many mornings, for so many years, with the thought that I was betrothed to you—to wake and feel that I am the betrothed of another! Kâmran, it's only this morning that I'm parted from you. I'm like a miserable refugee, who's lost the right to turn his head and look behind him, or reflect on what is the past; without the right to call up memories.

After my talk with Ihsan Bey this morning, I meant to take him to Doctor Hayrullah Bey's room and announce our engagement. On this great occasion, the nurse's overall I wore every day would look rather plain, and sadden my betrothed, perhaps; some slender convolvulus had blossomed in the garden, and I made a little posy of them, and stuck them in my dress. Again, this morning, I found Ihsan Bey dressed. When he saw me, he began to smile with child-like innocence; I thought to myself "It's my duty, from today on, to make him happy." I tried hard to laugh, and held out my hand.

"Bonjour, Ihsan Bey," I said. I took out a few of the convolvulus flowers, and tucked them into the front of his uniform.

"I believe you slept well last night."

"Very well. And you?"

"I slept as happily and as peacefully as a child six months old!"

"If that's so, why is your face so sad?"

"Don't forget that happiness can make a person sad."

After this answer we were both silent. Ihsan Bey's lips were white. A little silence ensued, and then he began to speak slowly. Now and again, as if he were afraid of a tremor in his voice, he hesitated for a few moments. This is what he said:

"Feridé Hanim, I shall be grateful to you for the rest of my life. You gave me a perfect night's rest, of a kind I never had even in the good old days. I didn't tell you the truth just now: I stayed awake last night, till morning. Your words, 'I beg you to marry me' kept sounding in my ears. I couldn't sleep, because I couldn't bear to lose one moment of the single night of happiness that I spent as your betrothed. I shall remain grateful to you to the end of my life."

I looked up at him. "I shall always make you happy," I said.

He was in a state of the deepest emotion. He wanted to take my hands, but he didn't dare. As though he were talking to a sick child, he said in a steady, persuasive voice, "No, Feridé Hanim. I knew such a night could have no morrow. I was very happy last night; but in spite of that, I'm going away today. In a few hours I shall have parted from you."

"Why, Ihsan Bey? Don't you want me? It's not right! After giving me so much hope, it's not right to go like this."

The officer leant against the wall and closed his eyes. "Ah, that voice!" he murmured. Then he shook himself suddenly, and said in a voice that was almost harsh, "If you try a little harder, sympathy will make you assert that you love me."

"But why shouldn't it be, Ihsan Bey? If I wanted to become engaged to you, there must have been some reason for it."

He answered with a kind of bitter mockery, "Yes. You agreed to marry me, and so it must mean that you love me. But I don't want to be loved to that extent by you. Had you really thought such a marriage likely, Feridé Hanim?"

No answer.

"Feridé Hanim, did you take me for the kind of man who has fallen low enough to accept a love which is nothing but pity felt for a hopeless wreck?"

I bent my head in a kind of boundless grief. "You're right. I'd thought to myself: 'We're two miserable creatures: if we share our sorrows, perhaps we shall be happy.' Evidently I was wrong. You still have one consolation left," I added, pointing to the sword hanging on the wall. "As you said, you can return to your duties. I'm a woman. I am worse off than you."

We two had met, that dark winter morning, as two people newly betrothed: each wearing a few frail convolvulus flowers, each with a false smile to match them, on the lips; and we parted, ten minutes later, parted as brother and sister, with tears in our eyes—an unhappy man, and a young girl with no possessions.

Kuşadasi, 2nd April

Three days ago they gave us back our school. After an interval of five months, we began lessons again yesterday. The old year, anyway, was done and finished with. Spring filled the dark rooms with bright shafts of sunlight and the scent of sweet flowers; the waving green of the

Mediterranean danced upon the wall. Neither child nor grown-up had any wish to work. The head teacher had no inclination to stay in Kuşadasi. They sent her to another district a month ago, and appointed me in her place, on condition that I changed my designation to that of "Mistress." From one point of view I was not too pleased, because my colleagues began to look askance at me a little. True, they were not persons of such great knowledge or attainments, but their age, all the same, had to be considered. As the Education officials had said, each one of them had some fifteen or twenty years' experience. If I had been in their place, and someone had brought along a child younger than my daughter one fine day, and appointed her as my superior, I think I too should have been somewhat disheartened.

At the beginning of March, Hayrullah Bey was pensioned off. He is a rich man, in no need of salary; he was sad, nevertheless. "I've closed the eyes of a great many of my dear little bears with my own hands," he said, "I should have liked them to have closed mine, and to have borne me to my grave. But no, it wasn't to be." Hayrullah Bey was a very cultivated man, as far as knowledge goes. He had spent his whole youth studying. He has a huge library in his house, and maintains that there's nothing in the world so useless and so vain as books; he claims that among those who write books, as among those who read them, there are a number of fools who pass through life perceiving nothing. I objected strongly the other day, and tried to confute him.

"If that's the case," I said, "why have you read so much yourself, and encouraged me, indeed, to do the same?"

My objections were so powerful that they should have stopped running water; but he wasn't in the least discomfited. On the contrary, he laughed cheerfully, and said, to tease me, "You're right of course. Who told you to listen to me, little one?"

I can't understand the old doctor. He denounces whatever he loves; indeed, I rather think he loves me most when he scolds me. From the day I left the hospital, he's either shut himself up in his house to read, or else he pulls on the soldier's boots which he still possesses, shouldering his gun like a gendarme, and mounts Düldul. (Düldul is his much-loved veteran of a horse.) He goes off, dressed like that, to look for sick people in the villages, and to find a little work with which to occupy himself. In his house he keeps a lame gardener whom he calls "Corporal," and an old nurse of eighty.

259

Three days ago he invited Munisé and me to his house. It was great fun. While I was turning over the books in the library, he played like a child with Munisé for hours on end. He gave her such strict orders that I was overcome with laughter.

"Now we're going to play hide-and-seek. But you mustn't hide in difficult places—you're only as big as my finger. If you go and conceal yourself somewhere you'll tire me out. And don't worry if you can't find me; I may go to sleep in my hiding-place."

For some days now I've been making Munisé wear a çarşaf. She's just about fourteen, and about the same height as I am. The child has blossomed like a flower; her small face with its dark blue eyes that change colour with the time of day, framed in hair so fair as to be almost white, suggests one of those fairies whose cheeks bloom like roses when they smile, and whose eyes weep real pearls. Hayrullah Bey is very annoyed about the çarşaf. I'm aware too, that she's very young for it, but what am I to do? I am afraid. Some of my friends tell me, "Feridé Hanim, you will lose that child; she'll get married, and you'll be a mother-in-law before your time." That puts me into a great state of delight and anxiety. It's not without reason that people say that mothers-in-law are particular. We were returning from school the other day; a rather good-looking schoolboy of about sixteen or seventeen was walking on the opposite pavement. I noticed that he was looking our way occasionally, and I stole a glance at Munisé under my veil. And what should I see? The deceitful little thing!—there she was, smiling at the young man out of the corner of her eye. I was so surprised that I nearly fainted in the middle of the street. I took the little savage by the waist and started giving her a real scolding. At first she denied that she'd done anything at all. And when she saw that I was not to be taken in, she began to cry because she'd lied to me. For she knew that I couldn't stand up to her tears and would start crying myself.

"I know what I shall do to punish you," I told her, and I began to make a çarşaf out of some dark green silk that I found in the market.

This morning we had a quarrel about heliotrope. Some months ago, in the course of conversation, I had told her that I was very fond of heliotrope. I don't know where he found it, but three or four days later, what should Hayrullah do but bring me a bottle! I used it sparingly, to make it last, but that wretch of a child gives me no peace. She's incorrigible. Leave her alone for a moment and the room's filled with the scent of heliotrope; and then with complete innocence she'll swear it wasn't she who touched it.

Kuşadasi, 5th May

This morning Munisé didn't seem very well. She had lost her colour. I could not stay at home, as I had a great deal to do at school; but I called in on Doctor Hayrullah Bey and begged him to look in on us and see Munisé. But as luck would have it, he had just mounted Düldül and gone off to some village. When I got home, I found Munisé in bed. I begged an old neighbour of ours to look in on the child occasionally, and indeed she did. She never left her, but knitted stockings by her bedside till the evening. Munisé's cold had got worse: her forehead was burning, and her cough was worse than it had been in the morning. Her voice was hoarse, and she said that when she breathed she felt a little obstruction in her throat. I put my hand at the base of her neck and made her open her mouth. Hard glands met the touch of my hand. The light of the lamp which I lifted to her face blinded her eyes. In her mouth and at the back of her small tongue, a white roughness was visible.

Munisé was amused at my anxiety. "What harm is there in a cough, abla?" she asked. "Have you forgotten that I had a cough at Zeyniler?"

The child was right. The night I found her half-frozen in the snow at Zeyniler, hadn't she a cough then? What was there in a child's cold, after all? The only thing that worries me is the absence of Hayrullah Bey. The Corporal whom I mentioned just now looked in again, and told us that his master had spent last night in the village. Pray God my child will be up and well by the time he returns.

Kuşadasi, 18th July

This morning I worked it out. Exactly seventy-three nights have passed since my little one was buried. I am gradually beginning to get used to it and master my grief. Is there any burden too heavy for man?

I went down to the sea with the old doctor; I began to collect pebbles and shells, and started skimming stones over the level water. Hayrullah Bey was as happy as a child: he laughed with those calm blue eyes of his from under his white eyelashes, "Ah—youth!" he said. "Thank God: we're over it. See—your spirits and your colour are both beginning to come back."

I laughed and said "That's natural enough, isn't it, when one has a doctor like you?"

He shook his head slowly. "It's not natural, my child; it's not natural. Doctoring, along with humanity, and books, and honesty, and loyalty, is just a baseless fabrication. What's the good of science, when I can't even save a slip of a child?"

"We can't help it, Doctor Bey; don't worry. It was God's wish, and it had to happen so," I answered.

He looked at me sadly. "My poor child; do you know why I really feel sorry for you? When you're in trouble, you forget that it's yourself that needs consoling, and you begin to console others. That pitiful habit of yours almost makes me weep, child." He was silent for a few moments, and then he began to scold himself. "I'm becoming an absurd old fellow; is that the reason, I wonder? Come on, my child; let's go."

We began to walk home through the fields; they were just turning yellow. All the farmers know the doctor: we had a few words with an old woman who was working alongside a great pile of cut corn. Hayrullah Bey had cured the woman's grandson a few years ago. The old grandmother offered up many prayers for him, and then she called a sturdy young fellow who was ploughing under the July sun: "Come here, Huseyin! Kiss your benefactor's hand. If it hadn't been for him, you'd have been a handful of earth by now," she said.

The old doctor stroked Huseyin's tanned and sweating face, and then said "Come on now: I don't understand this hand-kissing business. Take us for a ride on your threshing-machine!" We got on to the threshing machine behind two powerful oxen, and slowly revolved on the golden waves of a sea of straw, for nearly ten minutes. . . .

I find I have the strength, today, to write the story down. The morning following the night of my last entry in my diary, I found Munisé more unwell. Her voice was so reduced that she could hardly speak. Poor child! Her chest was suffocating for want of breath. Whatever happened, I must go and look for another doctor. But while I was putting on my çarşaf, Hayrullah Bey came in.

He gave the patient a brief examination, and said it was nothing serious. For all that, his face was frowning, and his eyes were thoughtful. I was afraid; I told him I did not like that look of his. He shrugged his shoulders as though annoyed. "There's no need to be lazy. I'm back from a four-hour journey; I'm dead tired. Can't I do you a service without your fussing over me?"

Hayrullah Bey was a man who invariably became brusque and irritable when confronted by serious illness. He was trying not to look me in the face as he informed me, "There's no need for it really, but I'm going to call in one or two of my colleagues; find me a pen and paper quickly."

Everything went wrong that day; three times, since the early morning, they had sent a servant over from the school. Two members of the Education Committee and an inspector had arrived and there were some things they wanted to ask me. I dismissed the woman servant who brought me word for the third time. Suddenly Hayrullah Bey got angry.

"What are you doing here? Go off to your work. I'm as tired as can be, and I've got enough to do. Am I to be bothered with you as well? Come on, make yourself scarce. Put on your çarşaf: march! You worry me by hanging about here. I swear I'll leave you and go." The old doctor gave me these orders in so stern and decisive a manner that it was impossible not to obey him. Weeping beneath my veil I went off to the school. If education were to overwhelm me with blessings, it would never be able to repay me for my sacrifice that day. The inspectors were going round the classes, examining the pupils, asking to see the files, and propounding a thousand and one impossible questions. How I was able to think with my head all in a whirl, and how I answered them, I really don't know. It was getting on for twelve and they still hadn't gone. At last one of them noticed the state of misery I was in. "Aren't you well, Hanim?" he inquired. "Judging by your face, you seem very upset." Well, I couldn't keep it back. I bowed my head as though asking for mercy, and clasped my hands together. ". . . At home," I said, "—my child's dying. . . ." They were very sorry; and with a few meaningless words of comfort, they let me go.

It takes about five minutes to reach home from the school. I took half-an-hour, perhaps more, to walk the distance. Although I'd been agitating and fretting ever since morning, to run home, when it came to the point I wasn't at all anxious to go. I leant against the wall in the Penertee streets, and sat down on the well-stones like a weary traveller. Through the open windows of my house strange masculine heads were visible. The "Corporal" opened the door to me. I didn't dare ask any questions. Rather than say anything, I besought him with eyes and by my manner.

"The poor child is rather ill. God grant her health," he said.

Suddenly, the ceiling shook, and Doctor Hayrullah appeared at the top of the stairs. His chest was bare, he had no fez on his head, and his sleeves were rolled up. "Who's there, Corporal?" he called out. I had dropped on to the steps of the staircase, defeated; when he saw me in the darkness of the passage, he said with much concern "Is it you, Feridé? All right, girl—all right," and then came slowly down to me. My attitude showed him that I knew everything.

He took my hands and said in a broken voice, "Courage, my dear. Set your teeth. If God please, we shall save her. We've made serum, and we're doing all we can. God is great. We must not give up hope."

"Doctor Bey, please let me see her," I begged.

"Not now, Feridé; a little later. She's a bit delirious. Nothing has happened, I swear to you. It's delirium." But with quiet obstinacy I said, "I insist on seeing her. Doctor Bey, you've no right," I complained. And then, drawing a deep breath, I added "I'm stronger than you think. You need not be afraid of my doing anything foolish."

Hayrullah Bey thought for a moment, and then with a shake of his head, he gave in. "All right, my dear. But don't forget that futile wailings will scare a sick person."

However bitter it may be, once a necessity has been accepted, one finds tranquility and resignation. As I leant my head on Hayrullah Bey's shoulder and entered the room, there was neither tumult in my heart nor a tear on my face. I can still see that room, although seventy-three days have passed—seventy-three days which feel like seventy-three years. There were two young doctors in the room with their shirt collars unbuttoned and their arms bare, and an old woman as well. The midday sun shone through the leaves of the tree and filled the whole room with a brilliant light. Outside, the birds and the insects of August were chirping, and the sound of a gramophone could be heard in the distance. The interior of the room was all confusion. Bottles and cotton wool stood on the chairs and on the shelves. A thousand varied things belonging to Munisé were on the floor or against the walls. At one corner of the looking-glass was a posy she had made with her own hands, from flowers out of the doctor's garden; on the little table were a handful of coloured stones she had picked up on the seashore, and under one of the chairs a single shoe. On the wall there was a painting of her, that I had done in watercolour at our house in B., with a crown of wild flowers round her head, and Mazlum in her lap; and countless trinkets, bits of stuff, glass vases, as well—all the innocent little things so dear to a child's heart. "Munisé is a young lady in a çarşaf now." I had bought her a yellow gilt bedstead, and decorated it myself with muslin, taking endless trouble, as though I were preparing a baby's cot. My little one was lying, white as a sheet, with her head turned a little on one side, in surrender to some oppressive dream. On the shelf at the head of the bed was the doll I had bought her, its face smeared with the kisses my little one had given it, with its bright blue eyes fixed on her. All the pain and misery of the illness was over; the last breath of life played about her mouth, now relaxed in sleep; her slightly parted lips seem to smile, and showed the pearls of her teeth. It was all those same poor things that had so pleased me, from the moment they first touched my heart in a dark village school, until today. The birds were still making merry, the gramophone was still playing. The rays of the afternoon sun filtered through the leaves of the tree, touching the child's pale face with a colour like the gilded dust left on the finger by the bruised wings of a butterfly, and played a little with the strands of golden hair on her forehead.

My arms were locked around the neck of the old doctor, and my head was on his shoulder; I had no impulse to cry nor to fling myself upon her, but gazed at the lovely sight with a kind of bitter happiness. Death was approaching the child with the softness of a ray of moonlight; it was to kiss her on the forehead and mouth like the lips of a mother, and cause neither fear nor recoil.

The doctors had approached the bed. I saw that one of them had taken the child's bare arm from under the silk counterpane, and was inserting a needle into it. Hayrullah Bey turned slightly and shielded my eyes with his body. One of them said "Some eau-de-cologne, a little cologne. . . ." The doctor pointed to one of the shelves. The birds were still singing; the gramophone went on playing more and more cheerfully. Suddenly a strong smell of heliotrope pervaded the room. They had been unable to find any eau-de-cologne, and had used heliotrope. Heliotrope—that bottle I'd taken from the child's hands by force. Had I been so heartless, in return for all the joy she had given me, as to begrudge her a little of the scent she loved? My voice was breaking as I spoke: "Sprinkle the rest of the bottle on the bed, doctor. My little one will die all the happier for the scent of it." Hayrullah Bey was stroking my hair. "Come now, Feridé; come, my child—it's time we went out of the room," he was saying. I wanted to kiss Munisé for the last time; but I hadn't the courage. I only took her bare arm. The child used to take my hands from time to time, and turn them over to kiss my palms. I did the same to her. I kissed the inside of those poor little palms again and again, and thanked her for all her kindness to her abla.

From that moment on, I never saw Munisé again. They laid me on my bed and left me alone. I was trembling and damp with sweat. The strong smell of heliotrope that pervaded the house engulfed me like a wave, and suffocated me. It seemed to me that the scent, and the midday light, and the voices of the birds, went on for years. And then, gradually, it got dark. Memories came to me of that night when Munisé was lost in the snowstorm. I could hear the child knocking on the door; I could hear her little voice wailing in the storm.

I don't know what hour of night it was. A strong light blinded my eyes; I felt a hand touching my forehead and my hair, and I opened my eyes. The old doctor was bending over my face with a lamp in his hand; tears were glistening in his half-closed blue eyes with the white lashes.

"What time is it? It's all over, isn't it?" I remember saying; and then I was swept back into the darkness of that night at Zeyniler.

When I next opened my eyes I couldn't make out where I was. It was a different room with different windows. I leant on my elbows, and tried to rise, but my head fell back on to the pillow as if it didn't belong to me. In a stupefied way I looked about me. I saw the doctor's blue eyes once more.

"Feridé, do you recognise me?"

"Why shouldn't I, Doctor?"

"Thank God—thank God! May we all be better."

"Has something happened, Doctor?"

"Nothing of importance for a child of your age. You've slept a bit, girl; you've slept a bit. Nothing of importance."

"How much have I slept?"

"A good deal—but no matter. A matter of seventeen days."

Seventeen days' sleep! How strange . . . The light worried me, and I closed my eyes again. I laughed at the seventeen days' sleep: but my laughter made funny sounds, as though it was coming from the lungs and through the lips of someone else. Then I went to sleep again.

I had had rather serious brain fever. Doctor Hayrullah Bey had taken me to his house, and for seventeen days he had not left my bedside. It was the first serious illness I'd had in my life. My convalescence lasted over six weeks; for days I was unable to move. After my illness, my hair began to fall about me in great locks: one day I asked for some scissors, and cut it off short, at the base of my neck.

What a delightful thing convalescence is! One is, so to speak, born again; one looks with joy and with happiness at the most unimportant things, like a child looking at coloured toys. A butterfly fluttering against the window; the coloured rays of the sun reflected in the corners of the mirror; the faint tinkling bells of a flock of sheep, were enough to make my heart beat unsteadily. My illness had removed all the poisons of the last three years. My memories, even, seemed to belong to someone else. They awakened in me neither grief nor emotion. From time to time I urged myself wonderingly "Take care; this may be just memories of a long dream, or something read in a forgotten novel." Yes; I seemed to see the old events in a dream; old pictures whose faces and colours were faded, their frames covered in dust.

Doctor Hayrullah Bey was my companion during this time of convalescence. He never left me for a day. Sometimes he would tell me stories, sometimes he read me novels, and tried to amuse me and make me laugh. Poor thing, he tired himself out for me. "Come on now—you get up," he said; "God knows, even if I'm not sick, *I'm* going to have a white cambric nightgown made, and *I'm* going to lie in bed for three months."

Now and again I had a kind of trance-like sleep: and then I would remain for a time with the light of the sun just piercing my half-closed lashes. Hayrullah Bey would be reading a book or dozing in an armchair at my bedside. During these times of unconsciousness I felt that my spirit had left my body, and was roaming through space, like a light or a voice. Where did I go? To what lands did I wander? And then suddenly, with a feeling that I was about to fall over a precipice, I would give myself a shake, and wake again, to feel that I was returning from some far off, distant place. Wind sang in my ears, as if that distance had been covered at lightning speed; and faint memories of the misty countries I had seen in the lofty air, would tremble before my eyes.

"My little Doctor," I said the other day to Hayrullah Bey, "I'm quite well again now. We can go and visit it."

He wouldn't agree at first, and told me I must wait at least a week or two. But no one can resist the obstinacy and the caprices of people who are ill. At last I convinced my old friend. We gathered two bunches of flowers from the garden, and a great many coloured pebbles from the seashore: my little one loved them more than flowers. Munisé lies on a hillock facing the Mediterranean, under a small cypress tree as delicate as herself. We sat beside her for hours. For the first time since my illness I talked about her with the doctor; I wanted to know how the child had died, and how she had been buried. In spite of all my insistence, Hayrullah Bey didn't give me all the details. I was only able to learn one thing. After she had been buried, the Imam asked the name of Munisé's mother; and of course no one knew it. The doctor remembered that I had been almost the same as a mother to her, and he gave my name. She was laid to rest under the name of Munisé, daughter of Feridé.

Kuşadasi, 1st September

This morning Doctor Hayrullah Bey spoke to me in the following words: "My child, I've been sent for again from one of the villages. I entrust Düldul to you. Mind now, you don't leave the bandaging of the animal to that bear of a Corporal. I wonder if he's determined to have Düldul's leg amputated as he's had his own? That leg won't get better. You know how to bandage; but you ought to begin to walk the horse about slowly. After you've bandaged the wound, give Düldul a turn in the garden for five or ten minutes; indeed, if you can, trot him a little. But not much, you understand. As for the second job, the baker, Hurşit, will bring the rent of the bakehouse today; it's about £28. Take the money on my behalf, Feridé. Thirdly—what was it I was going to say? I've no head left—Ah yes. Move my library downstairs: I'm going to give you the room on the side overlooking the sea. It's better, and faces the south wind in winter. You won't be cold."

The moment had come for me to say what I had long wanted to tell him. "Doctor Bey," I said, "don't worry about Düldul; and I'll take the rent. But is the other really necessary? After all, my stay as your guest has been sufficiently extended already. If you'll let me, I'll go."

The doctor put his hands on his hips and mimicked my tones with a good deal of annoyance. "'My stay as your guest has been extended

268

enough; if you'll let me, I'll go,'" he repeated, and then, with a sterner gesture and a shake of the fist, he went on: "What did you say? Going? Look here, you perverse girl; I'll give you something to laugh at, if you're not careful!"

"But Doctor Bey," I said, "I've been your guest too long."

He put his hand on his hip again. "Very well, young lady," he said; "you want to go. Good: and where do you think you're going to?"

I smiled. "I've been wondering myself, Doctor Bey. I can't stay with you forever, that's obvious. You've helped me at a time when my fortunes were at their worst; but. . . ."

"My little girl, there's no need for all this talk. You and I are 'two old soldiers' now; come, drop the nonsense."

I went on insisting, but Hayrullah Bey put his hand under my chin. "Doctor Bey, I'd like very much to stay; you may be sure of that. I've been very happy here. But why should I be all this burden to you? I know how humane you are, and the sacrifices you make. . . ."

The doctor tousled my cropped curls and continued to tease me, drawing in his cheeks and pursing his lips to mimic me in an assumed voice. "Humaneness—self-sacrifice? Are we playing in a tragedy, you crazy child?" he asked. "You don't understand in the least. Humaneness and self-sacrifice are nothing to me, child. I've lived for pleasure; I've served you for pleasure. If I'd not liked you, do you think I'd have even looked at you? If ever you hear that I've thrown myself down from the minaret on the top of the hill, don't you believe even then that I was making any sacrifice. This selfish old fellow knows just how much he'd enjoy doing it. One of Molière's heroes used to give me immense satisfaction; while they were beating the fellow, first one and then another ran up to save him, but he sent them all off, saying, 'Mind your own business, sir! How do you know I don't like being beaten?' Come now, my dear; drop all this nonsense. If those rooms aren't ready when I get back, look out for yourself. There's a tough young watchman here; I swear I'll send for him and make you marry him. You see what you'll be letting yourself in for?" Knowing that Hayrullah Bey would start making coarse jokes until I blushed, as he did from time to time, I ran away at once.

Hayrullah Bey has become both a father and a friend and companion to me; I don't feel a stranger in his house. As far as happiness is possible for a girl like me, whose heart and whose life have both been broken, I am happy. I invent a thousand different occupations for myself: I help the old nurse, I tidy the house, I keep an eye on the garden and on the food and even on the doctor's accounts, and a whole number of things of the kind. What shall I do when I leave? I shall still have to be regarded as an invalid; my health is improving, very slowly, but to little purpose, for I feel as if something within me is destroyed for good and all. I shall never regain the old health and the old happiness that used to make everything a pleasure to me. When I laugh, I cry; when I cry, I laugh; I'm not the same from one moment to another. Yesterday evening, for instance, I was in very good spirits. I really felt happy again as I closed my eyes. But towards morning, when it was still dark, I woke up crying, for no apparent reason. What was wrong with me? Why was I crying? I didn't know myself. I felt as though I'd been visiting, last night, all the houses in this great world one by one and had gathered together whatever there was of grief and hopelessness, and brought it back to bury it in my own heart. And in this state of misery, unfounded, nameless, and unexpressed, I cried out, "Mother, Mother!" I put my hand on my mouth, in case I should cry louder still. Suddenly I heard Hayrullah Bey's voice from the next room, "Feridé, is that you?—what's happened my dear?" The old doctor ran to my room with a candle in his hand; he didn't bother to ask me what was the matter, or why I was crying, but he comforted me with simple, even meaningless, words.

"It's nothing, my dear—it's nothing: a mere attack of nerves. Ah—my poor child!" I was shaking with sobs; I could feel them choking in my mouth like young birds suffocating. My old friend turned to the window and shook his fist at the distance, in the dark: "God!" he said, "like a beast of prey: you've done for this child."

What shall I do, when once I am alone again, if I have another bout of illness and despair of that kind? But why think about it now?—the doctor won't let me go, anyhow, for a month at least, and perhaps longer.

Alacakaya Farm, 10ᵗʰ September

I've been at Alacakaya farm for a week. Ten days ago Hayrullah Bey said to me, "Feridé, I've a farm at Alacakaya,—I have, really—and it's a long time since I've been to look at it. It's no good leaving things undone. I'm going to take you there for ten or fifteen days; it will be a nice change of air for you. It will open your eyes a bit, and your heart too. And remember, the school's opening soon. You'll be shut up for the rest of the year."

"Doctor Bey," I said, "I'm very fond of the open air; but the school is about to re-open; I don't quite know what to do."

He shrugged his shoulders angrily. "I never asked you whether you'd go, nor invited any observations from you. I'm going to take you, I said. What do you want to interfere for? This is a matter for a doctor; otherwise I shall make out a report and wash my hands of you. Come on now—get a few clothes together, and my copies of Rousseau from the library."

Oh well! Hayrullah Bey was treating me like a school child. My resolution was weakened after my illness, and I couldn't stand up to him. And the strange thing was, I felt no impulse to complain of it. Submission seemed to suit me.

The doctor's farm had been neglected. But what a lovely place it was! Even in winter, the place had all the appearance of spring; there was a rocky hill there too, which was a joy to see. The rocks would change their colour with the sun, at morning, noon and evening, and with dull or brilliant weather, and be all sorts of red, rose, violet, white or black, in turn. That's why the place was called Alacakaya. The farm took up more of my time than I'd expected. I milked the cows, like the other farmers; and on Düldul, who was now becoming a real friend of mine, I used to visit the plantations in the neighbourhood. The country life, in fact, that one dreams of. All the same, my mind was not at rest. The school was to open in a few days: I ought to be at work, cleaning and sweeping the building. But it was impossible to make Hayrullah Bey understand such things.

At night he used to read a novel with me. "This meaningless stuff is intolerable," he said, "but from your mouth, the ordinary becomes a pleasure." I was reading to him again last night. There are some rather outspoken passages in the book: I was ashamed to repeat them, and either tried to substitute other words for them quickly, or skip the sentences altogether. Hayrullah Bey used to notice my embarrassment, and made the ceiling shake with his roars of laughter.

Suddenly the dogs began to bark in the darkness. We opened the window. Someone on horseback was coming through the farm gate. "Who's that?" Hayrullah Bey called out.

271

The Corporal's voice came back "It's not a stranger; it's only me." It must've been something important to make the Corporal come out here from Kuşadasi at such an hour.

"I hope everything's all right," he said. "I'd better go down and see what's the matter. If I'm late, you go to bed, my dear."

Hayrullah stayed nearly an hour with the Corporal. When he came up, his face was red and frowning. "Why did the Corporal come, Doctor?" I asked.

He almost shouted at me "You go to bed—didn't I tell you? I never saw anything so scandalous! The tricks these little girls are up to! This is a matter for me." Well I knew his nature by now. At times like this there was no getting round him—nothing for it but to take my lamp and go to my room.

When I awoke this morning, they told me that Hayrullah Bey had gone off on an important piece of work, but had said I was not to worry if he didn't return. It was clear that the doctor had received some news that had upset him. About noon, I was tidying up his room, when my attention was attracted by a torn piece of an envelope, which had fallen beside the bed. I picked it up: only the words . . . "Head of the School, Kuşadasi," were legible. The envelope obviously belonged to me. This piece of paper gave me much food for thought. Was this what the Corporal had brought last night, I wondered? If so, why had Hayrullah Bey kept it from me? And how was it he came to open an official communication addressed to me? I couldn't believe that he'd done so. Another thought struck me: this envelope must have been among the books we brought from Kuşadasi.

Kuşadasi, 25th September

I am recording the last event as though it were on the last page of my diary. For myself, I don't want to add either tears or reproaches. Hayrullah Bey kept me waiting two days on the farm; on the third night, I was so anxious that come what may I was determined to get out the carriage and go down to the town myself. But the following morning when I awoke, I found he had returned. I don't remember ever seeing the easygoing, carefree Hayrullah Bey so utterly weary and exhausted. He put his lips to my hair, as was his custom; and then, looking at me intently, he said "May God punish them."

I realised that some new danger threatened me, but I didn't dare ask what it was. Hayrullah Bey walked up and down with his hands in his pockets, deep in thought. And then, putting his hands on my shoulders, he said: "My child, you know something."

"No, Doctor Bey."

"Yes you do; if you didn't, this queer state of affairs would have attracted your attention. You were certainly going to ask me something."

Slowly and seriously I replied "No, Doctor Bey; I know nothing. All I know is that I see you very worried and upset; you've got some trouble, and since you're my protector and almost my father, your troubles are mine. What's wrong?"

"Feridé: do you feel strong enough, my dear?"

My curiosity was stronger than my fears. I made an effort to appear calm, and said, "I'm a determined girl; you've had several proofs of it. Tell me, Doctor Bey."

"Feridé, take this pen and write what I tell you. Come on now, my dear; trust your old friend." Slowly and thoughtfully, Hayrullah Bey made me write these lines:

"To his Excellency the Chairman of the Kuşadasi Education Committee: As my state of health no longer permits me to remain in the Educational Service, I beg you to allow me to resign from the post of Headmistress of the Kuşadasi High School."

"Now, my dear, without any reflection, without asking any questions, put your signature to it, and give me the paper. Your hands are shaking, Feridé. You dare not look me in the face. It's better so, it's better so, my dear. Because if you look at me with those honest eyes of yours, I shall get confused. You understand, don't you, that you've been through some extraordinary times! Isn't it true? Listen to me now, Feridé. If you show excitement or emotion, I shall have to stop. All the same, it's necessary for you to know everything. Feridé, in the three years since you started out into the world, you think you've learnt what men are made of, don't you? Never believe it! This life of mine has lasted nearly sixty years, and I've not learnt it yet: I, who have come across every kind of ugliness and scandal in the world—I still can't absorb it all in this old head of mine. You and I are the world's best and truest friends, aren't we? For months on end I held your sick body in my arms as I would my own child; and do you know what people have said—and are saying—Feridé? No: you could never guess. It seems that I was your lover. Don't cover your face with

273

your hands: on the contrary; keep your head erect. That's the action of those who have something to be ashamed of. No: look into my eyes. What is there to make us turn from each other? Listen to me, Feridé, listen; let me tell you the whole story. This cursed calumny started first at the school. Your colleagues began to say impossible things about us to one and the other. The reason is obvious: you became headmistress, and they were left standing. Six months ago, without saying anything to you, I'd wanted to render you a small service, and with that in mind I'd written a letter to a friend who was Treasurer in Smyrna. The fact that your promotion was due to me increased their suspicions. The flames of this conspiracy have been burning for months. The matter reached the ears of the Education Committee and the local Governor. A local correspondence followed, and enquiries were instituted. They studied your record as found in the Directorate of the Province; and it seems there were a lot of obscure points. Your arrival in B. from Istanbul, for instance, and then your resignation from the Central School, and departure for a village in some remote spot, looked surprisingly like running away. A few months later you had some help from an unknown quarter; you were promoted with a speed for which there was no precedent in the educational world, and you rose from being a village teacher to a post in a Teachers' Training College. There again you resigned without reason: and this time you went to another district, but you didn't stay there either. A reply came from the Education Committee of C. My whole being turned to poison as I read it. They pretend that there . . . But no, no! I cannot say it. My soldier's lips daren't utter the words that fell from the mouths and the pens of those men of education, learning and culture, though you know I say whatever comes to my lips and can't prevent the most shameful expressions escaping me. In a word, my little Feridé, they've cornered you, as hounds will corner a stag. Your most innocent actions have been interpreted as evidence against you; they have gone upon reports and enquiries. Your invitations to me to come to the school from time to time, to attend to your children who were sick; your laying your tired head for an instant on my shoulder at the time when our little one was dying; and then, when you were ill, the hours I spent at your bedside: all this was criminal! We've shown such lack of shame that the customs, the conventions, the honour and the chastity of the country was brought into contempt. We took no account of those around us. After announcing to everyone that you were sick, we rode arm in arm on a threshing-machine in the village. Instead of occupying yourself with your duties, you exercised the horse in my garden. And as if all this were not enough, we retired to a farm outside the town. My little Feridé, I tell you all this in its raw and naked state. I might have deceived you a little longer by spinning it out with well-chosen words. I might have destroyed your hopes gradually, one by one. But I've not done so. Do you know why? My age and my profession have brought me to the same conviction: it's better to swallow poison at one gulp; one either dies of it, or one is saved. To mix your poison with syrup or some other concoction and drink it sip by sip is a vile and loathsome thing. To announce a disaster very slowly is like cutting a man up with a saw. Yes, Feridé; you've suffered the severest blow of your life; had you been alone, it might have killed you. Yes, it's true. What happens if so many people attack one small child? God be thanked that chance has thrown up an old man who'd been cast on one side. The clock of my life is about to strike eleven; but what does that matter? Even this small space of time will do to render you a service. If I succeed in that, I shall not mourn over the days I've wasted in a whole lot of stupid experiences. Don't be afraid, Feridé; this too will pass. You're young; don't give up hope of spending happier days. I was going to take your resignation, but I've given up the idea. I dare not leave you in this state. Children have all kinds of obstinacies and intractable qualities. Come on, Feridé: let's go out into the open. Let's get among the sheep and the cows. You may be sure those creatures will show more gratitude for what we do for them.

The old doctor put my resignation paper into the envelope, and gave it to the Corporal. I saw in that paper not only a portion of my life but the final consolation of my heart. Oh God! What a tragedy: whatever hope I cling to comes away in my grasp; whatever I love seems to die. Those dreams of a young girl, that passed away one spring evening three years ago; my little children; then Munisé; and now, after her, my students, who might, I'd hoped, distract the loneliness of my heart. I had watched over all these things, trembling, with the tenacity of a mother bird that sees her young in danger, and one by one they were all fading, falling, dying, like autumn leaves. I had not yet reached my twenty-third year; traces of childhood were still discernible in my face and body; but my heart was full of the deaths of all those whom I had loved.

For three days Hayrullah Bey never left me. He found it hard to credit the calm and the patience with which I faced so enormous a disaster. At

275

night, after I had gone to bed, he would come to the door of my room, and call out "Feridé, do you want anything? If you can't sleep, let me come in."

It was the morning after the third night; I awoke early to a fresh warm day—a real May morning. I got some milk for Hayrullah Bey, and brewed his coffee for him. The doctor was very glad to see me as I entered his room with the tray in my hand, and what was almost a smile on my tranquil face. "Well done Feridé—I'm so glad. So you've been left to bear the ills of the world alone?"

I opened his window and tidied up a few of his scattered things. I talked about farm matters and about the sheep and the shepherds. I went on talking and laughing without a pause, and from time to time I actually whistled, as I used to do in the old days at school. I can't describe how pleased Hayrullah Bey was; and when I saw how pleased he was, I became happier still. At last I judged that the moment had come. I drew the doctor's armchair alongside the window, and threw a wrap across his knees. And then, seating myself on the edge of the parapet, I said, "I've a few things I want to say to you, Doctor."

Hayrullah Bey covered his face with his hands. "Say on," he agreed, "but for God's sake get down—you'll fall off!"

"Don't worry; my youth was spent on the trunks of trees. I'm going to talk to you now about a decision which I think will please you. You see how calm I am, don't you? Yesterday evening I made an important decision."

"What about?"

"About living."

"What does that mean?"

"It's quite simple. Not to kill myself. Because for a few days I had seriously thought of it." I was smiling as I said so, with the lightheartedness of a child who is joking. The old doctor leapt from his place in a state of great excitement. "What are you saying, you wicked child? What's all that? If I'd been where you are just now, I should have fallen, from sheer astonishment, and been smashed to pieces. But for God's sake come in: do—whatever else may happen."

"When I've told you that I've decided to live, surely it's rather foolish to be afraid that I shall fall, isn't it, Doctor?" I said cheerfully. "Why did I make that decision? Let me tell you. There are a great many reasons. In the first place, I shouldn't dare. Take no notice of the fact that I talk of death now and again. I'm very much afraid of it, for all that. And besides, even if my last chance had gone, I shouldn't have the courage. . . ." I'd spoken the words with my hands outstretched and my head bent in a calm, simple way. In great excitement, Hayrullah Bey seized my wrists and forced me down from the window sill. He almost pushed me into a low chair.

"What an unintelligible creature you are, Feridé! Sometimes nothing but a bit of nonsense; other times, such depths and peculiarities; and then—incredible courage. All right, Feridé, go on. I'm listening."

"You're my only friend, my protector and father. I must go on living. Good! Once I've discovered that I've not the courage to die, what more do I need? But *how* to live, that's the point! Show me the way. If you can find an easy way out, that will be perfect."

Hayrullah Bey knitted his brows. He was thinking hard. "Feridé," he said, "I've been thinking about all this too. I wanted to wait a little before talking about it; but seeing that you're quite master of yourself now, very well—let us talk of it my dear. You must absolutely renounce any hopes of being a school teacher again, once and for all. I can give you a few details about what has happened. Ten days ago, an inspector came from provincial Headquarters; an evil-looking kind of fellow with his few teeth sticking out like a walrus. They had set up a committee of enquiry under this inspector's chairmanship, and before dismissing you, they wanted to interrogate you. The paper that the Corporal brought that night was a kind of summons. Just think of it, Feridé. How could you have appeared before a committee of that kind? How could you have answered the vile calumnies you'd have heard from the lips of strangers? As soon as I'd heard about it, I nearly went out of my mind. I pictured to myself the committee room; I saw you in my mind's eye, in your black çarşaf, with your poor little child's face and bent head, facing those walrus teeth. Whatever happened, that man had decided to tear you into little bits, like the monster in the tale of the wolf and the lamb, and he'd have been looking for the smallest excuse for repeating those slanders, which are as repellent as they are stupid. To leave you alone in the presence of that walrus, with that innocent face of yours that changes colour at an old soldier's somewhat careless talk, and your frightened grey-blue eyes— never!" Hayrullah Bey shook his fist. He was trembling all over, grinding his teeth, and coughing up his words with difficulty; and there was an alarming gleam that I'd never seen before, in those usually calm blue

277

eyes. "I opened my beautiful mouth and said what I thought of the walrus; and—well, if a bullet had struck him at that moment, not a drop of his blood would have flowed. . . . I learnt that two days earlier he had appealed to the Court against me; I'm waiting impatiently for the day when I can repeat their handsome behaviour to the customers, in the presence of the Court!"

The old doctor was silent until the wild gleam in his eyes and the alarming flush on his temples had disappeared. And then, in his usual quiet voice and simple, honest manner, he continued: "In the meantime, whatever happened to you, it is you who have suffered. I don't want you to think badly of me in the future, for having almost forced you to write your own resignation. It was essential that you should sever your connections. God made those eyes and lips to smile, and give happiness to others; it's not merely a question, Feridé, of your weeping and trembling again before the same sort of creatures. There's something else I want to say to you. My responsibility towards you has now increased twofold; because I was the cause of this calamity descending on you, and it's necessary therefore, that I should be the one to repair the damage. As I said, you've nothing further to expect from your profession. Even if we found an opening today, they'd find an excuse to strike you down tomorrow. Moreover I might not be there, by that time. Come now, let's go on thinking together. Is there any chance of your returning to your family in Istanbul?"

I bowed my head. "No, Doctor; I've quite finished with them."

"One other possibility: what about your getting married to some nice young fellow?"

"No, Doctor. I'm determined to remain an old maid."

"I'm not so sure that you'd be happy, even if you did marry, Feridé; that cursed fellow has rooted himself so deep in your heart that one can't tear him away."

"Doctor, I kiss your feet: talk of anything you like but that!"

"Very well then, child; very well."

"Thank you, Doctor."

Hayrullah Bey chewed his white moustache; he was thinking again. "Very well, then. If that's how things are, what shall we do? You need have no fear of want, or anything of that kind, because half my small capital will suffice for us both; in any case I'd been wondering what I should do with my money. How can I spend it better than on your happiness?"

I knew that my answer would make him angry, but it had to be said. With a sinking heart, I said it, stroking his knees as I did so. "But listen, Doctor. In what capacity am I to receive financial help from you? What sort of position am I to descend to?"

Hayrullah Bey didn't get angry; but he looked me in the face a little sadly, and a little resentfully. "For shame, Feridé, for shame; when we've understood one another so well, to go and say a thing like that! Shame on you. But it can't be helped; for all your carefree independence of manner, you're really a single-minded, domesticated girl, modest and rather limited in outlook; the kind of girl they call 'Kinali kuzu': a dutiful little lamb. It oughtn't to have been so, but that's how it is. Now, Feridé, listen to what I have to say. How is a proud girl like you, who can't even accept a little help from a sincere old friend—particularly after all this fuss and gossip—how's she going to live on her own? That's why I've been thinking again of getting you married, Feridé. You don't want to be helped by anyone, and if you want to work, that's out of the question. If I were to say 'Let's live together: don't leave me,' you'd never consent, would you? But you bow your head; to tell you the truth I don't look on this as a very secure possibility. Why shouldn't we speak openly to one another at a time like this? A deputation went to the Governor on behalf of our quarter of the town. They said that my living in my home with a young girl who was neither one of my family nor a relation was, in their opinion, contrary to custom and Moslem law. Indeed—indeed, they wanted you to be sent elsewhere. I'm one to tell everyone his faults openly to his face, so very naturally no one loves me; why not, therefore, use this pretext to aim another blow at me? In a word, little Feridé, it's not possible for you to live either with me or by yourself; groundless suspicions will poison your life. This cursed stain will follow you wherever you go: this doubt about your past will give every knave and good-for-nothing the right to insult you. What are we to do, Feridé? What action ought we to take? How are we to defend you?"

I gazed at him with the defeated expression of a suffering person condemned to die. But in spite of my deep sense of hopelessness, I smiled and said "You admit, at last, that I had some right to think of death. Look, Doctor: look at that sun, those trees, the sea we catch a glimpse of in the distance. Does anyone who hasn't been through as

much trouble as I have, willingly consent to give up loveliness of that
kind?"

Hayrullah Bey covered my mouth with his hand. "That's enough,
Feridé; that's enough. You make me swallow the sort of impertinence
I've never endured before. You'll have me weeping like a child." He
stretched his hand out to the autumn sun that shone down on us through
the bare branches; their leaves were fallen now. "I am pretty old. I've
seen the many forms your misery and pain have taken. How often have
you closed your eyes in my arms? I've never seen anything more tragic
than the face of this lovely child opposite me, who speaks so calmly of
having to die, or those quivering mischievous lips, still looking for
laughter." Hayrullah Bey threw the rug off his knees, and began to walk
up and down the room.

At last he stopped. "That's that," he said. "We'll have to take the last
resort. I shall keep you in my house, and I shall defend you too, in a
manner which conforms to the religious law. Get ready, Feridé.
Thursday next week!"

I've been in Kuşadasi for the last week. Tomorrow I become a bride.

Hayrullah Bey went off a day ago to Smyrna, partly to see to his
private affairs, and partly to get a few new things for the house. I've
received a telegram to say that he will return this evening. I had told him
that there was no need to buy anything new: but he objected in rather an
odd manner: "No, my bride: that would be a rather rude way of calling
attention to my age. True, the Almighty has erred, in putting between us
an interval of thirty-five or forty years; but that's of no consequence. My
real youth is the youth of the spirit. Don't look at me: I'm more of a man
than any youth of twenty; and I want to see you decked out as a proper
bride. As for me, I'm a bachelor, more or less. My wishes will not be
fulfilled. I'm going to bring you a real bride's dress from Smyrna."

I could say nothing; I looked straight before me. Hayrullah Bey went
on, "I'm making you a wedding present, but *what* a wedding present!
Come, now—guess! Earrings—a ring—pearls—diamonds? No, not one
of them. Don't weary your brain. You'll never guess. An *orphanage*!"

I looked at him in astonishment. He was beaming with pleasure.
"Haven't I discovered something to please you?" he asked. "I'm turning
our Alacakaya farm into an orphanage for thirty or forty children. We
will gather together there such orphan children as we find around us in

the neighbourhood. I shall be their doctor; you shall be their teacher and their mother."

I am writing these lines in front of the window of the room where I spent my convalescence. In the garden, from the branches of the trees, a ceaseless rain of dry leaves is falling. Some of those leaves fall from the bare branches and are being blown by the wind through the window, and on to the faded leaves of my diary. And like the last of the green leaves, there flourished in my heart the fatherly affection—so real, so disinterested—the pity, and the tenderness, visible in the dim blue eyes of my old companion. Ever since the day when I was first bound to look upon him as a husband, that last leaf withered like the rest. What is one to do? That is what life is like.

I have come to the last page of my school copy-book, filled by now with writing as fine as spiders' legs. What a melancholy coincidence! My notebook and my biography come to an end together. I cannot start to write my new life in a new diary. What would there be left for me to say? Moreover, tomorrow I shall be the wife of another, and I should have neither the right nor the courage to do it. What connection will there be between the life of that young woman, who will wake, on the morning after tomorrow, in the room of another—and Çalıkuşu, of whom nothing will remain but a tune or two and a few teardrops? Çalıkuşu dies today, forever, among the autumn leaves that fall on the pages of her diary, already stained with her tears.

Why should I conceal the truth, at this hour of parting? I wrote this diary for you, Kâmran, who will never read it. Yes: whatever I have said, and whatever I have written, is for you. Yes: today I will admit that I acted wrongly—so wrongly! I might have been happy with you, in spite of everything. Yes: in spite of everything, I was loved, and not unaware that I was loved; but that was not enough for me. I wanted to be loved *greatly*—to be loved, if not as much as I myself could love (no chance of that)—at least almost as much. Had I the right to be loved as much as that? I don't think so, Kâmran. I am a young and ignorant girl. There is a way to love, and a way to make oneself beloved, isn't there, Kâmran? But I knew nothing of all that. How lovely she must have been, that fair flower of yours; I'm not saying that to reproach you, Kâmran, believe me. She made you happy, so I'm making friends with her in my imagination.

Who knows what lovely things she said to you—what lovely letters she may have written? I might have been, perhaps, a good mother to your children—to our children. So much—Kâmran, I learnt to love you after I had left you. But don't believe that it was only after the experiences life gave to me, or from the love I gave to others. It was by loving your image, which, though I had no hope, I cherished in my heart. In the darkness of the graveyard at Zeyniler, in the long nights when the wind cried and moaned till the early hours of morning; in the wide spaces where the faint, doleful chime of the coachbells echoed; along the roads filled with the warm scent of the ju-jub trees of the gardens of willow: through it all I lived face to face with you, in the arms of your image. The poor man whose wife I shall become tomorrow believes me a girl as innocent as a lily; and how wrong he is! I don't suppose that love could have wasted and wearied the soul and body of any widow as much as it has mine. Kâmran, it is only today that we part from one another. Today I become a widow. In spite of all that had happened, you were a part of me. With all my soul I am yours.

END OF FERIDÉ'S JOURNAL

❧ PART FIVE ❧

I

"Kâmran, I swear being your travel companion is torture. I asked maybe a hundred questions without getting a single reply for two hours. I could get no answer other than a 'Yes' or 'No.' Pull yourself together, son."

Kâmran was absently watching the Marmara Sea, sitting in the corner of a carriage which was travelling on a rough road. He raised the collar of his coat to block the blowing evening wind. Hardly taking his eyes off the sea, he said with a smile: "I believe two hundred answers in two hours is not bad, Uncle, even though they were short 'yes' and 'no' words."

"Fine, but you don't even give those answers by thinking thoroughly . . . you say the words like a machine."

"Good treatment and a change of air, Uncle . . . you must have an intention to tire me out for no reason."

"No, Mr. Ungrateful, it really is not possible to satisfy you . . . I actually want to make you think. Although my intention is not to tire you out, but to prevent you from thinking about the other thing.

However, I'm giving up hope from now on. It is impossible to cheer you up. For example, under the pretext of a wedding, I took you to the village three days ago. You saw all kinds of people; you listened to drums and zurna; you watched köçek dancers and wrestlers; on my account I really enjoyed it; but you didn't have any fun—don't deny it, it's quite obvious."

"It is not possible to explain to you, Uncle. My nature is different."

"No, son, you have let yourself go. Look how I'm getting on in my sixties, I'm getting younger day by day."

"I hope Aunt Ayşe doesn't hear this."

"I couldn't care less if she hears. Didn't I look older than today, when I first came here?"

Kâmran laughed. "It's been ten years since that visit to Tekirdăgi. It's still in my mind. It was an August day just like this one."

Aziz Bey clapped his hands together: "Don't, for God's sake! Years go by so fast! You're right. Today, you have a four-year-old but I still remember when you were engaged to little Feridé for about four to five years. Ah, Kâmran, I still can't understand how you sacrificed Feridé. My heart aches when I remember hearing Çalıkuşu's nightingale voice and her sweet face. It's been ten years, and my heart still can't bear looking at the backyard. You know, if I died, I wouldn't forgive you, Kâmran."

"Uncle, is that appropriate to say to someone you invited to your hometown for a change of air?"

"Yes, but your life problems have nothing to do with it. You married a woman you loved, and you couldn't be completely happy even for a year. Münevver fell ill, and you spent three years of your life as her caretaker. You tried treatment in Buyukada, Switzerland, and who knows where else. Can you defy fate? Your wife passed away last winter, which caused some kind of decay to happen to you from which you could not recover and pull yourself together. You still look sick. What does it have to do with Feridé? You were in love with someone else."

Kâmran responded with a bitter smile: "Uncle, nobody believes me. You, of course, will not believe me and will find it strange. I've had some adventures in my life; in fact, quite a few exciting ones. However, let me assure you that I never loved anyone as much as Feridé."

Aziz Bey mumbled through his teeth: "Great passion, great love! ... "

"I told you, Uncle, you don't believe me. No one believes me anyway. Müjgan has been resenting me for years. She doesn't let me talk about Feridé at all, knitting her eyebrows together as she says: 'No, Kâmran, you have no right to talk about her!' Just like mother, just like Aunt, just like everyone. There is only Nermin here who I can talk about Feridé with. Nermin is seventeen years old today. When Feridé came here Nermin was only seven years old, and she only remembers Feridé vaguely. To her, Feridé is 'The sister in the red dress who pushed me on the swing.' I have such days, where I harness all my language skill and power in order to make Nermin talk about her red-dressed sister."

284

"What a strange person you are, Kâmran. Well, what about the other one?"

"She was a sick patient and she could have died because of me. After I lost hope in Feridé, I wanted to fulfill a humane and compassionate duty towards her. That's all."

"It's an incomprehensible case. You are a complex-spirited person, Kâmran."

"You're right, Uncle. I have never known what I wanted and what I did. There is only one thing I'm sure of: my weakness for Feridé. She had such personality and gave me such memories that it is not possible to forget. I suppose if I recall those memories when I am dying, I'll cry myself to death.

Let me give you one more piece of evidence, Uncle. When they told me I needed a change of air, the first place that crossed my mind was Tekirdăgi. Do you think it was your invitation that brought me here? Do you think I've been staying here for a month because of village weddings? Please don't be offended. I came here to find the first few broken memories of my youth, that's all."

"So, you were impertinent; was it not possible to repair the damage?"

"What I did was wrong, Uncle. Horribly wrong. When Feridé left us she was so indignant that when I found her tracks, I was afraid of putting pressure on her. It was not only her heart but also her pride that was hurt. Who knows how much grief forced her to go to a foreign country by herself? If she saw me again before six months had passed, she would've been combative and would've done even wilder and crazier things. I could barely wait for spring to come. Finally, I was preparing to catch Çalıkuşu at her village school. Around that time my damned illness began. I stayed in bed for three months. Moreover, when I took off to find her in B., it was too little too late. The ship had sailed. They told me of Feridé's love for a sick composer; placing her unfaithful head on her lover's knees by the waterfall, as he played his tambur while staring into her eyes. Think, Uncle, after years of waiting for that very head which I had thought of as 'Mine, only mine,' and then this happens..."

Kâmran did not continue. Trying to avoid the chilly evening breeze from the Sea of Marmara, he hid his neck in the collar of his coat, watching the freshly-lit bonfires of fishermen in the distance.

Aziz Bey's joy faded too.

"Kâmran, son, I'm afraid you have acted like a fool for the second time. I wish Çalıkuşu was a type of girl that could soothe herself so that she could at least be happy; but I really don't think so."

Kâmran nodded with another bitter smile: "You should put that point of view to rest, Uncle. Feridé has been very happy for two years. I have heard from others who have witnessed as such. Her husband is an old but rich doctor. The wife of a friend of mine—she happens to be an old friend of Feridé's—encountered Feridé in Kuşadasi, and told me that Çalıkuşu was constantly laughing, singing and making jokes. She said she is very happy on a farm three to four hours away from the city center, where she cares for approximately twenty children. Apparently, she couldn't stand being separated from her husband for even half an hour. The friend wanted to talk about relatives in Istanbul. Feridé quickly hushed the conversation. 'I don't even remember that city, nor those people!' she said. I am to blame because of my injustice against Feridé, Uncle, that much I know. However, take pity on me. Was she right to forget me so quickly? At the same time, these are unnecessary words. Let us not continue anymore. I bid you farewell. I'm getting out of the car and I shall walk home. These damaged roads have left me badly shaken."

Aziz Bey sighed: "These administrators really are miserable people. Years ago, I built these roads myself. Worked as a foreman and burned under the sun. But it was probably not the roads that shook you. Kâmran, don't blame others. What good work they've done in dismissing me from the governor position. Go on son, but don't be late, because old age has ruined me as well as your aunt. If you're late, your aunt would faint from worrying, and I from hunger."

Kâmran got out of the carriage at a familiar bridgehead. It was an August afternoon, just like this one, a decade ago when he came here and sat on the rotten wood bridge deck, swinging his feet.

He has formed a habit for nearly twenty days since he's been to Tekirdăgi. He has come here every afternoon, only to return back slowly, enveloped in the twilight of the road, deep in thought.

After her husband went off to Anatolia for a temporary civil service post, Müjgan lived with her children in Tekirdăgi. Earlier on she had asked Kâmran: "You look so tired, did you go far away?"

Kâmran had replied, smiling ruefully: "You guessed that right, Müjgan. I went too far, to some distant past ten years back."

He was going to say more, but Müjgan made a face as if she didn't understand a single word and said only, "Is that so?" then turned her back to him. Müjgan felt a stubborn indignation hidden deep in her heart towards Kâmran. She would not say another word about Feridé.

As Kâmran slowly ventured home from the garden, the sky began to darken into night. But the sun hadn't set on the mountains yet. The darkness was filling in the sides of the night sky, turning it into a magnificent violet flower.

The young man stood next to one of the garden paths and watched the greenish darkness of the path sparkling with the glow of fireflies for a long time. That evening, he saw Feridé emerge on the path. He could still see Çalıkuşu in front of him, dressed in white, curls coming out of her headscarf, in her flat-soled child's boots, skipping stones with the tip of her foot.

It had gotten quite late. He did not want to go back into the house despite knowing that the household would wonder. He was looking for traces of an old dream, killing time on the way.

In the distance, he saw a ghostly female figure in a white dress in front of the street gates. It was Müjgan. She would usually would go out on this street with her youngest child to practice walking while holding the little one under the arms.

Upon seeing Kâmran, she started waving.

"Kâmran, how slow you are walking. What have you been up to until now?"

"Nothing Müjgan, the weather is wonderful."

Müjgan did not have a child with her tonight. Strangely, there was some excitement on her usually calm face.

"Müjgan, something is going on with you!"

The young woman wanted to say something but could not find the exact words. She took one step back, pointing to the corner between the door and the inner wall.

"Look who's here today, Kâmran!" she said.

Kâmran turned his head and to his amazement saw Feridé's hazel eyes in the bluish light that shone through the door. Those eyes, shining like a blue star, were smiling. That beautiful face, looking a little faded and drawn, was smiling. Feridé's smile was still inside his heart, just like each time he had shut his stargazing eyes for the last six years. Kâmran swayed slightly, like those who fear losing a beautiful dream for a moment. He closed his eyes and looked for a place to lean on. They could not find words to say, and could only stare at each other, trembling. They attempted smiling at each other despite the tears that curtained their eyes. Müjgan felt the difficulty of the moment. She took Feridé's hand and brought her in front of Kâmran. Her voice heavy with meaning, Müjgan announced: "Cousins are almost siblings. Since Feridé doesn't have a brother, you would be considered a brother to her; tell your sister 'Welcome!'"

Kâmran still could not say anything. Gently leaning towards her, he touched his lips to Feridé's hair. Then he slowly said into her ear: "I cannot find the words to say how pleased I am to see you again, Feridé Hanim."

These words gave Feridé courage. With a voice that had lost some of its old crystalline harmony, she replied: "Thank you, Kâmran Bey. I too, am very pleased."

"When did you arrive?"

"Today, at noon. I arrived in Istanbul ten days ago. I got the news that none of you were there. However, I really had to see my aunts and all of you relatives. 'Maybe there are those who want to see me as well,' I said. Anyway, how big is Tekirdăgi for someone who is accustomed to traveling, is it not so, Kâmran Bey?"

Müjgan interfered again: "That's fine, but there is no need for formal words like 'hanim' and 'bey,' as I just told you before. You are almost considered real siblings. In fact, you should call Kâmran 'big brother,' Feridé."

The two lowered their eyes to the ground. Feridé, in a state of fear, asked, "Really, will you allow me to call you 'ağabey,' Kâmran?" She waited for his reply without looking at him, instead searching for something in the darkness swarming with fireflies.

Kâmran replied, disgruntled: "As you wish, Feridé . . . however you like."

They were able to speak calmly at this point. Feridé explained her journey with a few words: "I had some business in Istanbul; and then as I said, I came to see you all. The doctor gave me permission to be away for two months. I'm so glad I found my aunts and you all in good health.

However, you have suffered a tragedy, Kâmran. I heard about it in Istanbul, and I am so sorry. What a catastrophe to lose your wife in such a short time! But you have a little one. God bless Necdet. What a beautiful child you have, Kâmran. I like him so much, we are already friends, and he's already sitting on my lap. Anyway, I'm such a quick friend with the little ones . . ."

As she continued to talk, Feridé slowly opened up, and her words and personality began to take on their old mischievousness and lightheartedness again.

Listening to her voice, watching her lips, it was such a joy to see her hazel eyes glittering in the night that the young man did not think of anything, even if she was someone else's wife. It was such a moment of joy that he did not even give thought that it would be a dream again after a month and a half. There was only one fear: that those inside would realize she was here.

As it was with everything he feared, the discovery of Feridé's presence eventually happened. Nermin was the first to see them near the door. The young girl ran to them after she announced loudly that Kâmran was coming. She took Feridé into her arms: "I have not forgotten you, Feridé abla, and my brother is a witness. We used to talk about our red-dressed sister the most, didn't we, Kâmran ağabey?" she said.

II

That evening, dinner was like a wedding feast. Aziz Bey was like a playful child at the head of the table: "Ah Çalıkuşu, how you've made me suffer! I'd be crying whenever I would imagine hearing your voice. It turns out I loved you after all."

Seeing each other again after years, Çalıkuşu returned to the nest on a day when all hope was lost, bringing not only a little joy, but also remnants of the old days' love and kindness. All the faces were laughing, and in all the hearts—like fireflies coming in through open windows and whirling around lamps—something quivered with happiness. It was just at the end of the meal, when Besimé Hanim started to cry suddenly at saying something unimportant. But she immediately wiped her eyes: "Nothing, I just remembered her mother Güzide," she said.

289

Feridé, who was feeding grapes to Kâmran's child on her knees, bowed her head, and for a moment hid her face in his golden curls. Then her previous festiveness came back again.

For a while, Besimé Hanim talked about Nejmiye in Trabzon with her husband. Feridé sighed: "I know the pain, Aunt, I lost my little one to illness."

Everyone else in the room looked at each other with amazement. Aunt Ayşe asked, "You had a child? We did not know."

Feridé sadly shook her head: "A girl like a pearl, you should have seen her. What a beauty! There was no way to save my baby."

Aunt Ayşe asked another question: "How old was your child when she died, Feridé?"

Feridé's lips curved downwards again with the same sadness: "She just finished being thirteen years old. I was sewing her first çarşaf. She said I was to be a mother-in-law."

Laughter broke out at the table. "Ah Çalıkuşu, if you reach a hundred years you still won't stop your jokes and pranks," Aziz Bey remarked.

Everyone was laughing at the thought of Feridé having a thirteen-year-old daughter. But Feridé's eyelashes were full of tears. She held Necdet tighter to her chest, and then told them the story of Munisé with growing sadness.

That night, they stayed up late. Aziz Bey would occasionally say, "Feridé, my daughter, you are tired from your journey, you should go to bed now."

Feridé would laugh, without releasing sleeping Necdet from her arms. "No matter, Uncle. I am resting here with you, it was the loneliness that was truly tiring," she would say.

With brilliant hazel eyes, she spoke for hours with a little smile that never died. The old Çalıkuşu was completely awake. Realizing that she had enraptured her audience, she started chewing her words, talking with cute, coy movements that only loving and adored children know: pursing her lips, biting her lips with her teeth and sucking in her cheeks. It was such that the old uncle, who could not be separated from his joyful exhilaration, was not able to resist the desire to repeat an old joke. When she was little, he would squeeze Feridé's upper lip between his fingers: "You naughty little brat, you took my cherries—give them back!" He would then force the tip of her squeezed upper lip to be kissed.

Laughter propagated throughout the room. "Don't, Uncle!" she cried. He held Feridé's jaw with force, repeating the old joke.

He looked carefully at Feridé's face: "What should I do, Çalıkuşu? It's your fault; you are married, but still a child at heart. Even your face is that of a child's. Who says this is a young woman's face?" he said.

Sitting in the corner, Kâmran turned pale. At that moment, it was the first time he understood that Çalıkuşu belonged to someone else.

III

Within the next two days, Kâmran could hardly see Feridé. Ten years ago in Tekirdăgi, Feridé was friends with many girls of her age. These girls were now married ladies. They did not leave Feridé alone, as if it was not enough to come and sit for hours, and would drag Çalıkuşu wherever they would go, door to door, touring gardens.

As Müjgan realized Kâmran's secret sorrow, her eyes laughed while she complained: "They will not leave Feridé to us. Nevertheless, first and foremost she should have fun and loosen up."

During those two days, Kâmran saw Feridé once at lunch and once in the street, catching a glimpse of her in her çarşaf as she was returning home.

On the third morning, Kâmran woke up quite earlier than usual. The sun was rising, illuminating everything around him. The rest of the house was asleep. He opened one of the window shutters and saw Feridé in the garden. She noticed the open window and lifted her head, using her hand to shield her face from the sunrise.

"Are you awake, Kâmran Bey? How much your nature has changed. In the past one had to throw handfuls of rocks at your blinds or a heap of snowballs in the winter to wake you up. You've become a bit Anatolian. When I was there and woke up at this time, they would scold me by telling me, 'You lazyhead, would a human being wait for the sun to cast its light on her?'"

Her words, reminiscent of the former mild, mocking Çalıkuşu, were a clear stream of harmony that refreshed the heart. Kâmran, a little afraid, asked, "Shall I join you, Feridé?"

With hands still shielding her eyes against the sun, she was secretly having fun like she used to: "It wouldn't be bad if you weren't afraid of a little moisture hurting your delicate body. I'll make you some Anatolian treats."

She led Kâmran under a big walnut tree, and made him sit on a chair that had been forgotten in the garden the previous evening: "Now you will have to wait for me, Kâmran Bey."

"I thought you were going to stop using formal words with me."

"A little patience, and it'll come on its own. I do not dare to suddenly be disrespectful."

Kâmran laughed: "But this is a greater injustice, Feridé. I forbid you. It sounds like you are having fun when you say 'Kâmran Bey.'"

Feridé also laughed: "True, you are correct, sir . . . I mean, you're right, I will make an effort. Now excuse me, I will heat you some milk."

"Feridé, please."

"It's useless, do not insist. It is the best compliment you can give an Anatolian woman; to allow her to work, to allow her to serve."

She continued, enjoying herself, but also a little sad: "We as women do not have any other charm other than our housework to appreciate . . ."

She was walking in and out of the garden, copper bucket and dry branches in her hands, and her voice could be heard conversing with the newly awakened gardener.

Finally, she came with a glass of steaming milk.

"The milk is not how I wanted it," she said, disappointed.

"Kâmran, but three days later—what is today? Monday. I invite you to breakfast on Thursday morning. You will drink milk from the same sheep, but you will see that it will be completely different, almost like a beautiful fruit. This is my big secret! Do you not wonder how it will be? Oh, what ignorance . . . I'll tell you in advance. I will feed the sheep with pears for three days. I think you're going to be cold, the air is a little chilly. Do you want Aunt Besimé to say, 'Crazy girl, you got my son sick!'? Wait, I'm used to the humidity. I'll give you my scarf."

She pulled a red wool scarf from her neck that was attached with a pin and covered Kâmran's shoulders and chest, which were shivering slightly as if he were suffering from morning dampness.

In Kâmran's eyes, a dream from a decade ago was resurfacing. In front of the door of the house in Kozyatağı, he saw the little blue coat on her shoulders, her short skirt, her black apron and her tiny, tiny fingers stained with purple ink. He heard himself trying to be a man: "It's my duty to take care of you now!"

"Kâmran, you're going to drop your milk like a dotard and burn your knees! Why are you so dazed?"

"Nothing, something came to mind . . ."

Feridé, as if to block any further explanation, quickly blurted out, "Something came to my mind too. Seeing you with a scarf on your shoulders, made me think of you as Kâmran Hanim."

After she finished the chores, Feridé sat on a low kitchen stool across from Kâmran. The coarse, dull Bursa silk—outdoor style—in the form of a baggy dress, covered Feridé's neck and body with wide, slight folds. With elbows resting on her knees, wrists united under her jaw and cheeks cradled in her open palms, she began to speak.

Kâmran saw her face up close for the first time, bathed in such a clear light. He could see that Feridé's face had lost a little weight and she was thinner overall. The weight loss enlarged her eyes, which were bleary and shadowed with dark circles. Five years ago, Çalıkuşu's eyes were filled with a gilded light, and now the scorched forgotten flowers had fallen into her hazel eyes. Those eyes smiled and stared with bold innocence like her old self again. However, Kâmran realized that it was no longer possible to see their limits and depths like it was before.

Her hair was parted in the middle with two thick braids like the girls who dress up to go out and visit. The braids were so tight that they pulled at her forehead, her brow and her temples, slightly lifting the scattered tips of her eyebrows and revealing thin blue veins under transparent delicate skin.

Kâmran was listening to her voice rather than her words, watching her beautiful face. He noticed something: Feridé's colour was not that of a happy young woman living her everyday life. In her skin glowed a secret fire, a scalding redness similar to the fever of women like uncut roses left to dry, women who grow old without love.

The morning sun caused sunbeams to illuminate such subtle and expressive lines on her face that the effect engaged the young man so, making him want to cry. Kâmran had never in the world imagined that suffering could make a young woman's face so beautiful.

293

Feridé, with her everlasting smile, was talking about her childhood memories with the voice of broken crystal, lifeless and quivering.

Mustering up courage, Kâmran asked for more recent memories.

Feridé shook her head solemnly. "It is not in my mind, Kâmran. I remember events until the age of fifteen, but further than that it's all foggy and I can't see."

Talking about these newer, foggy memories caused her to start daydreaming. She turned her head to the side, looking away.

After these older childhood memories, she suddenly jumped to the last five years of her life. As she recalled sayings from Hadji Kalfa, a phrase from the Zeyniler muhtar, and the oddness of Director Rejep Efendi, there was no doubt that a tiredness was infusing her smiling eyes and vibrant gestures. At that moment the vague shakiness in her voice deepened and quivered like a sad heart.

When she started talking about the water's edge, Kâmran closed his eyes and wondered to himself, "Please don't let this be the edge of the waterfall where you put your head on your beloved's knees as you looked into each other's eyes while he played the tambur."

After talking about some of the most meaningless and innocent parts of her life, Çalıkuşu suddenly said, "Kâmran, I haven't shown you the photo of your Uncle, my husband." She held out the gold medallion that was attached to her neck with a thin golden cord.

The young man grabbed the photograph, trying to hide his pale and trembling hands. Feridé stretched out her head to look at the photograph with him, bringing her face next to his face: "Look at that face, Kâmran. Isn't it such a noble and beautiful face?"

Instead of looking at the photograph, the young man gazed at Feridé. She was completely unaware as she admired the photo.

That moment was the most painful and rebellious minute of Kâmran's life. Feridé's slender, delicate and innocent beauty had become food for some white-haired and rough-faced old man.

A crazed dream formed before his eyes: Feridé's tears, dripping down from her half-closed hazel eyes onto her blushing cheeks due to shame. He saw her with trembling, begging lips like an innocent child getting mauled in the arms of some old man.

Çalıkuşu shook off slightly, as if she had felt these thoughts without looking at him, and slowly put the medallion back on her chest.

"Excuse me, Kâmran. I suppose there will be guests today," she said.

IV

It had been ten days since Çalıkuşu had returned to the nest. Every evening, Aziz Bey repeated, "Are you paying attention, everyone? There's a change in the house. This time Çalıkuşu looks like a swallow bird. She has brought springtime under her wings. It's a pity that another day has passed."

Feridé laughed. "It doesn't matter, Uncle. After a few years, I'll get permission to come back. Don't be sad. While there are so many days ahead . . . why must we make life unbearable?"

Çalıkuşu was back to being the old Çalıkuşu. After being clouded over by a temporary storm, she was opening up day by day, like fresh flowers that had been restored to the sun.

Once again, she was the ringleader of the children in the house. Müjgan's three-year-old daughter and all the children, big and small, from Necdet all the way up to seventeen-year-old Nermin, were tied to Feridé; they would not let go of her skirts from morning until evening. The house was filled with laughter.

The elders sometimes complained about this level of mischief. But on the other hand, they were delighted. Feridé and Kâmran were after all, ex-fiancés, afraid of reopening their old wounds from five years ago. But Feridé's overflow of joy and Kâmran's mild, calm happiness, wanting nothing more than to watch her from afar, began to give the elders some peace.

At the same time, erring on the side of caution, they tried to bring back the old feelings of "Big Brother" and "Little Sister." Like those who abstain from talking in a sleeping patient's room, they feared they would wake this sorrowful past with a reckless word.

"Is it not possible to extend your stay a little longer?" Aziz Bey would occasionally ask. He would always get a little sad at Çalıkuşu's response:

"No way, Uncle. Çalıkuşu, after all, is now mother of another nest and there are those who wait for her."

What touched Kâmran the most was the great friendship between Feridé and Necdet. To separate them, he had to wait for Necdet to fall asleep in Çalıkuşu's arms.

One day, Kâmran heard Feridé arguing with Necdet.

Çalıkuşu was laughing and kept saying, "Necdet, say it one more time: 'Aunt, aunt, aunt!'"

But Necdet would not obey her. Shaking his stubborn blonde head, he cried, 'Mother, mother, mother!'"

It scared Kâmran somewhat. "Leave it alone, Feridé. What if he says so? What's the harm? Maybe the poor boy needs to say it."

Feridé bowed her head without saying anything, and caressed Necdet's head for a long time.

V

One morning, Kâmran woke up again to the sound of small stones hitting his closed window shutters. He knew this was Feridé's wake-up ritual. Çalıkuşu was inviting him to another morning feast under the big walnut tree. As she promised in the early days of her visit, there was milk next to the mini buns—which smelled like a nice pear—and there was a pink dessert that looked like jam.

Feridé spread the pink jam on the buns, with which she served Kâmran: "These are the products of my skilled hands . . . I do not know the name of these buns, but they call this dessert 'Gülbeşeker'."

After she finished serving him, she found her low kitchen stool again and sat close to Kâmran.

"Now tell me and look at me, Kâmran: do you like Gülbeşeker?"

The young man laughed and replied, "I like it."

"Do you love it?"

"I love it."

"Say it again."

"I like it and love it."

"Not like that, Kâmran. Say 'I love Gülbeşeker.'"

Kâmran laughed, not understanding this childish insistence. "I love Gülbeşeker."

With shining eyes and flushed cheeks, Feridé was fluttering her eyelashes shyly, bringing her face closer to him, and bending her neck like a pleading child. With the last breath on her lips, she begged, "One more time, Kâmran, say 'I love Gülbeşeker very much.'"

The young man bent down and looked at her trembling lips with amazement. He didn't know the reason he himself was shivering.

"I love Gülbeşeker very much, I love it as much as you want me to," he said.

Feridé clapped her hands with the joy of a child, but as her lips were laughing, her eyes started to cry. Like lecturing a stranger not to cry over something trivial, she exclaimed: "What madness, how crazy it is to be so pleased that you made someone else appreciate one of your skills!" She was struggling, trying to show she was having fun, trying to dry her eyes with her fingers. But the tears did not stop. A sob escaped; and then her face was in her hands and she ran inside, weeping.

One afternoon, Kâmran returned from the bazaar with his uncle. The children had begun to form a habit: they could be seen coming from afar, lining up at the door for fruit, candy and chocolate. While giving each child a share, Kâmran felt small stones hitting his feet. After giving away the last of the treats, his eyes searched and found Çalıkuşu. She was a little further away, standing by a huge chestnut tree and pointing at him with her hand:

"Do you know what it means, Kâmran Bey? I am here too." When she was about to have fun or play a prank, she always called him "you" in its plural and formal form. She laughed and continued: "You have neglected me too much. Where is my share? Do you think old misdemeanors are forgotten, sir? Either give me my cut to shut me up, or the story of that old cherry tree comes alive tonight at the dinner table."

Just as she did next to this door ten years ago, she squeezed her tongue between her teeth, laughing while showing the sharp red tip of her tongue.

Kâmran laughed as he pulled out a box from his coat pocket. "I got lucky. Feridé, what a wonderful coincidence. I bought a box of fondants today. I was going to eat it myself without showing anyone, but if I am threatened so, what should we do?"

Feridé's face shone with a child's joy: "How beautiful! How beautiful!"

"But on one condition, Çalıkuşu. I will feed them to you again."

"How?"

"In the past . . . when you were twelve or thirteen, how did it go?"

297

When he said that, he extended one of the fondants to Feridé. Çalıkuşu hesitated for a few seconds; then she stretched out her head and gently opened her mouth, lips slightly trembling. But despite Kâmran's insistence, she did not want to eat a second one.

"Give it to me. After dinner I will eat it with Necdet."

"Let's go to the wall, Feridé. Look, the sea is beautiful. We'll talk and watch."

"Okay, but I'll leave this box inside. Give me a minute."

Kâmran dared to touch her for the first time; he held her wrist. "No, Feridé," he said. "I don't trust you. You will say 'Wait a minute, I'm coming now' and you won't come back. Or if you go inside, who knows what time you will come? You see that I have no faith in you anymore."

Feridé bowed her head without saying anything and slowly began to walk with him.

That evening there was a wistful sadness in Kâmran. He could not control himself, constantly complaining in clipped and jumbled words. For a moment, he pointed at the birds flying through the open sky, which was starting to darken.

"Feridé, you will fly away like that after a while, won't you?"

". . ."

"Well, would it be so sweet for you to leave behind your aunt, your aunt's children, your old friends and your childhood?"

". . ."

"Will you not worry about the other nest you left in ruins while you happily live in your own?"

Feridé did not answer or even listen, drawing shapes on the underside of the candy box with a pencil fragment, scribbling at random.

"You're not answering, Feridé." Kâmran complained bitterly.

Çalıkuşu looked at his face distractedly. "Forgive me, Kâmran. My mind was somewhere else. I did not hear what you said. There was an old song I once listened to and had forgotten about and I don't know why, but suddenly it came to mind. I wrote it out so that I should not forget. Read it if you want. It's getting cold, I'm going inside."

Kâmran saw four verses written in Feridé's scribblings underneath the candy box:

298

Do not make me open my mouth, never ever,
Cruel tyrant, do not make me say what is in my heart;
Don't I know what you've done, do not deny it,
Cruel tyrant, do not make me say what is in my heart!

VI

Four days had passed. Feridé all but ran away from her old friends. Despite all the excuses she made to be alone, her cunning was wasted. When she had to talk to others, she was afraid to look at their faces and make eye contact.

It was the fourth evening. No one was home—the whole family had been invited somewhere. There was no way they would come back before the evening call to prayer. Despite the fact there was a violent wind that was kicking up dust, Kâmran did not dwell at home and went out to wander.

The wind whistled in the distant hills. Trees rustled with gusts of wind, as if they were under invisible rain. Dust rattled over a path that reached out as far as the eye could see.

Kâmran's eyes were filled with dust and he had to stop every few steps to turn his back to the wind. He saw a huge hollow in a rock at the edge of a naked hill. A scrawny little tree constantly fluttered, shaking its skinny branches. Kâmran went to the hollow, changing his direction. He sat at a corner of the rock, using it to guard against the wind.

It seemed so empty today, despite so much noise . . . empty and flat, like a desert.

He had never before seen nature so soulless, its beautiful things so useless and life itself so hopeless!

From a distance, he noticed a colourful female figure on the road, at a point near the sea that seemed to pass through the waters. He went down the hill for no reason and started walking towards her.

A little later he recognized Nermin's rose-coloured çarşaf. The young girl must have seen him. Was she waving her umbrella out there?

Why was Nermin separated from the others? Why did she come alone? Wondering, he began to walk faster.

The young girl was tilted against the wind, trying to hold her skirts with one hand and hanging on to her cloak with the other. Her çarşaf was fluttering like the wings of a bird.

The sight of her face sent a jolt through Kâmran's heart. It was Feridé, in Nermin's rose-coloured çarşaf.

When they closed in on each other, the wind took away Feridé's umbrella. Çalıkuşu yelled and tried to hang on. But suddenly her skirts scattered; her cloak was flapping in the air and her hair whipped loosely around her. Kâmran was just in time. He caught her umbrella near a bush. He used his coat to shield Feridé from the wind so she could fix her çarşaf.

"You got here just in time, Kâmran! The wind would've blown me away like a real çalıkuşu," Feridé said. She wanted to say something more. But the wind forced her head to bow down, with her eyes and her lips closed. They started to walk while Kâmran shielded her with his coat.

At one point, Feridé was finally able to say something. But it seemed she needed to overcome a fit of laughter first. She could not control herself, laughing as if caught by another heavy wind. In intermittent bursts, she eventually got out what she wanted to say.

"Do you know why I'm laughing, Kâmran? We were invited somewhere as guests. But I remembered that I had to run some errands at the bazaar. I had my cloak on my back. Of course, I did not dare go with that outfit. Poor Nermin wanted to do me a favour. She offered me her çarşaf. I was just leaving the bazaar with my face covered. I noticed an officer coming from behind me and as he passed by, he said 'Nermin Hanim! You are here—what an unexpected pleasant surprise! Wouldn't you say, ma'am?'

Nermin gave herself away when she offered to do me a favour and I found it so strange that I could not control myself. I laughed. The officer noticed the mistake. He ran away so fast . . . Oh yes! Seeing an old woman instead of Nermin . . ."

Kâmran listened with a smile. Feridé continued: "But I feel sorry I told you her secret. My babbling tongue does not stop . . . My dear, for God's sake, please don't tell anyone! Only in the future, who knows, what if this girl wants him too? . . . If we could do them a favour . . ."

"I promise you, Feridé, but Nermin is so childish . . ."

Feridé complained feebly: "Possibly, the heart of such children is never the way it seems."

After that, both of them fell silent; they started to walk side by side again.

The wind subsided and they slowed their steps accordingly, afraid to end the walk. Kâmran thought sadly to himself, "Just a moment ago, I saw nature as empty, and I saw myself as a useless person . . . now, protecting this gentle, tiny and beautiful thing—trembling in a child-sized rose-coloured çarşaf—against the wind, it gives me such unbelievable happiness. This, it could have always been like this. This beautiful little creature. I, if I wanted, I could have made someone happy and I would have been happy too. Pity!"

In contemplative thought, Feridé gradually started to walk even slower. She began to talk again, about irrelevant things.

"Despite everything, this little change of air kept me very entertained. Probably enough for a year or two . . . Then, my aunts and relatives, I will see you all again when I start to long for you too much . . . so the years will pass, my hair will slowly start to turn grey . . . you too, of course. We will be glad to see each other again. Maybe we will be less sad when we separate . . . who knows, I might even be back in the future, right? That's life, everything is possible . . . Then you, you will be my big brother completely . . . As the elders are lost one by one, we appreciate each other more. We start to see our little flaws as more pleasant. The last years of our lives, where we spent our childhood . . ."

The invisible wound in her voice grew deeper, tingeing her words with sadness, revealing a hidden testament.

Coincidentally, a beggar woman with her children appeared on the road. A child ran around in bare feet, stroking Feridé's skirts with dry hands.

Kâmran stopped to give the children money. Feridé, by habit of contact with little wretches, was repulsed as she stroked the child's head. When they started to walk again, the beggar woman prayed out loud: "May God never separate you, may God bless your beautiful lady!"

They stopped abruptly. All the pain of Kâmran's heart gathered in his eyes. "Feridé, did you hear what that woman said?"

Two large tears responded to his question.

They continued on their way, not daring to approach each other.

When they arrived in front of the house, it was evening. The weather was now quite calm and the howling of the wind had stopped. After such a long weariness, the trees fell asleep with their calm shadows on the rocks. A gentle light leaked through them, flashing gently like pearls.

"It's still early, Feridé. They have not returned from the city. Do you want to go to the rocks?"

With her head bowed, Feridé sluggishly made a request. "If you please, Kâmran. I want to go and change. The wind has made me dizzy."

Feridé's çarşaf was alive just a little while ago, like a playful creature around her, flying from her shoulders, fluttering to her knees like a delicate, flirtatious hug. Now the rose-coloured çarşaf hung limply from her shoulders down to her knees, like faded hopes and dreams.

As if there were no force to go further, she sat on the edge of a large rock in front of the door. With her umbrella she began to draw lines in the sand, lines as deep as her hopelessness, as fractured as her life.

A little later, when Kâmran sat next to her, she felt his shoulder touching her shoulder and him holding her hand, which slightly excited her. Confused, she looked around, wanting to escape. But she gave up.

Kâmran saw her take a few deep breaths, and suddenly he saw her violent eyes submit to a desperate defeat. He left his trembling, ice-cold hand in the hands of his ex-fiancée, and they both closed their eyes. In the darkness of his eyes filled with flying sparks, Kâmran thought to himself: "This hand trembling in my palm is Feridé's hand. So, it is possible that an impossible dream at night might just be real!" He opened his eyes again. Feridé, like children who fall asleep crying, was sighing every now and then, leaving her increasingly heavy head on his shoulder. There was a quiet surrender in her when she let her hands relax. Kâmran occasionally felt her get closer whenever he moved, squeezing his hand harder. The young man, not knowing why he said it, very slowly spoke:

"I love Gülbeşeker."

The sudden opening of the door next to them awakened them from this sleep. Feridé jumped with the lightness of a bird burst out of its place, as if there was a gunshot. Nermin had arrived first. Çalıkuşu, thrilled with joy, threw herself at Nermin. She was squeezing the young girl in her arms, burying the young girl's hair and eyes in her chest, overwhelming the young girl with kisses on the hair and eyes. No one understood the reason for this joy. There was no trace of the previous exhaustion. She was grabbing the little ones by the arms, throwing them

302

into the air and making them shout with joy. As everyone came in, Feridé lingered behind a little and waited for Kâmran to approach. Then, in the dark of the inner door, she slowly spoke.

"Thank you, Kâmran," she said.

VII

The next day, Feridé went to the city again and when she returned to the house in the middle of the afternoon, she looked very tired. Nevertheless, the children gathered around her again, and she built a large swing in the backyard.

Just as Kâmran freed himself from an old chatty friend of Aziz Bey, he came across Feridé and Necdet on the swing. Feridé was moving the swing with such a force that Necdet was climbing her neck like a kitten, screaming.

Kâmran imitated Aunt Ayşe just like she would have scolded ten years ago: "Feridé, my daughter, stop this madness! You're going to drop the child!"

Çalıkuşu, completely carefree, was amused with her entire soul: "Oh Aunt, what do you want? Necdet's owner is not complaining! Right, Kâmran?"

Feridé finished with one child and then took another, making sure to accommodate the whole line of children.

Nermin was the eldest of the children but the most cowardly. She jumped from the swing, screaming. Her sweaty hair was sticking to her forehead and her cheeks, and she rubbed her palms together to get rid of the rope burn.

"I suppose there is no one left anymore," Feridé concluded.

Kâmran was hesitant: "You forgot me, Feridé," he said.

A colourless smile formed on Çalıkuşu's lips. She was unwilling to say "No," but she didn't dare say "Come on." Instead, she examined the rope and the branches of trees with her eyes, waiting for encouragement from the others.

"But how? I don't think the ropes are going to hold the both of us, right, Müjgan?"

Müjgan held the rope with her hand, her eyes meeting Kâmran's eyes.

"Never mind the ropes . . . Feridé is very tired. Look at her, Kâmran. I think it's a sin to make a weary woman even more tired," she said.

At first, Feridé responded, "It's not significant. Does it matter?" But then she understood the meaning of Müjgan's words and eyes. Embarrassed and scared, like a child at fault, she lowered her head slowly.

"Yes, I'm too tired. Maybe I'll get sick," she said. Tiredness descended on her, and her eyes faded out of the previous joy that existed just moments ago.

Müjgan, still looking at Kâmran, slowly spoke: "You're more heartless than I thought, Kâmran!"

Just as slowly, Kâmran responded, "Why?"

Müjgan forced him to walk across the garden with her. "Can't you see the poor girl's condition? Haven't you upset her heart and life enough?

"Müjgan! . . ."

"None of us called her once in so many years. She couldn't resist the painful longing. She returned to us by forgetting her resentment, her rebellion. She was almost alright when she arrived. You re-opened this newly-closed wound."

Müjgan continued to keep her eyes down: "I'm thinking about the agony the poor wretch will suffer when she leaves tomorrow . . . Yes, Kâmran, Feridé leaves tomorrow. Everything is ready. I didn't know either. Feridé doesn't tell me anything about her heart or her life at this time. I just got word; I asked the reason for this sudden decision. She told me about a letter from her husband. I'm sure it's a lie. Feridé's avoiding you. She can no longer endure this. I'm afraid that your necessary separation will be a little difficult. Feridé is a very diligent, incredibly diligent creature. However, she is a woman after all. You owe a debt to this wretch whom you've destroyed, to be strong and calm in these days of separation; you must make an effort for her as much as possible . . ."

While listening to these words, Kâmran's whole being, including the green of his eyes, turned pale. "You're talking about the fractured life of Feridé. What about mine?"

"You asked for it yourself."

"Don't be so heartless, Müjgan."

"Do you think if there was anything to be done, I'd stand back? But we have no choice. Feridé is now someone else's wife. The wretch's foot is tied. I see that you are also miserable. I'm not offended by you anymore. But there's nothing to be done."

Everyone heard that Feridé was leaving the next day. But no one was talking about it. They ate supper in a deep silence. That night, Aziz Bey, who looked older and more exhausted, took Feridé aside. While patting her shoulder, he grabbed her chin, turned her head and looked into her eyes.

"Ah! Çalıkuşu," the elderly man said, "You are giving grievance to my heart at this old age."

That night, everyone went to bed early.

VIII

The time was past midnight. The house was already asleep. Müjgan came out of her room with a thin scarf draped over her shoulders and a small candle in her hand. Walking on tiptoe, she stopped at Kâmran's door. There was neither sound nor light in the room. The young woman gently touched the door and called out in a whisper.

The door opened quickly. Kâmran was still dressed. In the candlelight, his face looked more pale and tired. He was blinking, as if dazzled by the faint light.

"Haven't you slept yet, Kâmran?"

"You can see that I haven't."

"Why did you put out your lamp?"

"Brightness burns my eyes tonight."

"What are you doing in the dark?"

He smiled bitterly. "I'm trying to digest my despair, my poison. But why did you come at this time? What did you want?"

Müjgan tried to suppress her excitement. "There's magnificent news! Don't worry, Kâmran. Pull yourself together, I'll tell you."

They went into the room. Müjgan left her candle on the floor and slowly closed the door. She hesitated, not knowing where to start. In a voice that tried to appear calm, she assured him: "Don't worry, Kâmran my dear. I am not going to say anything bad, but rather a good thing. But if you get too excited . . ."

Çalıkuşu

The young woman was trying to calm him, but her teary eyes and trembling voice gave away her unusual anxiety.

"Kâmran, Feridé just came into my room. There was a strangeness in her behaviour. She said, 'Müjgan, I've only ever opened my heart to you in the world. I have no one closer than you. I have a secret to tell you, so you must hide it until tomorrow, when I go. Then you can reveal it. When you saw me arrive suddenly that day, you were surprised. I told you I couldn't stand the longing anymore and that is true. But that's not the real reason. I'm here to fulfill the promise I gave to a man I loved most in the world, three months ago, on his deathbed. Müjgan, I was forced to lie to you. I'm a widow now. My husband died of cancer three months ago.'

"When she said those words, Feridé put her head on my shoulder, sobbing. She continued in tears: 'The day my doctor died, he said to me, 'I'm not afraid of your financial distress any more. Because whatever I have will stay with you. A simple, calm woman like you can support yourself for the rest of your life. But there's something else, Feridé. It's not easy for a lonely woman to live alone, even if she is rich. Money and compassion are different things. Feridé, if you want me to die comfortably, swear to me now. After I die, you will return to Istanbul to your family. If you don't want to stay with them for good, at least stay with them for two or three months. You never know, maybe one day you'll need them. You might need a bit of family compassion someday. Shortly, little Feridé, if I'm sure you'll be able to make peace with your family, I'll die comfortably, without the worry of leaving something undone.'

'I told him, crying, that I would fulfill his last wish. But my doctor didn't think that was enough. He wanted me to make peace with my ex-fiancé, saying that one day he might be a big brother to me. He gave me a sealed package to be handed over to Kâmran with my own hands:

'There's an old book of love in it, which at one time made me very regretful. I want your ex-fiancé to read it.' He said, 'Swear you'll deliver it to him like this.'

'That's the truth, Müjgan. Now you know everything. My doctor was a pure and clean man. He thought that me making peace with my family would cure my life as an orphan. He couldn't imagine how painful it would be for me. After I put my doctor to rest beside Munisé, I went to Istanbul. The things I learned there showed me that fulfilling this will

306

would be very difficult. I learned about the death of Kâmran's wife. Then I heard bad words being spoken about me. If Kâmran's wife was alive, I as a new widow staying over as a family guest would seem natural. However, now all of you, even Kâmran, even you, Müjgan—you know me better than anyone—what terrible things you must think of me. 'She travelled all over, wandered, had all sorts of adventures . . . who knows with what kind of motives she sold herself to an old man?' Now upon hearing that her ex-fiancé was free again, you'd say that she came back with those petty motives to the house she left with insults and curses five years ago. I'd be crushed even in front of those who are too compassionate and sensitive to think otherwise.'"

Müjgan continued to speak with growing excitement and enthusiasm:

"Ah! Kâmran, if you heard Feridé say these things in my arms, shaking with such desperate tears! I'll never forget her last words. Feridé said, 'I have no way to tell you how I ran away from the family, with what kind of miserable feelings, how my life is full of sorrow, what obligations I was under that pushed me to get married. Twenty-five years old, a woman who has spent five years of her life, some of which she spent in her husband's house and some of which she drifted into adventures; if she claims to be a young girl who has not been exposed to male lips on her face, everyone would laugh. Everyone would call her a lousy liar wouldn't they, Müjgan? There's no way to prove otherwise. I'm not going to tell you. I don't know what is in the package the doctor left for Kâmran. But maybe there's something surprising hidden in it. I've fulfilled his last wish with so much sadness and misery. But I have no strength to do it. You give it to Kâmran after I get on the ferry tomorrow.'"

Müjgan fell silent. This woman, who could maintain a great depth of calm and endurance when facing the most painful events, was crying like a child.

She extended her trembling hands.

"We're not leaving her anymore. Kâmran, if we need to we will force her. No matter what happened in the past, you should no longer be separated. As far as I can see, both of you will not survive."

Kâmran was almost asleep. It was so much hope for a dreamer who for months consumed even the most insignificant daydreams and dimmest memories as food for his sick, ambiguous soul. With the eyes of patients waking from long comas, dull and unable to understand anything, he was not looking around in the dark but instead kept opening and closing his eyelids.

Müjgan took out a large envelope from her scarf. It was sealed with a red candle. She said, "I will give it to you now, despite my promise to Feridé."

She was preparing to leave the room and was fixing her scarf. Kâmran stopped her with his hand.

While Müjgan lit the extinguished lamp on the table, Kâmran opened the envelope. Inside there was a second large envelope along with a letter. The letter, written in bold writing, was addressed to Kâmran.

Kâmran Bey, My Son,

The man who writes you this letter, a hermit who has dedicated a piece of his life to books and another piece to the wounded in this blind birth we call life, is an old man who, in a long time before his letter touches your hand, will have given the last blow on his Yuf pipe for the world. It is in the hope of a last favour to a beloved poor girl that this old man has bothered to write you these lines in his last breath. Listen:

One day in a remote village I stumbled upon a beautiful little Istanbul girl who was as pure as light and as beautiful as a dream. What do you hear when you open the window of your room in the middle of a winter night, when snowflakes are falling, and the sound of a nightingale comes to your ears from the darkness? That is what I heard that minute.

This innocent, kind, polite girl . . . what cursed fortune would throw such a beautiful and rare ornament of God into this dump of a dark village? She was trying to deceive me with stories but her soul was crying. Oh, poor little girl! Am I the unwary, stupid boyfriend you left in Istanbul, to fool me with these stories? Her movements told me everything: Her bleary eyes, like children awakened from their sleep, sloppy movements like she didn't know what she was stepping on, the lips that appeared to be trembling with the dream of a kiss from imaginary lips, the feeling she invoked when she acted and moved like she was hugging an imaginary someone.

I used to remember Majnun, who succumbed to the Sahara in order to look for Leyla in ancient tales, occasionally, with compassion. After that day, I stopped. I began to remember often this clear hazel-eyed, silk-coloured, innocent, gentle "Leyla" in the dark villages of new times, full of cemeteries, looking for an impossible love dream.

Two years later, another coincidence and our paths crossed again. The sickness had not stopped, hollowing her inside. Ah, the first day I saw her, why didn't I put her on my horse, why didn't I bring her to my house in Istanbul? . . . Heedlessness! . . .

At the time of the second coincidence, the damage was already done. You were married. I thought to myself that she was still a young girl; maybe she would forget over time. But a notebook that I accidentally came across while she was sick showed me how deep this wound was. She had written her whole life in this book. At that time, I stopped hoping. I wanted to treat her like my own child. But the people gossiping around us did not allow it. I thought about finding a man for her to marry. But it was dangerous. Her husband would want her love, no matter how benevolent or mature he was. Although my little daughter was meant for love and was dying for it, the love of a stranger would be a sad chore for her. Falling into someone else's arms while she loved another might have killed her. Helpless in the face of this danger, I took it upon myself to marry her. I was going to defend her as long as I was alive. My insignificant wealth and few pieces of real estate would provide for her after my death. It would be easier for her to live as a confident widow than to live as a suspicious girl. There was still a chance that one day her dream could come true. What's impossible in life? As a matter of fact, your wife's death revived my hope. I kept watch on you in Istanbul. Her death might have hurt you deeply, but if I said the same for myself, it would be hypocrisy. I was thinking of a proper remedy. I was going to divorce Feridé at the marriage registry, a marriage which was folly anyway, and have her directly returned to you. I don't know, what would people have said about my actions? I am a man who has already spit on what people say and think about me, and at that time my illness had also started to worsen. At last, in three or four months, I was convinced that the issue would resolve itself. I don't think there is any need to go into details. With an excuse, I am placing Feridé at your doorstep. I have no doubt she will hand over my letter. I have learned her nature well, she's a strange girl. In case she acts difficult, don't pay attention and don't let her go. If necessary, be wild and rough like the mountain men, so that if she dies in your arms, she will die from pleasure.

Çalıkuşu

And I'll let you know that I didn't think about you at all. You know, with all due consent, I wouldn't even give you a house cat, never mind a rare girl like Feridé. What do they like about inexperienced and heartless men like you? I don't know ...

The Late Hayrullah

NOTE: Feridé's diary is in the envelope. Last year, when she went to the farm, I made it disappear with the chest it was in and said, "The coachman probably stole it." I sensed that she felt really upset. But she didn't make a sound. I was right to think that this diary would come in handy someday!

IX

By the time Müjgan and Kâmran finished reading Çalıkuşu's blue-clad school notebook, they were weeping, and the birds were chirping on branches outside the window.

Kâmran's head was heavy with fatigue and anguish, and he rested it in the yellow pages of the notebook. He kissed these words of love, throughout which there were spots wiped out with tears, over and over again.

When they were about to close the book, Müjgan made a slight movement, taking the blue book closer to the lamp and looking at it.

"The book is unfinished. There is also writing on the cover, but it is hard to distinguish the blue ink on the blue cover," she said.

They increased the brightness of the lamp, reading the following lines with difficulty, their heads close together:

I closed my notebook yesterday, forever. The morning after the night I was married, not only could I not write my memoirs but I also did not dare see my old face in the mirror or hear my old voice. But ...

Yesterday I became the bride. I humbly gave in like a flood-struck dry leaf. I was doing everything I was told, and I wasn't objecting to anything. So much so that I agreed to be dressed in the long white dress that the doctor brought from Izmir, and I even agreed to attach a pinch of ribbon to one side of my hair. However, after they brought me in

310

front of a large mirror to see myself, I kept my eyes down. That is all that is left of my rebellion.

Many strangers came to see me. Even my old colleagues were among them. I didn't listen to the words and instead tried smiling at them all with the same shaky smile. An old woman, against my face: "How fortunate is that dotard? He hit the jackpot."

Hayrullah Bey came home for dinner. He was dressed in a frock coat, which squeezed his fat body like a corset, and his strange, poppy-coloured tie was resting to one side. Although I felt melancholy, I couldn't help but laugh lightly, thinking I had no right to leave this man in such a ridiculous position. I removed the red tie and put on another tie instead.

He laughed and said, "Good girl, you're going to be a great housewife. See the virtues of being a young wife?"

The guests had left. We sat across from the dining room window. "Child," Hayrullah Bey said. "You know why I'm so late? I went for a visit. I left the tomb of Munisé with a few flowers and piece of your bride's ribbons. Poor thing, she wouldn't have dared tell you, but when we were alone she would never stop saying 'When my abla is a bride and wears her ribbons, I too will wear a ribbon.' I was going to attach the ribbon to that yellow head like a canary but it didn't happen."

While the doctor was saying this, I couldn't hold back and I cried for a long time, turning my head towards the window. The hidden tears evaporated from my eyelashes like a sad autumn evening fog.

We spent the first hours of the night in the dining room, like every night. Hayrullah Bey, wearing his glasses, put the thick volume of Rousseau on his knees, sitting in the corner.

"Mrs. Bride, the newlywed groom shouldn't be reading but please excuse me. Don't worry, new bride, the nights are long, I'll have time to read the new bride epic love stories."

I bent my head over the handkerchief I was sewing. Ah, this old doctor! How much I had loved him. How much I hated him now. When I put my head on his shoulder due to pain and worry, he . . . these innocent blue eyes with their white eyelashes would tolerate looking at me as a woman, a future wife! I was overwhelmed with these thoughts until eleven o'clock. Finally, the doctor left his book on the table and stretched out.

311

Çalıkuşu

"Oh Mrs. Bride, it's time for bed. All right, let's go." He stood up. The needle and tangle fell out of my hands as I stood up and grabbed the candlestick which stood on the table.

I approached the window under the pretext of closing it and looked out at the vast darkness for a long time. My gut feeling told me to sneak out of the room, to go out on to the dark roads.

"Mrs. Bride, you've daydreamed too much. Go on right up. I'm going to go tell the Corporal something and then I'm coming," he said.

A neighbour and an old foster nurse helped me undress. They sent me to my husband's room, handing me back the candle. Hayrullah Bey was downstairs. I stood by the edge of the closet, holding my arms and covering my chest as if I was cold. I was shaking so hard that the candle would occasionally burn the ends of my hair. Finally, I heard footsteps on the stairs and then in the hall. Hayrullah Bey walked into the room and took off his jacket while humming a song. He was surprised to see me.

"Girl, you haven't slept yet?"

I opened my mouth to answer but my teeth were chattering. He was near me and staring at me with amazement.

"Girl, what is this? What are you doing in my room?" Suddenly his booming laugh rocked the room.

"Girl, don't! . . ."

He couldn't finish his sentence because he was choking on laughter. His hands were slapping his knees and then covering his mouth.

"So, you're here . . . Wow, you hussy! Is it because we are really husband and wife? . . . How immodest, how shameless! God punish you! I'm like your father, and you . . ."

The room was spinning around me and the ceiling was collapsing. Red with shame, he bit his finger: "Wow, you ill-hearted hussy! Girl, aren't you ashamed to come to my room in your nightdress like this?"

If only I could have seen myself at that moment. Who knows how many colours I turned?

"Doctor Bey, I swear to God, I didn't know."

"Come on, the servants ate up that drivel . . . but you? . . . I could have thought of everything in the world, and at this age I would not believe that such a brazen girl would rape my honour and chastity!"

Oh my goodness, what torture! I felt so cheap, I felt like I was falling through the ground, biting my lip until it almost bled. As I moved, he

312

mockingly ran away towards the window and hid his neck with the collar of his flannel shirt.

"Girl, don't come at me, I'm scared. I swear to God, I'll open the window and shout, 'Friends! And at this age . . .'"

I ran out the door before he could finish. But I don't know what happened—I suddenly came back. My heart commanded it and I had to obey.

"My father, my father!" I cried, throwing myself into his arms.

He opened his arms with the same deep-hearted bellow: "My daughter, my child!"

I will never forget the sweetness of my father's kiss on my forehead at that moment, not until I die.

When I walked into my room, I was crying and laughing. I was so loud, the doctor thumped the wall of the room next to mine.

"Girl, you're going to tear down the house, what's that noise? The gossiping ill-hearted neighbours will find me guilty. They'll say the old geezer made the bride scream until morning!"

However, he was almost as noisy as me. He was walking around in his room.

"O God, our virtue, chastity is in your safe custody from these end-of-time women!" He screamed shrewdly.

That night, he, in his room, and I, in my room, awoke ten times by hitting the walls and prevented each other from sleeping by making rooster, bird and frog noises.

There you are, the story of my bridal night. My doctor was so pure-hearted that he saw no need to tell me our marriage was simply a promise. How coquettish my soul was compared to his, my goodness!

In our sublime friendship, he had forgotten his manhood. But I hadn't forgotten my womanhood. Most men are so wicked, so cruel, that is certain. All women are good, but oppressed, that is certain. But there are a few men who live with their simple hearts and faith, and it is not possible to find the cleanliness of their hearts in every woman.

Feridé could not sleep that night, not until morning. When she woke up more sore and exhausted than the previous evening, the sun was high in the sky and she saw that the clock showed past eleven. She threw herself out of bed with a little scream, like a child late for school.

Müjgan was busy setting the table.

"Well done, Müjgan! Why did you let me sleep so late on the day of my departure?" Feridé's voice was filled with resentment.

Müjgan responded in her calm everyday voice. "I came to your room a couple of times. You looked so tired as you slept that I couldn't bear to wake you. It's not as late as you think, but I'm not sure if the ferry will leave. There's a storm in the Marmara Sea."

"It doesn't matter, I'm leaving now."

"I already told father and he went to the harbour to check for you. He said that if the ferry comes in he would send a carriage or come himself to pick you up."

Feridé didn't think the day of separation would turn out like this. Müjgan was busy with her children and the aunts talked just like they did every day, laughing, and it made Feridé sad and heartbroken that she was getting so little attention. Kâmran was nowhere to be seen. But Müjgan had a secret behind her words.

"Feridé, I did you a favour. I've managed to get Kâmran out of the house. He has agreed to this sacrifice to avoid bothering you."

"He's not coming anymore?"

"I think he will meet you at the pier to say his goodbyes and . . . of course you're pleased."

Feridé's eyes were preoccupied. There was slight droop to her lips and she pressed her finger on a painful point at her temple.

"Yes, thank you, you did well." She thanked Müjgan with broken, meaningless words, feeling that her beloved childhood friend was dead and could never be reconciled with again.

When they sat down for lunch, they received news from one of the neighbouring vineyards. The municipal chiefs, who were preparing to go back to their winter homes in the city, wanted to give the vineyard community and Feridé a final parting feast.

"How? I'm going to get picked up to leave soon."

"Shame on you, Feridé," her aunts scolded. "It's only five minutes away. Anyway, what more do you have to prepare, you can wear your çarşaf now."

314

She lowered her head in order not to look at the faces of her aunts, the half-mothers, who did not care about her, not even as much as if she were a sick cat.

"All right, fine."

At three o'clock, Feridé was observing the road near a gazebo wrapped in leaves.

"There's a car coming, Müjgan. I suppose it's for me."

But at that moment, there was a ferry that suddenly appeared in the distance, beyond a tree on the beach.

Feridé's heart was in her mouth.

"It's coming!" she cried. There was a mad rush in the vineyard. Young maids were running to grab robes. "I'll go earlier, you can catch up," she told her aunts. She ran with Müjgan through a shortcut between the vineyards. They were jumping over fences and passing through gardens. They ran into the cook in front of the garden door.

"Young ladies, I was on my way to get you. The men came by carriage, they are waiting for you," the old woman said.

Aziz Bey and Kâmran welcomed them on the second floor of the hall. Aziz Bey gestured towards the room with his hand.

"Two inconvenient guests have arrived. Do not make noise," he said. Then, he looked at Feridé.

"What is this, little lady, are you sweating blood?" He approached her, laughing, and held her jaw while looking into her eyes. "The ferry is coming, but not in your favour. Your husband does not agree."

Feridé withdrew rapidly, puzzled. "Uncle, what are you saying?" she asked.

"He is your husband, my daughter. I will not interfere!"

Feridé, with a slight wail, covered her face with her hands. She was going to fall, but a hand grabbed one of her wrists. She opened her eyes again . . . it was Kâmran.

Aziz Bey laughed excitedly. "So, did you finally get in the cage, Çalıkuşu? Go on, flap, flap those wings! See, is it going to help from now on?"

Feridé tried to cover her face again, but she could not free her wrists from Kâmran. She squirmed to move her head but could find no other

315

resting place than his chest and his shoulder. Aziz Bey laughed excitedly again.

"The people around you set you up, Çalıkuşu. This Müjgan traitor sold your secret. May God rest his soul, the deceased sent your book to Kâmran. I brought it to the judge and showed some of your pen's work. The judge, a broad-minded man, immediately legitimized the marriage; do you understand, Çalıkuşu? This man, your husband, doesn't look like he's leaving you anymore."

Feridé was so flushed that the colour of her face hit her hazel eyes, and red stars were vibrating in their pupils.

"Come on, Çalıkuşu, don't be coy anymore. We see you love it. Say, 'You've done no harm, uncle, this is what I wanted!'" Aziz Bey half-forced her to repeat the words. Then he opened the door to the room with a triumphant laugh.

"I have the Sharia regent, sir. Çalıkuşu—sorry—on behalf of Feridé Hanim, I'm marrying Kâmran Bey. You do the prayer, we can say 'Amen,' here." Then he turned to Feridé.

"How is it, Çalikuşu? You finger-sized brat, you fooled us for years, ha! See how many tricks I have played on you?" The children's voices could be heard from the garden.

"Now, congratulations, the hand kissing will take a long time. Keep it all for yourself. I'm going to make a terrific wedding supper with my own hands. Come on, son, you do not benefit from our chatter. Certainly, you have things to talk about. Get your wife out through those narrow back stairs. As far as you want, then you can come back together."

When Kâmran ran to the stairwell with Feridé in his arms, Müjgan caught up behind them. Two crying friends kissed each other.

Aziz Bey, who wiped his nose noisily to avoid showing his tears, shook his arm, pretending to be a preacher: "So, Çalıkuşu, who steals my cherries, it sounds like the time has come for others to steal your cherry-like cheeks. Give them to me and I will settle the account," he said.

There was no escape. Aziz Bey lifted her up in the air to kiss and pushed her back into Kâmran's arms.

"We rescued you tonight from the sea storm, but the blonde storm next to you looks even greater. God bless you," Aziz Bey said.

They were running down the narrow stairs so fast, they were practically flying. Kâmran had his arm around Feridé's waist, squeezing the young woman like he wasn't going to let her breathe, hurting his fingers inside his palm.

Feridé's skirt caught on one of the stairs. They stopped, gasping for a minute. As the young woman tried to save her skirt, Kâmran panted, "Feridé, you're mine! I can't believe it. I need your weight to convince my heart that you are mine."

He picked her up by force—like she was a little child—as she gasped for air, trembling with deep chills in her body. He continued down the stairs, his face covered by her hair spilling out of her çarşaf. Her weight strengthened him, and her movement set his blood on fire. The young woman was laughing and crying at the same time, letting herself go into the warm sensation of falling off a cliff. She started begging for the small rock near the door.

"Look at me, Kâmran. How can we go out looking like this? Let me go to my room for a minute and I'll change my clothes. I'll be right back."

Kâmran would not let go of her wrists. "No way, Feridé. It happened once before. Now that I have you, I won't let you go," he laughed.

The young woman put her head on Kâmran's chest, exhausted. Hiding her face, embarrassed, she confessed:

"You think I'm not sorry I left?"

Kâmran could not see her face. He only heard the warm teardrops falling on his loving fingers, caressing her chin and her lips.

On the way, the couple walked close together, in each other's arms, only separating when they saw two fishermen coming. Without talking, they continued walking, drunk on the bliss of walking next to each other. They came to the spot where, ten years ago, Kâmran first saw Feridé on the vineyard road. He held her lightly by the shoulders.

"You might not remember this place, Feridé," he said. The young girl smiled carefully, looking into the distance of the road.

"Your look is full of meaning. So, you do remember?"

Feridé gently sighed and looked into Kâmran's face with a deep, absent-minded expression, smiling at some nostalgic dream.

"Will I ever forget how happy I was at that moment?" she said.

The young man held her chin, so that her eyes would not be separated from his eyes, and with a heavy, deep voice said, "Feridé. All our adventures begin here. Listen to me, I see that these eyes have witnessed and suffered enough that they are able to understand me now. When I began to love you, you were a frivolous, mischievous girl who didn't think about anything else other than laughter and a little fun. A Çalıkuşu that was impossible to handle, like light or sound. I had a deep weakness for you. Every morning, when I woke up, I found the love growing in my heart a little more. This deep weakness embarrassed and scared me. At times you had such a look, you had such words that my heart was beating with deep hope. But you, you were changing quickly. The young woman was waking up in your entertaining, smiling childish eyes that darted about so swiftly. I said to myself, "She is a child who will never understand me, she will destroy my life . . ." I couldn't hope that you would give your life to me with such a profound fidelity. Maybe you were avoiding me to hide your blushing colours, your beautiful trembling lips. My thoughts were consuming me, reasoning that it was just the casualness of Çalıkuşu. Tell me, Feridé, where did you hide such a deep loyalty, such a kind soul, in the little chest of Çalıkuşu? . . ."

Kâmran became silent for a moment. Then he continued with a slower voice, tilting his head, with thin drops of sweat forming on his gentle white temples:

"My misery did not end there, Feridé. Towards you from myself, my life, I felt jealousy. I was jealous of your various states of happiness. There is no feeling in the world that doesn't lose its strength, that doesn't wear over time. 'What if I don't love Feridé so much after a while and lose this delicious, precious feeling of longing?' I said to myself. At those times, just like how one puts out lights that are feared to diminish, I was trying to keep the dream of you away from my eyes.

"There is a plant that grows in the mountains. I don't know its name. Feridé, when a person always smells something, they start to smell less of its scent. The cure is to deprive yourself of it. Even sometimes—with the ambition to re-discover that good old scent, one will smell any scent, even bringing himself closer to the face of a meaningless 'yellow blossom.'

"This herb sometimes suffers because of its good smell. People tumble it between their fingers and they crush it. Feridé, with your eyes, deeply tired of this agony, your eyes and your beautiful face weary of these sad thoughts, you resemble the smell of the flowers that have been ravaged. You understand me, don't you? Because now your eyes don't laugh. You're not having fun with my seemingly meaningless words."

Feridé, like a child who was prepared to sleep, had quivering tears on her eyelashes. Exhausted from this thrilling fatigue, her knees gave way, leaving all of her weight in Kâmran's arms. In this dreamlike state, only her lips moved:

"You see, Çalıkuşu is dead forever."

The young man moved his head closer. He continued in the same light voice:

"No matter what, I gave all of Çalıkuşu's love to someone else. Gülbeşeker."

Kâmran felt the exhausted young body, which had grown heavier in his arms, suddenly revive and curl up, writhing out of the dream.

"Kâmran, don't say that. I beg you." Her head still on Kâmran's chest, she leaned back and turned her face towards him. Her neck was throbbing, the veins turning purple with her panting. Her cheeks were burning and red sparks flashed in her eyes and around her face.

Kâmran stubbornly repeated himself. Feridé rose on to her tiptoes while her whole body trembled and pulled the young man by his shoulders. With all the blood of her body gathered in her lips, she extended her neck towards him.

After a minute, they separated. Feridé had come alive like a bird drinking water from a clear stream after a long thirst, stomping her feet and turning her head from side to side to avoid showing her face.

"What a shame, my goodness, what a shame! You caused it, you caused it!" she growled.

A wren was singing in the branch of the tree beside them.

THE END

Çalıkuşu

Reşat Nuri Güntekin

Source: Wikipedia

Reşat Nuri Güntekin was a Turkish author who published *Çalıkuşu* as a novel in 1922. *Çalıkuşu* started out as a serialized piece in a newspaper and gained Güntekin much popularity in Turkey. It became his first novel after which he wrote several more novels and plays throughout his writing career. Güntekin was educated at a French school in what was then known as Smyrna (now known as İzmir in Turkey). He graduated from the University of Istanbul's Faculty of Literature in 1912 and became a Turkish literature and French language teacher as well as a national school inspector. He became familiar with Anatolia while working as an inspector. In 1939 he stopped teaching when he was elected as a member of parliament. As a member of parliament, he was the Turkish delegate to UNESCO in 1950. He died in London, England at the age of 67 in 1956, while being treated for lung cancer.

Sir Wyndham Deedes

Source: Wikipedia

Sir Wyndham Deedes translated *Çalıkuşu* into English and published it in 1949. His other published translations are also of Turkish works: another novel by Reşat Nuri Güntekin and a memoir by Mahmut Makal. Deedes was a British army officer and civil administrator. In the early 1900s he learned Turkish and knew enough to be posted in Constantinople in 1910. After World War I he was posted in Istanbul as a military attaché (military expert attached to a diplomatic mission). During World War II he was the Chairman of the London Turkish House (Halkevi), created to help foster Anglo-Turkish relations. In his later years he continued to do diplomatic and social work but illness forced him to retire in 1946. He died in Kent, England in 1956.

Angel Garcia & Tugrul Zure

Source: Angel Garcia

Angel Garcia (left) and Tugrul Zure (right) met while working as electrical engineers at ABB in Edmonton, Alberta, Canada. Tugrul Zure is the main translator of Çalıkuşu's Part 5 into English and currently resides in Kitchener, Ontario, Canada with his wife and two children. Angel Garcia edited the translated Part 5 and published it together with Sir Wyndham Deedes' English translation of Çalıkuşu's Parts 1-4 after obtaining permission from the Deedes family. She continues to live in Edmonton (where she pretends to ignore the winter) with her husband and their wonder dog. This is Angel and Tugrul's first published work together.